Studs

and

Stilettos

Bev Pettersen

Editor: Patricia A. Thomas
Cover Art Design: Hot Damn Designs

DEDICATION

To Hans and Brenna, thanks for the long hours waiting on movie sets and for patiently answering every question.

ACKNOWLEDGEMENTS

Many thanks to Barb Snarby, Becky Mason and Anne MacFarland for reading the early drafts, to Cathy McDonald, Lexi and Ice for the dog walks and to Lauren Tutty for always making time to watch Revenge. Lastly, a big thanks to my readers and the warm welcome you've given my books.

Also available from
Bev Pettersen and Westerhall Books

CHAPTER ONE

The ball bounced across the pavement followed by a blur of brown. Emily yanked the steering wheel to the right and slammed on the brakes as the dog disappeared beneath her bumper. Her car skidded sideways, tires squealing, until it was stopped by a steel utility pole.

"What happened, Em?" Jenna's voice sounded discordant over the speaker phone. "What was that noise?"

Emily pulled the phone from the dashboard, barely able to breathe, let alone speak. "J-Jenna," she managed, battling to suck air into her lungs. "I just hit a dog. Can you look up a nearby vet? I'm close to Churchill Downs."

She unclipped her seatbelt and scrambled out, in such a panic that her heel caught and she almost tripped. She dropped to the concrete and peered beneath the car. Thankfully there was nothing by the left wheel. She rushed around the bumper and checked the front.

Steam hissed from her crumpled hood and the smell of rubber stained the area, but there was no sign of an injured animal. Except for a squashed soda can, the pavement was bare. She sagged against the fender, finally able to breathe.

Twenty feet away, a brown dog scooped up a rubber ball from the center of the road. His tail waved in a gay plume as he rejoined a group of playing children, all oblivious to the near miss. Clearly he wasn't hurt. He moved as quickly now as when he'd dashed in front of her car.

She adjusted the phone against her ear. Her hand was still shaking but she forced her voice to calm. "It's okay, Jenna. The dog's okay. No need for a vet."

"What happened?"

"He ran after a ball and I had to swerve."

"Were you speeding?" Jenna's voice sharpened. "Were you using hands-free?"

"Yes, of course. And I was way under the speed limit. The airbag didn't even inflate. Everything's fine." Emily pulled in a deep breath. "The car needs some work though. Guess I'll need a little extra cash this month."

Regret knotted her stomach. This was the third time this year she'd been forced to ask for money from the loosely labeled 'education fund.' And repairs on the Lotus were never cheap. If Burke hadn't bought the car as a gift, she would have sold it long ago.

Luckily Jenna couldn't see the wrecked vehicle. Her sister was incredibly generous, as was her wealthy husband, but lately telephone conversations had been rather strained.

"Of course, I'll pay you back once I'm working," Emily added. "I had another audition last week. For a real movie, not a commercial. Those acting lessons are finally paying off."

Jenna still didn't speak.

Emily rushed to fill the silence. "This role sounds super. It's about some Kentucky race family and has a bigger budget than *Secretariat*." She forced a shaky laugh but didn't slow. When life threw curve balls, she'd learned it was best to talk fast, act confident and hide her fear.

"I'll need something to wear though," she went on. "I was just driving to that boutique close to my apartment. Their knock-offs are a fraction of designer prices. Do you need a new dress? Now that I lost ten pounds, we're about the same size. I could pick something out for you."

"How many auditions have you had now?" Jenna asked, her voice subdued.

"Twelve," Emily said. "But my agent says it takes a ton of auditions before you land a job. Once I have a speaking role, I can join the union which helps getting roles. Of course, it all takes time." But the knot spread from her stomach to her chest, and she hated the desperation in her voice. Lately she despaired of ever landing an acting job, and it was becoming increasingly hard to act positive.

She turned away from the steam rising around the hood, determined not to agonize over the crushing rejections. No one ever said acting was easy. Usually at this point though, Jenna was offering counsel and boosting her spirits. Today she was quiet, almost resigned, not sounding at all like Emily's supportive big sister.

Emily stiffened, instantly forgetting her gloomy car and even gloomier finances. "What's wrong, sis?" Alarm filled her voice. "Are you all right? Is Peanut okay?"

"I'm fine. And Peanut is doing as well as any other aged pony. His breathing is okay but he misses you." Jenna's voice tightened. "Isn't it time you finally gave up and moved home? Burke is building a guesthouse where the old shed used to be. A place where he can put his cousin and other business associates. There's lots of room. He installed a temporary ceiling for now. We're not sure about skylights, since you always said natural light wasn't very flattering."

Emily bit her lip. She had a lot more problems than debating the pros and cons of skylights. And while Jenna and Burke were always gracious, she'd tried living with them before. It hadn't worked. They were too much in love, and she always felt like a third wheel. She certainly didn't want to crawl home to West Virginia and beg for her tour guide job back. She needed to accomplish something.

Besides, they obviously didn't want her underfoot. They were sticking her with Burke's business associates? She tried to shrug it off but the reality hurt.

"I'll visit in the summer," she said, "if that's a good time. If your new guesthouse will be finished by then?" She paused, waiting for reassurance that she'd misunderstood, and of course she was welcome to stay in the family home. After all, it was built on Emily and Jenna's joint land, and it had been Burke who insisted on demolishing their old trailer.

But the only sound was the tapping of Jenna's laptop.

Emily forced a quick laugh, rushing to hide her hurt. "Of course I can't come home until my car's repaired," she said. "So maybe you could lend some money?"

"No," Jenna said. "That's why you have insurance. Burke included a comprehensive policy when he bought the car."

Emily squeezed her eyes shut, wishing she hadn't cancelled the collision coverage. But audition clothes were expensive and her agent had stressed the importance of dressing for the part she wanted to play.

And if she received a callback for the Kentucky movie, yet another purchase would be necessary. Her agent would freak if she wore the same clothes to the second audition. And she needed to freshen her highlights. The movie was based on a true story from the nineties, and the casting director had stressed they wanted blondes.

She realized Jenna was still talking and yanked her attention back to her sister.

"Exams are a nightmare," Jenna said with a heavy sigh. "I can't wait for the spring semester to be over."

Emily made a sympathetic sound deep in her throat. Luckily she didn't have to cram for exams, not anymore. She'd already learned college wasn't her thing. It was ironic that Jenna was working her butt off to be a vet when Burke would happily buy her anything she wanted. Clearly studying was hard on everyone's head. Jenna hadn't sounded this subdued in years.

"Forget about college for a few days," Emily said impulsively. "Visit me in Louisville. You can have the bed. I'll sleep on the couch. And I promise to be quiet when you need to study. We can shop, do your nails, spice up your wardrobe. It would be loads of fun."

"Thanks, Em. But shopping is your fix. I'd rather massage a few animals, sit on the porch and maybe end the night with a beer."

Emily's shoulders drooped. She couldn't remember the last time she'd spent quality time with Jenna. "You mean end the night with Burke," she said.

"Yes." Jenna's voice turned husky as it always did when she spoke of her hunky husband. "He's definitely the best way to finish the day. But he's working in New York now. Some big merger that's going to take awhile. I miss him."

She misses him more than me. The realization made Emily's throat tighten. It was only natural—Burke was Jenna's husband. But Emily felt so alone now. Sometimes she wished they still lived in their sagging trailer, back when it was her and Jenna against the world.

Jenna had always been a rock, more like a mother than a sister, and the only person in the world who loved Emily despite her flaws. She couldn't imagine not having Jenna around to laugh with. To listen to her problems. To fix things.

She twisted a tendril of hair around her finger, painfully aware Jenna might win a sister-of-the-year award but she never would. No wonder Jenna preferred Burke's company. He gave back. He showed he cared.

Emily had trouble just remembering the details of Jenna's vet program. She gave her head a regretful shake, wishing she'd paid more attention. But it was difficult to ask questions when she couldn't even pronounce the course names. "Well," she said cautiously, "I hope the studying is going well. After exams are over, maybe you can take a break."

"Yes," Jenna said. "Now I really have to get back to the books. Glad you and the dog weren't hurt. See you."

"Wait," Emily said. "I need a tow—" But dead air filled the phone. She lowered her hand, blinking in hurt, unable to recall any other time when Jenna had been the first to hang up.

"Really?" Emily slumped against the window, her grip on the phone tightening. "Another rejection?"

"Sorry," her agent said, without sounding sorry at all. "They didn't want you. You might consider new headshots. I can refer you to an excellent photographer. His rates aren't cheap but all the successful actors swear by him. And how long is your hair now? It's probably time to consider a more innovative cut."

Emily stared down at the bustling street while her agent recited a list of Louisville's top hair stylists. So far, she'd followed every one of Tamara's suggestions. Clothes, classes, diction and diet. She'd never questioned the price. Of course, that was when Jenna and Burke were footing the bill.

She didn't want to beg for extra money, not after this morning's car crash. They already provided a reasonable allowance. But it was mind-boggling how much it cost to break into the movie industry…and okay, perhaps she had blown her budget on clothes.

There hadn't been much choice though. A makeup commercial for cable TV and two local car ads certainly didn't pay her rent, although she wouldn't have landed even those paltry jobs if her clothes hadn't hidden her dirt-poor roots. As Tamara said, appearances were critical.

If Jenna knew how broke she was, she'd simply tell Emily to come home. She'd be doubly insistent if she knew Emily's car was stranded at the mechanic's. Burke might even interfere with his own brand of persuasion. That man would do anything to please Jenna.

Emily squeezed the phone with a sticky palm, trying to quell her rising panic as Tamara lectured about 'imperative career investments.'

"Would it make any difference if I streaked my hair?" Emily finally asked. "Money's a little tight now but I can do that myself."

Tamara gave a dismissive snort. "A cheap home job isn't enough. Remember, you have to invest in your career. This is about contacts. Contacts, persistence and looking good." Tamara's voice faded then turned rushed. "I have another call. I'll email you if something comes up."

If something comes up, not when. Obviously Tamara was losing hope too. Emily swung away from the window, unable to hide her frustration. "Wait. Please tell me the truth. Is there much chance? Do any of your clients ever make money?"

"Absolutely." But Tamara's voice turned defensive. "In fact, I'm sending a busload of extras to the movie set tomorrow. Sometimes the casting director will spot a new face. That's what happened with Harrison Ford."

Extras. Emily sank onto the sofa. Background seemed to be the only work Tamara ever offered. And Emily didn't want to be one of those. She wanted to have lines, to receive a credit, to be someone Jenna would see on screen and proudly say, 'That's my sister.'

"Only last month one of my background performers landed a speaking role," Tamara went on. "I was the sole reason he was on set. Perhaps you should consider it? Background pays slightly more than minimum wage and it also provides meals. Of course, I do receive my agency's standard commission."

"Of course," Emily said dryly. However, she did a quick calculation. Nine days of background work would pay for her radiator. It wouldn't cover the bumper but at least the Lotus would be drivable. Best of all, she wouldn't be forced to crawl back to Jenna.

"They're shooting a party scene tomorrow," Tamara said. "We need more bodies to fill the room."

"How much work? Could I get nine days?"

"Doubtful," Tamara said. "They can't use the same background for the stables. But these things often stretch, especially when animals are involved."

"All right." Emily blew out a resigned sigh. "I'll do it."

"Excellent. Wear your best nineties party clothes, and wardrobe will top you off there. The movie site is north of Lexington, about a two-hour drive from Louisville. Be at the pickup point at four thirty."

"Four thirty?" Emily asked weakly. "In the afternoon?"

"No. Morning."

"Do extras get paid for travel time?"

Tamara only laughed, as if Emily had made a joke.

CHAPTER TWO

The bus jerked twice then rumbled from the dark parking lot. Emily yawned and relaxed against the seat. She hadn't been up this early since Peanut's bout with colic. Luckily she never had any problem falling asleep. Tamara had said it was a two-hour drive to the set, plenty of time to grab a nap.

"This is my ninth movie," the passenger beside her said. "How many have you been in?"

Emily turned toward the middle-aged lady in the adjacent seat. "This is my first," she admitted. "But I've been in a few commercials."

"A makeup commercial?"

"Yes." Emily nodded eagerly. "Did you see it?"

The lady shrugged. "I just noticed all the makeup you're wearing. You do realize they have hair and makeup on set?"

Emily stiffened, biting back a quick retort. She couldn't imagine going anywhere without fixing her face first. And this lady could certainly benefit from some makeup. Despite the bus's gloomy interior, crows' feet visibly edged the woman's eyes. She was attractive enough, with nice bones, but she had horribly bushy eyebrows and deep worry lines slashed her forehead. She certainly wasn't the glamorous type one expected to see at a movie site.

"I heard they offered George Clooney the lead," the woman went on, "but settled for Robert Dexter. I'm just thrilled to see a famous stud farm. I don't get close to many horses in the city."

Emily's tart retort died in her throat and she forgave the rude makeup comment. This lady wasn't mean-spirited, only talkative. And she couldn't be all bad if she liked horses. Emily hadn't realized Robert Dexter was one of the stars. It would be cool to be in a scene with such a famous actor. That might impress Jenna.

"Where exactly is the horse farm?" Emily turned slightly in her seat. "My agent only said it was a couple hours east of Louisville."

"Don't you know? It's being shot at Hamilton Stud. This movie is about Reckless. That's the name of the movie too. Maybe we'll even see his grave."

"You're kidding. That would be cool." Emily nodded in approval. Jenna would definitely be interested in anything about Reckless. The famous racehorse had been one of the most influential Thoroughbred sires in North America. His progeny were still burning up the track and his owner, Thomas Hamilton, had been equally flamboyant, cutting as wide a swathe with the women as his stud had with the mares.

She whipped out her phone and began texting. *On way to movie shoot at Hamilton Stud. Robert Dexter is playing Thomas Hamilton. Will send pics.*

"Just remember not to take pictures of the actors," the lady said. "That's forbidden. If you don't follow etiquette, you'll be blackballed."

Emily grimaced. "Wouldn't dream of it." She palmed her phone, hiding the screen.

"Shania Stevens is playing Hamilton's groom," the woman added. "Not sure about that casting decision. She's gorgeous but a real city girl. She doesn't even like horses."

"You sure know a lot." Emily nodded admiringly. "Your agent sounds way better than mine."

"I don't have an agent," the woman said, with a hint of a sneer. "Background performers can apply on the Internet. That way you don't pay commission. Kentucky has lots of film incentives so the industry is hopping. It just takes a little research. Stupid not to be prepared."

Emily's mouth tightened. She may not be a good student but she wasn't stupid. And this lady was as bossy as Burke, always preaching about preparation and the value of hard work. No way was she going to sit and listen to another gratuitous lecture.

She checked the back of the bus. There were no window seats left, but a couple empty spots remained on the aisle.

"My name's Judith," the lady said. "What's yours?"

Emily groped beneath the seat for her bag. "Emily," she murmured.

"That's a nice name. Does anyone ever call you Em? My parents used to call me Judy but that was long ago…" The woman's voice faltered and she clutched her hands, revealing nail-bitten fingers. She certainly had stopped talking now. But her silence was heavy with melancholy.

Emily fingered her bag. "My sister calls me Em. She's the only one."

Someone in the back snored, a deep nasal sound that made the people sitting behind them giggle. But Judith didn't crack a smile.

Emily pushed her bag back under the seat, scrambling for something more to say. She definitely couldn't switch seats now and leave this lady looking so sad. "Thanks for reminding me not to take pictures," she said. "I need more than a day's work and can't afford to upset anyone."

"Just stay away from the camera," Judith said, her voice regaining a touch of its earlier authority.

"What do you mean?" Emily asked. "Shouldn't we try to be noticed?"

"Not if you want to be called back. We're background for a house party. If your face is on screen, you won't be eligible for any track or stable scenes. Are you special skills?"

Emily wrinkled her nose. "Special skills. What's that?"

"Background who can ride or handle horses. Special skills might get up to twenty days' work as long as they're not filmed in the house. Grooms didn't mix with the bluebloods. Don't you know anything?"

Normally Emily had little patience for people who shot such rude barbs but this woman didn't seem malicious, only awkward. Judith definitely knew a lot about the movie, and if there was a chance for three weeks' work, Emily was keen to hear more. "I've been around horses my entire life," she said, leaning forward in the seat. "I definitely should be special skills."

"It's not that easy." Judith shook her head. "They'll check qualifications. Especially with Dan Barrett in charge."

"Who's Dan Barrett?"

Judith's forehead wrinkled. "Didn't you look up any of these people? He's the reason that mustang movie cleaned up at the Oscars. He can persuade a horse to stand up and talk. All the directors want him. But he insists on complete control over the animals, wranglers and stunts."

"But I really am qualified." Emily's voice rose. "I worked for over a year at the Three Brooks Equine Center. They have a training track and some of the top Thoroughbreds in the east." She paused, deciding it was best not to admit she was only a tour guide. "We even had a Kentucky Derby winner once."

Judith sniffed. "Then I'm surprised you haven't heard of Dan Barrett."

"Well, I have now." Emily crossed her arms and looked out the window, staring at the blur of pavement. Surely working at Three Brooks would qualify her for special skills.

She hadn't been an actual exercise rider of course, or even a groom, but she'd certainly given a lot of tours.

And she could honestly say she'd galloped on a track. She and Peanut had raced at the annual Stillwater Fair back home in West Virginia. No one needed to know the oval was tiny and not completely fenced. Or that they had come last— Peanut's legs were far too short to cover much ground. But they had almost beaten the potbellied donkey, and Jenna had waved a pompom and cheered from the finish line. She'd even bought Emily a triple chocolate ice cream cone that day. Peanut had helped eat it.

Emily's mouth curved at the memories. The Stillwater Fair and Steeplechase had always been a blast. Maybe they could go again and relive those carefree times. No way would Jenna worry about school when whooping it up at the fairgrounds.

They'd always dreamed of staying at the Steeplechase Inn and enjoying all the night festivities. That hadn't happened yet. It would be cool to do it for the first time, together.

Emily turned back to Judith, her voice hopeful. "How long is this movie? Would a wrangler have more days than background? Someone has to look after the horses, right?"

"Yes, but wranglers are already on site. And like I said, Dan Barrett only hires the best."

"Of course," Emily said, undaunted. Wranglers might already have been hired, but they still needed special skills. And if she snagged that job, she'd have more work than a single day of background. The director might even notice her and give some lines.

With a little luck, she could afford to fix her car and also book that hotel for Jenna. They could go to the steeplechase together, just like old times. It would be cool to finally be the sister who picked up the bill.

Jenna would be shocked when Emily drove home waving two weekend passes and an all-inclusive reservation at the Steeplechase Inn. It was hard to remember the last time she'd done something special for Jenna. Burke usually had that area covered. But not this time. He worked out-of-state a lot and didn't have a clue how much his wife loved the jump races.

Emily tilted on her seat, buoyed with fresh optimism. "When we get to the movie site, is there a place for the different background types to register?" she asked. "Because I'm quite certain this Barrett guy is going to want my special skills."

CHAPTER THREE

"Sign the non-union sheet, then follow the group." The man with the thin pigtail and headphones glanced up from the table and gestured at the snaking line of people. Several crude signs read 'BG' and crooked arrows pointed to a large brown tent.

Emily gave a breezy smile. "Could you please make sure my form says 'special skills.' That should have been added."

The man frowned. "You're here for party background."

"Yes, but it was an oversight." She signed her name with a flourish. "I just need my qualifications updated."

The man yanked at the form, pulling it from under her pen almost before she finished signing. "Fat chance," he said. "Now move along. You're holding up the line. And we're on a tight schedule."

"But if you could just write SS by my name, then I'm sure—"

"Go." He jabbed the air with a crooked thumb then muttered into the mouthpiece of his walkie-talkie.

Emily rolled her eyes and flounced over to Judith. "Sheesh. That guy at the table was so rude." She shot him a dark look that made her feel marginally better but unfortunately the man was too busy to notice.

"Anyone with a walkie is usually an assistant director, or an assistant to an assistant director," Judith said. "So be careful. And get used to the rudeness. We're just background. We wear what they tell us, stand where they tell us, and eat when they tell us. Some companies treat background better than others but generally we're just a body."

Emily stepped back, staring at Judith in consternation. "Then why do it? Will background help us become real actresses?"

Judith snorted. "Not likely. We're invisible. But it's fun working at movies. It's interesting seeing how they're made, how much footage they have to shoot for just a couple minutes. I'm not doing anything else with my time. Although I usually stick to jobs within an hour's drive of Louisville."

"This one is a lot further than that." Emily rubbed the back of her neck, still rather stiff from the bus ride.

"Yes, but I wanted to see the farm. Reckless was a famous horse but Hamilton Stud is closed to the public. With this movie being shot on location, it's a chance to make it through the gate. The production company made several proposals before the Hamiltons finally gave permission."

"A movie would certainly be disruptive," Emily said, peering at the rows of trailers and humming generators. Coils of black wire littered the ground and officious-looking people rushed past with headsets and strained expressions. "The Hamilton horses must be a bit rattled."

Judith gestured at the row of white barns standing in the distance. "The buildings are still here but there aren't any racehorses left. After Reckless died, they sold their broodmares. The Hamiltons have six offspring in training but they've been shipped to a dispersal sale."

Emily gulped. Judith was a walking encyclopedia. The research this woman had done for a simple movie left her feeling insecure. And she hated that feeling. She smoothed her hair, hoping to bolster her confidence. At least her makeup was carefully applied. She always felt braver when she looked her best—people treated her much better.

"Where's the coffee?" she asked, scanning the portable trailers. "I've been up since three and really need some caffeine."

Judith jerked to a stop, her voice lowering to a horrified whisper. "You can't just wander off. Coffee breaks are scheduled according to regulation. They'll tell us when it's time. Everything is preset."

Emily rolled her eyes. "It's just a little coffee. And look at the long makeup line. I'll be back in a couple minutes." She pivoted, scanning the area for posted signs. Crude arrows pointed in every direction: makeup, wardrobe, barn, party. But she couldn't see anything about food.

"Save me a spot in line," she added. "I'm going to scout around. I'll bring you back a coffee."

Judith opened and closed her mouth, glanced at the long makeup line and then back at Emily. "A coffee would be good," she admitted. "I take milk in mine."

Emily grinned. Judith wasn't bad, just a little uptight and clearly lonely. But it was nice to have a buddy.

She nodded and veered to the left, stepping over thick black extension cords and passing noisy generators that muffled the sounds of hammering. An arrow pointed to a long tent: Dining Room.

She strolled through the open door and up to a table laden with serving trays. Folks here had been eating well. The distinctive smell of bacon and eggs lingered in the air. Stainless steel coffee machines stood in a row—not just one, but six—offering every type of tea and coffee imaginable, both pod and drip. There was even Herbalife tea and that stuff was awesome. She felt herself recharging, merely from seeing the logo.

However, there were no paper cups, only china, and it was going to be awkward walking out with a dainty cup and saucer. She picked one up, handling it dubiously, but her hesitation was costly.

"Excuse me," an authoritative voice said. "This tent is restricted. Background isn't allowed."

Emily turned toward the woman, her fingers tightening around the saucer. She didn't want to get in trouble her very first hour. But she also didn't want to leave without two cups of this delicious-smelling coffee.

"Of course, I'm aware it's restricted," Emily said. "But I've been asked to pick up beverages."

"You're not cast or crew. Who sent you?"

Emily adjusted the cup in the middle of the saucer, stalling for time. But her mind blanked beneath the woman's gimlet gaze. Judith's name wouldn't carry much weight, and she couldn't remember any of the directors Judith had mentioned. She gave an airy wave of her hand. "You know…the assistant director. That guy who does the horses."

The attendant's gaze shifted to someone behind Emily. Her stony expression cracked into a surprisingly pretty smile.

"You'll need paper cups around the barn," a man said, his voice low and velvety but with an unmistakable hint of authority.

Emily turned, her breezy words stalling in her throat. He was so ruggedly handsome, he had to be a movie star. Striking cheekbones accentuated a chiseled jaw and perfectly cut mouth. Amusement edged his eyes as he reached below the table and pulled out a stack of paper cups. "How many cups do you need?" He winked. "You know, for that guy who does the horses."

"Two, please." She checked over her shoulder. The attendant had rushed away to challenge an unfortunate teenager by the doughnut table. "Thanks," Emily whispered. "I thought she was going to pry the cup from my hand."

"She's been known to do that. She's irritatingly vigilant." The man chuckled, such a warm and easy-going sound Emily stopped worrying about the Gestapo attendant.

Now that she had a chance to study his clothes, it was clear he was no actor. There was nothing fake about his faded jeans, his workmanlike tan or the layer of dust that covered his boots. His brown hair was slightly long, curling over the back of his collar and lightened from the sun. He was a head taller than she was, and had a big headset stuck in his leather cowboy belt.

Emily's tension eased. It would have been awesome to bump shoulders with a famous actor like Robert Dexter but she'd grown up among simple working folk. She was comfortable around this type of man. There was no need to pretend.

"This is my first time on a movie set," she confided. "They certainly have a great selection of coffee."

"It goes a long way in keeping people happy." His gaze drifted over her brand new silk dress down to her stiletto heels, his intelligent blue eyes seeming to absorb every detail. "You don't look like you're heading to the barn."

"No, I'm an actress." She laughed, but his gaze remained on her face. "Well, trying to be," she added. "I'm background, here for the party scene. Hoping to be moved to special skills."

"What are your special skills?"

Her smile froze. His simple question highlighted her unfortunate dilemma. She had no skills. Despite Jenna's support, her life had been a depressing string of failures. So far, her most notable achievement was holding her breath longer than any of the boys at the Three Brooks swimming hole.

Naturally she had an elevator pitch that, speaking fast, could be delivered in less than thirty seconds. And she was accustomed to fighting for attention. However, this man just waited, as though her answer was important and he wasn't going to be distracted by silly prattle.

Someone hollered. Cutlery rattled. But neither of them spoke.

"I'm guessing you're a very fine dancer," he finally said, his voice gentle. "Wardrobe gave you nice heels too. Perfect for the party shoot today."

She laughed then, a real laugh, despite her surge of despair. "I haven't been to wardrobe yet." She stuck out her foot and wiggled her toes. "These are my own shoes. But I was hoping my horse experience might qualify for special skills."

"You're experienced? With Thoroughbreds?"

"I worked for almost two years at the Three Books Equine Center."

"I've heard of the place." He gave an approving nod. "So you've handled some rough stock?"

She nodded. Not really a lie. When Peanut wanted to keep grazing, he was plenty tough to catch. And she'd often moved horses around for the technicians, collecting them from their stalls and leading them to the therapy rooms. Some of them were quite rambunctious, although it was probably prudent not to ask this man's definition of 'rough.'

"Drop by the main barn after the party shoot," he said. "If you can handle a horse, we might be able to use you. But dress appropriately." The corner of his mouth twitched. "And the assistant director has his own coffee girl and doesn't look after the horses. And we usually just refer to him as the AD. What's your first name?"

"Emily," she managed, her cheeks flushing with heat. She should have paid more attention when Judith was prattling about ADs and movies and Internet gossip. At least this man hadn't called her bluff in front of the coffee guard.

And 'dress appropriately?' She hadn't worn jeans since she left West Virginia, determined to leave her hick life behind. But this was a big opportunity…if only she could find suitable clothes.

"I'm Dan Barrett," he went on. "Here's my card. It will give you entry to the test site."

"Test?" The mere word turned her mouth dry. She tended to flunk tests.

"Just basic horse handling," he said. "We need background that can handle horses, not actors trying to pretend they know what they're doing. Can you ride?"

"Sure. I've been riding since I was two." She squared her shoulders in a show of confidence but inside, her heart was pounding. This was the Barrett guy Judith had talked about, the production manager for the horse unit. She hadn't mentioned he was drop-dead gorgeous with a voice so soft and silky it was almost hypnotic. Or that his cobalt blue eyes would leave her slightly unbalanced, as if they could see much more than she liked to reveal.

Judith had only said he was an industry expert. And certainly not the type to be fooled.

She knew she should grab the opportunity and leave, before she said anything more and screwed it up. But she lingered, palming the card around her warm cup. "I'm not really a fancy rider," she said. "I haven't had any formal instruction, not unless you count a big sister who always preached about not yanking on a horse's mouth."

"Sounds like a smart sister."

"Yes." Emily nodded. "Super smart. And the best horse masseuse around." She gave herself a mental kick, wishing she'd said Jenna was studying to be a vet. That was much more impressive. But there was something about Dan's eyes, so knowing and patient, not at all judgmental. He just waited, as though what she had to say was of the utmost importance. And she should be selling herself here, not drawing attention to her limited background.

"Jenna taught me a whole lot," she added lamely. "But you know, basic stuff."

He nodded, poured a cup of coffee and snapped on a plastic lid. She checked for a ring but his fingers were bare. And lean and tanned and rugged. Like he was capable of doing many things. A flush of awareness swept her.

She jerked her head up, realizing she'd been staring. And all he was doing was putting a lid on a cup. "Well, thanks very much." She backed up a step. "I appreciate the opportunity. Guess I'll see you later."

"Yes." He smiled. "This afternoon."

She nodded and walked toward the exit, unable to resist a last peek over her shoulder. Already he was surrounded by three men with headsets. For a brief instant though, his head turned and his piercing gaze caught hers.

His eyes seemed to skim over her legs in a classic male once-over. However, the moment was too brief and she brushed it aside as merely wishful thinking.

CHAPTER FOUR

"This has to be the most boring job in the world," Emily said, peering over Judith's shoulder into the makeup tent. "Has this line even moved since I left?"

"This is normal." Judith sipped her coffee, barely looking up from her e-reader. "We're getting paid now, so relax. But thanks for the great coffee."

Emily drained her cup and glanced around, searching for a sympathetic face. About thirty people lined up behind them, but each one seemed stoically resigned, either reading, texting or moving like the walking dead. Not a single person appeared ruffled.

At least this wait provided time to brush up on her horse knowledge. Nothing to it. A simple call to Jenna would do the trick. She tossed her cup into a nearby garbage can and pulled out her phone. Scrolled down to her sister's name then paused. Her finger wavered over the keys. Jenna still hadn't answered her earlier text and was obviously busy cramming.

It might be quicker to check the Internet for the proper way to lead a horse. Not that Emily was a total newbie. She'd participated in many 4-H activities and Wally, the Center's manager, had constantly lectured her on safe handling.

The movie people might even want Wally's reference. Heck, she'd better warn him. *On movie site of Reckless,* she texted. *May need reference. OK?*

Wally answered within a minute. *Yes. Will confirm A1 tour guide. Have fun.*

Not a tour guide, she clicked. *Horse handler.* She crossed her fingers and waited.

His next text was very short: *lol.*

She grimaced. Not much help there. Wally considered her a lowly tour guide; it would be impossible to change his mind. Jenna, however, could do it with one phone call. Wally would walk over hot coals for Jenna.

She scrolled back to her sister's name but again hesitated. Asking Jenna to speak to Wally would definitely disrupt her studying. It would also drag Emily back full circle to begging for help.

It might be better to call Wally's receptionist and have her handle any calls. Frances was rather ornery. However, she'd padded Emily's job description before in exchange for crossword puzzle help. Besides, the movie people might not check references, especially if she aced the skills test. And really, how hard was it to lead a horse?

Reassured, she scrolled the Internet and pulled up a horse site. 'Lead from the left,' it said. 'Hand six inches below the halter ring. Turn the animal away from you.'

Okay, she already knew that. And she always got along well with horses…normal ones, anyway.

She tapped Judith on the arm. "Can you tell me if Reckless was a normal horse? Besides being able to run freakishly fast?"

Judith impatiently lifted her gaze from the e-reader. "You're too young to remember his races, but I can't believe you didn't do any research. I'm not sure what you mean by normal, but Reckless was a terror in the starting gate. He didn't even run in the Derby. His groom disappeared and for a while he was unmanageable."

"Unmanageable." Emily gulped. "What exactly does that mean?"

"He reared. Charged. Bolted. I believe he was pining for his groom. He never made it to any of the three-year-old classics. All his races were won as a four-year-old. That's why this movie is so intriguing. People will finally hear the entire story."

"They should have paid the groom more money," Emily said. "I don't blame him for quitting." A rearing horse was scary. She'd been clipped once on the shoulder and had a healthy respect for flailing hooves.

Judith's mouth tightened. "The groom was female, not male. And she left two weeks before the Derby. Just disappeared."

Emily shrugged and returned to the search function of her phone. 'How to handle a rearing horse,' she typed.

The screen changed, offering a wealth of equine information, tips and opinions. There were plenty of pictures, video and instruction—some of it conflicting. But all the Internet experts agreed on one thing: a rearing horse was very dangerous.

"Size?"

The clipped question pulled Emily from her research. She glanced up. A lady with an iPad impatiently tapped a finger.

"Size seven," Emily said, disappointed now that the line was moving. Some of these horse videos had been extremely entertaining.

"Height and weight?"

"Five foot six inches, one hundred and nineteen pounds." She automatically shaved two pounds. One hundred and nineteen sounded much better than one twenty-one.

"Move along to the wardrobe counter," the lady said, barely lifting her head as she punched in the data.

Emily joined Judith who'd already been issued a beige dress with a rather ugly lace neckline.

"Try to get a neutral color," Judith whispered as she headed for a change room.

Emily grimaced. She preferred bright colors, not boring brown. But if she was prominent in the party scene, she might blow her chance at special skills. On the flip side, she might not even pass the horse test, and the chance to appear on screen with a famous actor—someone who even Jenna would recognize—hung tantalizingly within reach.

A harried wardrobe lady dropped a gold sheath on the counter. Emily brightened. She could live with that. The dress was beautiful yet wouldn't stand out in a crowd. "Do you have matching heels?" Emily asked, scooping up the dress. "Something strappy? And I think a gold necklace would add some flair."

"This isn't a fashion show," the lady said with an amused smile. "Move along now. The wardrobe supervisor is on the far side of the tent. She'll check you out."

Emily stepped into the next empty change room and tugged on the dress. It was beautiful with a timeless cut that fit the nineties yet wouldn't look out of place at a cocktail party today. And the shoes were okay, not as sexy as she'd like and a half size too large, but otherwise acceptable. She did a satisfied pirouette in front of the mirror then hurried out to join Judith.

"This is great," Emily said. "I wonder how they'll do our hair."

Judith shrugged. "You already look gorgeous. I doubt they'll do anything more. Just leave your bag on the bench and get in the makeup line. After approval, we're allowed to wait in the lunch room until our call time."

Emily grimaced at the prospect of another lineup. At least there was something interesting to watch in this tent. There were six makeup stations and it looked like they did hair at the same time. One woman, obviously the supervisor, made last-minute adjustments before nodding curt approval.

All the makeup artists were extremely quick. And talented. But one poor woman was being rubbed with far too much rouge. "What are they doing to her?" Emily asked in horror. She certainly hoped they didn't put that clownish red on her cheeks.

"It's probably for the pool scene," Judith said, keeping her voice low. "That's when Thomas Hamilton brought Reckless to the house and announced he'd win the Derby. The poor colt was terrified and leaped into the pool. A couple guests were hurt, but they managed to get Reckless out okay."

"It looks like that woman hit the side of her head," Emily whispered, staring in awe as the lady's face was transformed into a bloody mess. "They even made a line down the side of her cheek."

"Probably supposed to be the horse's hoof," Judith said.

"What happened to Reckless at this party? I remember his name," Emily said, "but I'm a little fuzzy on the history."

"The pool incident is a famous story." Impatience edged Judith's voice. "He was drowning, and his groom jumped in and saved him. Animal experts think that's why he missed her so much when she disappeared."

"So, if Robert Dexter is playing the Hamilton guy, he'll be in this scene?"

"Yes. There was some sort of party, lots of drinking, and then the horse was led up to the house. That's when the trouble started."

"Pool trouble?"

"Not just that." Judith fiddled with the neckline of her dress. "Rumor was the groom and Thomas Hamilton were having an affair. The wife noticed and wanted the groom fired. I'm not sure if all that will be in the movie though. It'll probably focus on Reckless jumping into the pool."

"Wow." Emily shook her head, unable to imagine a horse leaping into a pool. It had been tricky persuading some of the Thoroughbreds to enter the whirlpool at the Center. And that pool had a rubber ramp.

She inched another step forward in line, keeping her gaze on the woman with the bloody face. So far, everything on the set was fascinating—except, of course, for the waiting. But she was going to be in the same room as Robert Dexter and Shania Stevens, huge Hollywood stars. This could be her big break.

"Next." A makeup artist gestured.

Emily stepped forward and sat in the chair, pleased to recognize several beauty brands crammed on the table in front of the mirror. "I'd like my eyes darkened a bit," she said, tilting her head and studying her reflection. "Maybe add a little more charcoal eyeliner on the sides with just a touch beneath."

The artist laughed. "Sorry. You're okay as is. We're not doing much for the extras, just making sure there's enough party look. You won't be that close to the cameras. Not unless you've been chosen for special effects. Have you?"

"No. Not chosen," Emily said, rather deflated. It had been six hours since she left the apartment and her makeup needed refreshing. She'd packed her bag with essentials but this was her first chance to look in a mirror. It wasn't at all reassuring. "Perhaps I could just sit here and fix my face myself?" she asked.

"Sorry. No time." The artist tugged her out of the chair and Emily reluctantly rose, appalled at the noticeable shine on her cheeks.

"Come on." Judith waved an impatient arm. "The quicker we get to the lunch room, the longer we'll have for a break. They still have about twenty people to get ready."

Emily took a last glance in the mirror but shook off her disappointment and followed in Judith's wake. No hair, no makeup but at least she wore a very elegant dress. "The dining room is the other direction," she said to Judith, remembering the tent with the delicious coffee…and Dan Barrett.

"We're not allowed in that one. Background has their own lunch room." Judith pointed toward a 'BG' sign. The crude letters were painted on a piece of plywood in bold green and a trail of well-dressed people filed into the drab tent.

Sighing, Emily stepped over a cluster of thick yellow wire then followed Judith inside. This place was much different from the dining room. It was poorly lit, the floor was merely dead grass flattened by countless feet and the musty air reeked of mold and onions. Wooden tables stretched in uneven rows. No chairs, only worn benches. Three metallic urns squeezed onto a wobbly stand. Coffee, tea and hot water: a much more limited selection than the dining room.

"Hurry," Judith said. "Grab a doughnut before they're gone."

Emily picked up a plain doughnut then filled her coffee cup. "I hope my dress doesn't pick on those benches." She eyed the rough wood with suspicion. "We look much too nice to be stuck in this place."

"At least you can have coffee," a woman behind Emily said. "I was ordered to avoid drinking and not mess my makeup."

Emily turned, recognizing the woman with the bloody face. "Your makeup does look realistic," she said. "They did an excellent job. Do you get hurt in the pool?"

"I have no idea what I'm doing. I just stand where they tell me."

Emily enjoyed a rush of relief. She wasn't so ignorant. This woman knew even less than her. Probably nobody had researched the movie as much as Judith. "I heard we're guests at the house party," Emily said, trying to be helpful.

"Apparently Reckless is scared and jumps into the pool. I can't imagine a horse doing that, can you?"

"Doesn't matter." The woman pushed past her and scooped up three chocolate doughnuts. "The longer the day, the more money I make."

"Exactly." Emily nodded agreeably although she'd been so entertained by all the activity she'd forgotten she was here to earn a paycheck.

She edged onto the bench beside Judith and checked her messages. Still nothing since she sent the text on the bus. Maybe Jenna didn't believe she was really working on the *Reckless* movie?

"Would it be possible to snap a picture of the set?" Emily asked. "Not the actors. But I need something to send my sister."

"You still have your phone?" Judith's eyes widened in horror. "They told me to leave mine in my bag."

"They told me that too." Emily shrugged. "So I stuck it in my shoe. It's very expensive. I'm not going to just leave it."

Judith's lips clamped so tightly they turned white. "Don't even think about taking pictures," she hissed. "Your sister will have to understand. We could be kicked off. It's not done."

"She didn't ask for a picture," Emily said. "I just want to send one."

"Why? Are you trying to impress her?"

"No, it's not that," Emily said. "Movies stars wouldn't impress Jenna. But I want her to see what I'm doing." *And maybe a picture would validate my education allowance.*

Her hand shook so abruptly coffee splashed her wrist. It hurt to admit most of her energy was spent figuring out how to justify handouts from her wealthy sister.

"Jenna really likes horses," Emily added defensively, "so she'd be interested in this type of movie. That's why I took the background job, so I can take her to the steeplechase back home."

"I see." Judith's voice softened, her expression turning wistful. "Family is important. But now that you've met Dan Barrett, at least you can try out for special skills. Just make sure you get back to the bus by seven."

"Sure," Emily said. "And maybe you can get more work too. Will they need party background another day?"

Judith shrugged. "Who knows? But if this scene is based around an unpredictable horse, it might take days to get it right."

"I hope so," Emily said. Maybe she'd make enough money to book a deluxe room at the Steeplechase Inn. The end suite had a balcony overlooking the parking lot. There'd be at least fifty trucks at the tailgate party, all within shouting distance. The suite had a big fridge too so there'd be no problem keeping Jenna's beer cold. She rubbed her hands with anticipation.

A man with a mike bustled through the doorway, interrupting her daydreams. "You're heading to the set now," he called. "Bus is waiting."

"Show time." Judith rose to her feet. "And if you're going to sit with me," she warned, "make sure that phone is turned off."

CHAPTER FIVE

"Wow." Emily pressed her nose closer to the bus window and peered at the huge mansion with the six white pillars. "That place is amazing. Do the Hamiltons still live there?"

"Yes. The movie is using the ballroom but none of the other floors. The barns and track are unrestricted though. That's one of the reasons they were able to proceed with the film. Shooting on a single site keeps production costs lower."

"What kind of budget are we talking? Ten million?"

"More like thirty," Judith said. "And Mr. Harrison is one of the backers. So it's doubtful the movie will reveal his many affairs. Rather a pity."

Emily nodded, more at ease now with Judith's detailed knowledge. Earlier, it had made her feel unprepared, stupid even, but now she realized the woman was simply an avid movie buff. Besides, whoever had slept with Harrison almost a quarter century ago didn't matter much, although it was certainly remarkable that Reckless had jumped into a pool. And survived.

The bus shuddered to a stop.

She rose from her seat and followed the line of extras into the house, her heart pounding. It didn't matter now that she was only background. She was going to be working with genuine movie stars.

A frowning woman with a dangling headset herded them into an airy ballroom. And now Emily really felt like she was on a movie set. Lights, cameras and faces crowded the area. Three of the cameras were in a semi-circle around a smiling man at the front of the room.

"Is that Robert Dexter?" she whispered to Judith. "He looks smaller than I expected."

"Shush," Judith said.

Camera crew surrounded Robert Dexter and the regal lady beside him. Obviously the lady was Liana Mason. Emily rose on her toes, craning to see past all the heads. Liana Mason had been in several of her favorite movies and appeared just as classy in the flesh. Dexter was disappointing though—not nearly as charismatic as she'd imagined. Certainly not as attractive as Dan Barrett, who wasn't even an actor.

Someone rushed up and brushed powder on Dexter's forehead. Emily edged closer until she was only twenty feet away. Her fingers itched to pull the phone from her shoe and snap a picture. Anything to prove she was really here.

"Spread out, please," an authoritative voice directed. "Stand in groups of two to five." A man carrying a loaded champagne tray pressed a fluted glass in her hand.

"Stay away from the front." Judith tugged at Emily's arm. "We'll have a better chance of getting more work if our faces aren't seen."

Emily wavered. She understood the rationale, but it was incredibly tempting to squeeze closer to the action. Already many extras had pushed to the front. Besides, how would she be offered a speaking line if the director didn't even see her?

"You'll blow your shot at special skills if you go any closer," Judith warned. "And you already had your share of luck meeting Dan Barrett this morning."

Emily clasped her champagne and reluctantly followed Judith to the back of the room.

"Picture is up," a man yelled. "Quiet everyone!"

At least she had a good view of the set. But it was difficult to hear the words and it seemed as if the two actors said the same lines over and over again. Her drink wasn't even real, just some colored water in a plastic glass. And every time the assistant director yelled 'action background' she had to tilt her head and pretend to be having a fabulous time.

"This is boring," she whispered. "How many times are they going to shoot the same thing?"

"Until they get it right," Judith said, her voice rather distracted. Emily followed Judith's gaze to an older man with silver-streaked hair and a rather pompous expression.

"Is that the real Mr. Harrison?" Emily asked.

"Yes. Apparently he watches most of the scenes. That's his wife standing beside him."

The wife looked younger than Harrison or maybe she was just better preserved. "It must be neat seeing two famous actors pretending to be you," Emily said. "To have done something so important that it warrants a movie."

Judith sniffed. "All they ever did was own a fast horse. And Hamilton was such a playboy, I'm surprised his wife didn't leave him."

The assistant director gestured at the background performers. "Reckless will be introduced now. When you see the signal—we'll wave a yellow paper—rush to the pool window. Remember to keep your eyes on the horse."

Emily glanced over her shoulder. The pool behind the clear glass was a hubbub of activity centered around a compact brown horse with a distinctive white stripe on his forehead. A striking blond lady stood by his head.

"Wow. Is that Shania Stevens?" Emily whispered, recognizing the gorgeous actress.

"Yes, she's playing the part of the groom. The one that disappeared." Judith edged closer to the window.

"How do they get that horse to stand still with all this commotion?" Emily asked, unable to remain silent. Her gaze shot to the man beside the director. "Oh," she blew out an appreciative breath, absorbing Dan Barrett's chiseled face. No wonder the horse was relaxed. She'd already experienced Dan's super-calm vibes, his velvety voice.

"That's the reason all the directors want Barrett," Judith said. "His horses do the job right. And so far his stunts have been injury free."

The wiry director was gesturing now, obviously more tense than in the ballroom. Even the camera crew appeared strained.

"Is there a problem?" Emily asked.

Judith shrugged. "I don't know. But it's a complicated scene. The Humane Association always has a safety rep on location. Maybe the rules say a horse can only jump in a pool once a week or something like that. This would be a pain to re-shoot, with all the background. There are another twenty extras outside."

Emily glanced around. As directed, everyone was watching for the signal. Most people had drinks in their hands, although a few held cigars. They really did look like a roomful of partygoers being introduced to their host's horse for the first time. A few lucky extras had been chosen to stand by the pool. The woman with the bloody makeup was quite close to Dan.

"Quit drooling and look at the horse," Judith said. "Besides, Robert Dexter is happily married."

Emily jerked her head away. She'd actually been admiring Dan, not Dexter. And now she regretted listening to Judith. If she'd followed the cameras, she might have been chosen as part of the pool background. Maybe even had a chance to see how Dan directed his horse stunts.

A man in front of the camera slapped his clapperboard. Someone shouted, "Action!" A yellow paper moved above the window and the background performers surged forward.

It wasn't hard to pretend interest. Robert Dexter gestured at the clump of guests crowded around the horse. The colt pawed and jerked at the lead line, his eyes rimmed with white. Shania pulled at the line. It looked like she was in trouble.

Suddenly there were two blond handlers, but neither could hold the horse. He tossed his head and abruptly shot forward. Water cascaded around him as he leaped into the shimmering blue pool, accompanied by his waving mane, a snaking rope and scores of screaming people.

It was pure bedlam. The horse thrashed in the pool, his head disappearing beneath the water for long seconds, his hooves flailing amidst a frantic spray of white. Ladies screamed and Robert Dexter looked horrified.

Emily clasped a hand over her mouth, stifling her groan. This was horrible. The poor horse was drowning in front of them. And the brave groom was trying to lift his head. Had actually untangled the lead line from his front legs. And now the horse's head was out of the water and he was swimming. Shania swam beside him, guiding the colt to the extra wide steps in the shallow end.

The horse scrambled out, paused and shook like a dog.

"Cut!"

"Well done!" The assistant director rushed over to Dan Barrett and pumped his hand. The director looked at a screen, grinned and announced they were moving on. Everyone around the pool smiled and slapped backs.

Emily lowered her hand, shaking in disbelief. "Wow. I thought that was all real."

Even Judith remained silent for a moment. "They got it on the first take," she finally said, rather grudgingly. "They'll be happy. Unfortunately that means we won't be called back."

Emily lingered by the window, still in awe. The horse stood quietly now, completely unperturbed. In her opinion, he was the best actor here. Dan spoke with a blond lady, obviously the actress's double. It had been the stunt double, not Shania who had jumped into the pool but the action had been so seamless, Emily hadn't noticed the switch.

Three people dampened Shania's clothes, spraying her hair and face and adjusting her makeup. She looked drenched but utterly beautiful. Emily glanced back toward the horse who was being led away by a wrangler.

"That is the neatest thing I ever saw," she said. "I really want to keep working here."

"We all do," Judith said. "It's easy money, getting paid for standing around. This will end up being about ten hours' work. With the overtime, I might be able to pay my rent."

"If I didn't need the money so badly, I'd do this for free," Emily said, still staring as Shania posed in front of the cameras. "This is fascinating. Especially the horse jumping into the pool. What happens now?"

Judith didn't answer.

Emily glanced over her shoulder. Judith had already moved away, threading through the crowd but moving against the flow of people. Maybe she knew of another entrance, or a way to get closer to the action.

Emily charged in her wake, trying to stay close to her knowledgeable friend. It took a little bumping and several apologies before she reached Judith's side.

"Why did you leave so fast?" Emily asked. "Can we get closer to the pool?"

Judith shook her head. Her gaze cut to the left. Thomas Hamilton and his wife lingered by a side door, less than three feet away. He exuded satisfaction while his well-groomed wife appeared slightly aghast at all the strange people in their ballroom.

"So the interior shoot is finished?" Mrs. Hamilton asked. "Those cameras won't be back?"

Thomas Hamilton nodded. "Yes, but that was brilliant. The horse was a mirror image of Reckless." He patted her arm. "Remember how much fun that boy was?"

"It's not something I'll ever forget," Mrs. Harrison said. "I'll have refreshments readied for the director and his crew. Perhaps he'll leave a schedule of tomorrow's scenes." She exited through the side door, moving so smoothly she seemed to be gliding.

Emily watched the door shut, admiring the lady's grace. It wasn't just her clothes and carriage that portrayed impeccable breeding but also her manner of speaking. Such poise would take a lifetime to copy, and even then Emily feared her roots would always show. She gave a wistful sigh then realized Thomas Hamilton was staring.

"My wife wasn't so happy about this movie," he said, "but she intends to watch every one of Reckless's scenes. What role are you playing?"

"Just background," Emily admitted. "But I'm taking acting lessons."

"I'm Thomas Hamilton. I owned Reckless."

"Yes, I know. He was an amazing horse. Did he really jump into the pool like that?"

"Almost exactly like that." Hamilton's eyes settled on the plunging neckline of Emily's dress. "If you're going to be around this week," he added, "I can show you his grave."

"We'd love that," Judith said, abruptly stepping in front of Emily. "I'm a big Reckless fan too. Is it true you named him after Sgt. Reckless, the Korean war hero horse?"

Judith almost stepped on Emily's toes in her eagerness, and her voice sounded unusually husky. Flirtatious even. Emily edged back while Hamilton explained the origins of the horse's name. Thomas Hamilton wasn't a movie star but he was wealthy, and Judith was close to his age. Maybe Judith was more starstruck about meeting Reckless's owner than the younger actors.

Judith turned, her hands fluttering around her face. "Emily, can you take a picture?"

"Sure." Emily kneeled down and slipped the phone from the side of her shoe, feeling rather vindicated. It was a good thing she'd brought her phone.

Judith squeezed in beside Hamilton who adjusted his white collar and expertly posed. Clearly he was a man who loved having his picture taken—expected it even. Emily framed the pair in her phone screen. *Click.*

"Got it," she said, checking the picture. She shot a wistful look toward the pool deck, wishing she had a similar close-up of Robert Dexter to send Jenna.

"I'll look for you ladies around the set," Hamilton said. "Maybe we can chat more between scenes." His gaze shot back to Emily's chest.

She forced a polite nod, resisting the urge to tug up the neckline of her dress. It seemed strange that with all the exciting people here they were hanging around with this man; Judith had said he was a hound. But Judith was batting her eyelashes and acting surprisingly vivacious. Maybe she thought Hamilton would help her secure more work, although the trade-off would suck. His attention was clearly focused below the neck.

Emily crossed her arms. She'd had a few boyfriends like Hamilton, much younger of course, but they'd been nothing but an aggravation, messing up her life and her confidence. She gestured at the emptying room. "They're calling for background to leave now, Judith. We should join them."

"You go on without me," Judith said, barely turning her head. "You have that special skills audition. I want to hear more about Reckless. Besides, it doesn't matter if I miss the shuttle, as long as I catch the Louisville bus tonight."

Emily's eyes widened. Judith had preached about following movie protocol yet now she intended to linger. On the other hand, why should she be concerned? The woman was a virtual stranger; they'd only met ten hours ago. Maybe she enjoyed flirting with married men—ones who were film financiers.

"Okay," Emily said slowly. "Guess I'll catch you later. Do you know when the bus leaves?"

"Seven thirty," Judith said. "They have to feed us supper first. You should just go now."

She tilted her head back toward Hamilton. "However did you cope with missing the Derby?" Judith gushed. "It must have been frustrating owning the best three-year-old in the nation. Knowing he couldn't run."

Emily stepped back, rather hurt by the abrupt dismissal. She'd been dumped, just when she was learning to appreciate her friend's company. On the other hand, she now faced a pressing problem, one where Judith's bossy presence would be a definite hindrance.

'Show up in appropriate clothing,' Dan had said. She certainly couldn't audition for the groom's role in heels and a golden cocktail dress. Since there was nothing in her day bag, there was only one option. And persuading the wardrobe department to lend her suitable jeans was probably a job best tackled alone.

CHAPTER SIX

"We have no record of any jeans requirement." The wardrobe lady pursed her lips, scrutinizing her iPad. "Besides, background shooting is finished for the day."

"It's a new scene where I lead a horse." Emily leaned further over the table, fighting a rise of panic. Wardrobe was the only place where she could scrounge up a pair of jeans, but she hadn't realized the clothes were so strictly monitored. "They probably didn't have time to add it," she went on. "It shouldn't be a big deal. I just need some jeans…and boots and a shirt, socks and a belt."

The woman studied Emily, her eyes narrowing. "My supervisor is on a break. You better wait until she returns."

"Oh, but there's no time." Emily waved her hand, rather relieved the supervisor was absent. "*He* wants me ready in fifteen minutes."

"Who?"

"Dan Barrett. Look, here are his instructions." She tugged out Dan's business card, embellished now with a time and scene number penciled on the back. She wasn't certain how movie scenes were actually numbered, but the clapperboard by the pool had read one hundred and forty, so she'd jotted down one hundred and sixty-two.

The woman's mouth tightened. "Scene one sixty-two. I hate it when they reschedule and don't tell us." Shaking her head, she handed the card back and turned to the clothes racks. "What are the specifics? Groom or exercise rider?"

"Groom," Emily said, taking Dan's handy business card and slipping it back into her pocket. "But a well-dressed one. No ugly jeans but a designer type. And those tooled leather boots on the second shelf might fit. I like the silver belt on the hook too."

The woman's brow furrowed and she shot Emily an odd look. However, she gathered the items and handed them over with a tight smile.

Emily scooped them up and hurried into a change room, eager to escape the tent before the supervisor returned.

The shirt fit nicely and the boots were lovely, with leather soft enough to be comfortable but certainly not too worn. However, the pants weren't flattering at all. She certainly couldn't appear around Dan Barrett in ugly jeans.

She spent several precious minutes trying on more jeans, stoically resisting the compulsion to check over her shoulder for the supervisor. Finally the patient wardrobe lady—after the first five minutes she introduced herself as Maggie—dug up some lovely Hudson jeans that outlined Emily's legs perfectly.

Emily gave a satisfied thumbs up to Maggie and rushed from the tent, bolstered by the knowledge she was now suitably dressed. If a hunk like Dan Barrett had to see her looking like a groom, at least it would be as a well-dressed one.

"We're a day ahead of schedule." Anthony Jenkins rubbed his hands and gestured at the whiteboard. Dan had never seen the director look so pleased.

"If the weather cooperates, we'll switch back to the track tomorrow," Anthony said. "Where Dan can show us more of his magic."

The nine other people in the trailer turned and smiled at Dan. He shifted in the chair, always a bit impatient during the daily production meetings. Much of it related to interior scenes that didn't involve him—or the horses.

And he was concerned about Bruno. The gelding had been over zealous with his rearing and needed more work in the round pen. Tomorrow's scene with Ice should be a cinch though. Ice was a pro; that horse never put a hoof wrong.

"We'll be shooting out of sequence this week," Anthony said. "Shania has a cold and needs some time."

"She didn't like the splash from the pool," the AD said, rolling his eyes. "And unfortunately she's allergic to horses." He shot a snide look at the casting director who appeared unfazed by the criticism.

Anthony shrugged. "Shania's a box office draw. It's important to keep her happy." He flipped through the storyboards then tapped with an authoritative finger. "I'm going to jump ahead and shoot Reckless's behavior following the disappearance of the groom."

Dan kept his face impassive but inwardly cursed. Bruno was going to need his A-game this week. He was playing the 'bad' Reckless. Unfortunately Bruno was more intuitive than the actors and had quickly learned how to intimidate. He behaved perfectly with Dan, and the stunt doubles loved him. But his rearing was much too enthusiastic.

Maybe Ice should sub for Bruno. He could also rear on cue. However, Ice's maneuvers were submissive and much more mechanical. He was the type of horse who wanted to please. He definitely lacked Bruno's air of menace.

Dan dragged a hand over his jaw. A sigh leaked out.

Anthony swung aggressively toward Dan. "I assume you're okay with this?"

The director had mercurial mood swings but Dan liked working with him. Anthony was an award-winning director and a genius for capturing emotion, but what Dan appreciated most was that he didn't generally interfere with the horses.

Dan gestured at the whiteboard. "Can a male groom lead Reckless to the track? With the rear by the barn door?"

"I prefer the rear be in the aisle," Anthony said.

Dan shook his head. "Too dangerous. The horse could slip. It has to be on dirt. And the same horse can only rear twice in one day, unless we get special permission from the Humane Association."

"All right." Anthony blew out a long-suffering sigh but turned and jotted a notation on the board. "That entire scene will be shot outside, depending on the weather. But I want a female groom. And use background, not union. We have to stay in budget."

"Better make her young too," the AD suggested. "The public knows about Thomas Hamilton and his womanizing. Big boobs would be good."

Dan glanced at the casting director who now looked slightly concerned. They needed a new face. Three of their special skills background could handle Bruno, but two were males and the third groom wasn't young. Dan certainly couldn't remember the size of her boobs.

Fortunately they had a cattle call scheduled that afternoon. He could only remember one of the applicants though— Emily, the pretty blonde with great legs, mischievous smile and a penchant for director's coffee.

She was certainly attractive enough for the role. However, after fifteen years on movie sets, he'd grown immune to the lure of beautiful women. It had been her body language that intrigued him, bold but oddly wary, as if she was more inclined to fight than flee but with a hint of vulnerability. He'd never seen a background performer plucky enough to wrangle a coffee from the director's table. He'd always been drawn to courage. Time would tell if she could handle a horse.

He checked his phone messages, more impatient now with the meeting. It was almost four and the special effects details were always tedious. They had to find a new groom and Bruno needed a tune-up. Even the casting director was twitching.

"That's it for now," Anthony said, correctly reading the mood in the room. "We'll go over footage later after I finalize tomorrow's schedule. It's been another good day. Thanks, everyone."

Dan rose and stepped from the trailer, not surprised to see his top wrangler lingering outside. Lizzie was super efficient and had a sixth sense about when the meetings would end.

"We put Bruno and Ice in the end stalls," she said, hurrying to his side. "The eight for the track scene tomorrow have been exercised and are ready to go. Not sure who you want for the interior shoot but that last Reckless lookalike is dead lame. I stuck him in the stud barn by the caretaker's cottage. Looks like a tendon or ligament."

"Front left?"

"Yeah."

Dan grimaced but kept walking. The new gelding had looked a little sore when they led him off the trailer. Damn shame too, since he was a movie pro and a dead ringer for Reckless, right down to the blaze and two white socks. Now they'd have to paint some markings on another horse.

"Call the stock contractor," he said. "See what else they have. I'll look at the leg later. And put another horse in the barn for company. Use the quiet chestnut that came on the trailer with him."

"Okay," Lizzie said. "Want to grab a coffee? Go over the rest of my notes?"

"Not now. I have to look for some special skills."

Lizzie's head tilted in confusion. "I thought the track scenes were on for tomorrow."

"Anthony's made some adjustments," Dan said, as they rounded the corner of the building. "We're shooting out of sequence." He scanned the group of hopefuls gathered in front of the main barn. About fourteen performers had shown up. With a little luck, one of them would fit.

Scene changes always created challenges, and the casting director had made some questionable choices. An actress who refused to get close to a horse? Stunt doubles were working overtime. But to keep costs down, they urgently needed more extras who could handle a horse...a rambunctious horse like Bruno.

His gaze settled on Emily, the girl who'd braved the dragon lady for a cup of coffee. She'd swapped her skimpy dress for boots and jeans but the set of her shoulders remained the same, hinting at a steely determination. He hadn't even been sure she'd show up. She must be a local since extras didn't stay at the nearby hotel, or even on site like the wranglers.

He altered his course, joining the casting director who was already addressing the group.

"We need a female between the age of nineteen and twenty-nine who can be available at eight tomorrow morning," the casting director said. "Silent on camera but able to lead a horse. Bonus if you can ride."

Someone complained about lack of transportation and a wiry man with bowlegs muttered about discrimination. However, from the group of fourteen, six women stepped forward.

The casting director numbered them quickly, spoke to them for a moment then turned toward Dan. "Can you check out one, two and three? Any of those would fit."

Dan nodded, glad Emily had made the cut. He gave her a reassuring wink and gestured toward the barn.

"Follow Lizzie," he said to the three approved women. "She'll assign you each a horse to lead. Then we'll have you walk in a line toward the track."

He crossed his arms and waited. Minutes later, the three girls reappeared, each leading a horse. Lizzie and two wranglers hovered beside them. Girl one was technically competent but looked tentative, something any horse person would pick up on screen.

The second girl was a little too poised, and her artificial smile suggested she was a pro at showmanship. They might be able to work with that though. Her horse responded well, following as though confident in her direction.

The third girl—oh, damn. Emily had been assigned Bruno, the trickiest horse to handle. And she sauntered as though out for an evening stroll, her legs long and loose, curvaceous hips swinging, as though fully expecting her horse to behave. She definitely possessed the racetrack insouciance, relaxed and unconcerned, as if big bad Bruno was her pet poodle. The wind lifted her hair, the lighter streaks glinting in the sun. This would make a great pet commercial; however, Bruno wasn't anybody's pet.

Dan's gaze flashed to the horse. Bruno wore a curious expression as though still evaluating his handler. He hadn't done anything wrong, not yet, but there was a familiar trace of mischief in his eyes. Dan stopped breathing and waited.

He didn't have to wait long. Bruno's neck abruptly snaked, his big teeth flashing as he reached for Emily's wrist.

Her arm moved so swiftly it seemed like a coincidence. But at the same time that her elbow met his nose, she snapped the lead. Bruno jerked his head and blinked, looking utterly hurt, as though he would never dream of nipping his handler.

Dan exhaled. His biggest fear was that someone would get hurt, and he tended to worry more about the women than the men. He stepped forward, smiling his approval. "Number three," he said to Emily. "You ended up with the barn brat. But if you can handle him like that tomorrow, you're our new background groom."

He glanced at the other two applicants. This was the part he hated. He always felt rotten about sending people away and completely understood their disappointment. "We can't use you as special skills," he said, "but leave your name at the sign-in desk. They might need some extras later. Thanks for coming."

He motioned to his wranglers who took the lead lines and led away the two horses. Bruno and Emily remained. Her eyes glowed with lively intelligence and she looked even prettier now than she had this morning. The rosebud shape of her lips was more prominent without the bright lipstick...and he couldn't help but notice she fit the boob requirement.

Bruno stood patiently beside her, accepting her leadership and not even reacting when the other horses disappeared into the barn. It was amazing what one well-timed correction could accomplish.

Dan chuckled. "You have a very fast elbow."

Her eyes widened as if she'd expected a scolding and was rather taken aback by praise. "I wasn't sure what to do," she said. "It wasn't on the video—" She paused then continued in a rush. "But I can certainly let him bite me, if that's what you want."

She gave a flippant smile but he guessed she'd made a habit of hiding her feelings. "We definitely don't want him sinking his teeth into your arm," Dan said. "Did you have a lot of biters at the last place you worked?"

"Oh, yes. Heaps." She nodded, but the toe of her boot scuffed the dirt for a telltale second before she managed to still it.

He waited, sensing she had more to say, and if given time, the truth would come out.

"Well, one little guy was pretty bad," she added, "but I haven't handled that many tough horses before. Not really."

He edged closer, drawn by the conflicting emotions playing over her face. He'd made a career of working with horses, reading their body language, and humans weren't much different. Usually he preferred to focus on the animals, but this girl possessed an effervescent energy that sparked the air.

"Then you're a natural," he said. "Your correction was perfect. Even the wranglers have trouble with Bruno. He's one of the lookalikes for Reckless."

"Really? But my friend said Reckless had two white feet."

"Yes, and this guy will have white feet tomorrow. We'll paint him up. Especially if he does the rearing scene."

"He rears." Her eyes glinted, their color shifting from brown to warm caramel, and her voice had a mischievous lilt. "I tried to teach our pony to rear but my sister made me stop. She thought it was too dangerous."

"It is dangerous," he said. "But it's the quickest maneuver for portraying a mood, and audiences love it. Bruno can hang in the air for almost fifteen seconds."

"Great. Will I get to do that tomorrow? Hold him while he's rearing?"

He smiled. If Shania Stevens had half of Emily's spunk, the movie would be much cheaper to film. Shooting the pool scene had been a challenge—Shania hadn't even wanted to hold the lead rope. Luckily Shania's stunt double was immensely capable.

He dragged a hand over his jaw. It might be possible to use Bruno tomorrow, now that they'd found Emily. But it was essential that she trust the horse so she could concentrate on the director's rapid-fire direction. He waved off a hovering Lizzie and turned back to Emily.

"Let's go to the round pen," he said. "You can watch Bruno and decide if you're comfortable. If not, we'll use another horse. But I'd like to use this guy."

She hesitated, nibbling at her lower lip as though considering a more pressing engagement.

He crossed his arms, making no effort to hide his irritation. "We need to find this out now. So do you have time, or not?" Earlier she'd acted delighted to be chosen for the background work, flashing him such a luminous smile it had made his breath quicken. He liked keeners, preferring to work with performers who put in the extra time to ensure a smooth scene. Her gumption was obvious but perhaps he'd misread her desire. "It's no problem if you're busy," he added. "I can call back one of the others."

"No need." She tightened her hand on Bruno's lead. "I'm totally free tonight."

CHAPTER SEVEN

Emily shaded her eyes from the setting sun and watched the man and horse in the round pen. The responsiveness of the big bay was amazing. This was the same gelding, Bruno, that she'd led for her audition. However, he behaved very differently now. His eyes and ears were locked on Dan, attuned to his handler's slightest command.

Dirt sprayed as Bruno slid to a stop, turned on powerful hindquarters and cantered in the opposite direction. Such beautiful movement. His back was rounded, his body so light and coiled it seemed he could move, catlike, in any direction.

He had no bridle, saddle or halter, only the laser focus of his trainer—that same concentration she'd felt when talking to Dan. She'd lunged horses before, had often chased Peanut around, but it hadn't been like this. Never like this. The communication between man and horse was inspiring. It was hard to spot Dan's signals: a head tilt here, a drop of the shoulder there, occasionally an open palm.

The fact that she was on a movie set suddenly became secondary to the magic of observing an elite trainer partnering with his magnificent horse.

She wasn't sure how much time had passed. Had stopped fretting about catching the bus to Louisville. And when Bruno stopped and Dan walked toward her, she still gaped.

"Would you be comfortable holding this horse if he were asked to rear?" Dan asked.

"I'd be comfortable crawling between his legs and holding his tail," she said.

Dan laughed then, a deep sexy laugh that left her appalled by her bluntness. She tended to speak and act too rashly. He was someone she needed to impress, the man who would decide if she could handle the role. But he had a rare quality that put her at ease, an astuteness that made her think he understood people—yet liked them anyway.

Even during the special skills interview, she hadn't been nervous. His presence had been comforting, almost like that of an old friend. And when he'd winked, her heart had given a little kick and her confidence had soared.

She'd sensed Bruno might be tricky judging from the sideways grins of the wranglers. And it was clear Lizzie, the wrangler with the Aussie accent, was extremely possessive of her boss. Not surprising. Dan was stunningly handsome and when he smiled deeply, like he was doing now, it left a giddy feeling in her chest. Dammit, even her breathing had quickened.

"I'll be behind you tomorrow, directing Bruno. Reckless's lifelong groom has just quit so we need the horse to act upset. The more aggressive, the better." Dan paused, as though studying her reaction. "And the director will want you close in order to emphasize the horse's size. It can be intimidating."

Emily glanced at Bruno who waited beside Dan, alert and ready for direction. He looked as dangerous as a lapdog. It certainly wasn't the horse who left her feeling unsettled.

"Bruno will appear different in the air," Dan went on. "Originally we had Reckless moping in the stall, but the director wants to emphasize how badly the horse acted with his new groom."

So they needed a different face. Emily nodded, doubly grateful for Judith's advice. If she'd been front and center in the ballroom, she wouldn't be eligible for this scene. "I'm happy to do it," she said. "Or anything like that. I'm used to rearing horses."

Dan said nothing, just kept his gaze on her face as if to make sure she was finished talking. She'd always thought a good listener was really thinking of something else. But that wasn't true with him. In fact, the sheer force of his attention pulled more words from her mouth.

"Those horses weren't rearing on cue though," she added. "Mainly they were scared or disobedient. But what you were doing with Bruno was amazing. He's a perfect actor."

Dan smiled, the lines around his jaw deepening. "We actually need six horses for the full-grown Reckless. A horse to rear, one to bite, one to lie down and two to gallop."

"That's five," Emily said. She liked it when Dan spoke. It gave her a reason to stare at his face.

"And one in the stall," he said. "A quiet one that even Shania can touch."

His voice had turned slightly reproachful when the leading lady was mentioned, and Emily felt a spike of relief that he didn't idolize the gorgeous actress. "What about the horse in the pool?" she asked, straightening her thoughts.

"That was Reckless as a two-year-old. Played by a Quarter Horse called Splash. He did a good job today."

"It looks like Bruno wants to do a good job too," she said, surprised by the gelding's submissive demeanor. "He wouldn't dare bite you."

"He's smart but headstrong. That's what makes him fun. Until you came along, I was considering using a different horse. Our earlier background performer was so intimidated, he dropped Bruno's lead line and jumped behind the cameraman."

Emily smiled and studied Bruno. Despite being free, the horse remained beside Dan, as though there were no other place in the world he'd rather be. She couldn't imagine anyone being afraid, not when Dan was around.

"Should I practice with him?" she asked.

Dan shook his head. "We want to keep your reaction fresh. And with the horses, too much practice can make it look artificial. The director will work with you tomorrow, tell you what he wants. Be flexible. Your call time is eight. It's just a simple scene."

A simple scene. Maybe to him, but not to her. She was going to be in a real movie, holding the horse playing Reckless. Sure, it was just background but at least Jenna would see her on screen, if only for a second.

She bounced on her toes, unable to hide her eagerness. "Thanks so much. I'm really looking forward to it."

"So you won't back out on me? On my horse?" He gave a teasing grin, his teeth flashing white. "You won't drop the lead line and run?"

"I definitely won't run," she said.

CHAPTER EIGHT

Emily burst into the background tent, flushed with elation. Fortunately everyone was still here. It was almost eight, but the extra time with Dan and Bruno hadn't made her miss the bus. She scanned the jumble of bored faces and spotted Judith sitting on a bench close to the coffee table.

"I got the job," Emily called, rushing toward her. "Special skills. I'm going to be in a scene with Reckless tomorrow."

"Wonderful," Judith said, although her smile looked slightly wistful. "You'll be able to see everything. His stall, the track, all the people. Hamilton showed me Reckless's grave and even checked on background for me, but the only part they need tomorrow is for someone who can drive a tractor."

Emily nodded, realizing now what had motivated Judith to stay and chat up Hamilton. "I wish you'd find something too. But maybe you could come on the bus with me tomorrow and watch."

Judith's forehead wrinkled. "But there isn't a bus tomorrow. No extras are needed. Only a few special skills."

"No bus?" Emily sank on the bench beside Judith. "But how will I get here?"

"Extras find their own transportation unless a lot of background is required, like today." Judith gave a sympathetic shrug. "Don't you have a car either?"

"Not one that's running," Emily said. "And I have to come. I promised Dan I'd show up."

"There's a hotel a few miles down the road. Most of the cast stay there. Maybe you could get a room."

Emily nodded, too proud to admit she was flat broke. Her last dollar had been spent on an awesome pair of shoes, perfect for the nineties. But perhaps Jenna could call the hotel desk and make a reservation. Burke and Jenna had stacks of credit cards.

She tugged out her phone. There were a couple of texts and finally one from Jenna: *Working with Robert Dexter. Yay. So proud of you, movie star!*

Emily studied the message, her throat tightening. She couldn't remember the last time she'd made Jenna proud. Unfortunately, her sister misunderstood. Emily wasn't actually working with Robert Dexter. She'd be lucky to even talk to him. And she certainly wasn't a star. It had been a major feat simply to be chosen as special skills.

She stared at the text, feeling herself shrink.

"You must have had a bang-up audition." Judith gave Emily a congratulatory pat on the back. "Being chosen by Dan Barrett is quite a coup. You definitely are scruffier now than when you were on the bus. You look like a real stable hand."

Emily swiped at the horsehair clinging to her borrowed shirt. Ironically the expensive shoes and dress she'd purchased hadn't helped land the job. Next time she'd save her money.

She shoved the phone back in her pocket. No way would she call Jenna for a loan. Her sister might ask deflating questions, like why the movie didn't cover a hotel. And right now, Emily felt better than she had in months. She'd actually landed work on a movie set.

At least Judith understood her accomplishment. "It's kind of a neat scene," Emily said, turning back to Judith. "I hold Reckless who's very upset after his groom quit."

"The groom didn't quit. I told you before. She disappeared."

"Right." Emily nodded, trying to appease Judith's sense of detail. "Anyway, after the groom *disappeared*, Reckless goes crazy. Dan said they have different horses to bite and rear and stuff. I get to hold the rearing one. His name is Bruno and he's gorgeous."

"You were with Dan Barrett? Or was it an assistant?"

"It was Dan. He let me watch while he worked with the horse. Wanted me to see that Bruno is obedient so I can trust him when he rears. Dan seems nice." Emily peered at Judith, hoping for some Internet trivia. "Dan seems really nice," she prompted.

"Oh, yeah," Judith said. "He knows his stuff. He's a Barrett, from one of the oldest families in Montana. When he's not on a movie set, he's at his ranch."

"Must be hard," Emily said. "Moving around the country, separated from...wife and kids." She held her breath and pretended to inspect her painted nails.

"Yes." Judith nodded. "According to Mr. Hamilton, Shania already complained about this remote site. Hamilton told me lots of interesting stuff. And he's going to try to get me another background job later this week."

"That's great." Emily waited a moment then tried again. "Are most of these movie people married?"

"Robert Dexter is. Shania isn't."

Emily gave a rueful smile. She wasn't interested in the marital status of Shania, or even Dexter. However, Judith's interest was clearly focused on the actors. Admittedly, Emily's had been too—until she'd met Dan.

Still, it was much more important to figure out where she would stay tonight, rather than waste energy wondering about a man who was so far out of reach, he might as well be in a different constellation.

She dragged her thoughts back to her current problem. "They're only using a couple barns for the movie. Does that mean the other buildings are empty?"

"Totally empty," Judith said. "Why do you ask?"

"I need to find a place to sleep...just in case the hotel is full."

Emily waved as Judith joined the line of weary extras and climbed onto the idling bus. The aisle light spotlighted Judith's drawn face until passengers streamed around her and she disappeared from sight. Most of the performers looked relieved to be heading home, in contrast to Judith's reluctant expression. One man was already asleep, eyes shut, his cheek flattened against the window.

Hopefully, Judith would land more movie work. Despite her eccentricities, Emily liked the older lady.

Minutes later, the bus rumbled away. A plume of gray exhaust spiraled from the tailpipe, marking its trail before fading into the night.

And then Emily was alone. She swallowed, hugging her bag closer to her chest. After the earlier frenetic activity, the movie site seemed deserted. The production crew had packed up for the day. Even the wardrobe tent was closed. Muted conversation drifted from a string of silver trailers beyond the tents but she felt isolated, and uncertain.

She never liked that feeling and squared her shoulders, trying to fool herself into feeling more confident. No way would she miss tomorrow's shoot. Her car was busted, she had no hotel money but according to Judith there were plenty of empty barns on the estate. And she had certainly slept in barns back home.

Grabbing her resolve, she started walking, skirting the tents and trailers and using the moonlight to pick her way over the thick coils of wires. Fortunately she still wore her groom's clothing. She'd forgotten how comfortable barn boots were. Navigating this rough ground would have been more difficult in heels.

The outline of a familiar building loomed—the main barn, the hubbub of activity and the site of her earlier audition. Stall windows glowed in a neat row of illuminated squares. A night watchman hovered in the doorway.

She veered to the right, trying to avoid his attention, and followed a rubber walkway to an adjacent barn. This building was unlit, and hopefully unmanned.

She stepped inside and waved her phone light. The long aisle appeared deserted. The stalls were empty of horses, filled only with moldy boxes and a string of dangling cobwebs. Something fluttered from the rafters.

She gripped her bag, trying to ignore her thumping heart. It was blindfold dark, and the weak phone light only extended a few feet. Bats and rodents—even an imagined bogeyman—had never scared her before. But when she'd slept in the shed back home, she always had company, if not Jenna then Peanut. Odd how a little pony could provide so much comfort.

And these huge barns were devoid of horses and not one bit friendly. They stretched in a lifeless line, their shadows silhouetted by an eerie yellow moon. Their stillness made her skin prick, like she was the only survivor in a hostile land.

A horse nickered in the distance, a faint but welcome sound. She hurried from the barn, trying to pinpoint its source. Definitely a horse. But where had it come from? Not the movie barn with the guard but from the opposite direction.

She edged through the shadows, following an equine walkway that hooked into the trees then turned into a crude footpath. Something rustled in the underbrush; a heavy rodent-like body moving scant feet away. Her stride quickened until she was moving so fast she almost tripped. And then, thankfully, she saw it—a compact two-story building tucked away in the trees. It was much smaller than the last buildings but bigger than a cottage. White-railed paddocks flanked the west side, matching the gleaming white shutters on the windows.

She stepped closer, peering inside. A night light illuminated the aisle, revealing six roomy stalls. The door at the far end was padlocked.

A bay horse abruptly stuck his head over the door, his eyes inquisitive. Then he nickered, such a welcoming sound that she smiled with relief and walked into the barn. She paused to stroke his neck, enjoying how his breath warmed her face. He had a distinctive white blaze and wore a blue blanket. His front legs were wrapped and the familiar smell of horse liniment thickened the air.

"Hi buddy," she said. "Want some company?"

She glanced around the cozy barn. The stall to his left housed a sleepy-eyed chestnut who barely looked at her. But other than the two horses, the building was empty.

She peered over the door of an adjoining stall, relieved to see fresh hay and six bales of straw stacked neatly against the wall. One bale was even open. Perfect. It would be possible to make a comfortable bed without leaving any mess.

Something brushed her ankle. She leaped backwards in shock. A gray cat with a ragged ear gave a plaintive meow and stared expectantly. Smiling, she scooped him up and headed for the straw. This couldn't get much better. Two horses and a warm cat for company. Best of all, it was within her price range.

"Look at Shania's horrified expression." Anthony gestured at the screen, his entire body twitching with energy. "This pool footage looks so genuine. And the double's switch is seamless." He gave an enthusiastic thumbs-up to Dan, then nodded at the department heads. "Keep it up. We'll have another good day tomorrow."

Anthony rose from the table, passed a progress report to the producer and turned toward Dan. "A slight change tomorrow. Shania is feeling better so I want to film the stall scene and the doorway shot. Forecast calls for red sky in the morning."

"Okay," Dan said. "I'll have both an old and young Reckless ready."

"No, we'll save the rearing scene for the rain, depending on what special effects can do."

Dan nodded. Anthony often adjusted his shooting schedule but never on such short notice. However, Ice was primed for his cuddly sunrise scene, and the production office would advise riders of new call times. The only performer they couldn't reach was Emily. He'd intended to take her phone number in case of a change but had been distracted by her throaty laugh, the hip-swinging walk, her tempting curves—she made the day more interesting and admittedly he'd been thinking of more pleasurable things.

Naturally he wouldn't pursue the attraction. He'd learned to keep his trailer door locked. Movie shoots had enough complications, and the hurt look in feminine eyes when it was time to ship out simply wasn't worth the sexual gratification. It was difficult enough to pat the horses good-bye.

Most women, despite pretty assurances to the contrary, wanted to prolong a relationship long after its due date. His business took him across North America while actresses were pulled in other directions. Long distance relationships always fizzled, no matter how much love and trust was proclaimed at the wrap party. He didn't have the time or inclination to worry about a demanding actress who was chasing her own agenda. And he hated telephone affairs. They turned people jealous, petty and paranoid.

Of course, Emily was a background performer, not an actress. She didn't face the same temptations as someone like Shania.

He snorted and gave his head a shake. Who was he kidding? Simply looking at Emily's lush mouth made him think of sex. Any red-blooded guy would hit on her in an instant. When she'd flashed that provocative smile and offered to crawl between Bruno's legs, he'd had a raunchy image of doing her against the rails. It was a good thing he didn't have her phone number.

Not so good for her though, considering she wouldn't learn about the change in call time until tomorrow. Of course, she'd be compensated. Most background performers didn't mind being paid to wait, especially if they lived in the area.

He scooped up a copy of the revised schedule, nodded goodnight to the script supervisor and strode toward the door. These nightly meetings could drag past midnight and it was his habit to slip out early after gathering feedback on his horses' performance. Anthony generally gave him free rein, one of the reasons Dan liked working with the talented director.

Dan yawned, grateful his trailer was on site. He needed to check back on the lame horse then catch up on some much-needed sleep. Traveling to a hotel cut into valuable time, and he always preferred accommodations close to the animals.

A narrow path edged from the back of the trailers to the more isolated stud barn, a short cut that reduced his walk by five minutes. The little barn was perfect for a lame horse or, God forbid, any animal requiring quarantine. It was conveniently close but removed enough from the action that the horse would have a better chance of settling, especially if given a quiet companion.

A gelding's blazed face stuck over the stall door, liquid eyes tracking Dan's approach. The horse gave a low nicker, his expression bright. Despite being restricted to stall rest, the animal seemed in good spirits. It was unfortunate he was lame; this bay was a dead ringer for Reckless.

Dan scratched the underside of the horse's jaw and scanned his legs over the stall door. One of the wranglers— probably Lizzie—had done a competent job. The wraps appeared firm and even, forming a perfect stovepipe pattern. The blanket was probably overkill but the gelding looked cozy.

He checked the tightness of the bandages then slipped a hand beneath the blanket, making sure the horse hadn't overheated. The temperature was about sixty degrees, a lovely spring night, and certainly comfortable enough without a blanket.

He gave the horse a final pat and moved on to check the chestnut in the next stall. This Thoroughbred had also been supplied by the stock contractor and, as promised, the gelding was very quiet. Life was easier when they possessed a good mind. Movie horses needed to be adaptable. This fellow was a perfect companion, not seeming to care about the barn change, as long as he was provided with plenty of hay. And right now, both horses clearly wanted more to eat.

It was hard to resist a hungry horse and neither of these guys were fat. It wouldn't hurt to toss them an extra flake, especially since they'd been shuffled away from the action. Unlike humans, they didn't care if they missed their shot at fame.

He turned to the hay stall, slid open the door and stepped in. A scruffy gray cat darted between his legs. His smile froze in surprise.

Someone slept in the corner, curled in the hay with an open newspaper spread over his chest. The retired caretaker perhaps? Dan hadn't met him yet but apparently a longtime employee still lived in the caretaker's cottage. The man had lived and worked on the estate for over sixty years. Poor fellow. Maybe he felt responsible for these horses and didn't realize they'd been shipped in for a movie.

But when Dan edged sideways, light from the aisle filtered past revealing the sleeping face. His eyes widened. This definitely wasn't the caretaker but instead his most recent hire, the woman who'd been coloring his thoughts.

Emily's eyes were shut, her dark lashes flattened against creamy cheeks. Stripped of makeup and that veneer of toughness, she looked younger, more vulnerable. But even asleep, her mouth looked…lively. He backed up, fighting the unwanted pull of sexual attraction. *Time for me to go.*

But he hesitated, his protective instincts surging. She must be uncomfortable, and cold. The urge to scoop her up and carry her back to his warm trailer was almost unbearable.

And why was she sleeping in a barn? There was a decent hotel only three miles away with a shuttle service for cast and crew.

He shook his head in pained realization. She was background. Extras found their own transportation unless numbers justified bussing. He'd asked her to watch Bruno in the round pen, assuming she lived close by. They both knew it hadn't been a request.

Had she missed the bus? He'd given her an early call time, for a scene that was now postponed. She didn't need to be here for at least another day. He jammed his hands in his pockets, battling with his conscience.

People did crazy things to get in the movies but this was background—merely holding a horse for thirty seconds. She must desperately want the job. And she didn't look *that* uncomfortable, more like someone accustomed to making the most out of a tough situation.

He stooped and adjusted the newspaper, pulling it higher over her chest. Her breathing remained slow and even. His knuckle brushed her cheek and he jerked his hand back. But she didn't move, and the peaceful look on her face remained unchanged.

He glanced at the open doorway. She was a sound sleeper. Anyone could walk in and clearly she'd be oblivious. The barn was probably safe enough—that lecher Hamilton was tucked away in the mansion with his highbrow wife—but it didn't feel right to leave a woman in isolation, sleeping under newspaper like a homeless waif.

He hesitated for another moment, then scooped up some hay for the hungry horses...and proceeded to look for a chair.

CHAPTER NINE

A familiar ring tone chimed. Emily groaned, too cozy and warm to move but the sound was irritatingly insistent. She fumbled for her phone and shut off the alarm. A horse nickered, jolting her awake. She jackknifed up.

This was the day she'd lead Reckless! Not a speaking role, but still a good start. She scrambled to her feet, dislodging a blue horse blanket, still warm from her body. She picked up the blanket and walked into the aisle, studying it in confusion.

The friendly bay nickered and pressed his chest against the door...his bare chest. She rubbed her eyes. Somehow his blanket had ended up on her.

"Sorry, fellow," she murmured. She wasn't a sleepwalker and certainly didn't remember borrowing his blanket. An empty chair sat against the wall of the hay stall. She couldn't recall seeing the chair last night either, but it seemed she couldn't remember a few things.

The bay nosed at her shoulder. It was tempting to slip him a flake of hay, a thank you for his hospitality, but it was early and whoever fed the animals might not be pleased. She considered putting his blanket back on, but entering a strange horse's stall, uninvited, was an even bigger taboo.

"I'll try to come back and visit later," she said. "Thanks for sharing your barn."

She left the blanket folded on the chair and stepped outside.

The sun poked over the ridge, the air crisp and invigorating. This area of the estate was especially beautiful with a secluded lane shaded by stately elm trees. Maybe this cozy barn was used by the Hamiltons and the two horses inside weren't involved in the movie. But someone must have covered her with that blanket. As a result, she'd had a wonderful sleep, and she was appreciative.

Voices and vehicles rumbled beyond the trees and she edged to the left, following a curving driveway toward the noise. Several portable toilets were on site. With a little luck, she might find running water. And breakfast. Her stomach rumbled at the thought of food.

She quickened her steps and rounded a bend, eager to spot a washroom of some sort. The movie site still wasn't visible though, only a small cottage that bordered the drive. A man with a wooden cane struggled to swing back a barred gate.

"Good morning," she said. She was about to slip around the bar and continue up the drive, but he looked feeble. She hesitated, then detoured to his side and helped push the steel bar back.

"Thanks." He grunted with satisfaction. "Mr. Hamilton wants me to open the gate every morning. They're going to make a movie of Reckless."

"Yes, it's started," Emily said. "They're shooting up by the main barn."

"They're going to make a movie," the man repeated. "And I have to open the gate."

"Yes." She slowed her voice. "It's good you're here to do that. Do you live in the cottage?"

"Yup. Not many people visit anymore but someone has to open the gate. Today my groceries are delivered." He gave an irritable tap of his cane. "Hope they bring everything. Sometimes they forget my doughnuts."

"I hope they bring everything too," Emily said cheerfully. "Thanks for opening the gate."

"Remember. I close it at dark." His caterpillar eyebrows drew together in a warning line. "You can't come through here all hours of the night."

"I certainly won't." She nodded, her opinion of Mr. and Mrs. Hamilton rising. The old caretaker took his job seriously, and it was kind of them to let him remain in the cottage and provide him with a job.

She waved and continued walking, following the driveway until it looped around the corner of the track. A starting gate gleamed whitely and a group of workers splashed fresh paint on a section of rail. A large barn, the first in a row of buildings was clearly the hub of activity. People and cameras rimmed the area. However, there was no sign of Dan or the casting director.

She blew out a relieved sigh. Her hair was a mess and she didn't wear a speck of makeup. She needed to find a bathroom. And quickly. If they saw her looking this ugly, they might fire her on the spot.

She strode into the empty dining room, head high and pretending she had a right to be there. It was easier now that she knew the layout. She ignored the squinty-eyed attendant, reached under the table and pulled out the paper cups and a tray. She made two cups of pod coffee while she scanned the walls for signs. Toilet and sink but no shower.

Disappointed, she trudged from the tent, balancing the coffee tray. She'd expected much better facilities at a movie site. *Not even a shower?*

She entered the wardrobe tent, blinking as her eyes grew accustomed to the different light. Luckily Maggie, the helpful lady who'd outfitted her in the groom's clothes, was already sorting shirts.

Maggie laid down a plastic hanger and gave Emily a cautious nod that blossomed into a big smile when Emily passed her the coffee.

"Thank you, sweetie," Maggie said, selecting a packet of sugar from the condiments on the tray. "I'm alone for the first hour and it's impossible to grab a coffee. Are you working as a groom again?" She tilted her head, her eyes narrowing. "Why didn't you return those clothes yesterday?"

"I was in a rush last night," Emily said. "This morning too. Even had to skip my shower. I'm surprised there's no running water on the grounds."

Maggie shrugged. "Anyone who's important has a trailer. Or a hotel room."

"I see." Emily swallowed. It would be impossible to primp in a portable toilet. Judith had warned about background's lowly status but the reality stung. "Do you have a bathroom here where I can clean up?" she asked, her voice small.

Maggie jabbed with her thumb. "Toilet and sink, second door. But you look fine. They want the grooms with basic hair and clothes. Let me check the wardrobe sheet and I'll fix you up."

"Okay." Emily paused, hating how she always felt like a bum. "But I'd hoped to keep these clothes from yesterday…in case of a later scene. It gets so busy."

Maggie took a thoughtful sip of coffee and nodded permission.

"Thanks," Emily said, vastly relieved to have a second set of clothes. "I'll be right back."

She left her coffee on the table and hurried into the bathroom. It was tiny, not much bigger than the bathroom on the bus, but she managed to squeeze out enough soap and water for a rudimentary wash.

When she returned, Maggie had already pulled out a faded pair of Gucci jeans and a clean shirt.

"I thought you'd appreciate the high end jeans," Maggie said wryly. "And I already had your sizes recorded. If you hurry over to hair and makeup, they'll check you out."

Emily nodded gratefully, then paused. She'd deliberately glossed over her clothes predicament, but without Maggie's support she never would have landed the groom's job. "Thanks for your help yesterday," she said. "Those boots and jeans were perfect."

Maggie gave a knowing smile. "Just make sure you return everything. I've never had so many people worrying about the fit of their jeans. My supervisor calls it the Dan Barrett effect."

"It's not him," Emily said. "I just like clothes."

"Good thing. Because he avoids actresses like the plague."

"But I'm not an actress," Emily said quickly. "I'm only background."

Maggie laughed, so teasingly Emily even smiled. But she honestly wasn't worrying about Dan Barrett. Not like that. And it wasn't his good looks she found attractive. It was his attentiveness and that super-calm vibe. Besides, she wanted someone who wore a suit, not faded jeans that molded long legs and emphasized the way a man moved when he was comfortable in his body.

Her skin tingled and she grimaced. Okay, admittedly he was droolworthy, but men like that always cracked hearts, and she couldn't afford to be sidetracked. This was a big day. She intended to stay focused. It might even be possible to take a picture of the horses so she had something to send Jenna. Perhaps people photography was forbidden, but surely it wouldn't hurt to snap a few photos of Bruno. After all, he wasn't a human actor.

And Dan might not mind. He was so kind, so accommodating...although obviously not when in full work mode. When he'd folded those ripped arms yesterday and quietly suggested she stay, she hadn't thought about anything but agreeing.

Besides, it turned out she hadn't needed to catch the Louisville bus after all. And it had been great fun watching him work with Bruno. She'd enjoyed a lovely sleep and now had a special skills job lined up for today. Life was looking up.

She strolled to the makeup table, eager to have her face fixed so she could report to set. Maybe she'd do such a good job holding Bruno the director would give her a line. Just a few words, but then she'd be eligible to join the union. That would jumpstart her career.

Perhaps she should find another agent too. Clearly Tamara wasn't top notch. Heck, Judith would make a better agent. At least, she kept up with social media, and frankly Emily had landed this job solely because of Judith's inside knowledge. Judith might even know about movies in more exotic locations. It would be nice to go somewhere hot, or even travel to a different country.

"No makeup for you," the artist said, yanking back Emily's attention.

"What?" Emily's jaw dropped. "But I never go anywhere without makeup."

"Today you do," the woman said, checking her notes. She gestured at someone behind the chair. Emily winced as impatient hands pulled her hair into a painfully tight ponytail.

"We'll just brush on a little anti-shine powder," the technician continued, flourishing a thick brush. "Then you'll be ready to go."

Emily stared in the mirror, recoiling with horror. She'd expected to have the full movie treatment. She already felt grungy without a shower, but to have nothing on her face— she was bat shit ugly without makeup.

"Maybe just a little foundation and blush?" She averted her eyes, unable to look at her reflection. "Please…I really would feel more comfortable."

"Sorry." The technician snapped the powder case shut. "We just follow directions. And this isn't about you. It's about the movie."

Emily jerked from the chair. No makeup. And now with her hair pulled back, it was as if she'd been stripped naked. And she was going to be on a big movie screen too. Everyone would see her. The back of her eyes pricked, and she blinked furiously, pressing a hand over her exposed face. The day that had started out so bright and shiny had turned disastrous.

The last time she'd gone anywhere without makeup, her father's punishing hands had taught her a memorable lesson. If she hadn't made a promise to Dan, she'd hide in the hay stall. But she had to show up; he was counting on her to hold Bruno.

She sucked in a fortifying breath and shuffled toward the set.

"Shania will have to step a little closer to the horse," Dan said, trying to keep the impatience from his voice. It was difficult to show the affection between Reckless and the horse's groom when Shania insisted on remaining two feet from Ice's head. The attentive horse was waiting for his cue, but Ice couldn't press his forehead against Shania's chest when she stood so far away.

"Move closer, Shania," the director called. "Perfect. Now reach up and smile. Action!"

Ice, a seasoned performer, immediately lowered his head against Shania's chest. Shania, showing the acting chops that had made her a box office draw, blinked prettily and wrapped her arms around his neck. It looked so real even Dan smiled. No doubt about it, the lady could act.

"Cut!"

"Did you get the sunrise? Let's see." Anthony adjusted his headset and bent over the screen while an assistant rushed up to Shania and offered her a sip of coffee.

Dan picked up the lead line and scratched Ice behind the ear. "Good boy," he murmured. The horse had been perfect. Anyone watching would never question his devotion to Shania. Ice was so savvy, he even knew the word 'action' and when to ham it up. Right now though, the gelding just wanted to return to his stall. He'd been outside the barn for the last hour and was due for his rest break.

"Moving on," the director finally called, to a collective sigh of relief.

Dan nodded at Lizzie who stepped in and took Ice's lead line. "Wash off the blaze and turn him out in the round pen for a roll," Dan said. "Have someone hand graze him for thirty minutes but keep him off the clover."

"Okay," she said with a smile. "He's a real lover boy."

"That he is," Dan said, with another pat for the horse. Ice had been in over ten movies and his specialty was his doglike behavior to humans. His trick of pressing his big head to a person's chest could soften the most cynical of hearts.

"Can you train your horse not to shed, Dan?" Shania asked, as she brushed at the hair clinging to her shirt. Two more assistants rushed to her side. One waved a damp cloth while another carried a box of tissue.

Shania waved off her entourage and smiled at Dan. "Contrary to what you might have heard, I do love horses. Unfortunately, I'm slightly allergic."

He nodded but his attention drifted sideways, drawn by the long-legged girl walking toward the set. Obviously Emily wasn't allergic. In fact, she looked fresh-faced and dewy after a night in the barn. But there was something different about her walk, about the way she held her head.

Shania tugged at his arm. "Are you joining us for dinner tonight? The hotel is flying in live lobster. I hope you'll make it."

"I'm busy with the horses," he said.

"Surely you can take a little time off." She gave a pretty pout. "Everyone needs to eat."

He gave a polite murmur but his attention shifted back to Emily. She probably wondered what had happened to the rearing scene. Maybe that's why she looked so subdued. Or perhaps she hadn't slept well, although he could have sworn she'd never once woken.

And he should know. The plastic chair had been too small, too hard and not at all conducive to a restful night's sleep. Probably that's why he was a tad impatient with Shania's attempts to pull him into her fan league.

She was still prattling about how she preferred lemon butter with lobster but never ate the tomalley. He simply crossed his arms and let his mind drift. A makeup person tilted Shania's head, brushing at her cheeks, and he seized the chance to escape. The next scene didn't involve horses anyway. They were shooting Shania in the aisle, hard at work loading a wheelbarrow with manure.

He strode toward Emily who watched him approach with something akin to panic. He slowed his stride, wondering if his impatience with Shania was evident on his face.

"Your scene isn't cut," he said. "It's only postponed until tomorrow. Sorry to drag you out so early today. I didn't have your phone number or someone would have called."

"Oh." She flashed him a relieved smile. "I wondered what happened. I've been watching the shooting though. Which Reckless was that?"

"That's the quiet one, Ice. He hugs on cue." His eyes settled on the cute dusting of freckles over her nose. He'd noticed them last night when she was sleeping. There was a little mole on the right side of her mouth too, just above the rosebud curl. Damn sexy, and he couldn't stop staring.

But she averted her head, her shoulders rounding almost imperceptibly. Definitely uncomfortable. And strangely tentative compared to yesterday. How the hell was she going to handle Bruno?

"Are you feeling okay?" He eased back a step, giving her more space.

She flinched, her hand sweeping to her cheek, and there was no mistaking the hurt in her big brown eyes. "I'm fine," she said quietly. "Sorry I look a little rough."

"If you want to go home, leave me your number. If you don't hear anything, you'll have the same call time tomorrow. But you'll be paid a half day rate for showing up this morning."

She blinked then gave him such a grateful smile, his chest kicked. "Really? I get paid for showing up? That's awesome."

"Or you can hang around and get paid for the entire day," he said impulsively. Obviously she needed the money, and in his opinion she deserved it. "Do you live close by?"

"I'd love to stay," she said. "I could clean stalls. Or wash dye off horses, bath them, whatever needs to be done."

She hadn't answered his question although her helpful offer was appreciated. Wranglers looked after the horses and delivered them for each scene, but it was always hectic, especially when animals needed extensive grooming. And Emily was obviously very capable in that department.

When they'd met in the dining tent, her shapely legs had been showcased by three-inch heels. During her interview, she'd flashed designer jeans and lipstick lips. She'd looked like someone pretending to be a groom. Today though, she was ponytail pretty in scuffed boots and faded jeans. She looked like a real horseperson, certainly someone who could bathe a horse. He already knew she was tough enough to sleep in a stall and skip a shower.

His eyes narrowed in sudden comprehension. Naturally she was eager to wash horses. There were no public showers on site; she probably needed soap and water. And her shirt today was typical groom issue. Clearly she'd been prepped by the wardrobe people. Maybe she was too proud to admit she had no place to stay...or that she couldn't afford one. He knew what it was like to be reduced to sharing a horse's bath.

"I could use some help later," he said, watching her reaction. "There's a wash stall in the stud barn past the caretaker's cottage. A horse there needs cold water treatment."

Her little shiver was almost imperceptible.

Almost.

"We'll get the warm water going too," he added. "The barn hasn't been used in years but it was built for Reckless. It's well equipped. If you can hang around for an hour or so, I'll show you where it is."

"Sounds good," she said.

Her words were simple but her grateful smile lifted his spirits, and he returned to the set feeling more enthused than he had all morning. He even managed a genuine chuckle at one of Shania's horse jokes.

CHAPTER TEN

"Roll camera!" the assistant director called, from the middle of the barn aisle.

Emily stood among a smattering of bystanders, surrounded by the smell of wood and paint and excitement, trying to resist the urge to pinch her arm. Dan had told her to watch the action from the periphery. There was no need to sneak or pretend. She actually had permission—such an odd and comforting thing. Already she'd learned so much.

This was the sixth take of Shania who played the missing groom, Tracey, with Robert Dexter, playing Mr. Hamilton. They hotly discussed the benefits of moving Reckless to a smaller barn. Apparently Tracey and Mr. Hamilton had enjoyed a very close relationship, and Hamilton had been almost as upset as Reckless when Tracey had left.

"Action!" the director called.

Shania dropped the wheelbarrow and jammed her hands on her hips. She wore a low T-shirt and her chest heaved with each impassioned plea. Emily blew out a wistful sigh. They hadn't skimped on Shania's hair, or makeup. The actress looked stunning. If the original groom had looked anything like that twenty years ago, there was probably some truth to the rumor that Hamilton had been completely infatuated.

At some point Emily had stopped feeling self-conscious about her own lack of makeup, mainly because Dan didn't seem to notice. He treated her the same way as he had yesterday. And while most men salivated over Shania, Dan seemed only interested in the welfare of his horse.

"Cut!" the director called. Shania immediately turned to a hovering assistant and accepted a glass of mineral water.

"That looked realistic," a satisfied voice behind her said. "Exactly as I recall."

Emily glanced over her shoulder, recognizing Mr. Hamilton and his wife. Mrs. Hamilton's expression was slightly bored while he wore a complacent smile. His eyes passed over Emily with a complete lack of recognition—obviously he didn't remember their meeting yesterday. Or perhaps her groom's clothes fooled him. More likely, he was only friendly to ladies with plunging necklines.

"Will they be shooting any gallop scenes today?" Hamilton asked, seeming to address no one in particular.

A pasty-faced man shrugged but nobody answered. It seemed Mr. Hamilton wasn't well liked. The silence lengthened.

Emily turned. "I believe the gallop scenes are scheduled to start tomorrow," she said.

"Good," Hamilton said. "My wife and I want to be here. Reckless was truly unbeatable once he settled down and decided to be a racehorse. Did we miss the rearing scene?"

"That's switched to tomorrow as well," Emily said.

"Thank you," Mrs. Hamilton said, politely inclining her head. "We'll come back then. Do you happen to know when the scene starts?"

Emily paused. Her new call time was eight but it was rather disconcerting how the Hamiltons considered her an expert. Still, nobody else seemed inclined to answer. "Eight o'clock, I think," she said.

"What about the scene when Reckless crashes through the rail?" Mr. Hamilton pushed in front of his wife, standing so close Emily could smell stale coffee and his liberal application of cologne. "Are they going to do that tomorrow as well?"

Emily doubted Dan would let one of his horses crash through a rail. He seemed very protective of anything under his care. "I'm not sure." She crossed her arms and edged back, trying to escape Hamilton's hot breath.

Suddenly Dan stood beside her.

"Morning." He nodded to the Hamiltons. "Tomorrow is the next scene with Reckless. We'll be using the horse you saw last week. Anthony's assistant has a revised schedule ready." He turned to Emily. "We need to go."

She followed him from the barn into the bright sunshine, not sure exactly where they were going but relieved to leave. It had been almost three hours of shooting for what appeared to be a one-minute clip. No wonder Shania looked grumpy off camera. There was a lot of standing around and waiting. Obviously it was the people behind the movie scenes, not the actors, who had the most fun.

"So, what did you think?" Dan asked, as though reading her mind. "Still want to be in the movies?"

"Of course but, well…" She hesitated but he remained silent, one of those rare people who didn't rush to complete someone else's sentence. "I was surprised it took so long to shoot a one-minute scene," she finally said. "Is the director always that fussy?"

Dan chuckled, and laugh lines bracketed his lean jaw. "Anthony demands excellence. That's why I like to get the horse scenes right on the first take. There's a strict limit to the amount of galloping or rearing they can do. And delays are expensive."

Emily clasped her hands, trying to control her flutter of nerves. She hoped she didn't mess up and cause a re-shoot.

But there were so many people and cameras and direction. So much confusion.

Shania hadn't seemed to notice the equipment focused on her face. But what if Bruno refused to rear? Worse, what if Emily dropped the lead line, or stumbled or didn't have the expression they wanted. So many things could go wrong.

"You'll do fine," Dan said. "Anthony wants us to do a run-through with Bruno today. You'll be ready by tomorrow."

"I'm starting to get scared." She blinked, rather shocked by her admission. She needed to impress this man, yet for some reason kept blurting out the truth. "Not scared of the rearing," she added. "I think it's the director and cameras watching every move."

"You'll forget them around a rearing horse. There's no time to pretend. Just be ready."

"That sounds like a warning."

A smile played around the corners of Dan's mouth. "Anthony often throws in an element of surprise so he can capture more emotion. Just get a good night's sleep and try not to worry. Do you live close by?"

"No. In Louisville," she said absently. "Good gosh, what's that?" They were skirting the track now and a wheelbarrow and pitchfork were propped against the outer rail. The wheelbarrow was filled with the strangest-looking manure.

"It's fake, made of paper," Dan said wryly. "Shania doesn't like the smell of the real stuff. And this section of rail is cardboard too. Bruno will be galloping through it later in the week."

"Oh," she said, still eyeing the paper manure in disbelief. "The Hamiltons were asking about the scheduling of that scene. Did Reckless really smash through a rail?"

"Yes," Dan said. "Apparently he was uncontrollable after his groom left. I was twelve at the time and remember hearing he wouldn't make the Derby."

"You'd think she would have returned," Emily said, "once she heard how much Reckless missed her."

"Maybe working for Mr. Hamilton wasn't the easiest thing for a young woman."

Emily glanced up, alerted by the change in Dan's voice. His jaw had hardened, his expression so cold it reminded her of Burke. Hard, tough, protective. "Did one of your wranglers have a run-in with him?" she asked, remembering how quickly Dan had whisked her away from Hamilton.

Dan's head swiveled. "How did you know?"

"Just a guess. It's clear he considers himself a bit of a stud. But he's probably harmless."

"Lizzie doesn't think so," Dan said. "She doesn't like being alone with him."

Emily hid a smile. Lizzie looked at Dan like he was a walking God, and it was doubtful the wrangler with the cute Aussie accent genuinely feared for her safety. It had been no coincidence that Emily had been assigned Bruno in the skills test, although that had certainly worked out in her favor. No, she sensed it had been Dan's encouraging wink that Lizzie resented.

Not that Lizzie had reason to worry. Emily touched her unflattering ponytail. She'd need considerable ammunition for someone like Dan to give her more than a wink. Maybe with makeup and proper clothes. Maybe if she were richer, smarter, skinnier…

"It's not a good idea for anyone to be wandering around here at night," Dan said. "There isn't much security for the size of the estate."

He sounded genuinely worried and she lowered her hand, rushing to reassure him. "I'm sure Lizzie has been in places far more isolated. Horse people are usually quite capable. Have you worked together before?"

"We met in New Zealand on the *Spartacus* set. She's part of the team I assembled for a couple movies." He pointed toward a footpath. "This is the quickest route to the stud barn. But at night, it's best to use the lighted driveway past the caretaker's cottage."

Emily had followed this same path yesterday and already knew it saved time. And she was extremely surefooted, even in the dark. Cutting through the woods was second nature to her and Jenna. They hadn't had a car when they were kids, so the path behind their trailer had been very well tramped.

Dan reached over her head, solicitously pushing aside a drooping branch. A flush warmed her face. She felt like she was fifteen again and on her first date with the quarterback of the football team. She scrambled for something to say. "This is a pretty walk," she said.

"Very pretty."

His eyes held hers for a heated moment. It was almost as if he was talking about her. But she wasn't pretty, not without makeup. Her father had always poked fun at her freckles and, except for Jenna, Emily didn't let anyone see her barefaced. She froze then turned so awkwardly she stumbled over a gnarled root.

Dan gripped her elbow, steadying her. He quickly lowered his hand but she could feel the imprint of each finger, and her skin still tingled. Unless it was poison ivy. She discretely checked both sides of the path but spotted only benign shrubs. Besides the tingle was nice.

Surprising but nice.

She considered stumbling over another root, just so he could help her again. But if she acted like a klutz he might pick someone else for the rearing scene. Ironically, she could have run over this path in two-inch heels and barely slowed.

And then they emerged from the path into a beautiful clearing and there were no more roots. Except for six fenced paddocks, the expanse of grass was completely manicured.

"That's the barn they built for Reckless." Dan gestured at the attractive building with the red tiled roof and white shutters. On the second level, French doors led to a cozy balcony edged with a wrought iron railing. "Reckless had his own paddock and sand pit, out of sight of the training track. I believe there are living quarters on the upper floor."

"It's lovely," Emily murmured, feeling rather guilty pretending she'd never seen the barn. Of course, it had been dark last night and barely dawn when she left this morning so she hadn't *really* seen it.

"Two of our horses are here," Dan said. "One is on stall rest with a strained tendon. The other is for company."

"Do you own them?" she asked, noticing he didn't call either horse by name.

"No, they were supplied by a stock contractor. It took quite awhile to find enough Reckless doubles, and I wanted some extras."

"Hey, Dan," an accented voice called.

They both turned as a breathless Lizzie burst from the path behind them.

"Thought I saw you going this way," Lizzie said. "I fed them this morning. Just came back now to give their noon hay."

"We can do it," Dan said. "Did the vet check the bay?"

"Yes. He suggested stall rest and wrap, cold water application and an anti-inflammatory. Hand walk if possible. The contractor will pick him up with the others once the shoot is over."

Dan dragged a hand over his jaw. "We'll have to work his care into the schedule. But it'll be tight."

"I don't have time to walk him," Lizzie said. "And it's not your horse. I tried to persuade the contractor to pick him up now, but he wants to save a trip."

Emily glanced down the aisle. The bay's head stuck over the stall door, his white blaze vivid. She already knew that one stall down, there was a very comfortable bed of hay, and she'd love a reason to hang around. Besides, after sharing his barn and blanket last night, she felt an attachment to the friendly horse.

"I can look after him," she said. "At least for the couple of days that I'm here."

Lizzie's gaze swung to Emily for the first time that morning. She didn't look at all pleased. "I don't think background performers are qualified to wrangle," she said. "Are you even in the union?"

Lizzie's dismissive tone rankled. Emily's fists tightened but she forced her voice to remain level. "I doubt the horse cares if I'm union," she said.

"I don't care either," Dan said, his voice decisive. "As long as you're working directly for me and don't handle a horse on set, there won't be a problem. Keep track of her hours, Lizzie. It'll save you from walking over here."

Emily relaxed, flattening the palms of her hands against her jeans. She'd hadn't expected to be paid, didn't need to be, but this was perfect. A sweet horse for company and a place of her own to sleep.

A grin cut the sides of her mouth, one that even Lizzie's dark scowl couldn't squash. There may have been a couple glitches but this day was definitely improving.

CHAPTER ELEVEN

"Are you sure the hotel's full?" Dan asked, speaking quietly into the phone.

"Absolutely. Shania uses the entire top floor." Anthony sighed. "But I need to keep her happy. She and Dexter don't have much chemistry. Hopefully the lobster dinner will help." His voice sharpened. "You *are* coming tonight?"

It sounded more like a request than a question.

"Wasn't planning on it," Dan said mildly. "I have a few injured horses." He glanced down the barn aisle to where Lizzie was outlining care and feeding instructions to Emily. "And I need to find someone a room for a few nights," he added.

He moved further down the aisle, distancing himself from Lizzie's rising voice. She didn't use that snippy tone often but Emily clearly knew how to get her riled, and neither girl was the type to back down. It probably wouldn't be wise to ask Lizzie to make room in her trailer for Emily.

He tucked the phone against his shoulder and fingered the padlock on the locked door. It must lead to the apartment upstairs although obviously it hadn't been opened for some time. "What's the deal with the little stud barn?" he asked. "Are we allowed to use the apartment above the stalls?"

"I assume so," Anthony said. "Hamilton gave blanket access to all the horse facilities. It's probably in the contract."

"Great." Dan rattled the padlock. "I'd like to put my background girl up there. Can you get the key to the door? Or send someone over with bolt cutters?"

"And then you'll come tonight?" Anthony asked. "We'll work together to humor Shania?"

"Sure," Dan said. "I'll even crack open her lobster."

He shoved the phone into his pocket and strode back to the two girls. The bay gelding was now tied to a ring in the stall. Emily wrapped his front legs while Lizzie watched with a critical eye. Clearly though, Emily was competent. Despite an unorthodox style, someone had taught her well. Probably the sister. Anyone who massaged horses tended to have a good foundation in horse care.

"You can go and grab something to eat now, Lizzie," he said. "I'll help Emily."

"But that bandage needs to be higher." Lizzie frowned at the left leg.

"Yeah. I'll check it. See you at the main barn in an hour. And make sure Splash gets turned out today."

Lizzie shot a disapproving look at Emily's bandaging then shuffled out the door.

"Should I start over?" Emily peered up at him, her cheeks slightly flushed.

He crouched down beside her and checked the bandage. Perfectly snug and even, perhaps a little low, but Lizzie was being unnecessarily fussy. "No, this is pretty good," he said. "Tonight you can hose and rewrap him for the night. Next time bring the wrap up another eighth of an inch. By the way, there's hot and cold water in the wash stall, along with shampoo."

Her face sparkled and she touched her hair in anticipation. She had the liveliest expressions. Her teeth weren't boringly straight, her lips had a rosebud shape and her bottom lip was big and full and sexy.

"Shampoo. Can't wait!" She clamped her lips, as if embarrassed by her enthusiasm. "I didn't have time to shower this morning," she added, "so it'll be great to wash my hair, along with the horse."

He nodded, completely understanding why she'd been so skittish. "One time in the winter I went six days without a shower. Finally stuck my head under a cold barn tap." He grimaced. "It was ice cold but worth the chill to get clean."

Her gaze shot back to him, the wariness in her eyes replaced by curiosity. "Was that on a movie set too?"

"Yeah, I was fifteen," he said. "Too young to be hired as a wrangler but I hoped by hanging around the horses, I might have a shot. My dad always said if I wanted something, I'd better be smart enough to grab it."

"My father always said I wasn't very smart, so I better slap on a lot of makeup." She laughed, but he noted the tightness of her mouth.

He kept his hands on the gelding's leg, resisting the urge to give her a hug. No wonder she'd looked uncomfortable this morning. "And is your father's advice usually good?" he asked gently.

"God, no. He was an asshole and a drunk."

"Then perhaps it wasn't the best advice."

She tilted her head, her mouth curving in a rueful smile. "You're right, of course. But it'll still feel nice to look better."

Her natural beauty didn't require much help. However, it was apparent she didn't feel the same way and he was sure she'd heard that opinion plenty of times before. He silently rose and untied the gelding. The horse flicked his ears, as if wondering why they lingered. Dan actually wondered himself. His days were already stretched, yet here he was, spending time he didn't have with a horse he didn't own. He'd sent Lizzie away and even switched off the volume on his phone.

"This horse's big trick is picking up halters," Dan said, ignoring the vibrating cell in his pocket. "He's going back to the stock contractor at the end of the movie."

"You don't keep them? After all the training?"

He shook his head. "I only hang onto a few, like Splash, Ice and Bruno. The rest I train as required." Shipping was expensive and at one point, his herd had numbered over seventy. He tended to get possessive of his animals so now he only kept the more advanced stunt horses.

"How do you train a horse to take something from your hand?" she asked.

"There are lots of methods. I usually start with some grain wrapped in a towel. A horse will automatically pick it up. After that, it's all about reward and consistency."

"So you could train him to pick up anything?" Her eyes sparkled with mischief. "Like a wallet or something?"

He gave her ponytail a teasing tug, guessing the direction her nimble mind was heading. "I had a cow pony who'd lift things from my friends' pockets," he admitted. "It was great fun."

She smiled up at him. "Wish I had done that with Peanut. We could have demonstrated at the fair and maybe raised enough to buy cotton candy. Who wouldn't want to donate to a cute little pony?"

I sure would have. He yanked his gaze away from her face and unbuckled the halter. But she looked so happy when she spoke of her pony and he wanted to keep her smiling. "How long ago did you have him?"

"Oh, we still have Peanut," she said. "He's part of the family. Even when we couldn't afford him, my sister somehow managed. I never realized we were so broke." Her voice trailed off but she certainly seemed more relaxed, now that she wasn't so preoccupied with her appearance. She even held the stall door open for him, smiling without a trace of artifice.

"Let's check out that wash stall," he said, reluctant to leave despite the insistent vibrations of his phone. "You'll need to be here early tomorrow if you're going to feed and be ready for your scene. Do you have a place to stay?" He hung the halter over the hook, watching her reaction.

"I certainly do." Her eyes flitted to the empty stall and then back to his face. "And I can be here as early as you want. Believe me, it's no problem."

But it was a problem. He didn't want to squeeze into a chair again tonight, and there was no way he was letting her sleep alone in this isolated barn. "We're trying to get the door open to the apartment upstairs," he said. "I don't know what the condition will be, but it's probably better than sleeping in a stall."

Her eyes widened. "It was you? The blanket?" Her mouth opened and for a moment it seemed she'd try to brush it off with a joke. But she gave a resigned sigh, her shoulders slumping. "Thank you. I'm sorry for barging into your barn like that. I really didn't have anywhere else to go."

"And now you do," he said.

Emily tugged at the taps, twisting until water streamed onto the concrete floor of the wash stall. The spray was discolored from years of nonuse but that soon cleared. And the hot water felt wonderful on her hands.

It didn't feel so great on her toes though. She backed away from the deepening puddle but already her boots were wet. The floor sloped unevenly and water pooled beneath the tap instead of flowing to the drain. It might be better to hose the bay's leg outside, rather than tie him in the wash stall and risk flooding the aisle. But she'd worry about that later.

Right now, she was simply delighted to have running water. And possibly a real bed.

She glanced toward the apartment door where Dan and a white-haired man from set construction were cutting off a padlock. Dan's eyes met hers and he gave a thumbs-up. She turned off the faucets and hurried to join them.

"Careful of mice," the man said with a grimace. He dropped the severed padlock into his toolbox, closed the lid and walked out of the barn.

Dan pushed open the apartment door and climbed the narrow steps.

"Has this place been empty long?" she asked, following, but keeping a wary watch for rodents.

"Apparently twenty years," Dan said. "Nobody used this apartment after Reckless turned incorrigible and was moved to the main barn."

"Too bad he didn't have a trainer like you," she said. "He might have made the Derby."

Dan smiled over his shoulder. "Trying to flatter me?"

"Maybe." She smiled back. She didn't know what it was that made her feel so relaxed, but she certainly enjoyed his company. "I do wonder what was bothering Reckless," she added. "My friend believes he missed his groom."

"A horse's problems can be physical, mental or emotional," Dan said. "Sometimes all three. The movie touches on the groom quitting but Anthony is letting the audience decide. Unfortunately, no one will ever know why she left."

Dan paused at the top of the steps, surveyed the room, then glanced back at her. "What do you think? Is this okay for a night or two?"

Emily just gaped, surprised he'd even asked. This place was stunning. A spacious sitting room included French doors that opened onto an intimate balcony. The white furniture still looked new and a throw pillow with a bay horse head, obviously handmade, lay on the sofa. A chair had been tugged over by the balcony where the view encompassed the entrance to the barn.

"It's beautiful," Emily said. "But it feels like someone still lives here."

"Hardly. The only thing left is dust." Dan ran a hand along the top of the railing then held up the tip of his finger for her inspection.

"Dust is fine," she said, still glancing around in awe, but unable to shake the feeling they were intruding. She tugged off her wet boots and stepped gingerly onto the pristine hardwood floor.

They explored together, checking out a solitary bedroom with cream-colored curtains and the large bed stripped of sheets, a bathroom empty of everything except a half-roll of toilet paper, and the sterile kitchen with granite counter and unplugged fridge.

"Guess it really is empty," she said. But it didn't feel empty and a little shiver ran down her back. "This is great," she added quickly.

"Ask Lizzie for some bedding," Dan said, bending down to plug in the fridge. "The wranglers have already been fixed up and there are plenty of sheets and blankets." His gaze drifted over Emily's soggy socks. "How did your feet get so wet?"

"The wash stall wasn't draining," she said. "It might be better to hose outside."

"The horse will like that better anyway. Just be sure to keep him from jumping around and hurting his leg." He scrolled though his messages then looked up, his eyes glinting with anticipation. "Your scene is a go for tomorrow. I'll have a wrangler bring Bruno to the pen. It's time for your rearing rehearsal."

CHAPTER TWELVE

"Keep your eyes on Bruno," Dan said. "No, you're too close." His hand settled on Emily's shoulder, and he tugged her back a step.

"This distance is good," he said, his minty breath fanning the top of her hair. "This is the scene where Hamilton realizes something is terribly wrong with Reckless. You're leading the horse from the barn. He goes up in the air. Keep your hand on the lead line."

Emily's heart pounded but she was more unsettled by Dan's touch than the big horse standing three feet away. She couldn't recall ever being so acutely aware of a man. "Should I look scared?" she asked, trying to ignore his proximity and focus instead on Bruno.

"Act natural. The cameras will be close. Anthony might put one beneath the horse. Or he may go with the back of your head or even a silhouette shot."

Emily nodded. But the back of her head or a silhouette... Would Jenna be able to recognize her?

"Don't think of the lights and cameras," Dan went on. "It's just you and the horse." His warm hand moved from her shoulder to her hip. "I'll be right here. Just ignore me too."

She gulped. It was impossible to ignore him, not the way his touch made her skin tingle. Even her breath had turned shivery.

It was also hard to ignore Lizzie's presence. The Aussie was definitely shooting her the stink-eye. And cow eyes at Dan. Of all the handlers who might have delivered Bruno, it was a downer that Lizzie had come, ostensibly to supervise the young wrangler with Bruno. But if Dan was aware of Lizzie's infatuation, he hid it well.

"All set?" he asked.

Emily nodded, determined to be unfazed by Lizzie's hostility—it would be good practice for the director tomorrow. She kept her gaze locked on Bruno, waiting for the signal. Dan's arm moved.

Bruno's ears flattened. His head lifted and he abruptly rose on his hind legs, towering over her like a mountain of muscle. Adrenaline jolted her, and she jerked back.

"Don't step back. Give him slack but make it look taut," Dan said, his voice low and calm. "Keep the line from tangling in his feet."

Emily adjusted the lead line, far too busy now to worry about facial expressions. Bruno literally hung above her, blotting the sun with his huge body. He was so close she could feel his primal energy, smell his salty sweat, see the glint of nails in his shoes.

He dropped to the ground, shaking his head, ears still flat and angry.

"Good," Dan said.

Bruno's ears shot forward. Emily assumed Dan was talking to her. However, he stepped past and stroked the horse's neck with a gentle hand, speaking in such a soft and approving voice, Emily's insides turned mushy.

"Do you give him a treat now?" she asked, slightly breathless.

"Some horses I do. But this guy works for love."

Bruno tilted his head. His eyelids lowered in bliss as Dan's ripped arms moved along the horse's neck, his fingers rubbing the crest of Bruno's mane. For a moment, Emily wished she were the horse. Her gaze flickered to Lizzie, their eyes locking in tacit understanding of Dan's blatant sex appeal.

"You did well," Dan said, finally turning to Emily. "Anthony will go over the scene with you in the morning. Hopefully we'll get it on the first take."

"And tomorrow night I can look after the horses in the stud barn," Lizzie called. "I juggled the schedule and freed up some time. It won't be necessary to use outsiders."

Outsiders? Emily's mouth opened but she swallowed her retort. Mouthing off at Dan's wrangler might make her feel better, but it wouldn't gain any extra work. And maybe if they didn't get the scene on the first couple of takes, she'd have to stay for another day.

On the other hand, if she didn't do a good job, Dan would replace her. It should be easy to find a background performer to hold a rearing horse, especially a well-trained animal like Bruno. Girl number two at the skills audition had looked competent, and her makeup had been flawless.

"Any questions before I go?" Dan asked Emily as he pulled out his phone.

"You better hurry," Lizzie called. "Anthony needs you. I can finish up here."

It was obvious Lizzie wanted to keep her away from Dan. And the knowledge that this scene would likely be finished tomorrow filled Emily with regret. This was the only job she'd had in a month. Lizzie might want her gone, but Emily was determined not to climb on the bus without a fight. She pulled in a fortifying breath.

"Just one question." Emily turned her back to Lizzie and gave Dan a flirtatious smile. "I couldn't help but notice Bruno is a gelding. Yet Reckless was a stallion. Won't the cameras show that he's missing the full package?"

"Geldings are more even-tempered," Dan said, not looking up from his phone. "Anthony is careful with camera angles. I only use a stallion when absolutely necessary."

"And mares?" she asked. "Do you have much use for…females?"

"Absolutely." He glanced up, amusement playing around the corners of his mouth. "But they can be moody. Especially in heat. I try to avoid them." He turned his attention back to his phone, as if aware she was flirting but wasn't at all affected.

"Good policy." She forced a flippant laugh. Well, that didn't go far. Clearly he was used to deflecting women, and of course he wouldn't be interested in a nobody like her. But even if there were no stalls to clean, there must be something she could do. Two days of work would never cover Jenna's steeplechase weekend.

She glanced over her shoulder. Lizzie sneered as if amused by such a pathetic attempt. Emily turned back to Dan, spurred by the wrangler's smugness.

"One last question," she said, remembering Judith's comment that Dan was a perfectionist. "I noticed Bruno doesn't have racing plates."

Dan's head shot up. "You noticed his shoes?"

She nodded. "When his feet were waving in my face, they were hard to miss. Aluminum race plates are shiny. But he had dull steel shoes. The real Reckless would have worn plates."

Dan rubbed his jaw. "Valid point," he said.

"You need to go, Dan," Lizzie called. "Anthony just sent another text. The big dinner—"

Dan raised his finger in such an authoritative gesture, Lizzie silenced. Even Bruno jerked to attention. "Anything else?" Dan asked, his laser attention on Emily.

"That's all for now," she said, "but with more time, I'd probably pick up other things. Most people wouldn't notice such tiny details. It's just that I've worked with racehorses for so long."

He smiled then. "How old are you, Emily? Twenty-four?"

"Twenty-five," she said quickly. "But I've been around the track since I was a kid."

Completely true. The school bus had dropped her off at the Center's gates; most of her homework had been done in an empty stall close to the track. The grooms always dropped by to visit and discuss the antics of their favorite horse. Occasionally they'd even bought her a Coke from the pop machine. She'd always envied the kids who lived in town, but country life hadn't been so bad. Jenna had made sure of that.

"Have you been around a starting gate much?" Dan stepped closer. Bruno followed.

"Absolutely." She gave a hasty nod. The gate had made excellent monkey bars until her back flips had spooked a horse and Wally had proclaimed it off limits. And she'd definitely been around the starting gate a whole lot the summer she'd turned sixteen and dated one of the exercise riders.

"Why don't you hang around a few more days?" Dan said. "Maybe you'll spot something we can make more authentic."

"So, like I'd be a race advisor or something?"

"Sure, we can call it that." His blue eyes glinted with amusement. "But the salary remains the same. You'll be on my payroll, same rate as non-union background."

She tilted her head, pretending the matter required a great deal of thought. "I suppose I could stay for a bit. Fortunately my agent said I'm free the entire week."

"How very fortunate," he said.

CHAPTER THIRTEEN

"Find a ladder and knock down those cobwebs," Lizzie said, scowling at the rafters. "This barn has been empty too long."

"Okay," Emily said. "I'll do that after supper." She'd already cleaned the stalls, walked the bay gelding for twenty minutes, hosed and wrapped his front legs and her stomach was growling. The day had been hectic.

She also felt rather lightheaded, no doubt from lack of food. It had been more than twenty-four hours since eating the doughnut in the background tent. This morning's coffee had given a temporary boost but if she'd known it was her main meal, she would have splurged and added milk.

She cast a worried look out the door. Dusk was falling and the dining room would be closing soon. Workers with trailers had their own kitchens, but she didn't have that luxury.

"Guess I'll bring the chestnut in now," Emily said. "He's been out awhile and the bay sure misses him." She draped the horse's lead line over her shoulder. "What are the horses' names? Dan only refers to them by description."

"That's because he never gets attached to contracted horses. Or to people. Everything goes back when the movie's finished." Lizzie gave Emily a pointed stare. "Everything."

Emily pretended to misunderstand Lizzie's clumsy warning. "And knowing their names makes it tough?" she asked. "Gosh, I'll just have to make up my own. Think I'll call them Barney and Ted."

"Don't be stupid." Lizzie's nostrils flared. "You can't just make up names. Besides, it doesn't matter. Your little scene will be over tomorrow."

The 'stupid' comment rankled but Emily had already discovered that the more she smiled, the more annoyed Lizzie became. And the sparring was kind of fun. "My acting scene might be over tomorrow," Emily said with a smile, "but the race advisory job will continue. And I'm looking forward to working closely with Dan…very closely."

Lizzie yanked off the bay's halter. "What are you talking about?" She flung the halter onto the hook so aggressively that Barney flinched. "Dan knows the race industry inside out. What can he possibly need from you?"

"I don't know." Emily shrugged. "Maybe you should ask him." She straightened the halter on the hook, annoyed Lizzie had startled this kind-eyed horse with her temper flare. "I'm going to bring *Ted* in now."

"Fine," Lizzie snapped. "But get rid of those cobwebs now. They can cause all sorts of respiratory problems. Plus they're a fire hazard. If you're looking after these horses, you better do it right."

"No problem," Emily said, trying to pretend she didn't mind hanging around the barn a few more hours. *I'm not hungry anyway.*

She strode to the paddock and clipped the lead line on the chestnut's halter. Ted seemed content with his new name and eager to return to his stall although grass stains on his back showed he'd enjoyed his brief freedom.

By the time they reached the barn, Lizzie was already stalking toward the path. It didn't seem a good time to ask for sheets and blankets. Besides, it was obvious Lizzie wouldn't grant her any favors. A part of Emily even empathized with the wrangler. It would be impossible to have a boss like Dan and not fall a little bit in love.

She gave a wistful sigh. If she'd met him when she was better dressed, with full war paint, he might have shown more interest. Even if it were only a fling. Obviously though, he expected perfection. And guys like him deserved it.

Ted gave her elbow an impatient nudge and she slipped off his halter, watching as he dove into his hay. Barney, however, stretched his head over the door, more interested in a pat than his supper. Of the two, the bay was friendlier and more eager to please. Barney seemed like a horse who might have performed a few tricks.

On impulse, she waved the halter. "Take it, boy."

He looked at her, ears pricked.

She waved the halter, extending it in her hand. "Get it."

He reached down and picked up the halter, holding it with an uncertain expression before dropping it in the aisle.

"Good boy." Grinning, she scratched his neck. Holding a halter wasn't much of a trick but maybe they could build on it. A girl had to start somewhere. But she needed to let him know he was doing it correctly.

She walked outside and picked some grass, filling her pockets with the greenest blades she could find. When she returned, Barney was waiting, his chest pressed against the door.

She didn't know what cues his former trainer had used but after only four attempts, promptly rewarded with grass, Barney grabbed the halter the instant she told him to 'get it.'

"You're a smart fellow." She scratched him beneath the jaw, pumped with success. Tomorrow she'd teach him to lift a brush from her hand. With a few more tricks, Dan might call the horse by name. Maybe even keep him. Being shipped to Dan's ranch seemed a far better fate than being turned over to a stock contractor. Especially considering Barney's injury and his labor-intensive care.

She reluctantly left the obliging horse and pulled out a broom and stepladder. There were too many chores remaining to dally longer. Besides, if cobwebs weren't good for Barney and Ted, she didn't want a single one left hanging.

Emily pressed a hand against her rumbling stomach and scanned the deserted dining room. Her mouth watered. Hot food had been served recently—the air still smelled of barbecue chicken—but she'd obviously spent too much time knocking down cobwebs. Only odors remained. Except for gleaming coffee machines the tent was empty.

Swallowing her dismay, she reached beneath the table and pulled out a paper cup. At least there was coffee. She debated the wisdom of caffeine free, but her head and body ached, and she chose a pod of dark roast.

She circled every table, hopeful for leftovers but found only napkins and a bottle of barbecue sauce. A doughnut box had been tossed on the floor and she kicked it in frustration. Something rattled. She bent down and yanked it open. Two plain doughnuts remained.

She blew out a sigh of gratitude. Not much but if she chewed slowly, she could make them last almost as long as a real meal.

She wrapped the precious doughnuts in a napkin, took a last look around then headed back to her barn.

Her barn. How cool was that? Two sweet horses for company, a background gig tomorrow and perhaps employment for a few more days. The pay was barely over minimum wage, but it was certainly more than she'd earned last week. Movie work, horse care and race advice—best of all, she'd done it on her own, without asking for Jenna's help.

Her steps lengthened. The wooded path was too rough in the fading light and she swerved to follow the paved drive.

She couldn't wait to sit down and enjoy her bounty but didn't want to spill a drop of the precious coffee.

After she finished her doughnuts, she'd check out more Internet sites. The racing consultant job was a bit over-reaching—Wally would have a fit—but she might be able to pick up some additional knowledge before tomorrow, enough so she wouldn't look like a complete fool in front of Dan.

She gave a contented sigh, savoring the silence. The reddening sunset reminded her of home. Their trailer had been a little rough but the view from the porch had always been first class. Generally she wasn't nostalgic, but the familiar sound of peeper frogs filled her with longing. It was comforting that the steeplechase was only four weeks away. She missed Jenna and Peanut. Best of all, when she finally saw them she'd have money to share.

"Hurry up!"

The sharp command startled her. She peered through the gloom. The old caretaker stood by the gate, gesturing with his cane.

"Hurry up," he repeated. "It's time to close the gate."

She obligingly sped up, even though the gate was only effective for vehicular traffic, and it would be simple to walk around the metal bar.

"Thank you," she said. "Guess I'm a little late tonight."

"You're always late," he grumbled. "Mr. Hamilton isn't going to like it."

She nodded, rather sorry for the confused man. At least he was in his own home, doing a job he obviously loved. Someone must be looking after him.

"Did you get your groceries today?" she asked.

"Yes. But they forgot my doughnuts." He thumped his cane in irritation. "And I really wanted some."

Emily's fingers tightened around the napkin. She was hungry. And quite likely this old man shouldn't eat doughnuts anyway. They were high in fat and sugar, not really suitable for aging arteries. But he looked rather distraught.

"I have an extra doughnut." She opened the napkin and thrust out her hand. "Do you like this kind?"

He nodded, his rheumy eyes gleaming.

She passed him a doughnut. He grabbed it without ceremony and stuffed such a large chunk into his mouth, it looked like a choking hazard.

"Let's eat slowly," she said, taking a dainty nibble, trying to set a good example.

He smacked his lips and took another giant bite. Crumbs dribbled down his shirt. "These are my favorite," he said, the words muffled.

"I love them too." Ignoring her good intentions, she chewed faster. It was impossible to go slow, not when she was so hungry. The doughnut was squashed and stale but quite possibly the best she'd ever eaten.

They chewed and swallowed in joint contentment. When he finished he wiped his mouth, his gaze locking on her cup. "Is that coffee?"

"Yes," she said. "If you get a cup, we can share."

He nodded and shuffled toward the cottage, leaning heavily on his cane. She followed him up the stone walkway.

"Visitors used to stop and bring me coffee," he said, huffing from exertion. "I hope it gets busier when they make the movie." He transferred the cane to his left hand and twisted the doorknob.

The movie was already half finished but Emily couldn't speak, too appalled by the stench oozing through the open door. She backed away, breathing through her mouth. "I'll just wait here," she managed.

After long minutes and much banging, he returned, carrying a stained and chipped mug. She poured half the coffee into his mug, trying not to recoil at the yellow particles caked on its rim.

"I'll bring you a coffee and doughnut tomorrow," she said. "And I won't tell the missus about you and Mr. Hamilton." He reached out, surprising her with a solemn handshake, and it was clear he considered his promise important.

"What's your name?" she asked, shaking his gnarly fingers then topping up his mug with almost all the coffee.

"Billy."

"I'm Emily. And I really do appreciate you opening the gate for me."

She gave a cheery wave and turned away. Her cup was much lighter but so were her steps. It felt good to do something nice. At least someone would miss her if she didn't show up tomorrow.

There was no danger of spilling her coffee now. Two sips finished it off. She drained the cup and hurried along the rest of the drive, eager to check the horses.

When she swept into the barn, both geldings poked their heads over the stall doors, looking for food. However, Barney further softened her heart with a welcoming nicker.

She gave them each another flake of hay—carefully following Lizzie's feed instructions—and walked down the aisle to the apartment door. After Billy's company, her loneliness had magnified and she scanned the barn for the gray cat. Despite her repeated calls, he didn't appear.

She drew in a resigned breath and pushed open the door. The apartment was unquestionably luxurious, but it hadn't felt welcoming earlier, even with Dan's solid presence. Now, in the utter darkness, it felt downright unfriendly. Steps loomed, black and silent as a crypt. She fumbled for the wall switch, relieved when the lights worked.

She locked the lower door, tugged off her boots and trudged up the stairs. The place was chilly, her toes already clammy from her wet socks, and for a moment she regretted giving away the coffee.

But the pleased look on Billy's face stayed with her. Besides, she was so tired, it was doubtful she'd have time to think about being hungry. She dropped onto the sofa and pulled out her phone. The battery showed a quarter charge, still some juice.

She sent a text to Jenna: *Love it here. Horses and people very nice. Hope your studying is going well. Good luck with exams!*

She scrolled through a few racing sites, trying to pad her knowledge. However, the information was too detailed and most of it centered on betting strategies rather than training methods. Her charger was back in Louisville and she didn't want to waste the limited battery so she turned off the phone and padded into the bathroom.

The tap was tight but water finally streamed from the faucet, murky at first, but eventually crystal clear. It wouldn't heat up though, even after running the tap for long minutes. She debated going downstairs and using the hot water in the wash stall, but was simply too tired.

She splashed her face with cold water, then shivering, dressed in every item of clothing she possessed. She shuffled into the bedroom and checked the closet for blankets but except for one lonely pink hanger, the room was empty. The stripped bed looked forlorn so she returned to the main room and curled on the sofa.

Barney and Ted shuffled in the stalls below, their sounds reassuring. Yawning, she closed her eyes. But in spite of her bone-deep exhaustion, it was impossible to fall asleep. It might have been the damp cold, or the caffeine, or perhaps her overactive brain scrambling for ways to stretch her employment...and impress Dan.

Dan. Sighing, she flipped onto her back, acknowledging the attraction. As well as the futility. Guys were like crows; they were attracted to flash. And she didn't have the necessary glitz and glam—none of her usual props. If she were a movie star like Shania, she'd have her own trailer and makeup attendant, even a hair stylist. She'd look stunning too.

But would he notice, even then?

She stared glumly out the French windows. A checkerboard of lights glowed over the tree line, obviously the Hamilton mansion. Whoever had lived here would have been able to see the top floor of the Hamilton's house. And vice versa. The hair on the back of her neck abruptly rose.

She scrambled to her feet and yanked the curtains shut, blocking her view of the house. Then curled even tighter on the sofa. She didn't know what caused the weird feeling. Was only certain that she felt it.

CHAPTER FOURTEEN

"Please help me with this lobster claw." Shania peered at Dan from beneath impossibly thick eyelashes.

He obligingly reached for her plate and cracked the claw open, not that it required much effort. The restaurant staff had prepared the lobsters beautifully. Anthony shot Dan a grateful nod from across the table then resumed his conversation with Robert Dexter.

Shania preferred to have her leading man dance attendance, and Dan knew he was a stand-in. But Dexter had maintained a prudent distance from Shania since day one. Actually Dan rather admired the actor. Dexter had been married for six years and was clearly devoted to his wife. However, Shania tended to sulk in the absence of constant adulation, and Anthony feared the lack of rapport between Shania and Dexter would be evident on screen.

"What did you think of my barn scene today?" Shania leaned forward, dipping the lobster in his melted butter, her breast brushing his arm. "Did you see how Robert stared?"

"Probably hard not too," Dan said, his gaze skimming the top of her dress. Very skimpy, very provocative. And her shirt this morning had been every bit as revealing.

"This isn't my idea." She dragged an elegant finger across her neckline. "The studio wants to jack up the sex appeal. They're promoting to a wider audience now. We have another boring media session following dinner, and we're supposed to appear in character." She shot a dark look across the table. "Robert is just so…"

"Married?" Dan asked helpfully.

"Yes, but it's not just that." She waved a hand. "He won't even sport flirt. The real Thomas Hamilton would have had me flat on my back before the horses were cooled out. He probably still would, even today, if his wife wasn't always watching. Robert doesn't play the role properly."

Dan made a non-committal sound, his mind drifting as Shania complained about her co-star, his lack of research and then randomly, how Dexter didn't use Twitter. Dan was grateful he dealt with horses. Far less drama, especially with the geldings. Of course, he avoided working with mares, unless one came along that was simply so special he had to have her. Sometimes that happened when least expected. Rather like Emily.

He slapped down that thought and turned his attention back to Shania, aware Anthony wanted her ego boosted. Daydreaming about another woman certainly wasn't part of the plan.

"I still think it's weird how that groom disappeared." Shania delicately pressed a white napkin against her lipstick-red mouth. "It wouldn't surprise me if he killed her and hid the body."

"Who?" Dan blinked in surprise. He really had been daydreaming. Seemed they were now discussing a murder.

"Thomas Hamilton, naturally." Shania frowned as though disappointed by Dan's mental prowess. "My assistant gathered a lot of research. It was classified as a missing person case although there was never much of an investigation. The groom simply disappeared. But she didn't collect her pay. No one ever leaves a paycheck."

Dan took a sip of wine, leaning back so the waiter could clear his plate. Shania made a valid point. He'd never had anyone walk away from a check, and grooms were notorious for living from payday to payday.

Grooms… He'd have to make sure Emily received her money on Friday. Otherwise, she might wait months for a check from the production company. She'd earned it simply by pointing out the discrepancy in Bruno's shoes. He'd already asked the farrier to make a switch.

Anthony rose, his chair scraping as he pushed back from the table. "We're going to take a break before dessert," he announced. "There'll be a short photo shoot in the foyer. We need all principal cast."

"Oh, I hate those things," Shania said. But she flung down her soiled napkin, rising so quickly Dan didn't have time to pull out her chair. "See you later?" She raised a questioning eyebrow.

"Tomorrow, bright and early," Dan said.

She gave a little pout but clearly wasn't at all heartbroken. She leaned down, brushed her mouth over his cheek then sashayed toward the door where she was immediately flanked by two burly bodyguards. Robert Dexter rose with much less enthusiasm and followed her into the media room.

Anthony slid into Shania's vacated seat. "How did it go? Is she any happier?"

"She's fine," Dan said. "Pro enough to do her job. But she wants Robert to stroke her a bit."

"I spoke to him. Reminded that she has top billing. And we need her happy."

"She's certainly researched her role. She said they never found that missing groom. You ever wonder what happened?"

Anthony shrugged. "Beats me. But I'm playing the sex angle. Luckily Shania has a nice rack. Old Hamilton can't take his eyes off her. At least she's getting attention from that direction."

Anthony's voice lowered. "I need another favor. My brother has a horse-crazy daughter. It's her birthday this month, and I want you to squeeze her onto your approved riding list. Just a quick shot so she's in the movie, my niece sitting on a horse. No problem?"

"No problem if she can gallop a racehorse," Dan said. "There's very little sitting."

"I'll embellish the scene." Anthony whipped out his phone and made an entry. "Show some horses walking before they go to the gate. Besides, if we use non-union, we can keep costs down."

Dan frowned, folding his napkin. "I'm not asking background to gallop through a rail."

"Of course not. We'll still use a stunt rider for Reckless. But the others can be special skills. Doesn't everyone in Kentucky know how to ride?"

"There are all types of riding," Dan said. "And race riding is the most dangerous. It has to be authentic. And safe."

"Agreed." But Anthony's voice rang with impatience. "So we'll work with what we got. Essentially I found you another rider. Besides, I've learned that if a woman's shirt is low enough, the audience doesn't notice how she sits a horse. This movie is total crap anyway."

Dan raised an eyebrow, reached for a bottle of wine and refilled his friend's glass. Anthony's anxiety always skyrocketed midway through a movie when he was convinced each picture would be the worst he ever directed.

Anthony grimaced. "Guess I'm a little stressed. But we're ten percent over budget."

"Was the dinner worth it?" Dan surveyed the room. Steak and lobster were extravagant and there must have been over eighty cast and crew invited.

"Definitely," Anthony said. "The producer wanted some team building. And Robert is going to play nicer with Shania. She looked much happier tonight by the way. She needs a man around." He paused, a speculative gleam in his eyes. "I don't suppose——?"

"No," Dan said.

"Not even for the good of the movie? Most men would salivate at the chance of tapping that."

Dan shook his head. Anthony had been married and divorced four times with numerous high-profile affairs. The man's personal life was in shambles. "I'm going back to check on the horses," Dan said. "Limo out front?"

"Yeah." Anthony pushed back his chair, shooting a regretful look at the media room. "But one of these days you're going to answer a booty call."

"Probably." Dan gave a wry smile. "But not tonight."

CHAPTER FIFTEEN

Emily woke, chilled and shivering. She wrapped her arms around her knees but it was impossible to ignore the cold. She groped for her phone and checked the time. Four thirty.

Her call time wasn't until eight but she'd need at least an hour for barn chores and somehow she'd have to coax more clothes from the wardrobe department. She remained curled on the sofa for another ten minutes, but she was truly freezing now and the thought of a hot shower in the wash stall was irresistible.

She pulled on her boots, still damp from yesterday, and headed down the stairs. Both horses blinked sleepily when the aisle lights flicked on. She tossed them each a flake of hay, pleasing them with their early breakfast, then prudently pulled the barn door shut and hurried to the wash stall.

She uncoiled the hose, waited for the water to heat before stripping, then stepped under the hot spray. She closed her eyes in appreciation, letting the water sluice over her body. Finally she felt warm. She didn't want to stop, but water pooled on the opposite side of the drain and spilled into the aisle. Much more and it would flood Barney's stall.

She reluctantly turned off the tap, then dried herself with a grooming towel and dressed. Her cold wet socks made her wince but at least she was clean.

She tied Barney in the corner of his stall and rewrapped his legs. It took her a couple tries but eventually the bandages were perfect. She doubted even Lizzie could find fault; the top of the wrap reached the exact point below the knee that Dan had specified.

She mucked out both stalls, grained and watered, then checked the time. Almost six. She planted a quick kiss on Barney's velvety muzzle. "I'm going to be in the movies today," she said. "Wish me luck."

She hurried from the barn, hopeful Maggie was working solo again this morning. She really needed clean clothes.

The sun hadn't yet edged over the horizon so she followed the paved drive, grateful for her borrowed boots. Despite her squishy socks, the boots were comfortable, similar to the leather pair Wally had forced her to wear as a guide. At the time, she'd thought he was simply being bossy, but now it was obvious boots were far more practical than shoes.

The door to the cottage rattled. Billy shuffled out, his scowl outlined by the bright porch light. "It's not time," he said. "I don't open the gate until six. You'll have to wait."

"That's okay," she said. "I'll just walk around the post."

"You can't do that." His voice quivered in agitation. "No one goes through until six. Mr. Hamilton said so."

The alarm in his voice made her pause. She glanced longingly at the path that circled the gate, wishing now that she'd taken the rougher trail through the woods. Time was critical.

"The gate is for cars, Billy," she said soothingly. "It's okay if people are walking. And you don't have to open the gate for me. See." She pointed at the gap between the steel post and the trees. "I can easily walk around."

Billy's forehead wrinkled in confusion. "But that's not the way it's done. Mr. Hamilton wants his privacy. You have to wait."

Emily tapped her foot. She didn't want to upset Billy, but she certainly didn't want to be late for her scene. "I'm on my way for doughnuts," she said. "Sure hope they don't run out."

"Maybe I'll open the gate a little early. Just for today." He creaked toward the gate, almost tripping in his haste, but righting himself with his cane.

Emily helped him push the bar back, wondering if this old guy really should be living alone. "How often do you have visitors?" she asked. "Do you have family close by?"

"No, it's just me. This area is my responsibility."

"But who brings your groceries?"

"Some regular people."

Her gaze swept his baggy pants, his stained shirt. Dirt rimmed the collar and threads dangled from his tattered cuffs. It was hard to determine the original color of his clothes. "Well," she said, "I'll bring some food later. Maybe a sandwich."

He scowled. "You promised doughnuts."

"Yes. One doughnut," she said. "But maybe some other food, to eat before the doughnut."

"I like doughnuts best," he said sulkily.

"Okay." She nodded, hiding her concern, and continued down the driveway. Once out of sight of the cottage, she turned on her phone and checked the time. Already past six. She'd wasted precious minutes but it certainly seemed that Billy needed more care. Back home, Jenna checked on their old neighbor regularly. Burke had even installed a downstairs bathroom so Mrs. Parker didn't have to climb stairs.

Billy had trouble staying upright on a paved driveway but at least his cottage was one level. And surely Mr. Hamilton was aware of his living conditions.

Shaking her head, she broke into a jog, trying to make up for lost time. Crew hammered nails by the racetrack and she cut along the trail behind them, returning their greetings with a breathless 'good morning.' A path edged between a row of trailers and led to an area filled with generators and the smell of bacon. She spotted the dining tent and slowed to a more dignified walk.

An officious-looking man with headsets draped around his neck strode in the same direction. She swerved to join him.

"Smells like another nice breakfast," she said.

"Sure does. But I ate too much last night." He groaned and rubbed his belly, then detailed last night's feast of steak and lobster.

Emily salivated, almost sick with longing. The door monitor eyed her suspiciously when they walked into the crowded tent but the friendly man was still talking, and his presence obviously lent her credibility. She didn't want to hear anymore about food though, and the smell of frying bacon sent her taste buds into a frenzy. However, she didn't have time to stand in any long lineup and she was used to skipping meals. It was much more important to be on time for her rearing scene.

She veered to the empty beverage table, made two cups of coffee and headed to the wardrobe tent.

Luckily Maggie was working. Her kind face creased in a smile when she spotted the coffee. She immediately dropped her bundle of clothes. "You're awesome," she said. "It's impossible to grab coffee when I work the red-eye shift."

Emily glanced around. Except for a lady washing makeup brushes, the tent seemed deserted. "Are you working alone again?"

"Yes, but tomorrow there'll be five of us. We have a busload of extras coming in. What are you here for?"

"More groom's clothes," Emily said. "My scene was postponed."

"But I gave you clothes yesterday. You don't need more."

"Yes," Emily said, automatically talking faster. "But this is a different scene—" She paused in the middle of her spiel. Maybe it wasn't necessary to embellish. After all, she hadn't done anything wrong. She wasn't trying to steal clothes, only borrow them. Besides, they were all working for the good of the movie.

"Actually," she squared her shoulders, "I didn't make it home the last two nights. I only brought a day bag from my apartment so the clothes I checked out yesterday are already dirty. Basically I have nothing of my own—except an entirely useless cocktail dress and a very pretty pair of shoes."

Maggie stared for a second then giggled. "You look darn good for not having been home in awhile. But I hope you know what you're doing." She shook her head, her face sobering. "Trust me. These movie people will break your heart."

"Oh, it's not that. It's pure work. I wish it wasn't," Emily said, indulging for a moment in vivid imagination of a shirtless Dan.

Maggie gave an understanding nod. "Yeah. Working these hours kills my love life too." She pulled two pairs of jeans off the rack. "Try these. In the meantime I'll find a couple shirts. Unfortunately we don't have any underwear, only some disposable stuff left over from a nursing home movie."

"I'd love them though," Emily said appreciatively. "And dry socks too, if you have any." She glanced around the tent, suddenly concerned for Maggie. Jobs were scarce in this area and working on a movie set had to be the best gig in the world. "You won't get in trouble, will you?"

"Thanks for your concern but I'm just doing my job." Maggie's eyes twinkled. "Didn't you say you were shooting three different scenes today?"

"Yes, I did say that."

"And that you need several changes of clothes?"

Emily gave a solemn nod. "That's exactly what I told you."

The director was hyper and unsmiling, and he spoke so fast Emily could barely follow his words. She'd already sneezed twice and her throat was desert dry. She was going to screw up this scene. She just knew it.

She swallowed, desperate to portray a cool professionalism. But her head throbbed, her nose was running and she was so terrified it was impossible to concentrate. Her eyes flickered to Dan, and his reassuring smile made her breathing steady a notch.

"The groom will lead the horse from the barn," the director said, pointing. "Here is where I want the first rear. Then another one here. Robert, you stand to the side and look worried. This is the point when you realize something is seriously wrong with Reckless. And remember, quiet. Turn off your phones."

Emily's hands fisted. Her nose tickled and it was torture not to rub it. Everyone else stood unmoving, absorbing everything the director was saying. Oh, damn. Another sneeze was coming; she could feel it. She raised her hand, desperate to stifle it.

Too late.

When she lowered her hand, the director was frowning and everyone else stared. "Excuse me," she muttered, her face flaming.

"Dan," the director snapped. "Don't you have any background that isn't sick?"

And suddenly Dan was there. "Hey," he said. He draped an arm over her shoulders, and it was so warm and comforting she wished it would never move.

"Sounds like you have a bit of a cold." His finger grazed her lower lip, his arm still exuding wonderful heat. He smelled crisp and clean and confident, and he was the best thing she'd seen this morning.

"Open," he said, brushing her lip.

His face was so close, his touch on her face gentle. If she looked into his warm blue eyes any longer she'd undoubtedly melt. Open her mouth? Was he going to kiss her? Here? Actually, she was fine with that, even though there were people all around, glaring at her because she'd sneezed.

She opened her mouth.

He popped a piece of gum on her tongue. "Just think of leading the horse, nothing else," he said. "It's just you and Bruno. You're going to do great."

His voice was so calm, she nodded and let him guide her to Bruno's side. Someone placed the lead line in her hand. "Walk," Dan said.

She walked.

But the horse stopped and pulled on the lead. She turned and Bruno reared, so high and menacing that her brain stalled. She couldn't remember a single direction, and it was obvious the director would fire her on the spot.

Dan's hand tightened reassuringly on her hip. "Watch the line," he whispered. Her skin tingled and his touch jolted her memory. 'Don't pull too hard on the lead but no slack.'

She tightened the line, concentrating on keeping it from tangling in Bruno's waving feet, but making sure she didn't pull on his halter. And then it was just her and Dan and Bruno. She forgot about the cameras and the dissatisfied director and her lack of makeup. She was only a groom trying to deal with a rebellious horse.

She even stopped worrying about acting or what type of expression to use. She just tried to avoid the horse's murderous hooves. And throughout it, she was conscious of Dan's guiding hand.

Bruno dropped to the ground, ears flattened. She coaxed him forward a few feet. But he reared again, looking so agitated she thought perhaps he really was upset. His front feet returned to the ground and Dan signaled for her to walk again.

She moved a few more steps and Bruno reared and it really wasn't scary at all.

"Cut!" the director yelled.

And then Dan was patting Bruno, and the director was talking to a camera guy and peering into a screen.

"If we switch the groom to the horse's other side, we can bring a camera underneath for a vertical shot," the director said.

The cameraman nodded and gestured at someone on his team. Dan, however, shook his head.

"Why not?" the director asked.

"It's customary to lead from the left," Dan said, his hand still on Bruno's neck. "It would be jarring to horse people to see the groom on the right."

"I can do the angle from the left," the cameraman said, "but it'll be tight for space."

"Let's try it," the director said, and an assistant director relayed the information to Emily as if she couldn't hear what was being said.

Dan stepped closer. "Just do the same thing, Emily. But the cameraman will get underneath for an upward shot."

She nodded, glad the scene would be re-shot. Dan's calmness boosted her confidence and despite her headache and runny nose, she didn't want it over too quickly. Besides, if they did a lot of takes, there was more chance Jenna would see her face.

They repositioned Bruno. Heads bent over cameras. Someone slapped the clapperboard shut. The director called 'Action!'

Emily stepped forward with Bruno and this time she didn't need Dan's guiding hand. She felt his calm presence though and knew Bruno felt it too. It was actually rather fun, now that she no longer agonized about the hovering cameras or the director's disapproval.

The lead tightened and she turned. Bruno's hooves flashed in front of her face. He wore shiny aluminum race plates today and seemed very proud of them, slashing the air with aggressive abandon.

"Cut!"

Dan's hand looped around her hip and he tugged her back. "You were too close on that one," he said.

"You changed Bruno's shoes," she whispered, smiling up at him.

"And you had too close a view." He smiled back at her. "If we shoot again, keep the positioning from the first time. You're not being paid for stunt work. I don't want my race advisor getting hurt."

"Moving on," the assistant director called.

"That's great," Dan said. "Anthony is satisfied with Bruno's scene."

Her chagrin at Dan calling it Bruno's scene was softened by his earlier reference to *my* race advisor. In fact, her heart was beating double time, something it always seemed to do when Dan was around. "Bruno was very careful not to hit me," she managed. "What happens now?"

"Bruno goes to his stall to relax." Dan handed the lead line to Lizzie who smiled prettily at Dan and promptly handed Bruno off to a waiting wrangler.

"I checked the small barn an hour ago," Lizzie said, her mouth flattening as she turned toward Emily. "I hope you intend to clean the stalls better. They're filthy."

"They were cleaned early this morning so they can't be too dirty," Emily said. "And of course I'll pick them out again later."

"As long as they're cleaned sometime today," Dan said, his gaze narrowing on Lizzie. "Are the horses ready for the track?"

"Mounted and waiting," Lizzie said.

"Good. Stick around, Emily. I'll need your opinion."

Emily nodded, ignoring her rumbling stomach. She'd hoped to grab some breakfast but the opportunity to stay with Dan was irresistible. Already, crew hustled toward the track, and there was a strange vehicle with cameras mounted on a boom. It would be interesting to see how galloping horses were filmed, and with Dan she'd be in the middle of the action.

Emily was so happy she even shot Lizzie a conciliatory smile. If she had an amazing boss like Dan, she'd probably be a little territorial too although it was crazy Lizzie even perceived her as a threat. There were too many other women around, stunning women with fashionable clothes and artful makeup and buttery soft Italian boots.

Her nose suddenly itched. She ducked her head, muffling another sneeze.

"Would you like a coffee," Dan asked. "Or perhaps some juice?"

She lowered her arm from her mouth, still blinking from the sneeze. "Is there time to go to the tent?" she asked hopefully.

"We'll have it delivered," Dan said. "Are you allergic, or sick?"

"Just what we need," Lizzie said darkly. "A flu bug."

"I'm not allergic," Emily said, "and sorry if I'm sick.'

"Tell Lizzie what you want." Dan's voice hardened, his eyes turning an icy blue. "And she'll get it for you. Whatever you want. Cough drops, Kleenex, coffee."

"Coffee would be great," Emily said. She wanted food too but she suddenly empathized with Lizzie. The wrangler looked quite stricken and no wonder. Dan's eyes and voice, so warm only minutes ago, now projected an icy chill. It was obvious why even the autocratic director listened when Dan spoke.

Dan was already moving away, completely dismissing Lizzie, his attention on the track. "Let's go, Emily," he said. "We need to make this track scene realistic. And I'm curious what an expert like you will spot."

Emily gulped. "Me too," she said.

CHAPTER SIXTEEN

Emily followed Dan's gaze, listening as he relayed information about each horse. It was a relief to be alone with him, away from the director. She hadn't sneezed since, although her head still throbbed. Clearly she'd caught some sort of bug but hopefully her headache would disappear with coffee.

"The first four horses will be on camera," Dan said. "Filmed walking in a line with Reckless in front."

"Is that the obedient Reckless?" she asked, studying the bay colt with the distinctive blaze and two white socks on his front legs.

"Yes. That's Reckless before his groom left. When Thomas Hamilton had high hopes for the Derby." Dan edged sideways so a harried camera woman could move some equipment. His hard thigh brushed Emily's hip. "So," his voice softened, "do you see anything that needs adjustment?"

Emily tightened her hands around the rail, struggling to calm her senses. But she could smell his subtle aftershave, feel his welcoming heat. And if she leaned two inches to the left, her elbow would touch his arm. His sleeves were rolled and for some reason, she couldn't pull her eyes off his ridged forearms, the tanned skin with the sprinkling of dark hair.

She jerked her gaze away and stared across the track, trying to stay grounded, desperate to find something—just one detail—that would help. Anything that would justify his faith. But everything looked authentic.

There were no obvious mistakes. The horses wore exercise saddles, the riders were properly equipped with race helmets and protective vests. The stirrups were short and the riders sat their horses easily. It could have been a group of riders from Three Brooks or any track in North America. Except something was missing—

"What about their whips?" she blurted.

Dan frowned. "They're not racing."

"But they're a necessary training aid. Especially with short stirrups, when you can't use your legs in the usual way. The riders at Three Brooks just tucked them in the back of their jeans but they always carried them, just in case."

Dan stroked his jaw, staring at the horses. "You're right," he said. "They should have them."

Emily's hands slowly loosened. He'd been quick to acknowledge the oversight. Most men would have scrambled rather than admit fault. At least, the men she'd known had been like that.

Dan was already signaling to someone—not Lizzie who was approaching from the other direction with a coffee tray and a forced smile—but to a man with a ponytail who sat in a golf cart.

"Here's your coffee." Lizzie thrust a cup at Emily. "And cream and sugar if you want it."

"Thanks," Emily said. She picked up the cup and took a grateful sip. It was strong and hot and would certainly ease the painful emptiness in her stomach. "I hope you didn't have to walk far."

But Lizzie had already turned away and was murmuring to Dan. He nodded, texted something on his phone then glanced back at Emily.

"Thanks for the tip. Can you be here tomorrow? Reckless is going to crash through the rail. Should be fun." He smiled, the cleft in his strong jaw deepening. "You did well today."

Warmth spread through Emily's chest. It didn't matter now that the director had been annoyed at her sneezing, or that her wet feet seemed directly attached to her itchy nose, or that Lizzie was standing behind Dan and glowering. He wasn't the type to throw out idle praise, and for a blissful moment even her head stopped pounding.

Dan turned away, still texting, with Lizzie scampering beside him. Emily felt slightly bereft.

Her hand drifted to the comforting phone in her pocket. Maybe she could whip off some texts too. Message Jenna and tell her about Bruno, about his rears. She wouldn't send any pictures, of course, or reveal any movie details. But a little text wouldn't hurt. After all, Dan used his phone on set all the time. And technically she was no longer background but a race advisor. Surely that gave some privileges.

She nibbled at her lower lip. Dan had been so respectful, almost as though he had high expectations. Odd since no one ever expected much of her. Generally they harped about the rules before she even had a chance to break them. She'd never forgotten Wally's words her first day on the tour guide job. 'I know you're going to screw up.'

It was amazing Wally had even hired her as a guide. Although he'd really done it for Jenna.

"Excuse me."

Emily gave a guilty jump, pulling her hand off her phone. Mrs. Hamilton stood about ten feet away, her carefully made-up face drawn in a slight frown.

"Did I miss Reckless galloping this morning?" Mrs. Hamilton asked.

"There was no galloping," Emily said. "Just the rearing." But it had been her scene and she felt a flush of pride.

"He didn't bolt and run through the rail?"

"Not yet," Emily said. "That's early tomorrow."

"Oh, good. My husband isn't feeling well but he didn't want to miss the action." Mrs. Hamilton stared across the infield, a faraway look in her eyes. "It seems like this all happened yesterday."

"Did Reckless really run through the rail?"

"Indeed he did. For a few months he was a complete terror. My husband almost gelded him. Fortunately, we didn't."

Emily shook her head, unable to imagine the number of talented horses who wouldn't exist if Reckless had been gelded. "How did you help him?" she asked.

"We moved him back to the main barn. Hired a new groom." Mrs. Hamilton gave a musical laugh. "Men rarely remain faithful for long and Reckless was no different. His next groom was a sixty-year-old woman who signed a contract saying she'd remain in our employ for as long as Reckless raced. He loved her, much more than the first."

There seemed to be no question that the groom's abrupt departure was what bothered Reckless. Mrs. Hamilton wasn't even speculating; she spoke as though it were fact.

"Were you tempted to offer the first groom a raise?" Emily asked, trying to choose her words carefully. "At least so Reckless could make it to the Derby?"

"I'm not sure why they couldn't make a deal." Mrs. Hamilton's eyes shadowed. "My husband was in charge of compensation. I wasn't…involved."

Emily took a hasty sip of coffee. It seemed the groom was a delicate subject. No doubt, old Hamilton had been having an affair. It made sense now. The elegant apartment, the private barn for Reckless, even Billy monitoring the gate. Clearly it had been an upsetting situation for more than just the horse.

Her nose itched and she averted her head but was unable to suppress a sneeze.

Mrs. Hamilton gave a sympathetic tilt of her head. She reached in her purse and pressed a soft tissue into Emily's hand. "My husband started sneezing yesterday. Now he's so chilled he can't get out of bed. I hope you don't catch it."

She snapped her purse shut. "I appreciate knowing the daily schedule. Anthony usually advises us of any changes but he's extremely busy. Now we won't have to call him."

Emily couldn't imagine picking up the phone and calling the director about scene changes. The man was a sparkplug of energy, and very volatile. She'd sensed the production crew's relief when Dan was present to act as a buffer.

Mrs. Hamilton continued talking but despite the lady's friendliness, it was hard to concentrate. Emily's stomach churned along with her head. She gripped her empty cup, wishing for another coffee. Or maybe food might help. Mainly she wanted to find somewhere warm where she could curl up and sleep.

"Well, I'll see you tomorrow," Mrs. Hamilton said, turning toward a stately silver Lincoln. "It was very pleasant talking with you."

"You too," Emily managed. But once Mrs. Hamilton closed the car door, she lobbed her empty cup into a garbage can and bolted toward the dining room. She'd pick up some food for Billy, clean the stalls and grab a nap. Sleep always did wonders.

She didn't want to sneeze tomorrow and draw more negative attention. No one was ever given lines that way.

She strode into the tent, past the monitor who eyed her suspiciously but didn't challenge her presence. Lunch was being served. However, the stagnant air still reeked of eggs, and nausea churned Emily's stomach, completely wrecking her appetite.

She picked up two sandwiches, ham and cheese and one that resembled chicken, wrapped two doughnuts in a napkin and hurried back outside.

The sun beamed overhead, warming the paved drive to Billy's cottage. Despite the heat on her shoulders, she shivered. She just wanted to curl up and sleep. But she stopped in front of the cottage, uncertain if she should knock or simply leave the food. The front and back yards were both empty. A large dog kennel had weeds entangled in the mesh, but the food should be safe on top of the wire.

Click. The door pushed open and Billy stepped out, as if he'd been watching the road. His eyes filled with anticipation. "Got my doughnuts?"

"Yes, and here's a sandwich you can eat first. Do you like ham or chicken?"

"I like them both," he said.

She passed over all the food. Her appetite had disappeared anyway. Now the only thing she wanted was solitude. "Maybe you should eat a sandwich before the doughnuts," she suggested, eyeing his baggy pants.

"All right," he said grudgingly. "But it would have been better if you brought more doughnuts."

"I need to look after the horses," she said, covering a yawn. "However, I'll bring more food, as long as I'm here."

"Mr. Hamilton wants you to stay." Billy took a big bite of doughnut, completely ignoring the sandwiches in his left hand.

"You should eat the sandwich first." She stopped making suggestions and gave a wry shrug. Nobody liked being told what to do. Besides, the order of the food didn't matter, as long as he ate something nutritious. "I want to stay until the movie's finished too," she said.

And maybe, just maybe, she'd land a speaking role. There weren't many special skills around and the director might need someone to say a line. Maggie had mentioned there was a lot of background scheduled for tomorrow. Emily would have to do something to get Anthony's attention though, something besides sneezing.

She rubbed her temple. Hopefully a nap would help her think more clearly. It wouldn't hurt to clean the stalls later. Barney and Ted wouldn't mind, as long as she fed them their noon hay. Right now, her arms felt too heavy to lift a pitchfork.

She forced a wave that Billy ignored. His head was still bent over the doughnuts, his jaw grinding rhythmically. And even though he was a cantankerous old man, his obvious satisfaction gave her a boost.

She continued her trudge along the winding drive, keen to flop on the sofa and catch up on some sleep. Maybe she'd borrow Barney's blanket. It was warm enough that he didn't need it. By now the sun would have heated the apartment. The wide French windows faced south so it should be warmer than last night. And in the daylight, the place might feel more welcoming.

She rounded the corner, swept with a swell of pride at the sight of the stud barn. She'd never been in charge of horses before. Never been in charge of anything important. She'd looked after Peanut, but Jenna had always checked, as though not trusting her to do it right. Dan had given her feed instructions, shown her how to wrap and then stepped back. Pretty cool.

Of course, she'd have to adjust the horses' schedule to fit her day. Before she went upstairs, she'd turn Ted out in the paddock and give Barney a flake of hay. Then, after she woke, she'd pick out their stalls and tend to Barney's leg. That would give her time to grab supper at the dining tent. Tomorrow she'd be rested and ready to smile for the director, hopefully without any disruptive sneezing.

Lizzie charged from the barn, shattering Emily's calm. "Where the hell have you been?" she hollered. "These stalls are still filthy."

Her accent didn't sound so cute when she yelled. "I'm going to do them," Emily said. "Soon."

Lizzie's scowl deepened. "This isn't some type of ranch vacation. If you're not going to work, you should leave."

"I just left the set," Emily said. "I've been working all morning."

"So have I," Lizzie snapped, jabbing a thumb over her shoulder. "And you have hay to stack."

Emily glanced to the left. A haphazard pile of hay bales had been dumped near the corner of the barn. It looked like enough to feed ten horses over a very long winter. And for some reason the truck had unloaded the bales fifty feet from the door.

Her shoulders drooped. The bales looked heavy, at least forty pounds each. "Why did they drop them so far away?" Emily asked, eyeing the extra distance.

"The ground is muddy everywhere else," Lizzie said. "And it might rain later so there's no time to waste."

Emily checked the clear sky. Not a cloud in sight. Sighing, she looked back at the stack. "Barney and Ted couldn't eat all that hay if they lived here a year."

"We might have a few more lame horses that need to be separated," Lizzie said. "But if chucking bales is too much work for an actress like you, just say so."

Emily's mouth tightened. Finally she was being called an actress, although in a very demeaning tone. A wrangler actually sounded more important. It definitely was more fun. But any work she did here was helping Dan so her nap would have to wait.

She forced an agreeable nod. "Where should we put them?"

"Use the empty stalls," Lizzie said. "They'll fit if you stack them properly."

"You're not going to help?"

"You offered to look after this barn," Lizzie said. "It's your responsibility." She turned and headed down the path, her back ramrod stiff.

Emily glanced wistfully at the sunny balcony. It was tempting to just feed the horses and grab a nap. But if by remote chance it did rain, the hay would be ruined. Besides, despite what Lizzie thought, she wasn't afraid of hard work. She and Jenna had lugged many bales before, although it was always more fun with company.

She walked into the barn, slightly mollified by Barney's welcoming nicker. She gave him a flake of hay, then turned Ted out in the paddock. At least she had the horses close by. They were much better company than grumpy old Lizzie.

She grabbed a broom and thoroughly swept the empty stalls, making sure the floor was clean before bringing in the hay. The wheelbarrow proved invaluable and after a few spills, she figured how to stack it so she could move four bales per load. Barney chewed hay, watching curiously as she pushed the top-heavy wheelbarrow in and out of the barn.

Earlier she'd been cold. Now she was clammy with sweat, and beads of perspiration trickled between her breasts. The hardest part was stacking. With no one to help, she had to wrestle the hay to the top of the rows, then climb up and adjust each bale. Her arms ached, four nails had broken and already blisters formed where the baler twine cut into her hands.

She took a couple breaks, twice sticking her head beneath the tap. The shock of cold water eased her headache, at least temporarily, and it certainly soothed her blisters. But her eyes and nose itched, and the dust gave her such fits of sneezing, she had to step outside and gulp in the cool fresh air.

She worried about Barney too. The hay was unusually dusty. She couldn't turn him out with his injured leg but it was becoming evident no one should breathe this air. His stall was close to the entrance where it caught a little breeze, but his flanks visibly heaved and his nostrils flared. When she leaned closer, she even heard a worrisome wheeze.

She walked outside and checked the paddocks. They were all too large for a horse with an injured tendon. He might run and buck, especially after being cooped up in a stall. If it were Peanut, she'd tie him to a post but she didn't know Barney. He might not be trained to tie, and if he panicked and pulled back, he'd hurt his leg even more.

There were still about ten bales left in the pile, but it seemed more important to look after the horse.

She returned to the barn, haltered Barney and led him outside. He was delighted to eat grass and immediately stopped wheezing. Ted was happier too, now that his buddy was in sight.

But she couldn't stand and hold Barney all day, not when she had so much work remaining. And already her body ached with exhaustion. It was times like this when she wished horses would behave more like dogs.

She closed her eyes, wondering if it were possible to sleep standing up. A fly buzzed around her ear. Barney chewed in the background, his steady chomping like a lullaby. She dragged her eyelids open and checked the horse. He looked as quiet as a puppy dog. She closed her eyes again, lacking energy to swipe at the persistent fly.

It was definitely peaceful here. No wonder Mr. Hamilton had built an apartment above the barn. The location was perfect, close to the track, yet isolated. And he'd even had a gate protecting him from unexpected visitors.

"There's been a change in plans." Lizzie's abrupt voice jerked Emily awake.

"The hay is too dusty so we're sending it back," Lizzie went on. "The truck will pick it up in about an hour."

Emily staggered, stunned by the pronouncement. All her backbreaking work, wasted. For a moment, she couldn't speak.

"It's really too bad you worked so fast." Lizzie gave a taunting smile. "But Dan trusts me to inspect the hay. It's part of my job."

"Apparently that job is above your pay grade," Emily said. "Most people wouldn't take an entire afternoon to notice bad hay."

Lizzie's smile faded. "Just get the hay back outside. If you want to quit, I'll be happy to take over."

"Hold my horse." Emily jammed the lead line in Lizzie's hand. "I can chuck hay all day, but it's too dusty inside for Barney."

She stalked into the barn, struggling to control her temper. At least Barney was safe, no longer breathing all this dust. Lizzie could figure out what to do with him.

Emily clambered up onto the top row of hay and pushed the bales back into the aisle. It was much easier tossing it down than dragging it up, but the complete waste of time and labor was devastating. It had been stacked perfectly too.

She trudged back and forth, pushing the loaded wheelbarrow, returning the hay to the pile outside. At some point, Lizzie disappeared, replaced by a wiry wrangler wearing a blue ball cap.

Let's switch," he called. "You can hold the horse for a while."

"Thanks." She walked over and gratefully took Barney's lead. There were only about fifteen bales left, but each one seemed to have tripled in weight. Every muscle in her body ached.

"Damn." The wrangler's eyes widened as he stared at her hands. "Why didn't you use gloves?"

"I don't have any," Emily admitted, ruefully inspecting her blistered palms. The baler twine had left angry tracks, and the skin on her exposed forearms was red and blotchy. "This job came up unexpectedly."

"I'm surprised Lizzie hired you." His gaze flickered over Emily's face and then back to her hands.

"She didn't hire me. Dan did."

"That explains it." He gave a wry chuckle. "Well, you just relax. My name is Monty. I'll move the rest of the hay. You look beat."

"I can do the job," she said defensively.

"So can I."

CHAPTER SEVENTEEN

"How far does the cardboard extend?" Dan studied the white strip of fence surrounding the track. It looked like a normal rail, but tomorrow morning a horse and rider were going to cause a spectacular crash. Any mistakes could be fatal.

"Twenty feet." The man adjusted his tool belt, his gaze sidling away.

"Dammit. I requested thirty." Dan calmed his voice, aware it wasn't the set crew's fault. "We need thirty feet minimum for this stunt. How long to add ten more feet?"

The man glanced at the setting sun. "Could start first thing tomorrow. Finish by noon. We'll need to add more foam grass though."

"Do it," Dan said. He turned to Lizzie. "Looks like we won't need Bruno tomorrow. Anthony wants this filmed at sunrise. Just a sec."

He walked a few feet away before pressing Anthony's number, conscious of the curious ears of the construction crew. "Anthony," he said into the phone, "I'm on the track now. We need more work on the cardboard section of rail. For some reason, it's way too short."

There was a long silence, punctuated by Anthony's resigned sigh. "A horse is only two feet wide. Twenty feet seemed like plenty."

A muscle ticked in Dan's jaw. "At a gallop. Dawn light. Be like threading a needle."

"That means we can't shoot it tomorrow."

"That's right," Dan said. "Unless it's done at a trot."

"No," Anthony said quickly. "I want it at a gallop. Go ahead and tell them to add the cardboard."

"I already have."

"I'm sure you did." However, Anthony sounded more resigned than irritated, and he was even chuckling by the time they cut the connection.

Dan turned, almost bumping into Lizzie. He hadn't realized she'd been standing so close. "No horses on set tomorrow," he said. "That gives us some breathing room."

"Okay," Lizzie said. "And I sent the hay back like you asked. Maybe we should inspect the next load before it's shipped. Drive out to the farm and take a look."

"Yeah," Dan said, absently skimming his messages.

"It would be nice to get away for a day."

The wistfulness in her voice made him glance up. She worked hard, always stuck close... Sometimes too close. She probably needed a day off. "You want a break?" he asked. "Go ahead. I'll have a rental car delivered in the morning."

"But I'm not used to driving on the wrong side of the road."

"Take Monty with you," he said. "Have some fun. You should do some sightseeing."

"What about you?"

He deliberately misunderstood. Had been avoiding far more aggressive women for so long, it was second nature. "I'll be fine," he said. "Going to work a bit with Bruno. I want the rail stunt to be perfect."

"Naturally you do," she said.

He caught something in her voice and glanced up. Lately she'd been on edge, snappy with all his crew. She was returning to New Zealand after this shoot and probably antsy about going home.

On the other hand, her tone had been borderline insolent and that was something he couldn't tolerate. "Something wrong, Lizzie?" he asked.

"No." She gave a quick smile and shook her head. "Not really. It's just...well, the new girl, Emily. She's neglecting the horses in the little barn. The bay was in distress today from the hay dust. I had to take him outside to breathe. She didn't even notice."

"Did you give him some Dex?"

"Not yet, but I'll check him again tomorrow. It's just that she creates more work." Lizzie paused as though reluctant to say more, then her words escaped in a rush. "I had to send Monty over to help. She's too green to understand how dust affects horses. And with the company trying to cut costs, she seems somewhat redundant."

Redundant. Not a word he'd ever attach to Emily. She had far too much presence, a vibrant energy that he appreciated. Granted, maybe his interest wasn't solely professional. "If someone's working hard to get ahead, I like to help," he said. "I recall you were in that position before."

"Yes, but I did my job." Lizzie's mouth pinched. "And I don't think I was in danger of getting hurt."

"Hurt?" He immediately stiffened. Now that was serious. His foremost goal was to keep his people and horses safe. No movie warranted an injury.

"She was almost kicked turning the chestnut out." Lizzie wrung her hands in agitation. "Stood right behind him. His hoof just missed her face."

For a moment Dan stopped breathing. He hadn't really vetted Emily, just watched her lead Bruno. But damn, she was plucky. He loved her buoyant spirit, that deep-throated laugh, the way she tackled life head on. Her sheer presence gave him a lift.

But he'd never forgive himself if she were hurt.

"She's an actress, not a wrangler," Lizzie added. "It's asking a lot for anyone to look after two spirited Thoroughbreds. And she's not the type to admit she needs help. She'll work until she drops."

Probably true. He dragged a hand over his jaw, warring with himself. Emily had looked so relieved that she could stay, seeming to need either the money or the job, perhaps both. He didn't need another race advisor, although her tips about the race shoes and whips had been helpful. Mainly though, he liked her company—and that was a damn selfish reason to put her in jeopardy.

Lizzie stepped closer. "Want me to talk to her? Let her down gently?"

"No." He blew out a regretful sigh. "I'll do it."

CHAPTER EIGHTEEN

The lights of the small barn shone through the gloom. Dan walked across the clearing and through the doorway. Both horses poked their heads over the stall doors. Hay protruded from their mouths and they chewed rhythmically, their eyes quiet and content.

Neither of them looked in respiratory distress. He checked the bay, but his vitals were normal. The horse's hay had been soaked and even the aisle gleamed, as though recently dampened.

Thank God for Lizzie. Whatever breathing problems the bay had experienced earlier, the horse was certainly stable now. Tomorrow, Dan would try to find a portable pen so the horse could stay outside. The pens were small enough so the gelding wouldn't be too exuberant and re-injure his leg, but at least he'd be in the fresh air.

And there would be better quality hay soon. Even though they were running low, Dan certainly wouldn't feed garbage. The delivery today had been so dusty he'd only cracked a few bales before rejecting the entire load.

He glanced over the door of the empty stall, checking if there was enough hay to last another day. His breath leaked in a groan of despair. Even though he'd found Emily a safe place to sleep, she was curled in the hay. Not really curled. It looked like she'd sat down in the corner and fallen asleep. A leather halter was still clutched in her hands.

He pushed open the door and crouched beside her, shaking his head with regret. The skin on her arms was red and blotchy, and welts laced the palms of her hands. She must be cold too. Her T-shirt was thin and though the days were comfortable, the temperature plummeted at night.

He touched her on the shoulder. She didn't move. He leaned closer, alarmed by her raspy breathing. It seemed she had more respiratory problems than either of the horses.

"Hey," he whispered, giving her a gentle shake. "You should go upstairs." She was the soundest sleeper he'd ever met. He shook her again. This time her eyelids drifted open.

"I have to watch the horse," she said before closing her eyes and snuggling against his arm.

"Emily." He tried to make his voice stern but at the same time couldn't resist tucking her into his chest. Her hair smelled of hay and sunshine, and he dipped his head a little closer, adjusting her in his arms. "The horse is fine," he whispered. "You need to go to bed."

Her eyes opened again although clearly it was a colossal effort. And while he appreciated her dedication to the horse, it was doubtful she'd notice if the bay toppled in his stall.

"Come on," he coaxed, rising to his feet and pulling her up. He half carried her down the aisle to the apartment, keeping his arms around her while she stumbled up the stairs.

He tried to guide her to the bedroom but she resisted so he scooped her up and carried her into the room. Paused in confusion. The bed wasn't even made. The mattress was completely bare.

"I sleep on the sofa," she said, her sleepy breath fanning his throat.

He turned and carried her back into the living room. The moon glimmered through the windows, but he didn't see any blankets. And the apartment was frigid. No wonder she hadn't been in a hurry to leave the stall, warmed as it was by the horses' body heat.

He sighed. It was probably best to move her to the spare room in his trailer. However she'd already fallen back to sleep, her cheek pressed trustingly against his shoulder, her blond-streaked hair fanning his arm. Something tightened in his chest.

He laid her on the sofa and draped his jacket over her. Stared for a moment, then stretched out alongside, tucking her in the warm spot between his chest and the back cushions. A tendril of silky hair curved over her eyebrow. He gently brushed it back. Her cheekbones seemed more prominent and her shadowed eyes increased that hint of vulnerability. She'd hate that, he knew. She made a habit of hiding behind a careless nonchalance, as if she had something to prove.

It was obvious she really wanted this job. And would work her fingers to the bone to keep it.

He lifted her left hand, examining the welts. He tried to be gentle but she winced and her eyes opened.

"Sorry," he whispered. "What the hell happened? Do they hurt?"

"Not one bit." Sleep thickened her voice. "I can still clean stalls or lift hay. Anything you want."

"It looks like you were already moving hay."

"The load was too dusty so I had to carry it back."

He frowned. The hay had been inspected before it was off the truck. Delivery had been refused.

"Barney is okay though," she added groggily.

"Who's Barney?" he asked, his confusion growing. He had no wrangler by that name although he didn't doubt that any member of the production crew would drop their duties to help Emily. Any male member. Lizzie clearly wasn't a fan.

"Barney's the bay. If you don't like that name, I can call him something else. But horses need names, don't you think?" Her question contained a streak of defiance.

"Names are pointless if they're temporary," he said. "It only makes it harder to say good-bye."

"You don't like good-byes?"

"You need to get some sleep." He realized he was still holding her hand and slowly released it. "I'll come back with some blankets and salve."

"Is that why you don't date actresses? Because of the good-byes?" She twisted and sneezed into her arm. "Excuse me," she murmured, turning back to him, her eyelids drooping. "You're lovely and warm. Hope my cold doesn't scare you away..."

She was so tired she couldn't finish her sentence, and he protectively wrapped her in his arms.

"Doesn't seem like it's going to," he said.

CHAPTER NINETEEN

Emily wiggled contentedly. She hadn't felt this warm in days, completely cocooned in strong arms and a chest that reminded her of a rugby player she'd once dated. Her eyes whipped open. Dan's face was only inches away, the dark stubble on his chin giving a rakish appearance. He looked sleepy and sexy and good enough to eat.

While she looked like a dog's breakfast.

She drew in a careful breath, trying not to wake him. Colorless light filtered through the windows but it was early dawn and the room wasn't too bright. Maybe he wouldn't look closely at her hair or face. Dammit. The nicest man she'd ever woken with and she looked like a witch.

She jammed her eyes shut. But then her awareness of him only rocketed. She could feel each strong heartbeat, the ridges of his toned chest, and how the third button on his shirt pressed against her breast. One muscular leg draped over her calf, and his body blasted heat like a furnace. He'd done her a big kindness last night, staying to keep her warm. She wished it had meant more.

It was tempting to linger in his arms but she needed to untangle and duck into the bathroom before he woke. Even if it was just to brush her teeth.

"Good morning. How do you feel?" His deep voice rumbled above her ear, and he lifted her right hand, the pad of his thumb inspecting her palm.

Darn. He was moving. And he'd already straightened his legs. Unlike her, he seemed to be one of those rare people who awoke to complete alertness.

"Nice and warm, thanks," she said, keeping her face averted. "You're much better than a newspaper."

"Don't knock paper. It's always good in a pinch."

Her eyes widened. "You've slept in weird places too?"

"My brother and I followed the rodeo circuit when we were young. We weren't very good so we didn't make much day money."

"Oh," she breathed, rather entranced. "That sounds like fun. Traveling around. Seeing new places and people."

"The life is fun but it was a lot of work for very little money. And it leaves worn and broken bodies."

"Broken? Are you talking about horses or people?"

"Both." He released her hand, setting it on her hip. "Some people I know can barely walk. Movies are much safer. And I can control the environment."

She tilted her head, curiosity now outweighing any concern about her appearance. "So that's why you hung around the movie set when you were young. What kind of movie was it?"

"A western. I dogged those poor wranglers." He chuckled, amusement crinkling the corners of his eyes. "They either had to run me off or shoot me. I'm glad Dad told me to be persistent."

"What about your mother?" Emily asked.

"She wasn't in the picture."

Judging by the hardening of his voice, he wasn't speaking literally. It was also clear he intended to rise. His entire body had tensed along with the mention of his mother. But she didn't want him to go, and it wasn't just because his body was a cocoon of warmth.

She gave an exaggerated shiver and just as she hoped, his arms tightened. It was probably an instinctive reaction—he was too chivalrous to let any woman freeze—but she was glad the apartment didn't have any blankets. She would have been happy to lie in his arms all day and share stories. Perhaps more. And the way he was staring at her mouth, it was obvious he was increasingly aware of her as a woman.

"I've been thinking," he said.

Her chest kicked with delight. He *was* going to kiss her. The signs were unmistakable. His voice had thickened, his eyes darkening as he studied her face.

"Yes?" She tilted her head another inch. If he didn't care she looked a little rough, she wouldn't either. Jenna had always said she shouldn't worry so much about her appearance.

"There's a background bus coming tomorrow," he said. "I think it's time for you to catch a ride back to Louisville."

Her head jerked against the back of the sofa. For an achy moment, her mouth was too dry to speak. "But who will look after Barney and Ted?" she finally managed.

"Lizzie will. Thoroughbreds aren't pet ponies," he went on, his voice oddly gruff. "They can kick and buck. You can't safely handle them, not with those welts on your hands. And we don't want you to end up with a hoof in the head."

A lump blocked her throat, making it difficult to hide her confusion. She'd been competent enough to lead Bruno…when they needed someone for their precious movie. She'd even bit her tongue around Lizzie, only snapping back a couple times. Yet despite working both ends of the day, she still wasn't good enough. Couldn't make enough money to give her sister a measly weekend away. Chalk up another failure.

She wanted to ask about the race-consulting job but feared her voice would crack. Besides, she refused to beg. "Whatever," she said, faking a nonchalant shrug.

He cupped her chin, tilting her head so he could see her face. "A friend of mine is involved in a Louisville movie about university hazing. He needs more background performers. It might last six weeks. I'll give you his number."

She blinked, struggling to control the odd pricking behind her eyes. It was brutally apparent she couldn't accomplish anything on her own. But she didn't want another handout. Especially from him.

"Thanks, but no need." She pulled away and jackknifed to a sitting position. "My agent is probably on that anyway."

He immediately rose, leaving a blast of frigid air where his body had been. It was damn cold, but she could feel his scrutiny and was determined to hide her shivers. Once he left, she'd go downstairs. It was always warmer in the barn and the horses, at least, would be glad to see her.

"I'll bring back some cream for your hands," he said. "And when Lizzie returns tonight, you can give her your banking information. We'll get you paid up before you go."

"Great," she said. At least Lizzie wouldn't be around her last day.

"You better keep my jacket. Don't you have any warmer clothes?"

The faint criticism in his voice stung. "Of course, I do." She thrust his jacket at him. "Take it. I'm already hot."

He ignored the jacket, reached down and felt her forehead with the back of his hand. "You feel warm." He frowned. "Better bundle up. It's chilly in the morning."

He walked toward the door but called over his shoulder. "Don't turn the chestnut out. I don't want you handling either horse alone. I'll come by later or send someone to help."

The door clicked and he was gone. She stared at the jacket in her hands, still warm from their bodies, then slowly slipped it on. Now she wasn't even trusted to lead Ted and he loved his grassy paddock. But at least she wouldn't be feeding breakfast in a thin T-shirt and for that she was grateful. Lizzie wouldn't be around either. Yes, she should be happy. There were loads of pluses.

She rubbed her nose, trying to be optimistic but her energy seemed to have vanished with Dan. Hopefully he wouldn't catch her cold. It wouldn't be much fun for him, working long hours on a movie set and feeling this sick.

She stumbled to her feet and trudged down the narrow staircase, chilled despite the jacket. As usual, the barn was damp and she glanced wistfully at the wash stall. But the thought of stripping in the crisp air made her cringe. Beside, the floor didn't drain properly and the last thing she wanted was to leave a flooded aisle. Lizzie would be downright gleeful if Emily made any mistakes.

Barney and Ted nickered impatiently, tracking her movements as she tossed hay in the plastic bin and then hosed the contents thoroughly with water. It probably wasn't necessary to wet Ted's hay since only Barney had reacted to the dust, but it was best to be cautious.

The barn still felt dusty too, despite that she had wet the floor last night, trying to reduce hay particles in the air. There didn't seem to be much else to do, although it might be worth a call to Jenna. Peanut always coughed in the spring. Fresh air and green grass helped him. However, Barney had to be confined because of his injury, and she was no longer allowed to lead Ted.

She reached up to pat Barney. He nudged her arm, hungry and impatient, obviously wondering why his breakfast was delayed. However, Wally had always insisted on soaking hay for twenty minutes, and she wasn't going to remove it from the tub a second earlier. One of the advantages of working at an equine wellness center, even as a tour guide, was that she'd absorbed a variety of knowledge.

Just not enough to satisfy Dan.

She blew out a mournful sigh. At least she'd managed to stretch the background employment into a few extra days. But now she had to leave, return to her boring apartment and hunt for another job. Or crawl back to Three Brooks and endure the condescending comments from old co-workers. A wave of self-pity swept her.

She gave an impatient shake of her head and pulled out her phone. It was pointless to worry too far ahead. The least she could do was take good care of Barney for her remaining day. She pressed Jenna's number, wincing at the low battery warning. Tomorrow though, she'd be back in her apartment and able to use her charger. The thought didn't give much comfort.

"Hi, movie star." Jenna's teasing voice instantly lifted her spirits.

"It's just a background part," Emily said quickly. "It was fun though. I held the horse playing Reckless. He was rearing and everything."

"Do you say anything?"

"Well, no. It's background." Emily hated how her voice turned defensive. "But I'm looking after a couple of horses too. I almost like that job more. One of them does tricks, like grabbing things from your hand. That's actually why I'm calling. We had some bad hay yesterday and he started wheezing. I'm wetting his feed but the air in the barn still feels dusty."

"Get him outside," Jenna said. "Twenty-four seven."

"I can't. He's on stall rest, tendon. He'll run around in the paddock."

"Then make sure his windows are open, that the bedding isn't dusty and wet his hay. If that doesn't help, start with a bronchodilator and then some Dex. The best thing though would be to find a way to keep him outside."

Jenna sounded faintly disapproving and Emily wanted to explain that it was impossible to keep the horse outside. Besides she was only looking after him for another day; she'd been fired that very morning.

But when she glanced over her shoulder, Barney watched with liquid brown eyes, totally trusting her to deliver his breakfast. And take good care of him. "Okay, thanks," Emily said. "I'll figure something out. How are your exams going?"

"Wrote a tough one yesterday. Wally is coming by for pizza later, and then it's back to studying. I'm finished tomorrow night."

"Is Burke still away?"

"Yes." Jenna's voice turned tight.

"That's good," Emily said, hoping to cheer her up. "Now you'll have more time to study. You and Burke would be doing other stuff if he were around."

"Probably." But Jenna's laugh sounded brittle. "I offered to fly out after my exams, but he said not to bother."

"Which makes total sense if he's coming home soon," Emily said. She wanted to ask if she should wet Barney's grain in addition to the hay, but it sounded like Jenna had her own problems. "You know Burke works incredibly long hours while he's away," she added. "So he can spend more time with you at Three Brooks."

"But he sounded almost secretive. So unlike him."

Emily paced a circle in the aisle. Burke dealt in black and white, and rarely was secretive. However, Jenna was clearly cranked from studying. And with Burke away, it seemed more important than ever to give her sister a carefree weekend.

"Just hang in there," Emily said. "Worry about your exams first. The other stuff will fall into place."

"Sounds like you're throwing my words back at me, little sis." But Jenna chuckled, sounding more like her old self.

"And I'm glad you found something you like. You were right about sticking with acting. How much longer does this job last? Another month?"

Emily winced. "I guess movie employment is always a scramble."

"What's that mean?" Jenna's voice sharpened. "By the way, you sound funny. Do you have a cold?"

"A little." Emily rubbed her forehead, then tugged the zipper of Dan's jacket higher. At least she wasn't sneezing. And she was no longer famished, even though she couldn't remember her last meal.

"You need to get rid of that cold," Jenna said. "They probably don't want sick people around a movie set."

"No, they definitely don't." Emily gave a wry smile, remembering the director's irritation when she sneezed. Dan though, had been sweet.

Not too sweet though. Her smile faded. After all, he'd just fired her.

CHAPTER TWENTY

"No problem," Monty said. "Construction is finished here so you're welcome to the wood from the scrap pile." He tossed three moldy bales from the back of a pickup then walked to the cab. "What are you building?"

"Just making a temporary paddock so Barney can get outside." Emily scanned the stack of wood. "I only need a few rails."

"Take as many as you want. All this wood is trash." He pulled open his truck door. "I'm going into Louisville, but I can help you later."

Emily politely declined, waiting until he drove away. Monty was already extremely busy. All the wranglers were. Besides, Jenna was correct. Barney shouldn't be left in the barn any longer than necessary. And Emily certainly wasn't going to twiddle her thumbs waiting for help.

There was an empty lane between two of the end paddocks. With the addition of a few poles, Barney could have the perfect turnout. And now that she'd found some properly sized rails, the air quality problem would be solved.

She balanced a rail on each shoulder and began the trek back to the barn. The poles weren't heavy but they were certainly awkward. Twice she dropped them on her toes. Eventually she gave up trying to move them in pairs and dragged them back, one at a time. It slowed her progress but forty-five minutes later, she had six rails piled in the narrow aisle between the paddocks.

She returned to the barn and gathered a fistful of baler twine. "You boys can both go out in a minute," she called to the horses. She and Jenna had often used baler twine for repairs. The stuff was free, plentiful and tough.

Twenty minutes later, she had a safe turnout, not much bigger than Barney's stall. She wiped her clammy brow, studying the pen in satisfaction. Now Barney could be outside in the fresh air but restricted enough that he wouldn't run around and foolishly hurt his tendon.

She quickly rewrapped his legs, eager to take him outside and watch his reaction. He followed her out the door, stepping carefully over the poles and into the turnout, then waited like a gentleman while she tied up the rails.

"There you are." She unsnapped his lead line.

He immediately dropped to his knees and rolled luxuriously. She watched with a twinge of fear, praying he wouldn't scramble up and buck. Or worse, try to jump out.

But he rose, shook himself like a dog, and began searching for patches of green grass, totally accepting of his new pen.

She hurried back into the barn, haltered Ted and led him into the adjoining paddock. Ted nickered to Barney, relieved to see his buddy, and immediately began grazing on the other side of the fence. They both looked happy to be outside, and it was certainly healthier.

She'd feed them noon hay in an hour, and at some point the stalls would have to be mucked out. Now though, she was exhausted. Her arms ached, and her eyes and nose itched. At least the day had warmed. The sun beat down, heating her shoulders and for the first time since Dan left, she wasn't cold.

She leaned against the fence post, reluctant to leave Barney unsupervised. However, he was a polite and obliging fellow and seemed to understand he was supposed to remain in his odd enclosure. Maybe later, when she had more energy, they could practice the grab trick.

She sank down on the grass and rested her back against the wooden post. A bee buzzed around her hand. She watched it cautiously but it was only exploring, and the familiar drone made her feel at home. It was extremely peaceful. The groom who had been assigned this apartment certainly had a sweet deal.

Last week she wouldn't have considered groom's work 'sweet,' but helping with the horses was far more inspiring than standing around for hours, only to be berated for sneezing. Here, she was her own boss. She definitely appreciated Dan's management style. It was way more motivating than the usual threats and lectures.

She tilted further against the fence, enjoying the sound of the munching horses. Probably she should text Jenna. Let her know Barney was outside and thank her for the advice. She also needed to figure out how to make some money when she returned to her apartment.

But for now, the sun was shining, the horses' contentment was contagious and there really wasn't any other place she'd rather be.

"This is the spot," Dan said, reaching into the back seat for the food and blankets. "Just drop me off by the barn door."

"Want me come back?" the driver asked.

"No. I'll walk. Just leaving some stuff for one of my crew."

"I've been driving people around for three weeks now," the driver said, glancing around curiously, "but this is the first time I've been here. Pretty spot. Is it part of the Hamilton estate?"

"Yes. The barn was originally built for Reckless but he didn't like it, so they turned it into a stud barn." Dan balanced the food on top of the mound of blankets and pushed open the van door.

"Spoiled horse." The driver peered up at the fancy balcony and gave a low whistle.

Spoiled something, Dan thought, but probably not the horse. If rumors were true, Thomas Hamilton had built this place so he could keep his groom conveniently close. Right beneath his wife's nose.

Anthony was pushing that angle in the movie too, leaning toward young and pretty grooms. Shania's necklines were constantly being lowered. And every day, Thomas Hamilton surveyed the action, beaming like he was king of the stud pen again. Clearly he loved having women around, especially if they showed a little flesh.

Lizzie didn't trust the man, preferring not to walk alone in the dark. Hamilton didn't scare Emily though. She'd been totally content sleeping in a stall…and then with him. Dan scraped a hand over his jaw. Damn, it had been a frustrating night, trying to ignore those tempting curves, the sweet way she'd curled against his chest. Luckily she'd been exhausted.

But no way was he going near a hungry actress. He preferred a simple woman, one not seduced by movie moguls or the lure of fame. A woman who wouldn't blow her kids a kiss and bolt for greener pastures. A woman he could trust.

And one who would trust him.

He shook his head, shoving aside old hurts. Most of the demanding horse scenes had been completed, but he still needed to focus. It only took a moment of inattention for someone to be hurt. Lizzie's admission that Emily had nearly been kicked still had his gut churning.

He shouldn't have put her in charge of the stud barn but had been swayed by her pluck and determination. And admittedly, he'd been attracted from the first moment they met. He couldn't stop looking at her. But that was a piss poor reason to hire someone.

Besides, Emily's end goal was to be an actress, not look after animals. And wranglers needed to have the horses' care as top priority. He strode down the aisle and inspected the stalls, shaking his head at their messy appearance. Almost eleven and she hadn't even mucked out yet. At least, she'd fed breakfast. Uneaten hay still littered the empty stalls.

Empty. He groaned, his irritation changing to concern. He'd told her not to lead the chestnut without him, and the Reckless lookalike was on strict stall rest. Irreparable damage could be done if the bay further strained that injured tendon.

He yanked open the apartment door and climbed the stairs two at a time, his steps deliberately loud. It was time for her to get up anyway.

But she wasn't napping on the sofa or holed up in the bathroom. He dropped the food and blankets on the table and went back downstairs, his steps not quite as aggressive.

Generally he liked his stalls cleaned immediately; a tidy barn looked much more professional. On the other hand, she wouldn't be working here much longer. He could hardly expect her to whip through her chores when she'd just been let go. And obviously she was sick.

This morning her throat had been raspy, her forehead feverish and her mouth...her mouth had been entirely kissable.

He sighed and stepped out of the barn, hating to admit he'd kept her around for selfish reasons. Movie sets weren't the place to pick up women, at least not the type of woman he wanted.

Luckily, Lizzie had noticed Emily was at risk. He'd been too busy noticing other things.

He rounded the corner of the barn and scanned the paddocks. If the bay had some grass to nibble he might not run and exacerbate his injury. Regardless, Dan resolved not to scold her for turning the horses out. He was late, and this was his fault for not checking her references. In fact, he'd completely disregarded his usual protocol. No wonder Lizzie had been huffy.

His shoulders jerked and he quit worrying about the horses. Could only stare in horror at the slender body crumpled on the ground. Emily was down. She must have been kicked. Lizzie's warning had come too late.

He charged across the grass. Dropped to his knees and scanned her head for injury. "Emily," he said.

Her eyes flickered open and she gave him such a beautiful smile, his breath stalled. "What happened?" he asked, his voice rough.

She blinked and tried to struggle to a sitting position.

"Don't move." He wrapped his arm around her shoulders, forcing her to sit still. "Did he kick?"

She rubbed at her eyes, still silent.

"Where did he get you?" He pushed her hair back, inspecting the skin around her temples. No mark, thank God. When his cousin had been dropped by a horse, the imprint of the hoof had been visible.

She tilted her head, her eyes confused. "Barney didn't kick me," she said. "Or Ted."

"Oh, sweetheart, that's good." He tucked her against his pounding heart, his hand still splayed over the back of her head. "I thought you were hurt. Lying in the grass like that."

She didn't say anything else but she didn't pull away either, just lay in his arms as she had this morning. Her hair was silky, her skin soft and warm and he tugged her even tighter, his relief overpowering his usual control. She wasn't shivering, not like last night, and even though they'd slept side by side, somehow this felt more intimate. He could almost pretend they weren't on a movie set, but back on the verandah of his ranch, surrounded by grazing horses and the sweeping Montana sky.

His jacket was rolled up a few feet away, the indent of a head still visible and he smiled into her hair. "What exactly were you doing out here?" he asked, trying to sound firm but unable to stop chuckling. Part of it was relief and the other part was simply that her free spirit left him light.

She lifted her head, her mouth curving into that irrepressible smile. "Okay, busted. I was napping on the job. But it's impossible to be fired twice. And I did move some poles."

She went on talking about why she couldn't wait for leading help because of Barney's breathing, but his mind quit processing. He'd been strung too tight and that rosebud-shaped mouth was too appealing. And so close their breaths blended.

She silenced, as if sensing the direction of his thoughts.

He caressed her bottom lip with the pad of his thumb, his eyes holding hers. Right now, it didn't matter that she was an actress and leaving tomorrow. He wanted her with a surprising ferocity. He slid his hand around the back of her neck and slanted his mouth over hers.

Her lips were sweet and inviting, her breasts warm and full against his chest. He coaxed her mouth open. Her breath shuddered out, and then she kissed him back, their tongues meeting in a slow erotic dance that left him hungry for more.

A truck roared beyond the trees and he reluctantly lifted his head. His pulse beat wildly and he drew in a ragged breath, wishing they really were back on his ranch. Alone.

"Obviously I don't want you to leave," he whispered, pressing his mouth against her neck, savoring the scent of her skin.

"Earlier this morning you did." He couldn't see her face but the hurt in her words was unmistakable.

"The last thing I want is for you to be hurt," he said. "This job isn't what you signed up for. You're an actress, not a wrangler." He couldn't keep the accusation out of his voice.

She pulled back, studying him with confused eyes. Not surprising. His ambivalence about this woman left him confused too.

"Let's go inside." His voice gentled. "I brought some food. Looks to me like you haven't been eating much."

"The dining room keeps closing before I get there," she admitted.

A painful band tightened around his chest. She didn't have a car or groceries, and the dining tent had limited hours. Food was always available at the hotel where most of the cast and crew stayed, and the wranglers had access to a trailer kitchen. But she was a background performer. An add-on. She certainly hadn't been eating steak and lobster.

"I assumed you had breakfast," he said, fighting his guilt, "but I brought soup and crackers. Stuff like that." It didn't sound like much now. He'd simply been thinking it made sense to have some food in the apartment. "Did you eat this morning?"

She scooped up his jacket from the grass, not meeting his eyes. "I often don't eat breakfast."

"But you like coffee. Did you even have coffee?"

"I've been busy."

"Not busy cleaning stalls," he said, slightly defensive. It wasn't *his* fault she hadn't eaten. It didn't take long to toss two horses some hay and grain. And the stalls were still dirty.

"I'm going to clean the stalls now." Her mouth tightened in a rebellious line. "I just wanted to have a little nap first."

He sighed and pulled her to her feet, careful to avoid touching the abrasions on her palms. "Eat something first. Then do the stalls. Don't take everything as a criticism."

But he had mentioned the stalls as a criticism. He didn't know what it was about this woman that left him unbalanced or why he couldn't keep his distance. But even as he mentally listed all the things he should be doing, he draped his hand

over her hip and guided her toward the apartment, knowing
full well he didn't intend to leave right away.

CHAPTER TWENTY-ONE

"This is good ham soup," Emily said, although her heart was drumming so fast she could barely taste it.

"It's chicken." Dan smiled and idly traced his lean finger over the inside of her wrist. Although maybe it wasn't idle. He had the look of a man who intended to take her to bed. For the last twenty minutes, ever since he'd splayed his big hand around her waist and walked her into the apartment, the air had been crackling. A touch here, the brush of his hand there, he certainly knew how to prime a woman. She was a bundle of anticipation, every one of her senses on high alert awaiting his next move. It was torture not to wiggle in the chair.

"Feeling better after the soup?" His hand shifted to her forehead and then curved lower, skimming the sensitive skin over her collarbone.

She shivered with pleasure, almost dropping the spoon. She'd never admit she was sick and risk him leaving. But it was rather disconcerting that he could skim a finger over certain spots and she was ready to hop into bed. He seemed very single minded once he made a decision. Of course, she was too.

She tried to match his boldness by hiding behind a flippancy she didn't feel. "I've been offered liquor and chocolate before, but this is the first time a man's tried to seduce me with soup."

His smile was quick and amused, as though he appreciated her bluntness. "And how's it working?" he asked.

"Very well."

He didn't say anything else, just leaned over and tenderly kissed her cheek. "Good," he murmured, his warm breath making her nerve endings tingle. "Eat up. I'll make the bed."

He scooped up the bedding he'd delivered and strode toward the bedroom.

She swallowed and set down the spoon. It was clear they both wanted to make love, but she'd never been with a man so certain. No alcohol, no games, no pretense. It was different, and wonderfully liberating.

Still, it wouldn't be wise to jump up and race him to the bed. Men liked a little challenge. She should at least nibble another cracker.

But she ignored the food, unable to hide her feelings. "Wait," she said. "I've been sleeping on the sofa. It's much more comfortable. The bedroom feels…occupied."

She expected him to argue, or at least roll his eyes, but he gave an understanding nod and veered back toward the sofa. It wasn't that she believed in ghosts, not too much anyway, but everyone whispered about Reckless's first groom.

Keeping a lover on the property had been the height of crassness. And Thomas Hamilton was definitely crass. The groom probably had good reason to vanish. Hamilton certainly wasn't Dan Barrett.

She felt an anticipatory squeeze as he flicked a sheet, then tucked it smoothly behind the cushions. He was competent, making up a bed as expertly as he'd kissed her. Clearly, once he decided to have a woman, he moved quickly.

Like all men.

She gave her head a little shake, still rather shocked this was going to happen. He was surrounded by movie stars, real ones. He rubbed shoulders with the most beautiful women in the world while she didn't even have her regular makeup. Or her nice clothes. Hadn't had a bath in… Oh my God.

She shot to her feet, sick with dismay. She hadn't shaved her legs in days. Her disposable underwear looked like it had been designed for the fifties. She'd stacked hay and shoveled manure and lacked even basic hot water. This was horrible.

He glanced up, raising an eyebrow as she skittered behind the table, her arms tucked over her chest. "Second thoughts?" he asked softly.

"Yes. No! I just remembered there's something I have to do."

"Something I can help you with?"

"No." She shook her head. "It's personal."

He stilled, watching her with his usual intensity. If he crossed the room and kissed her, she'd never be able to hold out.

"Do you feel okay?" His brow furrowed in concern.

She choked back a hysterical laugh. Clearly women didn't refuse Dan Barrett. And it wasn't even a refusal, only a postponement. "I have to see someone," she said, her voice rising in panic. "I just need a couple hours. And I'll finish making the bed."

The floor creaked as he walked toward her.

"I'm thinking you should stay at my trailer tonight." He touched her lightly on the shoulder. "This place feels cold."

"It is warmer in the stalls below," she said, relaxing with the knowledge he didn't intend to rush her. And he could, so easily. She felt his restraint, the tautness in his body, the sexual undertone in his voice.

But he just stood close, stroking the back of her neck, his fingers unhurried and gentle. She couldn't remember the last time a man had caressed her without trying to grope beneath her shirt.

She settled against his chest, not even worrying about her messy hair and the lack of a blow dryer. Maybe his eyesight was faulty but he didn't seem to care about the usual things. He'd never once criticized her appearance. She breathed a sigh of contentment, her cheek pressed against his soft shirt. She might not smell good but he certainly did, a mixture of leather and spice, power and patience.

"The trailer has my name on the door," he said, his breath warm and intimate against her hair. "It's the one closest to the trees. Key is underneath the bucket by the window. My meeting should be over by nine." His voice turned teasing. "Maybe you should have another nap and rest up."

She glanced up, slightly chagrined. "I don't know why I'm so tired."

"You're coming off a fever. And you haven't been eating. I'll send someone over to do the stalls."

"No, I'll do them," she said. And she wanted to check Barney's breathing and practice some tricks. She'd also like to watch Dan work with his horses and hoped to pick up some training tips. There'd still be plenty of time to visit Maggie in the wardrobe tent before it closed. Surely she could scrounge up some sexier undergarments.

But Dan picked up her hand and lightly traced her blistered palms. "Those two horses aren't your responsibility any longer. Neither is lugging hay. I'll help you with them at suppertime. Your skin must be delicate."

She stiffened at his implied criticism. Maybe she wasn't as tough as his wranglers, but there had been a lot of bales to carry and the wire-like twine stung. However, she gave a breezy smile and waved her fingers. "Even worse, I wrecked my nails. There goes that Dove commercial."

He stepped back, his eyes gentle, as if he saw past her flippancy. "Take it easy the rest of the time you're here. There's no need to break any more nails." He paused. "And there's no need to do anything you don't want to do. You understand that, right?" His meaning was unmistakable.

She rose on her toes and kissed his cheek. "See you tonight," she said.

Emily bounced along the drive with half the food Dan had brought cradled in her hands. There was enough to share and Billy could use the nutrition. The caretaker would be disappointed there weren't any doughnuts, but she could drop some off later, after she visited the wardrobe tent. Maybe he'd enjoy the soup if he wasn't distracted by dessert.

The chicken soup wasn't the best she ever had, but she certainly appreciated Dan's thoughtfulness. *Dan.* She gave a little skip, her entire body vibrating with joy. He was like no man she'd ever known. Smart, hot and sexy. Tough enough to keep her in line but kind at the important times. He could have his pick of women. Yet he'd chosen her.

There was still a month of filming so they'd be able to enjoy each other's company. Who knew where this new development might lead. He didn't want her working at the stud barn but there was always plenty to do. She might even learn some of his training methods and help turn Barney into a star. The horse might never jump into a pool, but he was plenty obliging.

Her stride quickened as she rounded the corner. The spring sun was pleasantly warm, and robins chirped with renewed optimism. It didn't matter now that freckles dotted her nose and she lacked even a speck of makeup. She must not look too hideous if someone as wonderful as Dan liked her.

Everyone said he wasn't the tomcat type so giving his trailer key was significant. Of course he hadn't actually given her a key, but at least he'd told her where it was hidden. Almost the same thing.

Movement flashed on the side of the drive. Billy. And he was walking past the gate. Strange he hadn't opened it. Maybe he was feeling a little weak.

"Hi, Billy," she called. "Do you need help with the gate?"

He turned, his forehead wrinkling. "I'm not sure," he mumbled.

"I can help you. That gate's awkward." She placed the container of soup and crackers on the ground and hurried to his side.

"But should I open it now?" Billy asked, his voice so plaintive it tugged at her heart. "I can't remember what Mr. Hamilton wants."

"He wants it open in the day and closed when it's dark," Emily said. "We can open it now if you like."

"Yes, it's important that I do my job right. Whatever he says." Billy's watery eyes gleamed. "But sometimes I get a little mixed up. I'm glad you came, Tracey."

"My name's Emily."

He jerked back, eyeing her oddly. "I know that," he said. "Tracey's gone."

Emily shrugged, deciding it was best to humor him. And if he wanted to call her Tracey, that was quite all right. She swung the gate back then gestured at the container. "I brought some chicken soup."

"Did you bring any doughnuts? That's all I want."

She sighed and picked up the soup. There was no way he was eating properly. Not unless someone dropped by and organized his meals. But she'd seen no sign of any domestic help.

She was in a hurry to reach the wardrobe tent, but it was impossible to walk away from someone in such need. He probably wouldn't eat the soup without encouragement.

"Let's go inside and you can eat," she said brightly. "Later this afternoon, I'll bring you a doughnut."

"I want a doughnut now," he grumbled. But he tugged up the waistband of his baggy pants, turned and shuffled toward the cottage.

A gray cat darted from the trees and across the walkway.

"Hey, buddy," she called, recognizing the feline friend who'd kept her company that first cold night. But Billy pushed past her, swinging his cane with surprising agility. The cat dodged to the left, avoiding his lethal blow, and Billy's cane smashed harmlessly into the dirt.

"Billy!" Emily stared in dismay as the cat streaked into the trees. "That's cruel. Don't you like cats?"

"Doesn't matter what I like." Billy scowled and pushed open the cottage door. "There were too many so Mr. Hamilton asked me to get rid of them. Nasty job, but I have to follow orders."

Emily pulled in a deep breath, trying to control her annoyance. Billy was rather nasty himself. Probably there was a good reason why he didn't have any visitors.

She checked over her shoulder for the poor cat, then followed him inside, warily watching his cane. The stench wasn't any better today and she left the door open, breathing through her mouth and praying for a breeze.

There was one main room, serving as a kitchen and living room with two more doors down the hall. But all she could see was a dump. Piles of muddy boots and clothing littered the floor, and dirty dishes crammed the sink and counter. An ancient television sat in the corner, the gray screen thick with dust. Columns of faded magazines teetered in mildewed stacks. It required supreme effort not to plug her nose.

Billy plunked down in the only available chair. "I don't get many visitors. I suppose you'll want tea."

"No, that's okay," she said hastily. "I'll just heat up this soup. You sit and relax."

Shuddering, she rolled up her sleeves. It was going to take a bit of cleaning before she could even find a useable pot and bowl. There was no microwave or any clean dishes in the cupboards. Even if he had food, there was no space to prepare it.

She peeked into his fridge, then quickly slammed it shut, repulsed by the mold-encrusted food. Someone needed to clean this place, and urgently.

"Do you have any family, Billy?" she asked, restacking the dishes so she could fill the sink with hot water.

"The Hamiltons. They're my family."

"Do you have any children?" She peered beneath the sink, relieved to find a selection of cleaning products. Thick dust around the sides confirmed they hadn't been used in years.

His irritable grunt was accompanied by a headshake so she silenced, relieved that at least he'd agreed to eat the soup. She cleaned a pot and some dishes, then struggled with the gas stove until the soup was safely heating. She dried the dishes with paper towel, the only thing that looked clean, then glanced dubiously around the room. It needed a thorough scrubbing, although the lemon smell of dish soap had somewhat improved the air.

She wanted to spend time with Dan, not this grumpy old man who had tried to kill a cat, but it was impossible to leave him in such a mess. Her family hadn't had much money, but she and Jenna always kept their trailer sparkling clean.

Billy's cottage would have to be decluttered before it was washed—it looked like he hadn't thrown anything away in decades. Broken bottles and yellowed newspapers covered every inch of space. One headline proclaimed a showdown between Sunday Silence and Easy Goer. When were those horses running anyway? Late eighties?

She tripped over a cardboard box bulging with cassette tapes and VCR recordings and pushed it further beneath the table, clearing another few inches of floor space. It was amazing that Billy hadn't fallen and cracked open his head.

"Would you like me to come back tomorrow and clean your house a bit?" she asked, half-expecting him to refuse.

But he just waved his spoon in an authoritative gesture, seemingly unaware of the soup splattering his shirt. "Bring doughnuts when you come," he said.

Emily stepped over a maze of wires and into the wardrobe tent, relieved it was still open. She hadn't intended to stay at Billy's for three hours, but she'd already made considerable progress cleaning his kitchen.

He hadn't objected to discarding the old newspapers as long as there wasn't a horse pictured on the front. But he'd whacked her arm with his cane when she tried to move the empty beer bottles. It was probably best to sneak them out when he wasn't watching. Tomorrow, she'd find some way to distract him.

There were several people in the tent, but luckily the ever-helpful Maggie was working. Emily waited behind two men who were returning shirts and sports jackets, then stepped forward.

"Are you turning in any clothes today?" Maggie asked. "I don't remember seeing you this morning. How's it going?"

Emily thought of Dan and couldn't contain her happy smile. "Everything is super," she said. "But I need some personal stuff. Like a razor, soap and nicer undergarments."

Maggie shook her head. "Can't help you. And I already said we only have the hospital issue stuff."

Emily's smile faded. She leaned forward, gripping the counter. "Please. You must have something. I met someone...very special."

"Sorry." Maggie chuckled, but not unkindly. "Besides, do you really think a guy is going to care?"

"But this one is used to the best. Please." Emily's voice rose. "There must be something. I'm desperate."

Steps sounded behind them and Maggie's eyes flickered. Emily's shoulders slumped with resignation. "Okay. But do you at least have a jacket so I can stay warm?"

"The weather's supposed to turn nice tomorrow," Maggie whispered, "so take these shirts too." She pushed over a coral jacket and two T-shirts. Her voice turned loud and officious. "Be sure to turn them in after your scene."

Emily checked over her shoulder. Mrs. Hamilton and a frowning lady with headphones stood less than four feet away.

"Yes, thanks," Emily said, picking up the clothes. She nodded a greeting to Mrs. Hamilton and trudged toward the door. The shirts were pretty, with lovely scooped necks, although they didn't help with the more immediate problem of cleaning up for tonight.

"Excuse me."

Emily swung around. Mrs. Hamilton gestured to a side door. "Follow me. My car's in the back." She smiled over her shoulder. "I couldn't help but overhear."

They stepped outside and into the bright sunshine. Her gleaming silver Lincoln was parked by the side of the tent. Mrs. Hamilton clicked a remote and the trunk silently opened.

"We fly so much," Mrs. Hamilton said, "that I always keep a travel bag ready. It sounds like that's exactly what you need."

She pulled out a soft leather bag from the cavernous trunk and pressed it into Emily's hands. "Take it. It's loaded with feminine necessities."

Emily stared, stunned and so grateful she could barely speak. "Thank you so much. I'll return it—"

"Keep it." Mrs. Hamilton gave an airy wave of her hand. "I have three other bags like this, packed and ready to go. My husband says I plan too much, but a lady always has to look her best. Especially when it takes longer each year to look presentable."

A warm glow filled Emily's chest. This lady was not only beautiful, but gracious and kind. Obviously she was unaware of Billy's living conditions. There must be a tactful way to mention the caretaker. However, Mrs. Hamilton had already slipped into her spotless car and pressed the ignition.

Emily stepped back, clasping the bag to her chest. She'd find another chance to broach the subject. It was clear Mrs. Hamilton was generous and would want to help. In fact, almost everyone involved with this movie was incredibly kind, almost like an extended family. It made her never want to leave.

CHAPTER TWENTY-TWO

Dan followed the tree-lined path to the stud barn. The production meeting had been tedious, and he'd found an excuse to duck out. Anthony's main message had been to sex up the scenes. Shania's necklines were about to plunge.

His mother had also believed a little cleavage went a long way. And when his father hadn't been around, it had been much more than a little. He snorted. Whoever said 'absence makes the heart grow fonder' had been a fool.

He glimpsed Emily moving in the barn aisle and his brush of melancholy vanished. She was plucky and resourceful, full of such radiant energy it was contagious…and she kissed like a devil-angel. For his last five or six movies, he'd been on autopilot, barely noticing the smorgasbord of women.

But she'd awakened him from a deep freeze and now he was horny as hell. For sure, he'd remember the filming of *Reckless*.

He only had an hour between meetings but he wanted to help her bring in the horses. And feel her mouth beneath his again. The night couldn't come fast enough. Fortunately his trailer had a queen-sized bed.

His stride quickened. Taking a break during the day was unusual for him, and he felt like a teenager playing hooky. But Emily had a way of lifting his sprits. However, his anticipation fizzled to disappointment when Lizzie—not Emily—stepped from the barn.

"You're back early," he said, scanning over her head for Emily. "Did you make it to Churchill?"

"Yes," Lizzie said. "And I took lots of pictures of the pointed spires. Monty went with me. He was a great guide."

"Good," Dan said, walking inside. Both horses were happily eating hay in pristine stalls. Emily must have led them in without him.

Lizzie gestured at the manure-laden wheelbarrow. "I mucked out. It seemed a shame to put the horses back into dirty stalls. Wouldn't want the Humane rep to get riled."

"The stalls weren't clean?" Frowning, he checked his watch. Four thirty. "Is Emily upstairs?"

"No, I already looked. Wanted to tell her we're in the process of transferring her pay. I calculated three days at eight hours a day...even though today shouldn't count." Lizzie gave a resigned shrug. "Oh, well. At least the bay is breathing better."

"Yes. That was smart to make a little paddock. I won't have to find a portable pen." He edged back toward the door. If he wasn't going to see Emily, he really should return to the meeting. "And if the horses are quiet," he added, "it's best to leave them out all night."

"The bay wasn't quiet though." Lizzie gave a mournful headshake. "He was rearing and bucking when I arrived. Too bad he was left unsupervised. I'm not sure how his leg held up."

"Damn." Dan turned and walked back to the stall. The Reckless lookalike raised his head, eyes inquisitive. Hay protruded from his mouth. There were no signs of sweat marks, and his respiration rate seemed normal.

"I cooled him out and groomed him," Lizzie said quickly. "Wet his hay and set out a soaking tub. *She* wouldn't think of doing that."

"Sorry you have all this extra work." Dan fought an uncomfortable tightening in his chest. "This was supposed to be your day off."

"It's okay. Usually I don't have to cover for such inexperienced help." Her words trailed off to a resigned shrug.

"It's my fault," he said. "I wanted to help Emily lead them in. I should have returned earlier. How were they to handle?" he asked hopefully.

"They definitely need an experienced groom," Lizzie said. "They're both rather pushy, greedy for grain."

Dan's mouth tightened, appalled he'd thought the two horses were so well behaved. It was fortunate Emily hadn't tried to lead them when they were in a hurry for supper. "I shouldn't have put a new person in that situation," he said.

"It's okay." Lizzie flipped her hair over her shoulder and stepped closer, her eyes earnest. "I can come back in the morning. Check the bay's breathing. Wrap his legs and turn them out. I checked out another hay supplier too. Even brought a bale back so you can give final approval."

He nodded, grateful but rather guilty about Lizzie's dedication. Especially today, when he was thinking about anything but horses. "You'll be busy tomorrow," he said. "It's the rail stunt and we'll need eight of the track horses, groomed and ready."

"No worries." Lizzie touched his arm. "I love animals. This is what I want to do with my life."

He gave her an appreciative smile. She never lobbied for a movie scene or chased after actors. Didn't need to be center stage. His father should have married someone like her; someone who'd be happy living on a ranch.

Lizzie's hand still rested on his arm and he turned away, scooping down to straighten an overturned bucket.

"Sorry about that," she said. "The aisle was a mess. I'm still cleaning. But I admire Emily for trying to do work she considers beneath her. This is her chance to be in the movies so it's understandable, I guess." She shrugged. "Some people will do *anything* to get what they want."

"Yes." He blew out a regretful sigh. "I suppose they will."

Emily jogged along the shaded path, leaped over a gnarled root and burst from the trees feeling as light as a gazelle. Someone stood in the door of the barn but the sun was slanting and all she could see was a dark silhouette. Probably Dan. He wanted to help bring in the horses tonight. Totally unnecessary, but very sweet. Her feet turned even lighter and her breath quickened with anticipation.

But the silhouette moved and Lizzie stepped from the shadows, hands on her hips. "It's past five. Where have you been?"

Emily's smile faded. Lizzie was such a buzz kill.

"I just dropped off some doughnuts for a friend," Emily said. She didn't want to mention Billy's name. Lizzie was the type who would gleefully slash her pay for feeding non-movie personnel.

"Well, you're late." Lizzie's voice sharpened. "I cleaned the stalls and grained them. Horses like a schedule."

"But five-thirty grain is their schedule," Emily said. "You even wrote down the feeding times."

"Yes, but their stalls were filthy. Or maybe you didn't intend to clean them?"

"Of course I did. But I thought the horses could stay out tonight. The weather's supposed to be nice."

"And as for that, there was an unfortunate incident here," Lizzie said. "They shouldn't have been left alone so long. And you shouldn't have built that paddock."

"Why? What happened?" Concerned, Emily brushed past Lizzie to Barney's stall. He flicked his ears in recognition, his jaw chewing rhythmically. He looked fine, and his flanks weren't flailing when he drew in air. "What happened?" she repeated, turning back to Lizzie.

"You didn't check the ground." Lizzie's voice turned accusing. "I found a piece of broken glass. And he was bouncing around a little."

Emily groaned and yanked open Barney's door. "I'm sorry. Did he cut his heel?" She dropped her bag and examined each foot. She couldn't see any injury but she wasn't an expert.

"I'm sorry, fellow," she murmured, replacing his hind leg and turning to Lizzie. "Should I soak his feet? Maybe he should have a tetanus shot? I'm so sorry," she repeated.

Lizzie shrugged. "It's okay. I took care of it. And I didn't tell Dan. As far as he knows, I'm the one responsible for that horse being in the paddock. He's a bit of a stickler about safety."

"Yes, I know." Emily gave a grateful smile. "He doesn't want me to lead them when I'm alone, even though they're both such gentlemen. Today I led them both at the same time and they were better behaved than my pony."

"Well, I didn't dock your pay. And I transferred the full amount to the email on file. So you're all paid up."

"Wow, that's great. Thank you." Emily's eyes drifted to the apartment door. She wanted to grab her phone and check the amount. Then transfer it to the Steeplechase Inn and reserve a room. But more importantly, she wanted to find Dan's trailer and clean up before he arrived.

"What's in the bag?" Lizzie asked.

Emily clasped Mrs. Hamilton's gift to her chest. "Just some stuff," she said. "A couple shirts and a jacket."

"Well, you won't need many clothes. Your job here is over and the bus to Louisville leaves tomorrow." Lizzie moved toward the door. "Gotta go. There's a meeting tonight and Dan likes me around."

Emily smiled but kept her mouth shut. Lizzie was absolutely correct; Emily probably wouldn't need many clothes tonight. However, there was no reason to flaunt her budding relationship with Dan. After all, despite the wrangler's abrasiveness, Lizzie had actually done her some real favors today.

CHAPTER TWENTY-THREE

Emily gripped her precious bag of toiletries and scanned the line of portable trailers for Dan's name. Most of the units were small but sparkling new. The biggest model actually resembled a compact apartment row and had five separate doors. She was tempted to send a picture to Jenna but her battery was dangerously low.

She'd already spent five long minutes on the phone with a clerk at the Steeplechase Inn. Deluxe race tickets, including unlimited beer as well as a corner suite, totaled four hundred dollars. Thanks to Lizzie's quick transfer, she was only eighty bucks short. However, the clerk knew Jenna and had agreed the remaining money could be paid next week. Emily gave an excited skip. The heck with fixing her car. Tomorrow she'd surprise her sister with an après-exam gift.

The ground was muddy and churned, rutted from heavy equipment, so she slowed to a more disciplined walk. She didn't want to drop Mrs. Hamilton's beautiful leather bag. She'd already peeked at the products and couldn't wait to indulge in a hot shower. There were still a few hours before Dan would finish his meeting. For now, she simply had to locate his trailer.

She skirted a humming generator and spotted a white trailer set apart from the others and close to a ridge of trees. Four black buckets were stacked neatly below the front window. She hurried toward the door and checked the printed sign. 'Dan Barrett.'

She lifted the rubber buckets. A lone key glinted in the dirt. She scooped it up, inserted the key and stepped inside.

Files were stacked on the kitchen table alongside a single coffee mug. The sink was empty but a beer can sat on the counter. She pulled off her boots and walked cautiously down the short hall, searching for the bathroom.

She peeked behind the first door on the right and grinned in delight. Not just a shower, but a tub. It seemed like weeks since she'd had anything but a hasty rinse in the barn. Now she'd be able to wash, wax and buff. If there were time, she'd even repair her nails. Mrs. Hamilton's kit included some very sophisticated products. Dan would be surprised. She might not be a movie star, but she knew a bit about glamour.

Two hours later, she applied the last touch of mascara and stared critically at her reflection. Damn, she looked good. Pursing her lips, she dabbed a bit more red gloss on her mouth. There, perfect. Even her hair had cooperated, falling in silky waves over her shoulders. Naturally when you have the best products money could buy, it was easier to look beautiful. *Thank you, Mrs. Hamilton.*

She zipped the leather bag, wiped the sink and wandered back to the kitchen. The clock said eight thirty. According to Dan, his meeting would be over by nine.

She sat at the small table and drummed her nails, then realized her pink polish was still a little wet. She wandered to the fridge and opened the door. There was plenty to drink— beer, water, juice—but she didn't want to mess her makeup.

The only thing she wasn't happy about were her clothes, but at least they were clean. She smoothed her T-shirt, wiped an imaginary speck off her jeans and rechecked the time. Eight thirty-three.

Maybe she should take off her clothes and wait in bed. Then he wouldn't see her granny underwear.

The door abruptly opened and Dan filled the doorway.

"Hi," she said, drinking in the sight. "I thought your meeting would go a little longer."

"I was in a hurry tonight." He gave a slow and meaningful smile. But his gaze swept her face, his smile fading. "You look different," he said.

"I had a bath. Put on some makeup." His eyes remained locked on her face and she touched her mouth, wondering if her lipstick had smudged. Or maybe he didn't like the bright red?

He turned and yanked open the fridge. "Want a drink? Something to eat?"

"No, thanks. That chicken soup was great."

He jerked around. "That's all you had today?"

She'd been too excited to eat, but she didn't want to admit it. Besides, any shred of appetite had vanished after cleaning Billy's kitchen. "I stopped in the dining tent around four." She omitted saying it had been to pick up doughnuts for Billy. "I often only eat once a day," she added.

His mouth tightened and he turned back to the fridge. "Well, I'm going to have a beer," he said.

She nodded but he wasn't looking at her, and she fought a stab of uncertainty. He'd wanted her this morning but now he seemed cool, almost indifferent. It was impossible to change that much in eight hours. Besides, it wasn't her nature to fake coyness.

She rose and crossed the small kitchen. Looped her arms around his tapered waist and pressed her cheek against his back. He stiffened. For a moment such tension radiated from him, she feared she'd misjudged.

Seconds later though, he turned and wrapped her in his arms. His head swooped, and his mouth covered hers in a raw hunger, kissing her as if he couldn't get enough. His mouth was hard and firm and insistent, and when his knowing hand caressed her breast, pleasure scooted through her body.

"Do you really want that beer?" she murmured, one leg entwined around his calf.

"Not one bit," he said.

He scooped her up and carried her down the hall, angling her so perfectly neither her feet nor head brushed the narrow walls. She felt a little pang, knowing how he'd perfected that particular trailer skill, but admittedly she had some moves of her own.

He laid her on the bed, his expert hands moving over her body, stripping her so urgently there was no time to worry about her granny underwear. No time to admire her waxing and buffing, her carefully shaped toenails with the intricate polish. His hands were slightly callused and the glide of his roughened skin against hers made her whimper with need.

His clever fingers caressed and probed and teased, exploring her most sensitive part, handling her like he knew his way. And when his warm mouth replaced his hand, she called out his name and her mind blanked.

CHAPTER TWENTY-FOUR

"I really have to go, sweetheart," Dan said for the third time that morning. But he made no move to leave. Instead he propped himself on an elbow, caressing her cheek with a finger, as though memorizing her face.

Normally she'd have dashed to the mirror for a pre-dawn makeup repair, but clearly he cared little for superficial trappings. Even her hideous underwear hadn't scared him off. Tonight, she wouldn't worry so much. Maybe just some blush and a touch of lipstick.

Her sister had always promised when the right person came along, she wouldn't obsess over appearances. She'd finally met that man.

And what a man. She couldn't remember ever babbling so much. Or being with anyone who listened so intently. She'd even confided that her father had died in prison, something no one outside of Three Brooks knew. They definitely shared a connection, using every minute of the night as if it were a precious gift. They might have slept an hour although that was debatable.

She ran a hand over his washboard abs, savoring her contentment. There were no secrets between them now. He knew she wasn't a big horse expert, knew what she looked like without makeup. Yet he couldn't keep his mouth off her.

The alarm had sounded almost an hour ago but he'd remained, making love to her with an odd desperation. Tonight it would be his turn to talk, her turn to listen. She hadn't meant to regurgitate her life story, but clearly he knew how to push her button.

Several buttons.

He skimmed his mouth over her lips and sat up. The mattress sagged as he pushed aside the sheets and swung his muscled legs over the bed. "I hate to rush off, but I'm going to leave a number. The director of that Louisville movie is a good friend. He'll make sure you get an audition."

The air in the bedroom turned stifling. Suddenly it hurt to breathe. "When does that movie start?" she managed, surprised she could even formulate a coherent sentence.

"Soon. They're auditioning now." He turned and cupped her face, his voice sweet and sincere. "I hope you find the breakthrough you're looking for. You'll make a fine actress. Don't give up."

She blinked, her throat so clogged she couldn't speak. She'd assumed she'd stay until this movie was finished. Thought he'd want her around a little longer, just to see how things went. They got along so well, both in bed and out. But he was finished with her. After one night?

Something itched at the back of her eyes and she averted her head, relieved he hadn't turned on the overhead light. She always fell too fast, making a man the center of her existence. And when they walked away, her life crumbled.

She'd thought Dan was different. Everyone said he didn't pick up women lightly. And the way he touched her, how he made her feel. Even now something glowed in his eyes. She was no fool with men—it was obvious he cared.

Clearly she'd misunderstood about this Louisville movie.

"I'm going to get up too," she said, watching his face. "And feed the horses."

"Not necessary." He bent down and scooped up his clothes. "We already have someone taking over. Lizzie will have your money ready before the bus leaves."

She squeezed her eyes shut, trying to blink away her tears. "Yes. She already paid me. But I could use another couple days' barn work." It was awful to beg. However, she raised her head, gulping back her tattered pride. "Please, Dan."

"Those horses need an experienced handler." He was already moving toward the door. "I don't want you to get hurt. Besides, you need to go after what you really want." He glanced over his shoulder. "How much money do you need? I'll have Lizzie top it up."

Her hands clenched the sheet so tightly, she could feel the bite of her nails through the fabric. *He wants to pay me?* This had to be a new low.

"No need." She hid her despair with a flippant laugh. "I don't generally charge for sex. And never with well-connected movie people."

He whipped around. The air in the room crackled. "Lucky for me then," he finally said.

He stepped into the hall. The door clicked shut.

She slumped back and yanked the sheet over her hot face. He was really sending her away, after one night. Groaning, she pressed the cotton against her eyes. Men tended to muck up her life, but this one especially hurt. She expected shoddy treatment from jerks. Could prepare for it even.

But Dan wasn't a jerk. Clearly, she had some fatal flaw, something that prevented people from caring.

Water splashed in the bathroom. She remained in bed, preferring not to face him again. It was definitely a speedy shower, four minutes max. A towel rustled beyond the thin bedroom wall and she guessed he was drying that hard body. The one that had done such magical things last night.

She straightened her thoughts and flung aside the sheet. Screw him. Which of course, she had. Several times.

A cupboard opened and closed. Footsteps thumped. She stiffened, hoping he wouldn't return to the bedroom. Praying that he would. However, the bedroom door didn't open.

Moments later the front door slammed and the compact trailer quivered. She scrambled from the bed and peeked out the window but saw only a dark tree line. To her right, the sun glinted just below the horizon.

She switched on the light and gathered her clothes, trying not to remember how feverishly he'd whipped them off. He'd acted so enamored. Damn, she was dumb. She hated when other people called her that, but clearly the label fit. She really hadn't seen this coming.

Maybe though, just maybe, he'd left a note. It was apparent he was exceedingly busy now, but maybe he'd want to see her when the movie was finished. Of course, that made total sense.

She rushed down the narrow hall and scanned the kitchen. Empty, except for a piece of paper on the table with a name and number scrawled in black.

The Louisville area code. Super. The movie might even be on a local bus route. She dropped the paper listlessly on the table and wandered into the bathroom. At least her agent would feel vindicated. Tamara had said background work would help with movie networking. Emily, however, couldn't summon up any enthusiasm.

She turned on the shower, knowing she had to harden her heart and put Dan in the business portion of her brain. This happened all the time. She'd heard enough gossip about the 'casting couch.' Besides, she now had a director's personal phone number. That had to be a plus. It certainly was thoughtful of Dan. Unfortunately it wouldn't be in time to pay for the rest of the steeplechase weekend.

And why the heck couldn't he angle her a job in *this* movie? Why one back in the stuffy city? She shook her head and huffed.

The ache in her chest loosened a notch so she blew out another huff. It was always easier to fan indignation than wallow with a broken heart. Besides, she'd been dumped by nicer men.

No, I haven't.

Sighing, she stepped into the shower and let warm water spray her face. At least she had this lovely private bathroom to enjoy. No worries today about frigid water or an overflowing drain. She didn't even have horses to feed now that she'd been fired. Just an entire day to wander around, watch the lucky actors who were still working—and wait for the bus.

She rubbed some of Mrs. Hamilton's aloe shampoo into her hair, resolving not to agonize about Dan. That never helped. Besides, there were lots of hours left in the day. And one thing she had learned, opportunities tended to pop up when a girl was alert.

CHAPTER TWENTY-FIVE

The mouth-watering smell of bacon wafted from the dining tent. Emily gave an appreciative sniff but kept walking. She'd enjoyed a lengthy shower in Dan's trailer, and the sun already poked over the eastern ridge. Her last day, and she didn't want to miss the stunt horse galloping through the rail. She wondered if it would be Bruno or a horse she hadn't met yet. It was fascinating seeing the animals perform, even more interesting than watching the people.

And Dan would be there.

A lump climbed her throat but she stoically shoved it back. He wanted her on the outgoing bus this evening—fine, but obviously they'd bump into each other sometime today. No doubt, he'd be cool and distant, the way men were when they no longer wanted a woman. And she could do cool. But her feet dragged and no matter how hard she tried, she couldn't find her usual bounce. It was much easier to pretend optimism to others, than to herself.

She rounded the string of trailers where a line of sleepy-looking extras stood in front of a registration table. It seemed a lifetime since she'd waited in that same line, naively believing she was on her way to box office fame.

"Emily!"

She wheeled toward the familiar voice, then charged forward to give Judith a warm hug. It was amazing how a friendly face could boost spirits. "I'm so glad to see you," Emily said, stepping back and smiling. "What scene are you in?"

"Reporter in a media scrum," Judith said. "I stand by the rail waving a notepad when Reckless bolts. You weren't on the bus. Are you background too?"

"I wish. But I'm finished here. I go home tonight."

"You stayed here for the last three nights? What were you doing? Where'd you sleep?"

Emily concentrated on smoothing a non-existent wrinkle in her T-shirt. "I did that groom scene and then I worked cleaning stalls in the little stud barn," she said. "It's over now though."

"Reckless's old barn." Judith voice rose. "You worked there? Can you take me to see it?"

"I guess." Emily shrugged. Dan hadn't said to stay away from the stud barn and there wasn't any security, other than at the estate entrance. And she wanted to say good-bye to Barney and Ted. "Sure, I don't see why not," she added with fresh confidence. "We can go there after you're finished."

"Great." Judith grabbed Emily's hand and tugged her toward the track. "This media scene shouldn't be more than a few hours and I want to see the rest of the estate. Has Thomas Hamilton been around?"

"A little. But I saw more of Mrs. Hamilton. She's very nice."

Judith's nose wrinkled. "I heard she's a society lady with old money and no interests but the arts."

"Maybe," Emily said. "But that doesn't mean she's not nice."

Judith tilted her head. "True. And you look nice toned down, without all the makeup. Are those groom's clothes?"

"Yes. I only used lip gloss today," Emily said. "Thought there might be an off chance of snagging some background work. They like the grooms barefaced, and I need to make a few more dollars. Do they have all the extras they need for the media scene?"

"I don't know. The bus was packed full of guys though. There were only five other women and one changed into a low-cut shirt—right on the seat beside me. Rumor is the director wants more boobage."

Emily glanced wistfully at her chest. She was adequate but not huge, not like Shania. In fact, this shirt barely showed any cleavage. A push-up bra did wonders. Dan hadn't seemed to find her wanting last night though. His hands, his mouth—

"Maybe Thomas Hamilton could help."

"Pardon." Emily yanked her attention back to Judith, irritated that her thoughts kept swerving back to Dan.

"Maybe Hamilton could help," Judith repeated. "He's a bit of a creep but he helped me with the casting people. That's why I got the second call."

"I'm not a poster girl for big boobs," Emily said.

"Too bad," Judith said. "Because that's what they need."

Emily experimentally pressed her arms against her ribs. Definitely some cleavage now, and the scooped blue T-shirt displayed it nicely. "I'll meet you at the track," she said, pivoting toward the wardrobe tent. "I need to make a clothing adjustment."

"You can't just wander off," Judith said, but her voice trailed off in a sigh of resignation. "Good luck," she called.

"You must have some bras with underwire," Emily said. "I don't care how uncomfortable they are."

"Sorry, we don't," Maggie said, her arms loaded with hangers. "And I'm in a hurry. I have to dress all these people." She slanted her eyes at the line of extras in front of the counter and nodded for the next man to step forward.

Emily shoved her hands in her pockets and trudged from the tent. There had to be another option. For the high school prom, Jenna had strapped tape beneath Emily's gown, rather than buy an expensive bra they could ill afford. However, it had been special surgical tape they'd borrowed from Wally.

The stud barn had first aid supplies but it was too far away. She paused outside the door, her mind whirling. She needed this job in order to scrape together the rest of the money. The remainder of the steeplechase package was due in three days. There could be no better present for Jenna. But time was running out.

Two men in coveralls walked past, carrying coffee and a green tool kit. "Nice morning," the shorter one said.

Emily nodded then spun around. "Would you gentlemen happen to have any tape?"

"Yup," the short man said. "But if you have any set repairs, call the supervisor. He'll have someone over within the hour."

"I just need to borrow a roll of tape for a spot repair." She gave them a hopeful smile.

The taller man set the toolbox on the ground, flipped open the lid and tossed her a gray roll of tough-looking tape. "Keep it," he said.

"This is perfect," Emily said. "Thank you."

Elated, she rushed back to the wardrobe tent clutching the roll. Ten minutes later, and after mangling several strips of tape, her chest was wrapped so tightly she looked like somebody else reflected in the mirror. Sure, she could barely breathe, but the transformation was astonishing.

She gaped at her chest, amazed by the eye-catching cleavage. Her push-up bras had never worked so well.

She stepped from the change room. "Thanks for the scissors," she called to a curious Maggie.

"Wait. Turn around." Maggie leaned over the counter, practically pushing aside a bearded background performer in an attempt to get a better look. "Did you use tape?" she asked.

"I did." Emily turned and spread her arms. "What do you think?"

"Amazing." Maggie smiled her approval. "Looks like a D cup."

The man with the beard nodded. "That's my guess too," he said with a grin.

By the time Emily reached the set, she was confident she'd nailed the look. Men's eyes simply locked on her chest. She could have egg on her face and they wouldn't have noticed.

"I should have done this before," she whispered to Judith, "and not bothered with makeup. Tape is much faster."

"Shush," Judith said. "He's coming."

"Good morning," Mr. Hamilton called. "Nice to see you back." His gaze flickered to Emily then lowered and locked on her chest.

"Remember my friend, Emily?" Judith asked. "She's already registered for background and has experience here. So if they need anyone else…"

"Yes indeed. Nice to meet you, Emily." Hamilton's gaze remained riveted to Emily's chest, and it was clear he had no memory of ever seeing her before. If it hadn't been amusing, Emily would have been insulted.

"Is that the casting assistant over there?" Judith prompted. "Should Emily report to him?"

"Yes, indeed." Hamilton wrapped familiar arms around their waists and guided them toward a cluster of people with headsets.

Emily fought the urge to shake off his arm, relieved she didn't have to work for the man. Expensive cologne couldn't mask his smell of eagerness. At least Judith was on his other side. But pity the female grooms who'd had to tolerate his pawing.

"Background for the rail scene," Hamilton announced, as though he'd conjured them up himself.

"Thanks," a man in a white jacket said, his head still bent over a monitor. "We'll put them along the rail, next to the reporters. Wait until you're called." He glanced up with a distracted smile. His gaze skimmed over Emily's chest. "We might be able to use you by the tractor," he added. "What scenes have you been in?"

"I only led a horse from the barn. I was background in the party scene but my face wasn't shown." Emily shot a grateful look at Judith.

"Okay, if you haven't checked in, sign this sheet," the man said. "Then hang around with the other background. Wait for your call."

"I'll be back," Hamilton said, his elbow brushing Emily's breast. "But first I want to watch Reckless go through the rail."

"Okay," Judith said. "See you later."

Emily gave him a polite nod, grateful for his help but relieved he was leaving. It was odd being restricted to the background area though, after days of wandering freely around the set.

"This is great," Judith whispered, her gaze on Hamilton's receding back. "Looks like you landed another background job."

"Thanks to you. Now what do we do?"

"We wait," Judith said. "Could be hours. Looks like they're filming across the track."

Emily peered across the infield, straining to see Dan. "Do you think we could walk over there?"

Judith scowled. "Don't even think about it. Isn't this what you wanted?"

"Of course," Emily said. But she fidgeted, fighting her boredom along with the growing discomfort around her rib cage. Perhaps she shouldn't have pulled the tape quite so tight.

At least this was easy work, relaxing beneath the warm sun. No stalls to clean, no horses to brush, no man to make her heart jump. She managed to wait another three minutes.

"Want me to get some coffee?" she asked.

Judith opened her mouth to protest then gave a wistful shrug. "That would be lovely. But the tent's too far away, and we're not supposed to wander."

Emily blew out a frustrated sigh. The time she'd worked as special skills, coffee had been delivered. However, the lowly group of background performers had no such perks. One actor, clearly union, sat beneath a shady umbrella with a hovering attendant delivering his drinks. But it wasn't really coffee Emily craved. She wanted a glimpse of Dan.

Plus there had been a lot of talk about the rail scene, and it would be exciting to see the runaway. Heck, she'd even watched the guys construct the cardboard rail, so naturally she had a proprietary interest. Even if Dan wasn't directing the stunt she'd rather be there. Not here.

"What's wrong with you?" Judith wrinkled her forehead in exasperation. "Robert Dexter is under an umbrella, only thirty feet away. And I'm sure I recognize that gray-haired man with him. Wasn't he in *Breaking Bad*?"

Emily gave a feeble smile. She'd never be able to match Judith's interest in the actors. She was more concerned about how the horses performed. Hopefully, they'd get the stunt on the first take.

She shaded her eyes and stared across the infield. It looked like eight horses were on the track, but none of them were moving. So either they'd finished or the scene had stalled. Maybe soon, she'd see Dan.

She turned back to Judith. "What exactly are we doing in our scene?"

"Reckless runs through the rail, dumps the rider, and is loose on the track," Judith said. "I think he acts up in the starting gate too."

"But what's the background for?"

"Mr. Hamilton invited press and other guests to watch Reckless train. His colt was the Derby favorite until the horse turned outlaw."

"Breeders obviously didn't worry that he'd pass on his uncertain temperament," Emily said thoughtfully. "I guess he did end up winning a lot of races."

"Yeah. He loved his groom," Judith said, "but like any male, he got over her quick enough."

Judith's voice sounded strained, a mixture of pain and bitterness. Clearly, she'd been dumped a few times too.

Emily gave her an empathetic pat on the back, determined not to dwell on Dan and the male species' deficiencies. Horses were a safer subject.

"I heard Reckless didn't like the little barn," Emily said. "That he bounced back to normal after they moved him. They turned the building into a stud barn, but it feels like that apartment was empty for years."

"What do you mean?" Judith frowned. "You saw the apartment above the barn?"

"That's where I slept. When I stayed for special skills." Except for the night she'd spent at Dan's. But Emily refrained from mentioning that. The pain was too raw.

Judith tilted forward. "Can you show me the apartment too?"

"Sure. No problem." There might be a problem if Lizzie saw them. However, Emily brushed away the concern. Judith had looked so sad when she spoke of men, and it was nice to be able to help her for a change. "Thanks for speaking to Mr. Hamilton about me," Emily added. "I really appreciate it."

"It helps to have contacts in this business." Judith's gaze drifted to the group gathered on the other side of the track. "What do you think of him?"

"Who?" Emily's voice gave a telltale quiver as she scanned the oval for Dan.

"Thomas Hamilton."

"Oh...I don't really know him. But I like his wife."

Judith's gaze shot back to Emily. "If you're politely reminding me he's married, there's no need. I really don't like the man. But he isn't happy. Rumor is he only married his wife because she owned the adjoining property. He couldn't have built this track without her land."

Emily shifted sideways, uncomfortable with the conversation. She liked Mrs. Hamilton. And despite Judith's denial, the gleam in her eyes revealed an unhealthy interest in Mr. Hamilton.

A tractor hauling a harrow rumbled up the track, cutting short their conversation.

"Background, move to the rail," the assistant director called. "We need two by the tractor, a driver and a groom. You, in the blue shirt, come stand here."

A man with headphones touched Emily on the shoulder. "This way, please."

She ducked beneath the rail and followed him to the green tractor.

"Stand there and wait." He pointed to a dark X on the ground.

Emily nodded agreeably. The air was still, a perfect morning for filming. But it was hotter on the open dirt track than it had been on the other side of the rail. Sweat beaded between her breasts and her tight jeans itched. She edged along the side of the tractor, searching for a cooling breeze, hoping the director would appear soon.

For the next forty minutes, a woman with a clipboard adjusted background performers against the rail. Judging by their clothing, it looked like media and casual onlookers sprinkled with barn workers. Cameras rolled into position. Robert Dexter still lounged beneath an umbrella, sipping on a clear bottle of water, looking crisp and cool. He must be in this scene, but obviously he didn't intend to move yet.

Emily blew out a bored sigh. She edged off the mark by the tractor and propped a hip against an enormous black tire. However, the rubber was burning hot and she quickly straightened. It seemed like hours before the man with headphones reappeared.

"Put some dirt on the girl's chest," he said. "We'll do a shot after the horse runs past."

A makeup artist hurried up. "Stand square please," she said, expertly brushing something on Emily's chest.

"What are you doing?" Emily asked.

"Making you look authentic. Reckless dumps his rider, then almost hits the tractor. People get dirty. Let's see." The lady tilted her head, studying Emily's chest. "Okay. That's good."

Emily glanced down. Her shirt was now stained and a line of dirt ran down her neck, disappearing between her breasts. Someone pressed a white lead line in her hands.

"What am I supposed to do?" she asked. "Do I catch the horse?"

No one answered and she blew out a frustrated sigh. It had been way more fun working with Dan, who'd let her know the procedure every step of the way. These people treated her like a mannequin. Or maybe they didn't know what was happening either.

"Just wait for the director," the man with the headphones said. "It might be awhile. There's a problem with the rail."

Emily shaded her eyes and stared across the infield. A chestnut broke away from the group and seemed to be heading their way, but the horse abruptly wove to the right and stopped. But that couldn't be the rail scene. Reckless was a bay.

She glanced around, hoping to find someone to talk to, but the rest of the background was positioned by the finish line. Judith now held a silver recorder and was talking animatedly with a man in a beat-up Fedora.

This is great, Emily thought. I'm being paid to do nothing. But her gaze drifted from the happily chatting Judith to Robert Dexter lounging in the shade, and it was painfully obvious some movie jobs were much better than others.

CHAPTER TWENTY-SIX

Dan groaned as the rider on the chestnut horse veered out of line and once again galloped past Bruno.

"Dammit," Anthony said, waving an arm in despair. "My brother promised she was a competent rider. Too bad we couldn't use stock footage."

Dan dragged a hand over his jaw. This entire morning was a fiasco, and it wasn't totally the fault of Anthony's inept niece. He'd been distracted, curt and surly, unable to forget the feel of Emily's mouth, the soft sighs she made in the dark, the trusting way she'd curled against his chest and spoke of her family. Thank God, she was leaving tonight.

"We can't work this group of horses any longer," Dan said. "I'll get a new batch."

"No. Background is in place." Anthony gestured at the colorful mob gathered on the other side of the track. "Keep your stunt horse out. We'll shoot the runaway scene now and finish this part later."

Dan flipped through his notebook. After Bruno crashed through the rail, he galloped riderless around the track, almost clipping a tractor. The incident was well documented since Thomas Hamilton had invited the media to watch the colt work prior to the Derby.

Dan had Bruno inked in as first choice and a second horse, painted and primed, as backup. No horse worked more than three furlongs a day, which meant Bruno would have to nail it on the first take, or step aside for his underling.

"Get the second bay ready," he said to Lizzie, hoping he wouldn't have to use him. The lookalike was rather lazy and didn't possess Bruno's wicked energy.

Dan walked up to the stunt rider, a fearless pro who he loved to work with. "Thanks, Mitzie. We'll shoot the stunt again tomorrow, along with the rearing in the gate. Bruno is going solo now."

Mitzie saluted and vaulted from the saddle, pausing to pat Bruno on the neck. "Not many horses are this versatile. Can we get together later so I can see the storyboard?"

"Sure. Drop by the production office about six."

She gave a knowing smile, probably aware his trailer was his refuge. But he'd learned never to invite anyone in, even someone as safe as Mitzie. Emily had been a rarity—but hell, he wasn't a choirboy. If she hadn't been leaving, he never would have touched her.

Bruno tossed his head, and Dan yanked his attention back to his job. The saddle would remain but the reins needed switching. The stunt reins would flap but break away if stepped on, keeping the horse safe and giving the illusion of greater speed.

"All done," the wrangler said, after making a final adjustment.

"Wait in the backstretch." Dan checked that the pickup rider was in place beyond the finish line then climbed into the golf cart beside Anthony.

"Wasted day," Anthony grumbled, as their driver turned the cart and headed to the front of the track. "We're going to have to get some of the extras back tomorrow. Gotta expect this once in awhile though."

Dan said nothing. They both knew the day would have been much smoother if Anthony hadn't insisted that his niece ride.

"The tractor is fifteen feet from the rail, and I want the horse to run through the opening," Anthony continued. "We have two people set up to wave their arms and look like they're trying to stop him. One of them is a stunt man who'll hit the dirt."

Dan nodded. This was a fairly simple exercise for Bruno. He'd be released at the top of the stretch, gallop riderless along the outside rail and across the finish line to where he'd be picked up by the outrider. The stuntman would be filmed up close. The background performer was only there to emphasize the danger of a loose horse.

"Just make sure the tractor guy stays well back," Dan said. "Bruno isn't going to stop. And I requested a bigger gap."

"Yeah, well, fifteen will have a bigger impact. But we shortened the run, like you asked."

Dan grunted. Bruno would have no problem with a fifteen-foot gap but if he had started at fifteen, Anthony would have cut the margin to ten, like he had yesterday with the cardboard rail. And ten feet was dangerous.

"We have some eye candy by the tractor," Anthony went on. "She's going to step out and wave her arms, instead of having the male driver do it."

"I take it she's not wearing a turtleneck," Dan said dryly.

Anthony laughed. "According to my assistant, she has beautiful tits."

"It'd be safer to have her up in the tractor."

"Precisely." Anthony gave a complacent smile. "But I want the movie popcorn friendly. Besides, she can't complain. She's not union."

Dan crossed his arms, unable to hide his disapproval. His tolerance level was razor thin today, a result of the botched rail stunt. His bad mood certainly wasn't related to Emily.

A handful of onlookers stood beyond the background at the rail, and he scanned their heads, searching for her face. He didn't want to see her. Not really. He just wanted to make sure she'd call about the Louisville job. She'd made this shoot very pleasurable and the least he could do was crack open a couple doors.

The university movie would be perfect for her, a fluff story about a student with sexuality issues. The director was screening a variety of pretty girls. Seeing Emily last night, all painted up, had provided him with a much-needed reality check. She was an actress who craved the lights, and actresses were out of bounds. He should have kept his belt buckled.

The cart bounced over a rut, knocking his knee against the frame of the front seat. "Dammit," he swore.

"What's wrong?" Anthony's eyes narrowed. "You've been surly all day. You need to get laid."

Dan snagged a bottle of water from the cooler and yanked off the top, trying to hide his despair. "That's the last thing I need," he said.

Sweat trickled and Emily's T-shirt was soaked. She wiped her forehead then brushed at a bloodthirsty fly, wincing as the duct tape cut deeper into her skin. The technician had warned her not to touch the makeup, but the brown stuff on her chest was itchy and drew insects like a magnet.

She glanced wistfully at the tractor seat. Up there, she'd have shade and a chance to catch the breeze. But she was being paid to stand so delays were good. Another day of this, and she and Jenna would be off to the races.

Clearly there was a glitch on the far side of the track. The slowdown wasn't good for Dan or the budget, but it was excellent news for background performers. As Judith had emphasized, they were paid to wait. For the sake of the horses though, Emily hoped the stunts went smoothly.

"Okay, gang," someone hollered. "They're on their way."

The announcement was accompanied by a flurry of activity. Even Robert Dexter rose from his umbrella chair. Seconds later, a dolly truck rolled up and positioned a camera. To Emily's right, a tech bent over a steady cam and refocused the equipment. She glanced down, checking that her feet were back on the mark.

Her heartbeat revved. Dan would show up soon. If there were horses in the scene, he'd definitely be with the director. It didn't matter really—they'd already said their good-byes—but it would be comforting to see a familiar face. Being left isolated for so long was rather depressing.

However, it looked like this upcoming scene might be very short. There were certainly fewer animals around. Only two horses circled near the starting gate, one without a rider. She strained to distinguish horses and faces. Possibly the lady in pink was Lizzie. The riderless horse might be Bruno. But the distance was too great to be certain.

Twenty feet away, a golf cart rolled to a stop. Dan unfolded from the back.

Every one of her senses kicked into overdrive. Her breath caught so sharply it hurt. She could see the pulse beating at the base of his throat, smell the spicy scent of his skin, almost taste the cool water dangling from his hand. She smiled, unable to hide her sheer joy at seeing him.

The hubbub around them faded to gray. His eyes locked on her like a laser, sharp, hard and angry.

She jerked back as if slapped.

He turned to the man beside him. "*That's* the girl?"

The director gave a dismissive shrug. "Oh, damn, it's the sneezer. She'll have to do. At least, there's no dialogue."

"Get someone else," Dan said flatly.

"No, she has the physical appearance. I like it." The director turned to a hovering attendant. "Put more dirt on her chest, a mark on her cheek. We'll take a medium shot."

Something withered deep in Emily's chest, but she forced a brittle smile. They spoke as if she weren't there, and at that moment she resented the director, resented the movie but most of all, she resented Dan.

"We have to move the tractor out another five feet," Dan said, turning from Emily and striding after the director.

"Look at me please." The makeup artist yanked at Emily's chin and brandished a black brush.

Emily raised her head, uncaring now how hot and grubby she was, or what they rubbed on her skin. It didn't matter anyway. Dan had barely looked at her. And when he had, it was with open hostility. Even horror.

Had he expected her to lay low until the bus pulled out tonight? Maybe he was embarrassed. After all, she wasn't a sought-after movie star, only a lowly extra. It was painfully obvious he hadn't expected to see her again.

I'll laugh about this later with Jenna when we're watching the races from our fifth-row seats close to the finish line. But she didn't feel like laughing now. In fact, she gulped twice, desperate to control the weird spasms in her throat.

"Would it be possible to have a drink of water?" she croaked.

"You don't have any lines." The woman deftly flicked some powder off her brush. "And I have to hurry. The director's in a mood."

"Isn't he always," Emily said, struggling to regain her usual flippancy.

"Still, no one dares cross Anthony today, except maybe *him*." The lady rolled her eyes meaningfully over her shoulder.

Dan still followed Anthony who flung a clipboard in his director's chair and wheeled, arms waving. It looked like a heated exchange. Emily couldn't see Dan's face but his muscles were bunched so tightly, his shirt strained from the tension.

Finally Anthony nodded and gave a curt jab of his thumb. A gray-haired man with a ponytail and white sandals ran over and clambered onto the tractor. It rumbled to a start, spitting exhaust and dust as it inched toward them. "Stand back, ladies," he called, positioning the trailer further from the rail.

"Maybe they won't need me out here," Emily said hopefully. It would be much more pleasant to stand with Judith and the other background people. They hadn't been dirtied up. Emily no longer cared about makeup and stylish clothes; she'd settle for a clean face and some shade.

"Quiet. Here he comes." The makeup attendant stepped back, nodding deferentially at Anthony, his assistant and Dan.

"Cue her when to wave her arms," Anthony said, his gaze raking Emily's dirty shirt. "Then she needs to step back before the horse hits her." He walked away without ever addressing her directly.

"Stand here," the assistant said, then glanced at Dan. "She's all yours now."

Emily's grip tightened around the lead line. She raised her head before turning toward Dan, determined to hide how much his antipathy hurt.

His gaze traveled over her chest then back to her face. He'd been animated with Anthony only minutes earlier, but now he stood silent, unmoving, other than one lean finger that idly tapped his water bottle.

"Was this scene explained to you?" he asked.

She shook her head, hoping he wouldn't insist she be replaced with another performer.

"Reckless," he said, "played by Bruno, rips through the rail and dumps his rider. A stunt rider. He bolts around the track. Someone tries to stop him—another stunt person. Bruno then gallops between the tractor and the rail, almost trampling a groom. You are *not* a stunt person." His voice turned accusatory.

She blinked. Perhaps she'd exaggerated a bit about her horse experience, but she was quite certain, almost positive, that she hadn't marked the stunt box on her application. "I never pretended to be one," she said cautiously, guessing he was searching for a reason why she wasn't suitable.

"That's not the point," he snapped. "Drink." He pressed the bottle into her hand, shocking her as much by the action as the abrupt cold against her skin.

She took a quick swig, then reluctantly passed it back, unable to keep her wistful gaze from following the water.

"Finish it," he said, his voice gruff.

She drained the bottle. At least they weren't arguing over this.

"Want more?" he asked.

She shook her head and carefully wiped her mouth, conscious of the makeup artist's annoyance.

Dan's gaze drifted over her chest and his scowl returned. "You have to follow directions. No thinking out of the box. Jump out of the way the second you're cued. Got it?"

"Of course. I always listen. I'll do whatever the scene requires."

"I think you have a skewed definition of 'listening' but you are definitely plucky." A corner of his mouth twitched. "And you do look like one of Hamilton's grooms."

She gave a cautious smile, relieved to see the return of his natural good humor. He, of all people, must know her shirt-popping cleavage required some assistance. But he was looking at her face and perhaps didn't notice. It didn't seem as if he'd insist on a replacement performer though. His anger had disappeared, replaced with a wry resignation.

"The assistant director will rehearse the scene with you," Dan said. "I'm tied up with Bruno and the stuntman." His voice lowered. "Did you take the number for the Louisville movie?"

"Yes, thanks."

"Good. It's an excellent opportunity. No stunts required. Nice wardrobe too."

Clearly he was poking fun at her dirty face. She raised a self-conscious hand to her cheek, then slowly lowered it. What did it matter? She'd primped for hours last night and it hadn't made a bit of difference. "We extras do love a nice wardrobe," she said, hiding her hurt.

"Look, Emily. I'm working flat out today." He glanced over his shoulder at the makeup artist. His voice lowered. "But I do apologize for this morning, for leaving the trailer so quickly...afterwards."

"No problem. It was a good chance to check for souvenirs. You'd be amazed how well movie stuff sells on eBay." She waved a dismissive hand, deciding she was a damn good actress after all.

Something flickered in his eyes. "You'll be okay. But I will miss you. Now get your head in the scene."

She blinked, absorbing his strange words, but he said nothing more. Merely turned and walked down the track.

"Move a step to the right and wave your arms," the man they called the AD said. She obediently followed his directions but wished Dan was working with her, especially when the director complained that her actions were too mechanical.

"She has to wave her arms so a horse would see them," Anthony said to his assistant, shaking his head as though she was an idiot.

Seconds later, she heard Anthony's strident voice again. "Switch the lead line to her left hand. And add a halter."

Then, "Focus the second camera on her chest."

Finally, after numerous comments and adjustments, she had the director's approval. "You know the horse isn't going to stop," Anthony said, walking past the assistant director and talking to her for the first time. "This horse is trained to run through a wall."

She nodded, rather shocked by his direct attention. He was even making eye contact.

"But if you stand still and wave your arms until the last second," Anthony added, "it would be way more realistic. Remember, you're a desperate groom, trying to stop a valuable animal from injuring himself. And Reckless's owner, your employer, is watching from the rail. So it's important you don't jump aside until the AD's signal. Can you do that?"

"Of course," she said, remembering how Bruno responded to Dan's direction. Dan might not want her around, but he would never let anyone be trampled.

"Right," Anthony said, turning to the crew. "Let's go for a take."

"Rolling," someone said. "Marker." A clap stick sounded.

"Background," the AD called. She swallowed, tightening her grip around the halter, surprised by the stickiness of her palms.

"Action," Anthony said.

A loose horse abruptly appeared around the turn, dark mane and long reins flailing. She glimpsed Dan's raised arm. Halfway down the track, a man rushed from the rail. It looked like he would catch the horse. But no, he was knocked over, his body flying in the air like a bowling pin.

She gulped, staring at the huge horse bearing down on her. Bruno had never looked so big, so powerful...so unstoppable.

"Wave arms," someone cued.

She frantically waved her arms, hoping Bruno would stop but knowing he wasn't supposed to. Damn, he was huge. And fast. He was tearing along the rail now, nostrils flared, ears back, clods of dirt flying in his wake. She wanted to leap behind the tractor but the stuntman had waited. So could she. The ground shook as Bruno towered over her—

"Move!"

She scrambled aside, tripping to the ground in her urgency, almost knocking down the wind fan.

She peered up in time to see Bruno's long streaming tail as he galloped in front of the spectators. Only background people. But they appeared genuine, watching the bolting horse with varying degrees of horror. Just past the finish line, a rider appeared alongside Bruno and both horses slowed to a controlled canter.

"Cut," Anthony called, his voice much lighter now. "The middle couldn't get any better," he said, peering over the cameraman's shoulder. "Circle that."

Anthony walked up to Emily, still smiling. "I like your guts, girl. Come back tomorrow. We'll find more work for you. Dress the same as today."

She nodded, too exhilarated to speak and still punchy with adrenaline. She glanced up the track, glad to see Bruno had already slowed to a trot beside the pickup rider. What an awesome horse. For a minute, he'd looked like a panicky runaway and she'd feared he truly was bolting.

She brushed the dirt off her jeans and glanced around for Dan. He must be so proud of his horse. And maybe, just maybe, he was a little proud of her.

"What the hell were you thinking? Are you a total imbecile?"

She spun around. Dan's face was ashen and he was breathing hard, as though he'd sprinted up the track.

Her smile faded. "I did what they said."

"Fifteen feet! You were supposed to jump aside at fifteen feet. Dammit. I'm sick of people craving attention. Always wanting the limelight." He jammed his fists in his pockets then yanked them out again. "You'll never work for me again."

"But I wasn't working for you." Her voice quivered with hurt, and anger. "You already fired me. Remember."

"Dan," Lizzie called, her voice breathless. "Why did you leave? I heard it was a wrap."

A muscle ticked in Dan's jaw. He didn't even look at Lizzie, just stared at Emily, his cold blue eyes filled with such contempt she feared she might cry. And she never cried.

"They must have liked it," Emily managed. "Doesn't a w-wrap mean it's finished?"

Dan just shook his head and strode away, shoulders rigid, fists clenched.

"What's going on?" Lizzie stared at his retreating back then glanced accusingly at Emily. "I've never seen him so upset."

Emily pulled at her lower lip, trying to stop it from trembling. "Guess I didn't move at the right time."

"You can't do anything right, can you?" Lizzie snapped. She pivoted and rushed after Dan.

Emily pretended to cough, fighting her shame. Reamed out on set. She glanced around, but no one appeared to be watching. The production crew was already headed in the same direction as Dan.

Moving on to the next scene.

She hugged her arms over her chest and walked across the track, shaken and confused. She'd tried to follow directions, to wait for the signal even though she'd been terrified. She'd even dared to hope for a satisfied nod. However, it seemed the harder she worked, the less Dan approved.

The other background performers moved in a cohesive group toward the lunchroom, still talking animatedly about the scene. She hunched her shoulders and joined the stragglers, hoping no one had witnessed her humiliation. But their carefree chatter only magnified her feeling of isolation.

"That was so exciting," a cultured voice behind her said. "You did an excellent job."

Emily swung around, so relieved to hear a kind word she almost gave Mrs. Hamilton a hug. "Did it look okay?" she asked, desperate for reassurance.

"Absolutely. That horse even moved like Reckless. Seems like yesterday." Her voice turned wistful. "He was our only chance at the Derby. We never had another three-year-old good enough. I remember my husband's despair when he realized Reckless wouldn't be able to run."

Emily nodded. Very few Thoroughbreds were good enough to make the Derby. Qualifying as one of the twenty three-year-olds to enter the gate took a unique combination of talent, training and luck. It was a shame the colt's groom had quit so abruptly. "Couldn't you have just hired the groom back?" Emily asked.

"We wanted to. But my husband couldn't find her. She'd packed her bag and left. It was a…difficult time."

Neither of them spoke for a moment, and Emily wished she could pull back her question. Hamilton was a lecherous creep. If only half the rumors were true, it must have been a challenging situation for Mrs. Hamilton. But why had the groom not stayed for the Derby? If she cared at all for Reckless—and what groom didn't love their horse?—she could have stayed a few more weeks.

"At least Reckless finally settled down and ended up racing again," Emily said lamely. "By the way, I thoroughly enjoyed your travel bag. Thanks very much."

"I'm glad it helped." Mrs. Hamilton gave a gracious nod. "I'm sure you made an excellent impression."

Emily forced a nod, waving as Mrs. Hamilton headed toward her car. But it was obvious any impression she'd made hadn't been a good one. Dan's eyes had been full of such contempt, she'd wanted to crawl beneath a rock. It wouldn't have hurt nearly so much if it had been the director who had yelled.

Dan's words played over in her head. 'You'll never work for me again.' Which probably meant sleeping with her was out of the question. A hysterical choke escaped. Because being with Dan was what she wanted. It didn't matter if she shoveled manure or jumped in front of a runaway horse, she just wanted to stay close.

Instead, she'd somehow managed to sabotage her career and earn his contempt. She jammed her hands in her pockets, fighting her misery, uncertain what to do or even where to go. The bus wasn't leaving until this evening, but she didn't want to linger around the set. Dan's scorn was too withering.

The director had invited her to work as background tomorrow, but it was clear Dan wouldn't let that happen. And so what. She raised her chin a notch. After all, she'd finally earned enough money for Jenna's weekend. Sure, she'd slept in a stall, shoveled shit and tried to flag down a bolting racehorse, but she'd done it. She'd earned her pay.

And she was going to help her sister. Jenna's happiness when she learned about the tickets would more than justify this aching misery.

CHAPTER TWENTY-SEVEN

Emily pulled out her phone and edged along the rail, away from two workers unloading a panel van. She eagerly pressed Jenna's number. This was the first sister weekend she'd ever paid for, and organized. Jenna would be shocked.

A horse vacation would be the perfect tonic. She and Jenna were both lonely. Burke traveled extensively, and the annual Stillwater Fair and Steeplechase wasn't the highlight of his busy calendar. However, Jenna loved the jump races.

There'd be other fun events too, like the three-legged sack race that Wally always sponsored. But this time, she and Jenna wouldn't have to get up early and drive to the fair. No, this time they'd be sleeping at the Inn, a first for the Murphy girls. She paced a circle, almost able to forget the disgusted look on Dan's face.

"Hello, Emily." Jenna finally answered the phone but she sounded breathless, as if she'd been running. "I tried to call but your phone is never on. It goes directly to voice mail."

"My battery's low. The charger is back at the apartment. They used me for more background today. I actually stood in front of a runaway horse." Despite Emily's disastrous ending with Dan, she experienced a thrill of pride.

"Do you like the work?"

"I love being here," Emily said. "And I like seeing the horses do such amazing things. But acting probably isn't the easiest career. I'll certainly never look at a movie the same way." She hesitated. "The director isn't very patient. He always yells."

"Yelling never bothered you before," Jenna said.

Emily scuffed her boot in the dirt. It wasn't Anthony but Dan's displeasure that left her stomach in knots. "How did your exams go?" she asked, changing the subject. "It must feel good to be finished."

"Yes. The last one was yesterday." Jenna gave a long exhale, sounding more relaxed than she had in months.

"You'll make a great vet," Emily said. "Those tips you gave sure helped the horse here." She paused, relishing her heady anticipation and the fact she was calling with a gift, not a request. "I was thinking we should do something special to celebrate. And it's not shopping either."

"Just a sec," Jenna said.

A man's familiar voice rumbled in the background.

"Burke says hi," Jenna said, coming back on the line. "He knows a producer in LA if you need a contact."

"Oh, that's nice." Emily swallowed. She appreciated Burke's help, but he didn't think she could accomplish anything on her own. Or maybe he just preferred that Jenna's sister live far away in California. "I thought he was working in New York for the next month?" Emily asked.

"I did too." Jenna gave a bubbling laugh. "But he tricked me. He came home last night, along with a big surprise."

"What was it?" For some reason, Emily's palms began to sweat.

"We're going to the Grand National in England." Jenna's voice bubbled with excitement. "Somehow he arranged for seats right beneath the Royal Box. I can't believe it. The most famous steeplechase in the world. Something I've always dreamed about but never thought I'd ever see in person."

Emily sagged against the rail, unable to speak. Her little gift seemed so mundane now. She'd been naïve thinking she could plan something amazing, especially when the richest man in West Virginia loved Jenna to pieces. But maybe they could still enjoy the local fair. The suite was plenty big enough for three. And it would be nice to see Burke.

"That's fabulous," Emily said, after a moment. "You always loved that movie *National Velvet*. When do you leave?"

"Tomorrow," Jenna said. "And then Burke arranged to cruise up the Thames and also visit Newmarket. He has a special invitation to view Stanley House Stud."

"Oh...so you'll be gone until the middle of next month. That's great." But Emily's voice cracked.

"The only thing I worry about is Peanut," Jenna went on. "He's been having trouble lately. I know Wally will take good care of him, but I'm not sure about leaving for so long."

Emily sucked in an achy breath, tempted to agree. However, Jenna always put everyone else's welfare above her own. She deserved a European vacation, certainly something more special than the local fair. "Peanut will be fine," Emily said. "You should definitely do the cruise."

Burke's low voice rumbled again.

Jenna's voice faded then became clear. "Burke promises we can be home in eight hours if I need to return for Peanut."

"See?" Emily said. "There's nothing holding you back." But she squeezed her eyes shut, unable to imagine the love of such a man. Burke was so tough but really a marshmallow inside, at least when it came to Jenna. It was astonishing how he'd quietly arranged the perfect vacation. Jenna sounded like she couldn't stop grinning. Of course, when you love someone, you want to make them smile.

"Take lots of pictures," Emily managed. "And check my boxes in storage. I have some gorgeous hats."

"I will, thanks. And hopefully you can visit this summer. But only if a big movie star like you can take a break." The misplaced pride in Jenna's voice made Emily wince.

"They won't even miss me," Emily said, blinking rapidly. "Now go pack and enjoy your trip. Love you, but gotta go. My battery's almost dead."

She turned off the phone and slowly tucked it away in her pocket. Then propped her elbows on the rail and stared across the expanse of dirt, feeling as lifeless as the deserted track.

"There you are," Judith called. "I've been looking all over."

Emily straightened, stepping away from the rail and swiping her cheeks with the back of her hand.

"Why are you standing out here all alone?" Judith asked. "You should have watched my other scene. They shot it in the second barn but made it look like the Churchill backstretch. The director even ordered coffee for everyone. I was only a few feet away from Robert Dexter during the break."

"That's great," Emily said.

"I'm finished for the day though," Judith went on, "so I have time to see the stud barn now, if you think it's okay to visit." Her eyes narrowed. "Are you all right?"

Emily averted her head. "I washed my face under a tap, but I think my eyes were a little allergic to that makeup they rubbed on." She jabbed her thumb toward the footpath. "The barn is that way. Let's go."

She no longer cared about annoying Lizzie who was probably still on the set anyway, panting after Dan. Besides, Emily wanted to see Barney and Ted one last time, and she also wanted to finish cleaning Billy's cottage.

"I need to help the retired caretaker afterwards," Emily warned. "His name is Billy and he's a bit of a hoarder." She glanced at Judith, guessing her friend would have no interest in spending time with non-movie persona.

However, Judith only shrugged. "I can help too. The bus isn't leaving until nine. They're shooting non-stop today."

"Great," Emily said. "We can clean up Billy's place a bit. Someone checks on him, but I think he needs more support." She shot Judith a hopeful look. "Maybe you could talk to Mr. Hamilton about him?"

"Shake that big chest and Hamilton will give you anything you want," Judith said dryly.

Emily glanced down. She'd forgotten about the irritating sting of the tape. Turned out it hadn't really been necessary. None of it was. "My sister's going to watch the Grand National in England," she said quietly.

"Nice. Is that the trip you're saving for?"

"No. Mine was the Stillwater Steeplechase. Unfortunately, it's at the same time. Jenna's husband surprised her with it, along with a cruise and exclusive visit to some famous race stable."

"Oh, no." Compassion filled Judith's kind face. "You've been working so hard too. But can you still go? Maybe take a friend?"

Emily nodded. "Yes, the tickets are non-refundable. Two nights at the Steeplechase Inn. Beer, hot dogs and horses. So, would you like to go to West Virginia with me? Everything's paid. And I'd love for you to come."

Judith just stared.

"I know you like movies more than horses," Emily went on, uncomfortable with Judith's silence. "And it's no big deal if you're busy. I totally understand. These horses aren't famous or really even all that fast. And sometimes the beer is a little warm—"

"Emily," Judith interrupted, her voice husky, "I'd love to come."

"You would?" Emily felt a smile crease her face. "Awesome. And you can meet Peanut. He's our pony and longtime member of the family. One Christmas we even brought him into the house. Well, not a house exactly, but a trailer. And we'll have to take the bus to Three Brooks because I don't have the money to fix my car."

"I'm used to taking buses," Judith said. "Never could afford a car. And I'd love to see all the Center's wellness features too, if we have time."

"We'll definitely make time." Emily grabbed Judith's arm with renewed vigor and tugged her along the path. "Most of the horses there are Thoroughbreds, like the two in the stud barn. Wally can be a wet blanket, but at least we won't have to sneak around. Not like here."

"Are we sneaking now?" Judith glanced sideways, her voice hushing beneath the tree-lined path.

"Maybe a little," Emily admitted. "But I don't think Lizzie's around and she's the only one who would mind." Except maybe Dan. He'd given her clear walking orders today. "But you want to see the stud barn, right?" she added.

"I certainly do," Judith said. "And especially the apartment if it's not locked."

"It only locks from the inside. Quiet now." She motioned for Judith to stop just before the path emptied into the clearing. They peered at the barn. There was no movement in the doorway, and the paddocks were empty. Apparently no one had taken the time to turn out Barney and Ted, which was unfortunate since it was a beautiful day.

"It looks deserted," Emily said. But she lingered, hesitant to step into the open.

"It's beautiful," Judith whispered. "I love French windows. But I think something moved above the balcony. Who sleeps there?"

"I did for a couple nights, but it's probably empty now. The wranglers have trailers."

"We better wait a minute," Judith said. "Make sure it's empty and then go in."

Emily scanned her friend's face. For a committed rule follower, Judith was being an excellent sport. "It doesn't matter to me if we're caught," Emily said slowly. "Dan says I'm through here. But you might be given more background work. There's no sense blowing it over an empty apartment."

"It's okay," Judith said. "It would be worth getting kicked out just to see the place."

"Really?" Emily asked. "It's not that special."

A door slammed and they both flinched.

Moments later, a man strode from the barn. Emily relaxed when she recognized Thomas Hamilton. "It's just your buddy," she said to Judith. "He won't care. Heck, he probably doesn't even know who feeds these horses."

"He's not my buddy," Judith said. She grabbed Emily's arm. "Let's wait. See what he does."

Emily shrugged. The only people she cared to avoid were Lizzie and Dan. However, they waited until Mr. Hamilton disappeared around the corner of the barn. A car door sounded from the parking lot. Seconds later, a sleek black car purred down the drive.

Emily stepped out from the shadowed trees, rather impatient with the delay. She hoped Barney's breathing was okay; he really should be outside. Hopefully he'd remember her but now that she wasn't feeding him, he might not care.

The white of Barney's blaze flashed from the aisle. His friendly whinny cut the air.

Emily grinned. "That's Barney. He loves people."

She rushed into the barn. Barney stretched his neck over the stall door, eager to greet them. His nostrils weren't flared and his respiration seemed normal. "I probably shouldn't go in his stall," Emily said, scratching the base of his ear, "but I want to pick them both some grass."

But Judith had already wandered down the aisle. "Is this the door to the upstairs apartment?" she asked over her shoulder.

"Yes, but there's nothing up there. Look at this." Emily waved the halter. "Barney can do tricks."

Judith fingered the knob of the door, obviously more interested in the apartment than equine tricks. "I want to go upstairs and take a picture of the infamous love shack," she said. "I wonder what Hamilton was doing here. If only the walls could talk."

Emily rehung the halter, rather relieved the walls couldn't speak. She'd barely been able to swallow her soup when Dan touched her in the apartment, and her intense physical response was embarrassing. More so now, since it had obviously been one-sided.

She gave Barney a pat and reluctantly followed Judith up the apartment stairs. "We shouldn't stay long. They might plan on putting another wrangler up here."

"I just need a couple minutes," Judith said. "But I'd like to see the place." Her steps quickened until she was climbing the stairs two at a time.

Emily followed more reluctantly, not wanting to dwell on the last time she'd slept here, back when she'd woken in Dan's arms. It had been a lovely interlude, but that's all it had been. And brooding didn't help.

"There's nothing here." Judith jerked to a stop at the top of the steps, her voice almost accusatory.

"There never was," Emily said. "But those flowers are new." She pointed at the vase of pastel pink roses by the French doors.

"Hamilton must have left them," Judith said.

"Yes, but how wasteful. They're only going to die." Emily had always considered cut flowers a colossal waste of money. And wild flowers were much prettier.

"This was the anniversary of Tracey's disappearance," Judith said. "Do you think he feels guilty?" She walked across the room and examined the flowers. "There's no card."

Emily remained rooted at the top of the staircase. This apartment had always felt occupied. Unsettled. She rubbed her arms, trying to ward off the chill.

Judith's suspicious gaze scanned the room. "Maybe Hamilton was so in love, he didn't want her to leave. He might have lost his temper and killed her. That would explain a lot." She disappeared into the bedroom, like a hound on a scent.

Emily's imagination raced, spurred by Judith's words. Billy was almost paranoid about closing the gate. Maybe he and Mr. Hamilton had kept that poor groom prisoner here. And then one day she got away… Or hadn't. Maybe Billy knew something important.

Judith reappeared, her face dejected. "Like you said, there's nothing in the bedroom. It's like she vanished into thin air."

Emily tightened her arms over her chest, hating the direction of her thoughts. But Billy had called her 'Tracey' once. And he was anal about following Hamilton's orders. "Maybe we should talk to Billy," she said slowly. "About the groom."

"Excellent idea," Judith said.

CHAPTER TWENTY-EIGHT

Emily held her nose, blocking the nauseating smell. She flipped the toilet seat back down and retreated into Billy's narrow hall, weaving around dirty clothes, magazines and a squashed box of mismatched nails.

"This isn't right," she whispered to Judith. "Nobody should live like this."

"I know." Judith's gaze shifted to Billy who sat in a wooden chair and stared morosely out the window. "He's not the most likeable man though. I've been stacking garbage for hours, but he refuses to let me take it outside."

"He's still annoyed I came without doughnuts. I should have gone to the dining room first."

"We were in a hurry," Judith said. "But clearly he doesn't remember a groom from twenty years ago. Besides, he'll barely talk to me."

Emily scooped up a sponge, wincing at the nagging pain around her ribs. They'd been cleaning for hours, ever since leaving the stud barn, and she'd forgotten about the duct tape.

Billy hadn't been able to answer any of their questions. But at least the strenuous scrubbing had kept her from agonizing about her useless gift for Jenna. And Judith had been amazingly kind, staying to help, although her efforts seemed focused on de-cluttering while Emily had a need to clean.

"Maybe I should talk to Louise Hamilton," Emily said. "She's very approachable. Maybe she hasn't seen Billy in awhile."

"I guess." Judith flipped open the top of a cardboard box, sneezing as dust clouded the air. "There's so much junk here. Look at this."

"Don't open his personal stuff," Emily said. "Just stack it—"

"Oh my God..." Judith's voice trailed off. Her face paled as she lifted a brown duffle bag with a horse head ID tag and a name written in cursive pink loop.

"What was the name of the missing groom?" Emily asked, her mouth turning dry. Judith traced the tag with a slow finger. "Tracey," she finally croaked. "Tracey Walker—just like on this nametag."

Emily pressed her palms over her cheeks and wheeled, eyeing Billy with horror. There were probably all kinds of reasons why the groom's duffle bag was here. However, her scrabbling brain could only think of one.

"It doesn't mean anything," Judith said quickly. "She might still be alive."

Billy stared out the window. Emily dropped to the floor beside Judith, reassured by his oblivion.

"Yes, this is probably just an extra bag." But Emily's hands shook as she tugged at the zipper. "Maybe we can find something important," she whispered. "Like makeup or birth control pills. No girl ever leaves that stuff."

They flipped through the contents but found only a toothbrush, assorted clothing and a yellow bottle of moisturizer cream.

"This ball cap looks like an original." Judith waved an inscribed cap: *Reckless, Kentucky Derby 1994.* "Bet there aren't many of these. The director would love it for the movie."

"You can have it."

Emily jerked around at the sound of Billy's voice. He stood above them, his eyes bright and lucid. It was surprising how he'd crossed the room so silently.

"We were going to order five hundred of those hats, but the damn horse went crazy. You can have it," he repeated.

"I'd love it," Judith said.

"Not you." He shook his head and pointed at Emily. "Her. She brings me doughnuts."

"That's okay," Emily said. "You keep the hat, Billy. It's special."

"No. I keep too many things." He reached down, pulled the cap from Judith's hand and plunked it on Emily's head. "It's new and needs to be worn. Reckless should have won the Derby."

Emily obligingly adjusted the cap, pulling her hair through the loop in the back. She'd never been a hat person. Fancy hats were different, of course, but she'd always thought it foolish to spend hours styling hair merely to hide it beneath a ball cap. Considering her hair and current clothes though, this was a definite improvement. "It's great, Billy," she said sincerely. "Thank you."

"Do you remember Reckless's groom," she added, her gaze shooting to the duffle bag. "A girl called Tracey?"

"Did Tracey give you some stuff to keep?" Judith chimed in. "Maybe you remember where she went?"

Billy just scowled. "Reckless should have won the Derby," he repeated. He shuffled back toward his chair, splaying a gnarled hand against the wall for support.

"We need to come back," Judith whispered. "And have a better look around."

"Yes, but Dan doesn't want me on site." Emily gave a nonchalant shrug, careful to hide her hurt. "Would they let me on the bus if I wasn't working background?"

Judith sighed regretfully and shook her head. "Not likely."

CHAPTER TWENTY-NINE

Dan fidgeted in his chair, unable to keep his mind on the camera team's analysis. He rarely lost his temper but he'd done so with Emily. When she'd planted herself in front of a charging Bruno, his raw fear had been gut wrenching.

He knew why she'd done it. Performers often took huge risks to further their careers. He understood that, respected it even, but he couldn't condone it. Not when the behavior could result in an injury. He'd watched that happen before; he wasn't going to go through it again.

And dammit, her cue had been to leap from Bruno's path at fifteen feet.

He folded his arms, staring unseeingly at the whiteboard. Anthony was talking again, smiling, obviously delighted with the day's shooting. *Bruno wouldn't have stopped.* The thought left Dan nauseous.

"Great footage today," Anthony continued, waving the remote. "The horse played a perfect rogue. Starting gate scene tomorrow. Is it the same horse, Dan?"

Dan jerked to attention and nodded. "Yes."

"Good." Anthony gave a hopeful smile. "You positive you can't flip him?"

Dan shook his head. Rearing in the gate was dangerous enough for horse and rider. And anyone else nearby. Anthony's request that the horse flip over was a joke. At least, Dan hoped it was a joke. He narrowed his eyes.

"I'm joking," Anthony said quickly. "How many times can your horse rear in a day? Eight?"

"Six max," Dan said. "But I'll have a second horse on standby."

Anthony nodded. "So twelve chances for the scene. Good. And I want the gates to open, and Reckless to come out rearing. Then we'll show Hamilton's horror."

Dan stiffened. Originally Reckless just stood in the gate, along with four others. Reckless reared and they backed the horses out, deciding he was incorrigible. "We only have one stunt rider booked tomorrow," he said. "The other three are just special skills. Including your niece."

Anthony shook his head. "I don't want my niece riding a galloping racehorse from a gate."

"No problem," Dan said. "I doubt she'd stay on."

The casting director laughed and even Anthony's mouth twitched. Unfortunately, Anthony's niece had stalled the first portion of the rail shoot. She could barely manage a trot, and it was clear her father had greatly exaggerated her riding ability.

"We have some cutting to do," Anthony admitted, "but we did get some good stuff on the other side of the track. Reckless looked like a mad runaway. Take a look."

Dan dragged his gaze to the screen, his hands clenching so tightly his knuckles whitened. He didn't need to see it; the footage was seared in his mind. Emily had looked utterly vulnerable standing in Bruno's path. She'd remained rooted much too long, although admittedly it was good stuff from the director's point of view.

But Anthony had never seen the damage a horse's hooves could do, and besides, it was Dan's responsibility to protect the stunt performers.

"This is awesome." Anthony gave another satisfied nod. "It really looks like she's going to be trampled."

Dan stared reluctantly at the screen. Bruno's ears were flattened, his neck stretched as he gunned toward Emily, galloping exactly as he'd been trained. To run by anything, through anything and over anything until he reached the pickup point.

Dan's stomach heaved.

"Look at that." Anthony blew out a satisfied sigh while onscreen Emily waved frantic arms. "That girl has guts."

"Great tits too," someone in the back said.

Dan's jaw clenched. He hated this part, and at the moment hated every smug smiling face in the room.

"Gotta love non-union," the assistant director said, giving Anthony a complacent smile. "They do what you tell them, no questions asked."

The comment jarred Dan. He leaned forward. "Can you roll it again, with sound?"

"We're dubbing our own sound later," Anthony said.

"I'd like to hear the original."

"All right." Anthony blew out a noisy breath. "But you need to know we changed her timing a bit. After all, this wasn't a stunt. Just a background performer."

Dan didn't need to listen to the audio. It was apparent now. He squeezed his eyes shut, sick with regret. Emily hadn't been showboating; she'd merely been following directions. And he'd been off balance all morning, still reeling from their memorable night together. He should have remained by the tractor rather than monitor the stunt man.

No wonder her eyes had been full of such bewilderment, such hurt. It was the hurt that bothered him the most.

"Next time for horse scenes," he said, cracking his knuckles, "please run all changes by me. As per the contract."

He scraped his chair back, picked up his notebook and stalked from the room.

"The bus is here," a woman announced from the front of the background tent. "Gather all your personal belongings. For those returning tomorrow, pickup will be at five a.m."

Emily scooped up her bag, joining Judith and the line of performers trudging toward the door. It seemed a lifetime since she'd arrived on set. She'd miss this place. In fact, she felt the same desolate feeling as at the end of 4-H camp, and the thought of walking into her stuffy apartment filled her with dread.

Maybe tomorrow she'd contact her agent. Obviously she couldn't call the number Dan had provided, not after his statement this morning. In fact, it was going to be hard to find a production company that wasn't influenced by Dan.

Dan. It hurt to brood, but it was impossible to block the memories. How could someone who had touched and listened to her like that turn so hateful? She'd followed directions, every one of them. She blew out a despairing breath, too sad to be indignant.

"You have to get back here," Judith said, her plaintive voice jarring Emily's thoughts. "The caretaker's cottage is too creepy to search alone."

Emily's arms tightened around her bag. Judith had promised to talk to Thomas Hamilton about Billy, but she knew Judith didn't worry about his living conditions like she did. "His name is Billy," Emily said.

"Yes." Judith compressed her lips. "And Billy might be a murderer. What if I asked Hamilton to get you back?"

"Could he override...Dan?" Emily didn't like how her voice wobbled over his name.

"Probably not," Judith said. "Dan's too powerful. If he's blackballed you in the industry, you're done."

The matter-of-fact statement made Emily's eyes prick, and she shuffled closer to the bus. "I only did what the director said," she muttered, fighting the sting of injustice.

"Well, you obviously didn't listen to someone. And Dan Barrett's a stickler for safety. You really should research these people before any future jobs. Hopefully some of the smaller productions won't hear about it..." Judith's voice trailed off, her eyes widening. "Oh, no. He's here. Talking to the lady with the clipboard."

Emily peered through the gloom, her heart thumping. Dan stood only twenty feet away, his imposing figure outlined by the powerful headlights of the bus.

"Maybe he's going to ban you from the bus," Judith whispered. "I heard of that happening before. But don't worry. If he does, I'll hitchhike back with you."

Dan abruptly turned, his gaze locking on Emily. He walked toward her with long purposeful strides.

Emily's heart squeezed at his grim expression, but she squared her shoulders and sucked in a fortifying breath.

He stopped in front of her. "I want to apologize. I just saw the dailies." He made no effort to lower his voice, and everyone in a fifteen-foot radius watched with avid interest. "The entire production team is impressed with the job you did today. And you need to know that before you go."

"If she's still on the background list," Judith asked, "can she come back tomorrow?"

Something flickered across Dan's face, a mix of emotions Emily couldn't read. "She's welcome here any time," he said.

"So she's allowed to ride the bus tomorrow?" Judith asked.

A middle-aged man tried to push around them, bumping Emily as he raced to get a good seat. Dan frowned. The man flushed and stepped back, suddenly electing to wait in line.

"It's a long ride to Louisville and back," Dan said slowly. "You're both welcome to stay in my trailer tonight."

Emily's cheeks burned. It was obvious he didn't want to risk being alone with her, and while she appreciated the apology she'd never been one to hang around when unwanted.

"That would be great," Judith said, jabbing Emily in her sore ribs. "We appreciate your offer."

Emily could feel Dan's gaze but didn't want to look at him. Didn't want to see the reluctance in his face. "We can sleep in the apartment above the barn," she said.

"No." Dan shook his head. "Hamilton has asked that it not be used. Apparently the apartment was always intended to be off limits."

"Oops." She looked at Dan then, unable to suppress her smile. "Guess we shouldn't have cut off that lock."

"Guess not," he said, his eyes glinting with a familiar mix of mischief and humor. "But I'm definitely glad we did."

CHAPTER THIRTY

"Don't you think that's weird?" Judith's voice lowered and she glanced down the hall, checking that Dan was out of earshot. "Hamilton putting the apartment off limits? There must be something there he doesn't want us to see."

"Flowers?" Emily joked, wishing Judith would ease up on the subject. It was impossible to concentrate on anything with Dan so close. So far, he'd been the perfect host, acting as though he was delighted to have two women for company. But she knew better.

Judith drummed her fingers on the kitchen table. "We have to get back in there. Have a better look."

Emily made an agreeable sound deep in her throat, her attention elsewhere. It sounded like Dan was in the spare room now, moving file boxes off the bed. He had the second room set up as an office so their presence in his trailer was surely an inconvenience. Yet he'd been nothing but solicitous since collecting them from the bus.

She ran her finger over the base of the wine glass, too drained to analyze his motives. She hoped it wasn't guilt. But one thing she did know, she had no desire to be anywhere else.

"You need to sneak back into the apartment," Judith said.

Emily yanked her attention back to Judith. "But it's off limits. You heard Dan."

"But you can pretend to visit the horses. And you have to do it quickly, before Hamilton padlocks the door."

Emily shifted on the chair, picturing Dan's scary look this morning. His eyes had turned so arctic cold. No wonder horses and people hopped when he raised his finger. "But we were both told the apartment was out of bounds," she said weakly.

"So what? Rules don't bother you. And this is an incredible opportunity." Judith shook her head, glancing around the kitchen in disbelief. "I still can't believe we're drinking wine in Dan Barrett's trailer. He's supposed to be reclusive. He must feel guilty about almost wrecking your career."

Guilty. Emily's hand shook with regret, and wine sloshed against the sides of her glass.

"This is so lucky," Judith continued, oblivious to Emily's distress. "Maybe we can finally figure out what happened to Tracey. I bet both Billy and Hamilton were involved. So be nice to Dan. Don't waste an important connection. Do what you have to do—"

She flushed and quit talking when Dan appeared in the doorway.

"There's a bed ready in the bedroom on the left," he said. "And the kitchen table folds out."

Judith jumped up. "I'll take the bedroom. See you both in the morning."

Emily crossed her legs, embarrassed by Judith's clumsy attempt to leave her alone with Dan. "She's really tired," Emily said.

"Clearly." His enigmatic gaze followed Judith as she rushed down the hall. "Let's go outside so we don't wake her."

He filled Emily's glass, snagged a beer and wordlessly guided her around the back of the trailer. A cooler and a wooden chair sat by a fire pit. A bundle of wood was stacked neatly on the side.

She glanced around in appreciation. Trees buffered the back, giving a sense of privacy, and the twinkling stars overhead created their own skylight. One never saw a sky like this in the city. "This is lovely," she said.

"I like my space, and trailers are cramped. This keeps me sane." He gestured at the lone chair. "Have a seat."

She sat while he crouched and expertly lit a fire. The sound of crackling wood filled the air and despite her hurt, her tension eased. She'd missed starry nights, the smell of smoke, the timeless comfort of a burning fire.

And the very best ones always had something to roast. She and Jenna had cooked many meals over their backyard pit. Her mouth salivated just thinking of hotdogs and marshmallows.

"Hungry?" he asked.

She turned away from the flames to stare at his shadowed face. He seemed to have read her mind. Already he'd pierced two hotdogs with a long pointed stick.

"Oh, boy," she said.

"And…" He scooped her up with one arm, sat down and replaced her on his lap. "I'll even do the cooking if you share the seat."

She allowed herself a brief second of savoring the feel of his body against hers before edging away. She knew men, and when the sun came down, they always turned less discriminating. But he'd said good-bye this morning, in no uncertain terms.

"I'll find another chair," she said.

His arm banded around her. "This is the only one."

"Bull—"

He abruptly angled his head, cutting off her words with a passionate kiss. By the time he raised his mouth, she could only blink.

"Look, Em, I'm sorry about yelling this morning. And I don't bring many people back to my trailer." He pressed his forehead against hers, his voice oddly gruff. "I'm very glad you didn't leave on that bus. But I don't want a woman with an agent. Really I don't."

"My agent isn't all that good," she said, distracted by the proximity of his mouth.

He chuckled but it lacked humor, and in fact sounded sad. However, she stopped wiggling, and let him readjust her on his lap. He didn't bring many people back. So why her?

They stared silently into the flames, but it was a comfortable silence. His heart pounded in tandem with hers, his heat forming a familiar cocoon. She couldn't recall a nicer fire.

He leaned forward and adjusted the coals for the hotdog stick, keeping her firmly wrapped in his left arm. "What are your plans for tomorrow?" he asked, settling back in the chair.

"I'm not sure." She paused, remembering Judith's insistence about visiting the apartment again. "Maybe visit the horses in the stud barn," she said. "Check with the set too. The director mentioned he might have more background work."

Dan traced his finger over the inside of her wrist. "About that university movie in Louisville, I called Tony this afternoon. He's agreed to give you an audition."

"You called him? This afternoon?" She tilted her head, struggling to understand, trying to ignore how his casual touch made her shiver with pleasure. "But that was when you didn't want me working again."

"I was just worried," he said gruffly. "Besides, you'll be safer in a union. I'm sure Tony will give you some lines."

A glow warmed her chest. Even when Dan believed she hadn't followed his directions, he'd still tried to help. He'd even called his friend. She understood he didn't want anything long term but he must care a little. And for the first time since he'd tugged her onto his lap, she completely relaxed. "Thank you," she said.

"Acting is a tough way to make a living." He cupped her face, his expression suddenly intense. "But that's what you want, right?"

"Yes, of course."

He lowered his hand and yanked the sizzling hotdogs further from the fire. "That's what I thought," he said.

Dan drained his beer, rose and tossed the can into the bin beneath the kitchen sink. The shower had stopped running. She'd be out soon. Four hotdogs, six beers and the most enjoyable campfire he'd ever shared with a woman, and he still didn't know what to do.

He hadn't made up the pullout bed in the kitchen. Not yet.

Two hours earlier, he'd resolved not to touch her. They had their night, and he didn't regret it. But he would never ask anyone to sacrifice her dreams. Forget the mind-blowing sex, the quicker he stopped this thing, the better.

Even if by some miracle she were willing to swap her stilettos for a Stetson, it wouldn't last. She'd turn bitter, wondering what might have been. Hell, she'd probably make a helluva actress. But he wouldn't be around to see it.

He sighed, trying not to picture her sleek body only fifteen feet away. One thin door, likely unlocked. Worse, he could hear every sound from the bathroom—the pad of her bare feet, the rustle of a towel…an agonized whimper.

He bolted down the hall.

"What happened, Em? Are you okay?"

The bathroom door cracked open, releasing a feminine burst of vanilla and lavender. She peered out, water still clinging to her eyelashes. "I'm fine," she whispered, "but could you come in and help me pull off some tape?"

"Sure," he said, immediately hardening in a mixture of memory and anticipation. He shoved aside his good intentions. One more night wouldn't hurt. He liked this girl, she liked him, and right now lust licked inside him like a hungry flame. His gaze lowered. She was practically naked. Her shoulders glistened invitingly, a tiny towel was wrapped like a sarong, and her beautiful breasts—

"Dammit, what have you done?" He pushed back the door and charged in, his eyes widening.

"I had to tape them. The director wanted big breasts. It was the only way to get the part."

His hands fisted. The line of skin beneath her breasts was raw and reddened. Blood trickled from beneath curled gray tape. Worse, the bottom of the tape seemed imbedded in her flesh.

"I'm a bit of a wimp about pulling it off," she went on. "But if you could find the end and yank fast... I think it's at the back." She glanced over her shoulder as though puzzled by his stillness. "The duct tape is really strong," she added. "It might need to be cut."

He automatically reached for the knife in his pocket, fighting the sick feeling in his gut. "How long did you have this on?"

"Since this morning. I forgot about it actually."

He gulped. She was no wimp. It must have hurt like hell although he shouldn't be surprised. She was resourceful, smart and courageous...and clearly would go to great lengths to break into the business. "I thought you looked a little different," he said.

"I didn't think you noticed."

"Oh, I noticed." So had every male with a pulse. And she was right. Anthony wouldn't have picked her for the part if she hadn't displayed such attractive breasts. He tucked the tip of the knife beneath the tape, forcing his hand to steady. "Don't you have a bra that does this sort of thing?" he asked.

"All my clothes are in Louisville. A nice wardrobe lady has been helping me out. They have quite a selection of jeans." She gave a rueful shrug. "But no bras."

He smiled, despite his despair. His mother hadn't been nearly as creative, insisting they sell half their horses, including his pony, to purchase her expensive show clothes. But it hadn't mattered. She'd still left.

"This is going to hurt." He paused for a moment, his fingers gripping the tape. "Is it worth it? Giving up your family for a shot at fame?"

She glanced over her shoulder, her eyes startled. "Of course not. I love my sister. And I'll go back and visit. But I need to succeed at something first."

He steeled his jaw and ripped. She winced but didn't make a sound. He dropped the tape in the trash can and gave a relieved sigh, impressed at her stoicism. "Well, you definitely succeeded in drawing Anthony's attention. That's going to take a few days to heal. Luckily you won't need to use tape again."

His left hand was still splayed over her ribs and he felt her stiffen. "Or do you? Did Anthony ask for the same look? Dammit. Look at those welts." He placed his hands on her hips, turned her toward the mirror and pulled the towel lower.

She tilted her head, frowning at her reflection. "Yes, they are bad. I'll definitely use a different tape."

He squeezed his eyes shut, then raised the towel and wrapped it around her, carefully avoiding the abrasions.

"I forgot how different I look without makeup," she said, still staring critically in the mirror. "Like a different person."

"Yes," he said. "You'll make a good actress." It ached to be this close and not touch her but if he did, it would hurt even more when she left. He backed out of the bathroom. "I'm going to make up the bed in the kitchen. You can sleep in my room."

Her head whipped around, her brown eyes so full of hurt, he had to grip the doorknob. "Not even a last night together?" she asked. "You care that little?"

"No," he said. "I care too much."

CHAPTER THIRTY-ONE

Emily pried open her eyes, clutching the pillow as memories of last night's rejection flooded back. The skin on her chest ached but not nearly as much as her heart. What man turned down strings-free sex? He must have been truly repulsed, whether it was her wet hair, lack of makeup or the ugly chafing below her breasts.

She thrust aside the sheets and immediately winced. Perhaps the skin was a little more than chafed, although it wasn't such a big deal. It certainly didn't justify Dan's expression. He'd looked stricken when he saw the tape.

Her mind still felt numb. At first she'd thought he was disappointed because her breasts were a bit smaller than initial appearances. But he'd already seen her naked and based on his performance in bed, he hadn't found them unattractive.

She squashed an ache of longing and impatiently swung from the bed. She didn't intend to moon over Dan. She'd been almost naked and he'd walked away. A guy couldn't be more blunt.

She pulled on her jeans and shirt, dragged a brush through her hair, and strode from the bedroom, feeling rather liberated. It was convenient to play a groom's role and not have to worry about hair and makeup. Certainly getting dressed in the morning was easier.

She pasted on a smile and walked into the kitchen, rather deflated to see it was empty. The pullout bed had been restored to a kitchen bench and the clock above the stove said six a.m.

Obviously, Dan was an early riser but this time he hadn't left a note. Hopefully she'd see him on set though, especially if Anthony chose her for background in a horse scene.

She moved to the kitchen window and peered outside, searching for a worker lugging a toolbox. Wrapping herself in tape again would be painful, but show biz wasn't for the faint hearted. It was too dark to see anyone so she walked down the hall and knocked on the spare bedroom door.

"Time to get up, Judith," she called.

"I'm up," Judith said. "Come in."

Emily pushed open the door. The narrow bed was made and Judith sat on the floor, surrounded by open boxes. "What are you doing?" Emily asked, her eyes widening. "That's Dan's stuff."

"He wouldn't have put me in here if it was confidential." Judith barely looked up from the papers spread on her lap. "And this explains the script. It says Tracey disappeared on a Thursday, ten days before the Derby. She was wearing a baseball hat when she disappeared."

Emily crossed her arms. "Put it away."

"But this will give us an edge. We'll know how the director wants us to look."

"Close it. Now." Emily's voice sharpened. She scooped up a picture and rammed it back into a box.

"Fine," Judith said, her voice sulky. "But that picture wasn't in the box. It was in the binder by your foot."

Emily yanked the picture out of the box and paused. A blue-eyed boy hugged a Shetland pony, his mischievous smile mirroring the pony's expression. He looked like a boy she would have liked to play with. She glanced at the lady beside him and almost stopped breathing. "Wow," she said.

"Gorgeous, isn't she? That's Dan's mother," Judith said. "She was a stunt rider and rodeo queen. She even worked in Vegas for awhile."

It took a moment for Emily to breathe again. "No wonder he likes perfect women," she managed. And Dan had the same profile, the same striking cheekbones, the same arresting eyes.

Judith snorted. "No wonder he distrusts them, you mean. His dad raised him. His mother just dropped in for visits. He wrote some cards begging her to come home and apologizing for making her sad—"

"Judith!" Emily dropped the picture back in the box. "Get out of here. Now!"

"There's not much about Tracey anyway. It's mainly horse notes." Judith rose and brushed off her jeans, not at all repentant. "Don't forget, we are here trying to figure out what happened to a missing person."

Emily shook her head, grabbed Judith's arm and yanked her from the room. "We're leaving Dan's trailer," she snapped, "and not looking sideways. In fact, we're walking out right now."

"Fine," Judith said. "But I'm surprised you don't want to read the script notes. It might help land more background, maybe even get you a line."

Emily pushed Judith down the hall and toward the kitchen door. "He trusted us."

A polite knock sounded and they both gave a guilty jump. Emily hesitated then reached over and cautiously turned the knob. A gray-haired woman in a blue windbreaker stood on the doorstep, a bulky envelope in her hand.

"Delivery for Emily," the woman said.

"That's me. Thanks." Puzzled, Emily took the package and closed the door.

"Who knows you're here?" Judith asked, watching as Emily ripped open the seal.

"Only Dan. But he wouldn't send anything. He didn't even leave a note…" Emily's words trailed off as she opened the envelope, her throat constricting as she pulled out a perfectly sized, lace push-up bra.

CHAPTER THIRTY-TWO

"We need a female groom to push a wheelbarrow to the manure pit," the casting director said. "It's a wet gloomy morning."

"That sounds easy," Emily whispered to Judith. "It's not even raining."

Judith pointed at the large industrial fan and extensive network of hoses. "Looks like they plan to do some drenching." Her eyes flickered over Emily's chest. "Bet you could get the job. That fancy bra is doing its thing."

Emily's gaze drifted toward the barn aisle. She hadn't had a chance to thank Dan for the thoughtful gift. However, it looked like he and Anthony were finally leaving the interior set and coming this way. She clasped her hands, surprised at her rush of nerves. This heart-pounding excitement was far worse than any high school crush.

"Do it," Judith said, giving her a poke. "You can check out Billy's cottage later."

Emily pulled her attention back to the casting director and stepped forward, joining a line of four other women.

"Any union here?" the man asked. No one answered. He gave a humorless chuckle. "Guess none of our union performers want the job. Okay, you're going to get a little wet. And the wind will be blowing."

One of the ladies shrank back, shaking her head.

The man was still talking but Emily could no longer concentrate. Dan had arrived. He spotted her and a slow smile curved his face. He looked deep in her eyes, not at her chest, despite the scooped shirt.

"Thank you," she mouthed.

He nodded. His gaze drifted to the black hoses. His smile flattened.

Anthony's assistant gestured at Emily. "You did a good job yesterday. We like you for this scene."

Dan abruptly stepped forward. "Pick someone else," he said.

The assistant shrugged. "How about you in the green shirt?"

The lady in the green tank top nodded happily.

"The rest of you can wait for the next scene," the assistant said, gesturing at the remaining background.

"Not you, Emily," Dan said. "I need someone else in the gate."

She stared blankly. Even Judith, who understood set procedures, appeared puzzled.

"Let's get a coffee first," Dan said. He slipped a hand over her elbow, gestured at someone and guided her to a spot at the rail. But he didn't speak, not until they each had a coffee in their hand and the attendant had shuffled away.

"Sorry," he finally said.

Emily studied his face over her hot cup. He looked rested, handsome and somewhat sheepish.

She shook her head in confusion. "I don't understand. Why did you send this lovely bra—thank you very much by the way—if you're going to stop me from getting these parts?"

"It's cold this morning. That rain machine can cause ear infections. You might be under it for over an hour. The water hasn't been tested." He paused. "And I guess I don't like to share."

"But you didn't…last night, we didn't." She stopped talking and pulled the lid off her cup, her confusion switching to annoyance. "So you pretend to need me in a gate scene knowing that completely blows the chance at any more groom background?"

He looked at her as if she spoke a foreign language. "But I do want you for the gate." He glanced at Anthony, his voice lowering. "You're non-union. I can look after you better if it's my scene."

"Oh," she managed. A warm flush spread through her chest. Suddenly she wasn't annoyed at all.

"With me, you won't get hosed." His gaze slid over her chest, his eyes glinting with amusement. "And you'll be wearing a protection vest. A really big one."

"I'll wear a suit of armor if necessary. And five layers of dirt on my face."

His smile deepened. "When we first met, you were dressed for a party shoot. You looked very different."

She automatically smoothed her shirt, swiping off a piece of straw. A week ago, she would have taken such a comment as criticism. Now though, she wasn't sure. There was too much approval in his eyes, in his voice.

"Jeans are more practical," she said. "Besides they don't want the grooms with obvious makeup or fancy hair. The wardrobe department is very strict." She gave a rueful shrug. "I already tried for more glamour."

"I bet you did." Still smiling, he glanced over his shoulder at the waiting golf cart. "I have to go. Don't get in any trouble, okay?"

"Will I really be breaking from the gate?" she asked, wishing he'd linger.

"Hell, no." He chuckled. "You'll just be sitting on a horse. We have to back them from the gate when Reckless, played by Bruno, rears."

"Okay," she said. "But if you need anyone to break from the gate, I can do that too."

"You've ridden from the gate? At Three Brooks?"

She opened her mouth then stopped, reluctant to stretch the truth. "Well, it was just a pony."

"Your pony? Peanut? He's probably not as explosive as a racehorse." But Dan turned back to her, ignoring the waiting golf cart. "How did your little guy do in the gate? He probably couldn't see over the bars."

"He couldn't. But he behaved very well when he was standing there. He wanted to eat grass though and was rather annoyed there wasn't any hay in the starting gate. When the door opened, he started bucking. I lasted maybe three seconds. It was still fun though."

Dan's eyes twinkled. "I had a Shetland pony who loved to eat too. I fell off every time he stopped quick. Mischievous fellow but damn fun. And so tiny I could almost pick him up."

"Yes." She sighed with nostalgia. "I didn't like it when I grew too big to ride. It was fun sharing Peanut with the other little kids, but I missed our adventures."

"That didn't happen to me," Dan said. "My mother sold Silver before I outgrew him."

"I'm sorry." She gave his arm a sympathetic squeeze. "My father did the same thing when we needed money. But Jenna found Peanut and somehow convinced the owner to sell him back on credit. We gathered pop cans for a year and half."

Dan's eyes darkened. She realized she was still touching his arm, and yanked her hand back. According to Judith, he was one of the most private people in the industry. Already she could feel curious stares.

"Sorry." She flattened her palms against her sides, appalled at her familiarity. "I know you don't want rumors—"

But she stopped talking, had to, because his mouth covered hers in a quick and totally tender kiss.

He straightened, his expression enigmatic. "See you in a few hours, Em."

Ignoring the gawking production crew, he stepped into the waiting golf cart. She stared after him in bemusement, her heart pounding, her hand pressed to her tingling lips.

CHAPTER THIRTY-THREE

Judith charged into the stud barn. "Did you check the apartment yet?" she asked, her face flushed from running.

"Couldn't," Emily said. "The door was padlocked when I arrived." She stepped back to Barney's shoulder. "But watch this trick. He can grab my empty cup and shake it, as if he wants more coffee. He even rolls his lip. I have to show Dan. I think Barney is definitely worth keeping."

"It's padlocked?" Judith clutched the stall door, ignoring Barney's inquisitive muzzle. "But I wanted to take another look at the apartment."

"There's nothing up there," Emily said. "The place is basically empty." She waved the cup again, keen to demonstrate Barney's ability. "Check this out."

"I don't have time for useless tricks," Judith snapped. "Not when a groom has been missing for years. Why are you in such a good mood anyway? Never mind." She blew out a resigned sigh. "Everyone's talking about how Dan kissed you. No wonder you both are walking around with foolish grins."

Emily stepped from the stall, rather guilty she was so happy. But Judith was right. For the last hour, ever since Dan had publicly kissed her, she'd been grinning in delight. She just prayed the kiss was as important as it had felt.

"It was just a little kiss," Emily said, unable to wipe the smile off her face. "It doesn't mean much. He probably does that a lot nearing the end of a shoot."

"No, he doesn't," Judith said. "Not according to my Internet research. I'm going to try that lock."

She stomped down the aisle to the apartment. Emily followed, hopeful that Judith would talk a little more about Dan rather than worry about a damp and deserted apartment.

"There's really nothing up there," Emily called. "The hot water doesn't even work. I had to shower down here. Did you say Dan was smiling too?"

Judith glanced sideways at the last stall then jerked to a stop, so abruptly Emily almost bumped into her.

"What is it?" Emily asked.

"Look at the heart carved in the wood." Judith pointed at the wall. "The T must be Tracey. Men don't draw hearts. But who's R?"

Emily stared at the crude heart carved on the side of the stall. She'd seen it earlier but hadn't considered it important: T loves R.

"Probably Reckless," Emily said, remembering all the hearts she'd drawn with Peanut's name. "Girls love their horses."

"Or maybe it was another guy," Judith said, "and Hamilton was jealous. If he set up Tracey in the apartment but she fell in love with someone else, he couldn't have been pleased."

Emily nodded thoughtfully. Billy *had* been weird about the gate. He would have known if Tracey received any visitors. Maybe Billy had served as Hamilton's watchdog. Maybe he'd been the one to tell Hamilton about Tracey's new boyfriend. After all, he had said something to Emily about not telling Hamilton the night she was late. Had acted like it was a big favor.

"I only have another hour before my scene," Emily said slowly, "but let's stop by Billy's cottage and try asking a few more questions."

"Good idea," Judith said, already turning toward the door.

However, forty-five minutes later they'd learned nothing about the possibility of a boyfriend. Billy barely responded to their questions, or their presence. He hunched in his chair and stared morosely out the window, his conversation reduced to grunts.

Emily shoved a strand of hair behind her ear and continued bagging old beer cans. At least she had the chance to clean a little more, with the security of Judith's company. And today Billy didn't seem to mind that they were removing his cans and bottles. The refund would pay for his groceries for at least a week.

She glanced at Judith who no longer pretended to clean, but instead was searching for more of Tracey's belongings.

"Billy," Emily asked, rather worried about the depleted contents of his fridge. "Have you had other visitors lately? Did anyone else bring you food?"

He looked up, blinking, as though surprised to see her. "Nope," he mumbled. "No visitors since the snow melt."

The expiry date on the milk carton showed that wasn't true.

Judith kicked a box in frustration. "We better go. He can't remember anything. Probably R was Reckless. Besides, you have to report to set."

"I hate to leave him," Emily whispered. "He needs help. Do you know if he has any relatives?"

"I did some poking on the Internet but didn't find anything." Judith pinched the bridge of her nose. "I put Tracey's duffle bag in the hall closet. We'll have to tell someone about it. I only wish we had found something else, something that would spark an investigation."

"Yes, but at least his place is cleaner."

"That's not top of my priority list," Judith said.

Emily smiled at Monty, recognizing the helpful wrangler. Today he led a very tall bay with a wide chest and thick black mane.

"Here's your horse," Monty said, stopping in front of her. "I'll be close by, ready to take him back to the barn when you're finished."

"Thanks." Emily gulped, staring up at the tiny saddle perched on the big Thoroughbred. The horse looked at least seventeen hands, and he was as solid as he was tall. "He's sure big. Will he even fit in the starting gate?"

Monty nodded. "Dan had us lead them in and back them out twice already."

"Where is Dan?" She glanced around for the golf cart.

"With the AD. They'll be along once we're ready. Lizzie is in charge right now." Monty chuckled. "She picked this big guy out especially for you."

"Isn't that nice of her," Emily said, unsurprised. The glare Lizzie had shot her when she assembled with the other gate riders had been noticeably hostile. "Does this fellow do something I should know about?" she added.

"Just watch your legs against the bars of the gate. He has lots of mane so you have plenty to grab when he goes up in the air. He knows his job. Just let him do his thing."

"What exactly is his thing?" Emily warily tightened her helmet.

"He's a copycat. He'll probably be in the stall next to Bruno. They want to show how dangerous Reckless was in the gate, how his rearing affected the other horses. You know how it spreads when a horse freaks out."

Emily nodded and squared her shoulders. "Okay. Can you give me a leg up?"

The obliging wrangler boosted her into the saddle. She guided the horse toward the four other riders. He had a lovely walk, alert and eager, and he veered toward the gate as though keen to do his job.

"Not yet," she said, lifting a rein and turning him back toward the mounted group of riders.

The lady on Bruno was clearly a stunt rider. She slouched in the saddle, sipping on a bottle of water and studying the teenager on the gray with relaxed good humor. "Don't you worry, sweetie," she said. "This is a simple scene. You just stand in the gate for a minute or two and then we're done."

The girl on the gray didn't seem at all reassured. Her eyes were huge in her pale face. She sat ramrod stiff, keeping a chokehold on her horse. Emily immediately felt better. She might not be the best rider today, but she certainly wasn't the worst.

The stunt rider gave Emily a quick perusal. "Great. We have our fifth rider. Although we'll probably have to wait another hour for Anthony." She twisted in the saddle and hollered at an attendant. "Bring these riders some water. It's hot up here."

The girl on the gray declined a drink, choosing to keep both fists wrapped around the reins, but the other riders quickly accepted.

"Thanks for getting us the water," Emily said, smiling gratefully at the stunt rider.

"No problem. It gets hot with helmets and vests, especially mid-afternoon. I galloped here when I was a teenager. Mrs. Hamilton made sure we had plenty of water. She was always doing nice things like that."

Emily leaned forward in the saddle. "Did you know Tracey, Reckless's groom?"

"Sure did." The stunt rider tilted her head. The muscles in her arms and neck rippled as she drained the bottle. She swiped her mouth with the back of her arm and resumed talking. "Reckless should have won the Derby that year. Sad about Tracey."

"Sad? But maybe she left with a boyfriend and is living happily somewhere."

"No way. She wouldn't have left Reckless. They had a real bond. That famous incident in the swimming pool really happened." The rider looked at Emily, a knowing smile lifting the corners of her mouth. "And she didn't have a boyfriend. Mr. Hamilton was the one who reported her missing. They were exceedingly close, if you get my drift."

"No boyfriend? Well, do you think he—?" Emily paused, scrambling for a tactful word.

"Killed her?" The rider shrugged and flipped her empty bottle to a watchful wrangler. "I don't know. There were always whispers but he appeared to adore her. And she seemed to feel the same way."

"What about Billy, the caretaker by the stud barn? Did you know him?"

"Don't remember him at all." She gave another dismissive shrug. "I was a rider. That's what paved my way into the movies." She glanced toward the starting gate and straightened in the saddle. "Here *he* comes. Let's make this good."

Emily glanced over her shoulder. Dan strode toward them, followed by the assistant director and two men in a dolly truck.

"I thought they'd use a steady cam for this shot," the stunt rider said. "Maybe the gate is going to open after all. The dolly can drive beside us but it leaves tire tracks."

Emily nodded, not wanting to show her ignorance. She didn't know the various camera names or methods, but it certainly was exciting to be in the middle of the action. There was even a fake horse with a moving head mounted on a truck. Obviously it was intended for actors, and simulated a galloping horse without the inherent danger.

One thing was apparent, the five horses chosen to enter the starting gate were all pros. They stood quietly, unfazed by the increasing commotion. It must have taken Dan a long time to find them, or maybe he had trained the horses himself.

"These animals are going to act a lot different in a few minutes," the stunt rider said. "Dan does awesome work. It's a huge boost to have his name on your resume. I bet he won't let the director's niece ride, even though Anthony ramped down this scene."

Emily glanced to her left. The nervous young girl was the director's niece; that explained a lot. Remarkably, the gray horse she rode didn't seem upset, tolerating the hammerlock on his mouth with amazing grace.

"Hello, everyone," Dan said, striding into the middle of the circle and looking at the stunt rider. "Good to see you on this one, Mitzie. We're going to load the first three, then pick it up with you and Reckless." His gaze shot to Emily and then to her horse. He frowned. "I had you on the gray, Emily."

He walked closer, patted her horse's neck then slipped his hand beneath the girth. "Your saddle is a little loose. Let's tighten this a few holes." His voice lowered. "We can switch you to the gray, if you'd like. He's more seasoned and extremely quiet. You'll be less likely to bang your legs too. "

"This horse is fine," she said, guessing the director's niece would be even more terrified on a bigger horse.

Dan gave an appreciative nod, his eyes as brilliant blue as the sky. "Okay," he said. "Remember, just hang on. And it's okay to look scared. In fact, we want that. The gate crew will lead you in, Reckless will rear, the others will get upset and then we back you out. Simple?"

"Absolutely," she said. His quiet confidence was infectious and she was eager to see Bruno's imitation of Reckless. She already knew the horse could rear when led, but it would be

much more dramatic in the narrow starting gate. And she'd
have a front row seat.

"Your hands are okay in those gloves?"

She nodded happily. Her hands were healing well and with
the riding gloves Dan had supplied, they didn't hurt at all. He
squeezed her boot, making her heart skip a beat, then turned
and headed toward the director's niece.

Mitzie frowned. "That's weird. I've never seen him stop
and personally check a saddle. Or are you a relative too?" The
condescension in her voice was unmistakable.

Emily paused. Back at Three Brooks she'd openly flaunted
her connections. Sure, people might resent it. But they tended
to give preferential treatment once they knew the powerful
Derek Burke was her brother-in-law. Here, she'd worked
harder than ever before. She'd actually achieved more without
Burke or Jenna's help. And it felt good.

"No, I came on the background bus." She raised her head.
"But I stayed to clean stalls and do whatever work was
available."

Mitzie's eyes narrowed. "Now I know why you look
familiar. You were the non-union girl in that bolting scene
yesterday. Why didn't you say so?" She gave an approving
nod. "I thought I was stuck working with a bunch of
weekend riders."

Emily gave a feeble smile. Weekend? She hadn't ridden in
years.

"You should ask Dan to get you a speaking line," Mitzie
went on. "That would get you in the union. He seems to like
you and he has tons of clout."

Emily glanced down, pretending to straighten her horse's
mane. Dan might like her and want to keep her safe, but
unfortunately his goal seemed to be getting her off the set.
And away from him.

"But maybe you don't like cameras." Mitzie shrugged. "I understand that. Not all beautiful people want to be in the movies."

Emily touched her cheek, remembering she wore no makeup, but the outgoing Mitzie continued talking, apparently sincere. "I have a friend who worked as a wrangler for twenty-four years. She loved it."

"I do like working with the horses," Emily said. "They're very relaxing. And Dan is…"

"On every woman's top ten-to-do list."

Emily flushed but Mitzie didn't notice her discomfort.

"Dream on," Mitzie said. "He doesn't takes advantage of his looks, or his position. He wants a stay-at-home ranch girl. His mother craved the limelight. Wasn't so happy about marriage and motherhood. Awesome rider though."

Emily pushed her feet further in the stirrups, uncomfortable with the gossip. However, the chance to learn more about Dan was irresistible. "You knew his mother?" She sneaked a peek at Dan. Luckily he was out of earshot, still reassuring the frightened rider on the gray.

"A little." Mitzie shrugged. "We worked together on some stunts before. She ended up in a chair."

"A chair?" Emily gaped. "Executed?"

"No, stupid, a wheelchair. She's in a bad way. Happens to a lot of people." Mitzie jabbed her thumb at the girl on the gray, her expression darkening. "And Anthony should have known better than to saddle Dan with such a timid and inexperienced rider."

Emily's hands tightened around the reins, but Mitzie didn't seem to mean anything personal about the 'stupid' comment. She seemed more concerned about everyone's riding ability. "I'm not so experienced either," Emily admitted.

"But you're not timid. And we're just sitting in the gate. It's like putting a quarter in and enjoying the ride. Who wouldn't like that?"

Emily laughed, enjoying this woman's attitude. She didn't even mind being called stupid. No wonder the wranglers always looked happy; they were able to hang out with Dan and all the cool stunt riders. Although Lizzie didn't look very happy, standing by the rail. The more Emily and Mitzie laughed, the more Lizzie glowered.

"Picture is up," someone called.

Emily turned away from Lizzie's sour face. A man appeared beside Emily's horse and slipped a leather line through the bridle. She assumed he was a real horse handler, not an actor. He moved with deft assurance, acting just like the gate crew at Three Brooks.

She gathered her reins and stared between the horse's ears, pretending she was about to break from the gate and ride in a real workout. A few things felt different. The saddle was smaller, the stirrups shorter. However, the horse was solid and real, and soon she forgot about the cameras.

She couldn't forget about Dan though. He moved with athletic grace, talking to each rider, communicating with each horse. He gave her a last encouraging nod, clearly trusting her to do this right. And she was determined to justify that trust.

A voice—sounded like Anthony's—called, "Action," and the attendant turned and led her horse into the first slot of the starting gate. It was definitely cramped. Her knee scraped the metal side, and for a moment she feared they wouldn't fit. But the door clanged shut behind her. The attendant jumped up on a narrow ledge, still holding her horse's head, and it was all so controlled her breathing steadied.

She stared through the grill. The dirt track stretched in front of her, vast and empty—except for several cameras in front of the gate. And of course, Dan. She tried not to think about him, didn't want to be distracted. Beside, this was a unique experience and with a little imagination, she could pretend the gates were about to crack open, releasing five thundering horses, including the Derby hopeful.

Her horse stared straight ahead, his ears pricked. He seemed poised to run. Did he think this was real? But no, his body felt as relaxed as it had outside the gate, as though aware he was a movie horse now. Not a racehorse.

"Get ready," the attendant murmured.

She glanced sideways. The girl on the gray was next to her but Mitzie and Bruno were four slots down, as far away as possible, which meant Emily's face wouldn't even be recognizable on the big screen. She and her horse were just fillers, pure background. Oddly though, it didn't matter. The satisfaction of being on set, of working together to make this movie, filled her with a sense of community and accomplishment.

Steel clanged. Someone shouted. Movement flickered in her right eye as Bruno rose in a perfect rear, his hooves waving threateningly against the door. Her horse tossed his head and clearly had been waiting for his cue. He gave a controlled rear, barely twelve inches off the ground, then dropped to the ground and reared again. But this time much higher.

It was totally awesome. She gripped his mane, stared straight ahead and tried not to grin.

Bruno was killing it. Dan allowed himself a brief moment of satisfaction then signaled again with his hand. The horse rose one last time, flailing his legs. Mitzie cursed, leaped from the saddle and scrambled nimbly through the bars of the gate. Bruno continued his rodeo, the impact even more powerful with an empty saddle. He looked like a rogue. Unrideable. Unraceable.

Emily's mount, the big bay from Churchill Downs, was totally hamming it up, tossing his head and giving his trademark baby rears. That horse was a pro and originally Dan had planned to load him in the stall next to Bruno.

There was always an element of danger though, especially in the confines of a starting gate, so he'd shuffled Emily further away from the action.

No need to worry about scaring her though. Her eyes sparkled. She may not be a stunt rider but she definitely shared their joy of an adrenaline rush.

Relieved, he glanced back at the perfect row of rearing horses, stunned to see tears dripping down the face of Anthony's niece. A little fear was good, but tears? Exercise riders were damn tough. They didn't cry.

"Cut!" Anthony called.

Dan signaled and the row of horses planted their feet, eyes glued to his hand.

"Did you bump your leg, Leslie?" Dan asked, stepping closer and peering through the grill of stall three.

She shook her head, tears tracking her cheeks. "I c-can't do this anymore. I'm too scared. Please don't tell my uncle."

Dan grit his teeth, then turned away. "Back this horse out," he said to the gate crew. "Send him back to the barn."

Anthony yanked off his headset and rushed forward. "What's going on?"

"This horse has reared six times today," Dan said. "He's done."

"It couldn't have been six," Anthony said. "We just started."

"Sorry. My mistake," Dan said. "I used him earlier this morning." His gaze met Emily's, and she gave him such a sweet smile, his frustration drained away. "We can move the bay up a stall," he added. "Would that work?"

"Let's hope so," Anthony snapped. "Back them all out and take a short break. We'll go with four horses." He stalked back to the cameras but his mild reaction made Dan suspect he was rather relieved his niece was out of the picture.

"Good job, everyone," Dan said, moving up the line, waiting until the horses had backed out of the starting gate.

He signaled to Lizzie for a dismount. Some people treated their mounts like rocking chairs. However, he liked his riders off whenever possible, in order to avoid unnecessary back and leg problems, for the horses.

"It's not a scheduled break yet," Monty asked. "Do you still want the horses watered?"

"Yes. And stand them in the shade." Dan frowned. "Next time, triple check the saddles. Emily's girth was loose."

"The girl on the big bay? The one who built the paddock?" Monty shook his head. "Wasn't me, boss. Lizzie saddled the bay."

Dan swung around. "Emily built the paddock? I thought Lizzie did."

"No. Emily dragged the rails from the leftover pile on the backstretch. Must have walked half a mile. She was worried about the lame horse coughing. Wanted to make sure he had a safe place outside."

Dan dragged a hand through his hair. His impressions of Emily were conflicting. He'd thought she wasn't safe handling the horses in the stud barn, that she didn't know much about horse management. Yet many of those impressions had been shaped by Lizzie. "Those two horses in the stud barn," he asked thoughtfully, "are they hard to handle?"

"Not at all," Monty said. "They're perfectly behaved boys. Probably why Emily cares about them so much."

"Probably," Dan said, his narrowed gaze searching the set for Lizzie.

CHAPTER THIRTY-FOUR

Emily pulled off her helmet and wiped her hot brow. She couldn't count the number of times they'd walked in and out of the starting gate. Judith estimated an hour of shooting resulted in a minute of useable film. Since it had taken four hours to shoot the gate scene, including the required breaks for the horses, that ratio meant approximately three minutes would be in the movie.

Dependable Monty led her horse back to the barn. She wished she could follow. But Anthony hadn't offered any more background so it seemed inevitable that she'd be returning to Louisville tonight. She fought a pang in her chest and glanced around for Dan.

However, he'd already moved down the track in preparation for the next scene. She understood now why he could pick and choose his movie contracts. His horses behaved perfectly, even under extraordinary pressure. But it was his kindness to the director's niece that had impressed her the most. He'd understood the girl's fear, covering for her even when questioned by Anthony. No wonder his staff adored him.

Sighing, she reached into her bag and pulled out Billy's ball cap. Her jeans were dusty, she wore no makeup, but at least the hat would hide her helmet hair. Besides, it wasn't worth the trouble to obsess over her looks; Dan didn't care about appearances.

The fact that he'd kissed her earlier, in front of the cast and crew, left her baffled. However, it had definitely raised her status on set. An assistant had already pressed a flavored bottle of water into her hand, making her feel as pampered as a real movie star. There was no doubt she'd be welcome in the big dining tent tonight. Maybe that's why he'd done it, to make sure she had a comfortable last supper.

"We better go," a lady said. "The theater fundraiser starts at seven."

Emily turned toward the familiar voice. Mr. and Mrs. Hamilton stood by the rail, only ten feet away. Emily smiled and Mrs. Hamilton waved a friendly acknowledgement. Mr. Hamilton, however, charged forward, his eyes riveted to her forehead.

"Where did you get that hat?" he asked.

Emily automatically reached up and touched the brim of the ball cap. "Billy gave it to me."

"You're lying."

"I certainly am not." Emily stiffened, annoyed at both his words and his aggression. However, this man was the property owner, a movie investor as well as Mrs. Hamilton's husband. She willed her voice to remain level. "If you want me to return it though, that's no problem."

She pulled off the hat, holding it in front of her.

"What were you doing in his cottage?" Mr. Hamilton snapped, his eyes narrowing to slits.

"Cleaning." She gripped the hat with both hands, trying to control her temper. Mr. Hamilton was acting like a first-class jerk, all upset over a hat while Billy lived in squalor. "While we're discussing Billy," she said, quite proud at how she remained calm, "you should be aware he needs more in-home assistance."

"Assistance? You were inside?" Mr. Hamilton's throat moved convulsively. "Did you find anything else...from Reckless's days?"

Emily shook her head. No way was she mentioning the duffle bag. Clearly Judith had been right to suspect this man. His mouth clenched so tightly, his lips turned white. And he only worried about what she'd found. He hadn't shown a speck of concern for poor Billy.

"Come on, Thomas. It's just an old hat." Mrs. Hamilton shot Emily an apologetic look and placed a manicured hand on her husband's arm. "Let her keep it. She's been working in the sun all afternoon."

She tried to urge her husband away, but Mr. Hamilton remained stiff legged, staring at the cap in Emily's hands as though he wanted to snatch it from her fingers.

"Hi, everyone." Judith walked over, her voice artificially cheerful. "That starting gate scene was fun to watch. Emily, your horse looked quite wild."

No one answered. Finally Mr. and Mrs. Hamilton turned and walked toward a waiting car.

"I heard him freaking out," Judith whispered, her face an oyster gray. "Was it the hat? Did he recognize it?"

"He sure did," Emily said. "Thanks for coming over. And now I really do believe he murdered that poor groom." Goose bumps chilled the back of her neck.

"I always thought so." Judith's pensive gaze followed the powerful car. "But it was a long time ago. And there's no way to prove it."

Emily glanced down at the cap, turning it over and examining the material. It appeared unworn, with no marks except a 'one size fits all' tag. "There must be someone who'd know more. What about Shania? You mentioned she always researches her roles."

"Yes, but she isn't in these scenes. Besides, she has bodyguards; she wouldn't talk to us peons." Judith hesitated, her eyes flaring with hope. "It's obvious she likes Dan though. Maybe you could ask him to call."

"I can't ask him to do that."

"But this is important. That man likely killed Tracey." Judith's voice rose. "And we can't let him get away with it. Don't you want justice?"

"Yes, of course. But I'm leaving tonight—"

"You have to do this first. You know Dan better than me." Judith's voice turned persuasive. "While you're at it, you could tell him about Billy. Take him to the cottage, show him Tracey's bag. Once he sees that dump firsthand, you know he'll help. Someone like Dan wouldn't leave Billy in those conditions."

Emily kicked at a pebble. Yes, Dan was tough but kind. He'd never stand back and ignore someone in need. She'd seen evidence of that firsthand. And he had the power to make things happen. *But Shania?*

She forced a strained smile and rubbed her mouth. The grit from the track seemed to be caked to her skin and teeth. "Great," she said. "You want me to ask him to talk to Shania, one of the most beautiful people in the world. Famous, rich and single."

"But it's for an important cause," Judith said. "Besides you're leaving anyway, so it doesn't matter if they hook up. And considering that he slept in the kitchen last night, I gather you aren't together anyway."

"Good point," Emily said.

CHAPTER THIRTY-FIVE

"Martini shot!"

The entire crew blew a collective sigh of relief at Anthony's pronouncement. The last shot of the evening was always a relief, but particularly for Dan. This was the second night in a row he needed to stop Emily from climbing on that bus.

He checked his watch then signaled Lizzie to take the horse. It took a few extra seconds to snag her attention. She'd been avoiding him all afternoon, ever since he'd grilled her with several pointed questions. She'd denied claiming she built the paddock, even suggesting he'd misunderstood, but her body language indicated otherwise.

He hadn't vented too much about her claim that the horses in the stud barn were dangerous—he should have checked that himself—but the hay fiasco was another matter. She was supposed to protect his wranglers, not bully them. No, his trust in Lizzie had eroded, and once that was gone, it was difficult to have any sort of relationship. Another warning and she'd be handed an immediate plane ticket home.

He strode from the interior set toward the door. The bus wasn't scheduled to leave until two hours after the last scene, but he hoped to find Emily before that. He skirted two cameras and a mock bale of hay, breathing a relieved sigh when he escaped into the relative quiet outside the barn.

He rounded the far corner so fast, so preoccupied, he almost bumped into Emily.

"Hi," she said. "I wanted to see you before I left."

"Don't go," he said. He hadn't intended to be so blunt, and his abrupt words obviously surprised her. Hell, they surprised him.

She blinked up at him. Tendrils of hair escaped from beneath her ball cap, dirt smudged her left cheek, and a smattering of fresh freckles covered her nose. She'd never looked more beautiful. Something yanked at his chest, and it felt like he had run a mile. "Stay with me," he said, "until the end of the movie."

"Stay?" Her eyes widened. "You mean in the guest room?"

He caught her hand, wincing at the reddened welts. "I was hoping my room," he said, "but wherever you want to sleep is fine. Just stay."

"I have to talk to you about something first."

He loosened her hand in resignation, knowing what was coming. She wanted his help getting a speaking role. He'd been asked to use his influence so many times before, it was par for the course. Expected even. But it still bothered him. "Go ahead," he said.

"Billy, the retired man in the caretaker's cottage, has some sort of dementia. He's a hoarder too. His place is a mess. He gave me this." She tapped the cap on her head. "This cap," she added, as though expecting a reaction.

"Very nice," he said cautiously.

Her grave eyes remained locked on his face. "I don't want to leave until he has more help. Normally we'd tell the Hamiltons. He's their responsibility, not the movie's. But when Judith and I were cleaning Billy's cottage, we found the missing groom's duffle bag." She sucked in a breath. "Judith and I think Thomas Hamilton killed her."

His hands dropped to his sides, and for a moment he couldn't speak. Emily always surprised him, but this...this was astounding. "You've been cleaning for this man?" he asked. For some reason, that knowledge was important. Actresses didn't scrub; at least the ones he had known didn't.

She nodded. "It's hopeless though. He's lonely and doesn't have any visitors, and he's not eating properly. His personal care isn't up to snuff either. I can't leave without telling someone." She nibbled at her lip. "And we think he knows something about Tracey. Mr. Hamilton turned white when he saw this hat. And Shania might know more but she's unapproachable, and the director doesn't even look at us—"

"Hey." He stepped closer and wrapped her in his arms. "We'll sort it out. Is the old man okay for tonight?"

She nodded. The brim of the cap hit his shirt and flipped backwards. He caught it in the air and studied the inscription. Typical Derby issue, year 1994. It looked authentic, definitely old style and not shaped like current ball caps.

"This is the hat Hamilton saw?" he asked.

"Yes. His face turned white, and he asked where I found it. Demanded actually."

"I see." Dan slipped his hand beneath Emily's hair, absently rubbing the base of her neck. Tracey Walker had disappeared two weeks before the Derby and never resurfaced. The duffle bag seemed more significant than the cap. She probably wouldn't voluntarily leave her bag. But anyone who knew Tracey was long gone.

"Mitzie, your stunt rider, worked here the same time as Tracey," Emily said, as if sharing his thoughts. "She might know something. And apparently Shania researches all the characters she plays."

He smiled, impressed with Emily's quickness. "Shania is known for her research," he admitted. "I'll talk to her and also Mitzie." He shook his head, still absorbing the information. "How did you run into the caretaker?"

"I met him walking to the stud barn. He loves doughnuts. So later, after you fired me, I had more time to visit."

His throat tightened. "Lizzie won't be around the little barn anymore," he said, dragging his gaze away from Emily's reddened hands. "Monty will be in charge. I mistakenly thought those horses were too much for you. I was mistaken about several things. I'm sorry."

"So I didn't do anything wrong? I was okay with the horses?" She tilted her head, relief coloring her face.

"More than okay," he said gruffly. "If you didn't want to be an actress, I'd hire you in a minute."

"But I don't want to be an actress. It isn't what I expected. And it's not nearly as much fun as wrangling."

"Hey, Dan." Anthony called, striding past with his hovering assistant. "It's all set. We can film the crowd at Churchill on Wednesday."

Dan nodded but looked back at Emily. It was hard to believe she no longer wanted to be an actress, especially after the way she'd worked. There hadn't been a thing she wouldn't do, from tossing hay bales to jumping in front of runaway horses. A paycheck had been important, but her career, more so.

"What about the university movie?" He tilted his head, studying her reaction. "It's a chance to audition for a speaking role. You won't get anything here but background."

The last wasn't quite true. He could ask Anthony to give her some lines. But he didn't want Emily to know that; experience had made him distrustful. People said anything, did anything, for a chance to be on stage. And later they pushed everyone aside running out the door, feverishly chasing the next big opportunity.

"A speaking role isn't important," she said. "I was a little lost when I came here. I wanted to make some money and do something for my sister." She flashed a rueful smile, but he caught a hint of wistfulness.

"And now?"

"Now if we can help Billy, maybe find out what happened to Tracey, that would be plenty."

Hope buoyed in his chest like a hot balloon. "Then I think you better stay with me until the wrap party," he said. "Twenty-year-old mysteries don't get solved overnight."

"Yes," Dan said, adjusting the phone against his ear. "It's a Derby cap with the horse's name. Mitzie said they were never released. Did they show up in any of your research?"

Emily sipped her wine and peeked at his face. Dan had been talking to Shania for at least fifteen minutes and it was clear the actress was delighted to hear from him. It was equally clear he was determined to keep the conversation on a business footing.

She shifted in the kitchen chair, still amazed that any man could remain immune to someone as beautiful as Shania. Emily had ducked into Dan's bathroom for a quick shower, but there hadn't been time for primping. He'd been in a hurry, insisting on grilling her a thick steak before going inside to make the calls.

Until now, she'd forgotten her face was bare, her hair still damp. It was rather intimidating picturing the beautiful movie star at the other end of Dan's phone.

As if sensing her thoughts, Dan leaned over and squeezed her hand. Her heart kicked with pleasure and she stopped worrying about her dripping hair. No doubt about it, he wasn't swayed by high fashion. Besides, he already knew the location of every freckle on her body.

"Thanks, Shania," he said. "See you later."

He cut the connection, his voice grave. "Those ball caps were ordered but never distributed to staff. Tracey had the only one. She wore it for the official photo with Reckless, taken the day before she disappeared."

Both of them were silent for a moment, staring at the hat lying benignly on the table.

"Tracey might have given it to Billy," she said, gripping Dan's hand like a lifeline. "Or she could have left it, or—"

"Or Billy might have killed her," he said gently.

"It wasn't Billy." She shook her head. "He gave me the hat. It was Hamilton who reacted."

"I think we have to consider all the scenarios," Dan said, his face grave. "Shania confirmed Mitzie's statement that it was Hamilton who reported Tracey missing. And you said Billy is forgetful. He may not have remembered he was hiding the hat."

She pressed her arms over her stomach, feeling slightly sick. "If Billy did kill her, what will happen? How can you question someone with dementia?"

Dan dragged a regretful hand over his jaw. "I'll visit tomorrow. Try not to scare him. It would help if you came along. There might be a simple explanation."

"Maybe. But it doesn't seem like anything good will come out of it."

"No," he said softly, "it doesn't."

Emily slapped down her ace with a whoop of delight and leaped on Dan's lap. "I finally won a hand. You're very good. Montana cowboys must play a lot of cards."

There was no question where she'd be sleeping tonight. And thanks to Dan's entertaining company, along with several highly contested card games, she'd managed to stop fretting about Billy's possible involvement in Tracey's disappearance.

She glanced down the hall to the spare bedroom, her smile fading. "There's something I have to admit. It's been bothering me all day."

She picked up the cards, shuffling the deck with studious concentration, afraid to see the condemnation in his face. "You know how a lot of people can get obsessed over movies," she said, "and anyone involved with them. It affects how they act, the things they do. Even though they're still a good person."

"Yes, I've run into that," he said.

"Judith was very interested in Thomas Hamilton," Emily went on, "and now she's turned her attention to Tracey. So this thing with Billy, the hat and bag…she's determined to uncover the truth. She thinks it justifies doing whatever's necessary."

"Go on," he said, his voice clipped.

Emily drew in a fortifying breath, then the words came in a rush. "I'm sorry but she looked through some of your personal stuff when she was in the guest room."

"And?"

"And, I'm sorry we slept here. I should have kept a better watch. She looked at your papers, trying to figure out how it would help get lines. I wish—"

"You wish you hadn't slept here? Or that it had resulted in a speaking role?"

She jerked her head back, blinking. His tone was so resigned she couldn't even feel anger at his assumption. Did he really think women hit on him because of his position?

He stared at her, his face impassive.

"If I wanted to sleep my way into the movies," she said, "I'd probably have gone for Anthony. Not someone who hangs out with horses and can barely beat me in cards."

His lip twitched, only slightly, but that hint of humor gave her the confidence to keep talking. To admit how she felt.

"The truth is," she added, not even trying to joke. "I quite adore you."

She leaned forward and kissed his cheek. But even though he obligingly tugged her closer, she couldn't shake her despair. He liked her well enough, and he'd go to considerable lengths to protect her. However, when this movie was over, it was clear he didn't intend to see her again.

"I don't want to be an actress, Dan." Panic sharpened her voice. "Really I don't." She knew he didn't believe her, knew she was protesting too much, but she couldn't stop babbling. "You think I do, and the audition you arranged for that college movie is appreciated. But everyone is different and just because when you were young—"

"It's been a long day. Let's go to bed." He lifted her to her feet.

"But we should talk about this."

"Maybe," he said. "But not tonight."

"Was it because your mother walked out? Or someone else? Because you should know everyone adores you." Her voice rose. "And it's definitely not because of your job."

"You're very sweet," he murmured. Then he slanted his head over hers. She automatically opened her mouth, welcoming his lips, his tongue. He cupped her jaw and deepened the kiss. Heat zapped through her, and she made a sound of suppressed need.

She rose on her toes, needing to get closer. His hand splayed over her back and pulled her against him. She could feel his belt buckle, his zipper, his growing desire.

His hand left her face and trailed down the column of her neck to cup her breast. Her brain always shut down when he touched her, but tonight every cell seemed to be vibrating. She suspected this was his way of avoiding conversation but it totally worked. Talking was overrated anyway.

They were both breathing hard when he raised his head. He dimmed the kitchen lights and when he offered his hand, she silently took it and followed him down the hall to his bed.

CHAPTER THIRTY-SIX

"Mr. Barrett asked me to deliver this box of doughnuts. Would you like your coffee refilled?" The fresh-faced attendant smiled at Emily, almost bouncing in her eagerness to please.

Dan glanced up from the monitor, his intimate smile making her heart skip. He'd joined her for coffee on his last two breaks, and now she was buzzed on caffeine. Of course, she needed the boost. It had been another wonderful night in his arms. He'd made love to her with a passion that left her both exhausted and ecstatic.

"No more coffee, thanks," Emily said, accepting the box of doughnuts and giving Dan a grateful wave, impressed he'd remembered Billy's favorite food. She'd planned to drop by the dining room before their visit, but clearly Dan was more organized.

He had hoped to finish before noon, but Anthony kept demanding a re-shoot. Once this scene was over, they'd head to Billy's cottage. The large box of doughnuts should put Billy in a receptive mood. And it would be comforting to have Dan's imposing presence at her side. Emily didn't like to admit it, even to herself, but Billy scared her a little.

She turned on her phone and scanned her messages. The battery was so weak, she was limited to infrequent checks. There wasn't anything to tell Judith, not yet. However, Judith was back in Louisville and bursting with impatience. Emily scanned her most recent text: *Have you found anything else in Billy's cottage? What's happening?*

Emily replied with a brief message and slipped her phone back in her pocket. It would have been nice if Judith was here, but no background performers were required today. As a result, there weren't many spectators. Even the Hamiltons were absent since the scene was fairly mundane—merely Robert Dexter, the trainer, three vets and two additional grooms crowded around Reckless, trying to pinpoint why the colt had turned so rebellious.

It was clever how the company saved time and money by filming in one location, simply by changing the layout. Reckless had actually been stabled in the stud barn, along with two other top three-year-olds in training. However, all the stall scenes were shot in the big barn beside the track. Dan said they were traveling to Churchill Downs the next day to shoot some crowd scenes and would rely on stock footage for Reckless's preliminary races.

She tugged the spare halter higher on her shoulder and blew out a contented sigh. Dan might not be convinced she didn't want to be an actress, but her work would prove it. He'd been relaxed this morning, even including her in some wrangling duties.

His mother walking out had clearly left him with a hang-up he didn't want to discuss. Totally understandable. She was getting over some issues of her own. She still couldn't accept that Dan thought her beautiful without the camouflage of stylish clothes and makeup.

"You can switch the halter now," an assistant said, turning down the volume on her walkie. "They're moving on. We'll add audio later. Anthony wanted Hamilton's input, but he didn't show."

Emily nodded and walked toward the horse. This was the last equine scene so Dan was finished for the day. There'd be loads of time to question Billy.

She stepped up to the horse and unbuckled the halter with the shiny brass nameplate, replacing it with a worn leather halter. Dan was deep in conversation with Anthony and the assistant director, and she paused, not certain which barn housed the gelding.

"He's in the second barn," Monty said. "First stall on the right. A car ran over a possum and he didn't like the smell so Dan had him moved." The wrangler gave the horse an understanding pat. "This guy is hyperactive, always searching for a reason to be upset."

Emily nodded, turning the fretful horse before he could start pawing. He looked a lot like Bruno except his neck was slimmer, his head carriage higher, and he studied the aisle as if certain meat-eating predators lurked behind every door.

It was fascinating how the animals had such different personalities. This horse had been chosen for the vet scene because he looked excited, even at a standstill, while Bruno was assigned the more athletic maneuvers.

"Should I let him eat a little grass before he goes back in his stall?" Emily asked.

"Sure," Monty said. "He'd love that. He's a bit of a pain so most of us don't want to spend any extra time with him."

"Okay. Come on, boy. You deserve this." Emily led the prancing horse outside. He was definitely a handful but it made her feel good to watch horses graze. To hear their contented sounds while they chewed. And it appeared Dan needed time with Anthony before he could leave anyway.

She paused along the walkway, letting the gelding eat where he pleased. The horse was picky, not wanting to stand still, but Peanut had been like that too. When she'd been younger, it had been frustrating when the pony wouldn't remain in one spot. Now she could relate. Horses were like people, simply searching for greener grass.

Other than being incapable of pausing for more than thirty seconds, the gelding behaved perfectly. He did snort near the entrance to the first barn, but she guessed that was related to the possum. Horses had a keen sense of smell. Peanut knew when she had carrots in her pockets and was like a bloodhound sniffing for treats.

"How are you two getting along?"

Emily turned toward Dan's deep voice. He always sounded so composed, despite the demands of his job.

"Be alert," he added. "That horse is spooky." Dan moved closer and she caught the concern in his eyes.

"He's behaving," she said. "We've already been out here about ten minutes."

"Did Monty ask you to graze him?"

She shrugged, afraid Monty might get in trouble. However, Dan was waiting as though her answer was important. "No," she said, "but I asked permission first, and he thought it was okay. We both thought it would be a good reward for the horse."

Dan inclined his head as if in total agreement, and it was then she realized he'd only been worried about her safety.

"Are you in a hurry?" she asked, her voice rather breathy. "Want me to put him in now? Go see Billy?"

"Give the horse another five minutes. It's nice of you to give him extra grazing time."

He sounded surprised but she didn't know why it was such a big deal. She gestured at the fence by the barn. "If you're hungry, I left the box of doughnuts by the second post. That was thoughtful of you. Billy will be happy."

"It's not Billy I'm trying to please," Dan said. His eyes glinted and his smile turned rather wicked.

"You pleased me last night."

"Good." He stepped closer and gave her a one-armed hug. "This horse ground ties," he murmured. "You can drop the lead line and he won't run off."

She tilted her head, studying the restless horse. His ears flicked, and he constantly glanced around, checking their surroundings. He didn't seem the type that would ground tie.

"You're not trying to get me fired?" she asked.

Dan chuckled. "I trained him last week so we could let him loose in the aisle."

She dropped the lead line, expecting the high-strung horse to sidle away. However, he turned stock still, standing better now than when she'd been holding him. "Wow," she breathed, "I'd love to learn how to train like that."

Dan stared at her for a long moment. "Maybe I could teach you," he said, his voice almost rusty. "And you could learn a little more about wrangling...if you like."

"I'd like that." Her heart beat a delighted staccato. "More than anything. Maybe I could apply for wrangling on your next movie."

"Maybe. Don't you want to know where it's being shot?"

"That doesn't matter," she said. And oddly enough, it didn't.

CHAPTER THIRTY-SEVEN

Dan guided Emily along the tree-lined drive, not that she didn't know the way to Billy's cottage, but he liked an excuse to touch her. She truly seemed content to work with horses. At least no actress he'd known had ever preferred to hold a grazing horse rather than brownnose with the director.

She was loyal too, not the type to disappear with a wave and a kiss. He liked how she'd defended her snooping friend as well as her reluctance to leave the ailing caretaker, even though the old man sounded like a curmudgeon.

And quite possibly a killer.

Dan stopped walking, his hand tightening around her arm. "Don't visit this guy alone again, okay? Not until we sort this out."

"I won't." Her eyes shadowed. "Do you think it can be sorted out?"

"If Tracey's bag is there and Billy doesn't have a reasonable explanation, I'm sure there will be an investigation." In fact, Anthony would be delirious with joy. Nothing sold movie tickets faster than a juicy scandal.

"Billy has a lot of stuff crammed in there," she said. "We might find some other things."

"Like other women's bags?"

"No, I didn't mean that." Her eyes widened in horror. "Just other items that belonged to Tracey. You think there might be other women missing?"

"I don't know. According to the Hamiltons, Billy has always been reclusive. He was raised in that little cottage. Never left. This estate is the center of his existence."

She looked a little pale so he pulled her in for a reassuring hug and then couldn't resist stealing a kiss. She tasted so sweet, her body molding perfectly to his. She'd like Hawaii, his next movie location, and he'd love rubbing coconut oil over her bikini line—

The ground rocked. His ears throbbed from the concussion. Something smashed on the driveway, ricocheting scant feet away. He yanked Emily behind an oak tree. Smoke rose in a black clump, so close he could smell the acrid burning.

"Stay here," he said, pressing her shoulders. "There might be another explosion. Take a picture if any vehicles go by."

"But we need to get the horses out..." She peered past him, staring at the rising smoke in disbelief.

"It's not the stud barn," he said grimly. "Stay here, Em." He pressed a hard kiss on her mouth then ran down the drive, pulling out his phone on the way.

He rounded the corner and jerked to a stop. The caretaker's cottage was a mangled frame, marked by a burning pile of wood, glass and debris. He pressed nine-one-one and reported the location, guessing emergency vehicles would be at least thirty minutes away. There didn't seem to be any need for an ambulance.

"Oh, no."

He turned at Emily's pained cry.

"Billy might not be in there," he said, tugging her back and pressing Anthony's speed dial with his other hand. He didn't want her anywhere near the debris field, at least until the fire was under control.

Anthony answered with an anxious voice. "What happened? I heard the noise. Are you anywhere near the smoke?"

"Right beside it," Dan said. "It's the caretaker's cottage. Burning fast. Send over our water truck and paramedic."

"Anyone in there?"

"Don't know yet."

"Okay," Anthony said. "Don't be a hero."

Dan cut the connection and began snapping pictures, keeping his left arm tightly wrapped around Emily. "Did Billy have a gas stove?" he asked. "Propane? Paint? What about a car?"

"Gas stove and paint," Emily said, her voice subdued. "No car. But lots of cans and stuff. I don't remember seeing a barbecue."

"Did he leave the cottage often? Go for walks?"

"I think he only left to open and close the gate." She looked up, her eyes dark with despair. "You can let go of me now. I'm not going to run over there. I know it's way too late."

He cautiously lowered his arm, but her devastated expression made his chest ache. It was agonizing to watch, to wonder if anyone was in that burning rubble. And it would be much worse for her. She'd befriended the old man. "Why don't you go and check the stud barn?" he said. "Maybe Billy's there. And the horses might need calming."

"Okay. I'll leave the doughnuts here." She placed the box on the ground, her hands and voice shaking. "D-do you think you could make sure the fire truck doesn't run them over? Billy wouldn't like them if they're squashed."

"Don't worry," Dan said gravely. "I'll keep everything safe."

Anthony stared at the smoldering cottage, shaking his head in dismay. "Was the old caretaker inside?"

"They don't know yet," Dan said.

"If Tracey's duffle bag was really in there," Anthony said, "this muddies the water. It could be arson. Possibly murder. Too bad this happened before you could retrieve the bag."

"Yes," Dan said dryly. "It does seem rather coincidental."

They both stepped back as a second fire truck left the scene, leaving a skeleton crew to watch for hot spots.

"Thomas Hamilton is on his way," Anthony said. "He drove to Louisville this morning."

"By himself?"

"Yes." Anthony's voice turned thoughtful. "Maybe he wanted an alibi. He always had an obsessive interest in Shania's scenes. He remembered the missing groom's hair, her clothes, even the songs she sang to the horse."

Anthony crossed and uncrossed his arms, as if unable to control his energy. "Shania said you asked about a Reckless ball cap. Nothing can be proven with just a hat, but we can definitely milk it. Hamilton is one of our movie backers so for now we'll look at the old man, enough to stoke questions. The girl can hold the cap, talk to reporters—"

"Absolutely not," Dan said. "Emily cared about Billy. And we can't make insinuations without proof."

A firefighter rolling a thick hose stopped and stared. Dan lowered his voice. "Also, assuming this wasn't an accident, whoever did it is still around. And very ruthless."

"Exactly." Anthony's head bobbed. "That's what I'm talking about. You can't buy this kind of publicity. What's that girl's name again? The one who found the cap? The girl who stood in front of the horse?"

Dan's mouth tightened. He had a bad feeling about this. But Anthony could unearth her name in two minutes simply by picking up the phone. "Emily," Dan said reluctantly.

"And the other background girl? The one who also saw the duffel bag?"

"Judith."

"I want them back on set. Keep them around so we can rev interest. I'll give them a line or two."

"Emily's still here," Dan admitted, "but she befriended Billy. This is going to be hard for her." He paused, warring with himself. "And I don't want her to have any lines."

"Fine. But she can do an interview. Just keep her around and happy." Anthony slapped Dan on the back. "She'll look good on TV. She's the pretty one, right? And it could help her career. It's a win, win."

"Not such a win for Billy," Dan said.

A black Bentley rolled up and jerked to a stop. Thomas Hamilton opened the door and stumbled out. Even from thirty feet away, his face looked ashen.

"Oh, my God." He pressed a hand to his mouth, staring at the rubble.

Anthony jabbed Dan in the ribs then rushed over, like a journalist on a story. Dan followed more slowly. Hamilton's shock seemed genuine but he'd seen Oscar winning performances before. Unlike horses, people could fake emotion.

"Sorry for your loss," Anthony said gravely.

"Billy was in there?" Hamilton's voice lowered. "You're certain?"

"Seems that way." Anthony made a sympathetic sound deep in his throat but didn't remain quiet for long. "Did he have any friends? An ex-wife?"

"No." Hamilton said, still staring at the rubble in apparent disbelief. "He stuck to himself. Never married."

"Did he like girls?" Anthony asked. "Young women always flock around horses, and he did have a private cottage. How well did you know him?"

Hamilton shook his head. "What exactly are you asking? And why can't you tell me if he's in there?"

"It'll take a few days before they can sift through the debris," Dan said.

"Not much chance Billy wasn't inside." Hamilton heaved a sigh. "He rarely left the cottage."

"What about his groceries?" Dan asked.

"The local store delivered them. Health problems kept Billy from doing too much." Hamilton jabbed a thumb at the open gate. "That gate was his job. And we were all happy with that."

"People are going to be curious," Anthony said. "I'm going to talk to the producer about adding Billy's character. Just a small appearance. After all, he would have been around when Reckless was here."

Hamilton shrugged. "Billy never had much to do with the horses. He looked after the grounds on the west side and monitored traffic to the stud barn."

Anthony stiffened, his excitement palpable, at least to Dan.

"That means he must have known the missing groom," Anthony said. "Were they friends? Tracey and Billy?"

"Not that I recall," Hamilton said. "Billy was always a bit gruff. Rather intimidating, especially to the girls. They tended to avoid him."

But not Emily, Dan thought. She'd been brave enough to bring him doughnuts, big-hearted enough to return and clean his cottage. She'd probably been the last person to show Billy any kindness.

But the girls finding the groom's bag had revitalized interest. Whether Billy had anything to do with Tracey's disappearance might always remain a mystery, but it was clear Anthony intended to cover all angles.

No one seemed too upset that Billy's body would probably be discovered in the charred cottage. No one but Emily. In fact, the conversation had already shifted to the best way to include Billy's character in a hastily added scene.

"I'm going to the stud barn," Dan said. Anthony merely grunted, his attention locked on Hamilton.

Dan walked away, relieved to escape the cloud of smoke and dust and suspicion. His throat and nose stung, and he wanted cleaner air. Cleaner emotions. He wanted Emily.

His stride quickened. It only took a few minutes to reach the blessedly fresh air surrounding the stud barn.

He stepped inside and scanned the stalls. They were both empty but clean. The aisle was freshly swept, and a huge shiny padlock now hung on the apartment door. Clearly that place was out of bounds.

He walked outside and rounded the barn. The chestnut grazed in the large paddock, his shiny tail swishing away flies. Emily was in the makeshift paddock with the Reckless lookalike, the bay with the tendon injury. His front legs were neatly wrapped but otherwise he looked happy and healthy. His ears were pricked, his attention locked on Emily. Neither horse looked upset, but they were movie horses, accustomed to commotion and the random explosion.

The bay's head abruptly snaked and he grabbed something from Emily's hand. Her words were too low to hear, but she gave the horse an approving pat. It looked like she was teaching him some sort of trick. And getting results.

Dan's tension faded, simply watching her. Obviously she liked working with horses—despite Lizzie's report to the contrary—and he didn't want to interfere. But the bay lifted his head, his nostrils flaring as he caught Dan's scent. Emily turned, following the horse's gaze.

She slipped between the rails and rushed toward him. "What's happening? Did you find him?"

"Nothing yet." He wrapped an arm around her waist. She vibrated with anxiety, and he slid a hand beneath her hair, automatically rubbing the back of her neck.

"It might be awhile before they sift through the rubble," he said, after a long moment. "But it seems like Billy was in there. I'm sorry, Em."

His own heart was beating faster than normal, and his hands tightened around her shoulders, taut with guilty gratitude. Because try as he might, he couldn't stop agonizing about one inescapable truth. If she hadn't waited for him this morning, quite likely she'd be tangled with Billy at the bottom of those sad and deadly ruins.

CHAPTER THIRTY-EIGHT

"Guess what! I have a line." Judith's voice bubbled with so much excitement, it was barely recognizable. "That means I'll be back on site. The casting director just called."

"You have a speaking role?" Emily leaned over Dan's kitchen table and checked her phone battery. She didn't want to leave it on too long. She'd already talked to Judith twice today, updating her about the explosion, but this was wonderful news. No wonder Judith was ecstatic.

"Yes." Judith paused to take a breath. "They're sending a car to pick me up—no more crowded buses. And I'm even doing an interview."

"Oh wow, that's great." Emily fought an itch of envy. "I'm really happy for you."

And she was happy. No one had researched this movie more than Judith. Besides, Emily had stumbled onto something much more important. She smiled across the table at Dan, who watched with an inscrutable expression.

"I'm glad they were able to recover Billy's body," Judith went on. "Is there a chance Tracey's duffle bag wasn't destroyed? Maybe we could go over tomorrow and poke around."

"The area is still restricted. There's yellow tape everywhere," Emily said. "They found his body but not much else. Certainly not a bag."

"But the explosion might have thrown it into the trees. I saw on the Internet where a gas stove exploded and a baby's crib was found fifty feet away, completely intact. And maybe there's something else." Judith's voice turned fervent. "It's up to us. You have to help me. Help Billy—"

"I will," Emily said. Judith had been rather subdued when she'd first learned about the explosion. Now she sounded almost desperate. Emily had been fortunate enough to spend the day with Dan whose caring presence acted like an anchor. But Judith was single, with no family, and this movie seemed to be her only interest.

"Tell me about your role," Emily said, trying to distract her. "Do you have the script yet? What do you wear?"

They spoke for another ten minutes about Judith's part and by the time Emily hung up, Judith sounded more like her normal self.

"Sorry," Emily said, putting aside her phone and turning back to Dan. "Judith just found out she has a new role. Acting, not silent. This is the first time she's been pulled from background. It's really quite cool. And she needed to tell someone."

Emily picked up her wine glass, but as usual Dan's unwavering attention kept her talking. "Jenna was keen to hear about the movie at first but didn't say much when she realized my role was only background. She still thinks I'm going to be a big star." Emily gave a little laugh, to prove it didn't hurt. Not one bit.

Dan said nothing, but his warm blue eyes filled with understanding.

"I've always wanted to make her proud," Emily said after a moment. "To do something important. She was…is the best sister. But now that she's married to Burke, she has everything.

"I planned to take her to the Stillwater Fair and Steeplechase. When we were little, we always dreamed of staying overnight. It seemed like the perfect gift. Who would have dreamed Burke would think of horse racing too? But he did." Emily shrugged but despite her best efforts, her voice turned wistful. "So now she's off to the races in England, one box down from the Queen. How can I ever compete with that?"

"It's not a competition," Dan said. "Just be there for her. Money, success—none of that is as important as being there."

Emily grimaced and reached for the wine bottle. 'Being there' might be important to Dan, but Jenna and Burke didn't want her around. They'd added a guesthouse so she wouldn't be underfoot.

"I just mean," she said, "that it would be nice to do something for a change. To prove I'm not a complete failure. Anything I've accomplished is because Jenna helped me."

"I doubt that very much," Dan said.

Emily shrugged. "Well, it feels that way."

Dan dragged a hand over his jaw and for the first time that evening seemed to be thinking of something else. He picked up his phone, tapped a message then turned his attention back to her.

"What about you?" Emily asked, trying to change the subject. "You've already accomplished so much. What do you want?"

"Dependable horses…dependable people. My dad was devastated every time my mother left." He paused. "Guess I was too."

"I'm sorry," she said softly. "We went through a similar thing in our house. I know how much it hurts. Mom should have left him. But Jenna said the song *Stand By Your Man* was written for our mother."

Dan chuckled, then picked up her hands and gently kissed her reddened palms. "There's a new cream in the bathroom," he said. "It worked well on one of the horses. Thought you might give it a try."

She nodded. Clearly he didn't want to talk anymore about family foibles but this was good progress. He actually looked relaxed when he mentioned his mother. His face hadn't turned to granite like it did before.

"That makes six creams and ointments you've brought. I'm sure—" Her phone rang. The screen flashed an unfamiliar number. The name was clear though: 'Reckless Productions.'

"Excuse me for a sec," she said, grabbing the phone.

She listened while the casting director spoke. But joy leaked out the sides of her mouth and she couldn't stop grinning at Dan. An offer! Five lines, enough to join the union. She wasn't background anymore. She'd have a screen credit.

She kept her composure long enough to politely thank the man. Then she leaped from the chair, shooting her fist into the air. "I have lines! The scene is being shot Thursday morning, only two days away."

She twirled around the kitchen, unable to stand still. Seconds later, she plunked herself back into the chair. "I'm an awful person," she groaned. "It's wrong to be this happy on the day Billy died."

"Don't be so hard on yourself. You're probably the only person who gave that man the time of day." Dan's voice flattened. "Besides, you should be celebrating. Those lines will get you in the union. Acting jobs will come much easier now."

"But I already told you, I don't want to be an actress. I only want this one movie part."

"Right." He rose and scooped his beer off the table. "But you don't have to decide that tonight. Let's go to bed."

Clearly he didn't believe her, but it didn't matter. There'd be plenty of time to prove she was happy to work behind the scenes. Not *in* them. Time to prove she was dependable. And it didn't matter where the next film location was, as long as she was with Dan. In fact, the idea of moving around the country—seeing different places and people—was rather exhilarating.

Maybe after more experience, she could even move from a wrangler's job and help with the training. Barney was an apt pupil. By next week she hoped to demonstrate he was worth keeping. That is, if Dan had any room on his ranch.

"How big is your place in Montana?" she asked, picking up her glass and following him down the hall.

"Ten sections."

"You mean ten paddocks?"

He took her left hand and led her into the bedroom. "A section is six hundred and forty acres."

"That means—" She stopped, unable to fathom that much land. She'd thought Hamilton Stud was huge. And she'd assumed Dan's family had been financially challenged, like hers. Not land barons. "So you have room for a lot of horses," she said weakly. "I mean, there's no reason not to keep an extra one, if you suddenly decided."

"Yes. But I never take the extras home. Only horses like Bruno and Splash." He tugged her shirt from the waistband of her jeans, and his hand slid along her bare back. "Shipping is expensive," he added. "It's best not to get attached unless you're certain they're worth keeping. Everything ends with the movie."

She suspected he was talking about more than horses, but now he'd unclasped her bra. His knowing hand drifted along the underside of her breast, making her shiver in delight. "Is that why you don't bother with names?" she managed. "You just call Barney the Reckless lookalike?"

He cupped her breast, his thumb stroking her nipple, and clearly he had other things on his mind. "Maybe," he said, rescuing the tilting glass of wine from her hand and setting it on the dresser. "Never thought much about it. Seems if I'm not going to keep them, descriptions are best."

Despite his expert ministrations, a coldness settled in her chest and she couldn't let it go. "But what about people? Do you even know my last name?"

"That's different," he said, but there was a trace of defensiveness in his voice.

"You really don't know it, do you? Is that because you're not certain I'm worth keeping?" She tried to keep her voice light, but he must have sensed her hurt.

He cupped her face, his voice thickening. "You're worth keeping. Nothing I want more. But people want different things. Often they collide. The very worst thing is to see someone you love walking around unhappy."

She had no idea what he was talking about—she was always happy around Dan. But his eyes had darkened so they looked almost black. His finger stroked her cheek, her mouth, her jaw, as though absorbing every curve of her face. And he stared down at her with such a hungry expression, it made her tremble.

Then he pressed his mouth against her hair, so tightly she could feel the rasp of his stubble. "Don't ever doubt how I feel, sweetheart," he whispered.

Seconds later, his hands moved over her with raw urgency, stripping her clothes and carrying her to the bed.

His lovemaking was expert and thorough and as usual left them both convulsing with pleasure. But her final thought before the orgasm rocked her was that he still didn't care enough to ask her last name.

CHAPTER THIRTY-NINE

"Can we read through the lines one more time?" Emily asked, adjusting her sunglasses and scanning the script. "I need to try it with a more serious expression."

Dan obligingly checked his sheet. Her unbridled enthusiasm was contagious. She'd been bouncing around the set all morning, ever since the script had been delivered. Any regret he had about texting Anthony last night had vanished.

He couldn't resist using his influence, not after she'd confided about her sister. She'd shrugged off the steeplechase fiasco with her typical casualness, but her disappointment had ripped at him. He understood now why she'd been so desperate for a paying job. Maybe acting really wasn't that important and this truly was about doing something for Jenna.

He could only hope.

But better she walked away now, rather than later. And the script was a simple one: a replacement groom looking for Tracey and questioning the actor playing Billy. Dan didn't like that Anthony was exploiting the girls for media purposes, but it was selfish to deprive Emily of this opportunity.

He'd been a little irritated when he discovered she'd be bathing a horse. But naturally Anthony would want Emily displayed in a wet T-shirt. At least he'd be present to make sure she wasn't shivering too long.

He'd order in some extra heat lamps. A quiet horse would help too. Splash would be the best. The gelding loved water and would stand for hours. It would be easier for her to concentrate on the lines if she didn't worry about a horse bruising her toes.

"Do you think I should act scared here?" Emily tapped a spot on the page, pulling back his attention. "When Billy enters the barn? Or maybe it's better to act irritated that Tracey didn't show for work? Or maybe a smile's best?"

"Don't worry." Dan chuckled and steered her out of the way of a sound technician. "Anthony will tell you tomorrow. I expect he'll want a little fear but maybe he's looking for something else. Remember, just say 'no' if you're uncomfortable with it. They're still working out the scene, based on Billy's...perceived interaction with Tracey."

She grimaced at his choice of words and he used the bustling production crew as an excuse to pull her closer. Damn, he couldn't keep his hands off her. Soon he had to drive to Churchill Downs and already he dreaded the limo's arrival.

"Do you think he killed her?" Emily asked, her eyes troubled.

Dan hesitated. Part of him suspected Billy was involved in Tracey's disappearance, but if it had been a sexual crime, it didn't make sense that the man had stayed away from women for the next twenty years. And Tracey had been tight with Hamilton who claimed she'd barely known Billy. "I'm not sure," he said slowly. "Apparently Billy worked normally that day. Hamilton said he fixed some plumbing in the stud barn. In fact, they're planning to use that wash stall for your scene."

Emily tilted her head. "Billy may have lied about his work that day. Because the stall still doesn't drain properly. I showered there and almost flooded the aisle."

Dan's mouth tightened. The realization that she'd showered in an isolated barn, slept in an apartment where a groom had gone missing—even sat down alone in Billy's cottage—now bothered him. Clearly she was single minded and brave. Her buoyant energy and resourcefulness were as much a part of her appeal as her bold heart. But those kind of people were hard to love.

She studied him with thoughtful eyes. "You're being very helpful for a man who doesn't like actresses. Are you trying to get rid of me?"

Every once in a while, she sucker punched him with surprisingly intuitive questions. Of course, he didn't want to get rid of her. But if she intended to chase an acting career, it was much better to find out now. He wasn't testing her. Not really.

He preferred to believe that if acting was her passion, he'd be chivalrous and help her succeed. However, he certainly wasn't going to invest any time or heartache in a relationship that was doomed from the start.

"I just want you to be happy," he said, a trite phrase he'd used on more than one woman.

"Excellent." She flashed a mischievous smile. "That's all I want too." But her big eyes softened with the same understanding she'd shown last night. "This will be my one and only time in the movies. I'm not going to get the acting bug and take off. I'm not a fan of long-distance relationships either."

Her gaze drifted past him, and she quit talking.

"Hey, Dan," Anthony called, pushing past a cameraman, his arms swinging with purpose. Hamilton trotted pompously by his side. "We're leaving for Churchill in ten minutes. Ride in my car so we can discuss the paddock scene."

Anthony gave Emily a distracted nod then looked back at her with a marked increase of enthusiasm. "Good morning," he said. "Would you be able to do a couple interviews later? Maybe talk about your conversations with Billy and what you saw in the cottage? Movie fans would love the inside scoop. I know you saw Tracey's bag," he added. "And that Billy said some things—"

"You saw Tracey's bag?" Hamilton asked, his eyes bulging. "Why didn't anyone tell me?"

Dan eased in front of Emily. "This is still under investigation. So any interviews should probably wait."

"Fine," Anthony said. "But I want her available to shoot footage at some point. The movie is trending on Twitter." He rubbed his hands in glee. "We'll keep everything quiet for a bit, then stagger enough tidbits to keep it in the news."

"How did you know it was Tracey's bag?" Hamilton asked.

"Her name was on it," Emily said. She glanced back down at her script, and it was quite clear, at least to Dan, that she preferred to concentrate on her acting role tomorrow.

Hamilton edged closer, his complexion pasty white. "But did you look inside? What was in it? What did Billy say?"

Dan's jaw tightened. Anthony shot him a warning look then placed his hand on Hamilton's arm.

"This will all come out later," Anthony said. "It's a difficult time, but we do have a movie to shoot. And scripts to study. So no more questions at this time."

Dan's jaw slowly relaxed. But he didn't want to drive to Churchill Downs and leave Emily alone. At least, police investigators made appointments. Hamilton, however, owned the property. He was also a movie backer. When the man spoke, people had to listen.

And despite Anthony's directive, Hamilton still stood too close, hoping to bully Emily into talking. It was a tough situation for an aspiring actress who had to please all three men. Dan wanted to whisk her from the set. But he certainly couldn't tell her to stay in his trailer all day. That would be like confining an energetic filly to a gloomy stall.

"Excuse me, Dan."

He turned toward the accented voice. He'd never been so happy to see Lizzie.

"Do you want six horses in the paddock at Churchill?" Lizzie went on. "Or the ten we discussed?"

"Ten," Dan said. "And, Lizzie, take Emily back to the wranglers' barn so we can check out a horse for tomorrow's bath scene. I'm thinking Splash but she's already worked with Bruno."

Anthony gave a knowing smile. But Hamilton's nostrils flared, and it was obvious he'd planned to grill Emily with more questions once Dan and Anthony left.

"See you tonight." Dan leaned down and kissed Emily's cheek.

She seemed startled but covered it well, perhaps understanding he was trying to extend some much-needed protection. Dan shot a look at Lizzie who gave a little nod.

"Okay, then," Anthony said mildly. "Let's go, Dan. It's obvious everything here is under control."

Emily dragged a sweat scraper over Splash's slick neck then gave the horse an appreciative pat. He'd jumped into a swimming pool before so it was obvious he was trusting and tractable. Now she'd learned he was bomb proof.

Lizzie had rang an ear-piercing bell and also hung a bucket over his hind leg to demonstrate Splash's calm nature. It would be a cinch to bathe him tomorrow, even when surrounded by cameras and a demanding director.

More remarkable was Lizzie's helpfulness. Although her mouth had remained in a flat line, she'd brought Emily to the wranglers' barn and served as a private assistant, even filling the bucket and mixing the frothing herbal soap.

"We won't completely wash Splash now," Lizzie said, handing Emily a dripping sponge. "But you could put water in his ears and he won't shake his head. So no matter what the director wants, you can concentrate on your lines. He's smaller than Bruno but the cameras can adjust the angles," Lizzie added. "He's really the best horse for any water scenes. I think you should choose him."

"I get to choose?" Emily's eyes widened. Most actors were just handed a horse.

"Yes," Lizzie said grudgingly. "It's rare but those were Dan's instructions. You're definitely being primed for success."

"What do you mean?"

Lizzie shrugged. "Getting you lines in that scene. I've never known him to ask a director for a favor."

"He asked Anthony? I didn't know that." Emily's hand fisted around the wet sponge, so tightly water dripped on her boot. Dan had sent a text last night. And almost immediately afterwards the casting director had called. "But that doesn't make sense." She shook her head in confusion. "He doesn't even like actresses."

"That's right," Lizzie said. "He doesn't."

A chill swept Emily despite the water warming her hand. She understood now why Dan had interfered. It was a test.

She gulped and tucked a strand of hair back in her ponytail. It hurt that he didn't trust her, but she understood his motives. He wanted someone dependable, someone who'd stick around. And she'd show him. Usually she flunked tests, but this one she intended to ace.

She tossed the sponge into the bucket and wiped her hands. "Thanks for showing me the movie horses. I'd love to use Splash. He'll be perfect for tomorrow."

"Okay. Now would you like a cup of coffee or something?" Lizzie asked.

"No, thanks. I'll put Splash back in his stall and then help you with whatever chores are left."

"Not necessary," Lizzie said. "Everything's done. They're using on-site track horses this afternoon at Churchill, and only Splash is working tomorrow."

"There must be something left." Emily checked the rafters. She didn't see a single cobweb, but her adrenaline was pumping. "Maybe I could wash the walls or scrub some buckets?"

"There's nothing. Dan wants you to have time to practice your lines. I can read them with you, if necessary," Lizzie added.

"But I'd prefer to help with wrangler stuff. What about cleaning tack?"

"Everything's done." Lizzie's mouth clamped in a stubborn line. "Dan will have my head if I make you work."

Emily wrung her hands, fighting a rush of panic. She didn't need to be an actress to be happy. And she was dependable. That was all Dan needed to know. Two simple things but very difficult to prove. And while she wanted to be dependable, she wasn't. Not really. She wasn't much of anything.

She slumped down on a bale of hay, cradling her head in defeat.

"Look," Lizzie said, her voice softening. "I just want to get along here. Sorry I was a little hard on you earlier. But Dan...spoke to me. He made it clear I can't assign you any work."

Emily glanced up. Lizzie actually sounded apologetic, and clearly she'd jump through hoops to please Dan.

"I'd really like to help with wrangling stuff though," Emily said. "And you're not assigning me anything. I'm offering, so it's different. Actually, I'm begging."

Lizzie heaved a sigh but seconds later she dropped two loaded buckets at Emily's feet. "Okay then. It would be a big help if you'd deliver these bath props to the stud barn."

"You're awesome. Thanks, Lizzie." Emily scrambled up, grinning. "Is that where they're shooting the rest of the movie?"

"Only the bath scene and the part when you bang on the apartment door." Lizzie gave a tentative smile. "Come back afterwards and I'll show you everything a wrangler does. If that's what you really want."

"That's what I want." Emily nodded gratefully. "I'll be right back."

She scooped up the buckets brimming with soap, brushes and a sweat scraper, and hurried toward the door. Lizzie wasn't so bad; in fact, she was rather nice. Emily shook her head. Maybe if she'd tried a little harder at the beginning, they would have made out just fine. It was clear she could learn a lot from the capable wrangler.

She cut though the woods to the stud barn, swinging the buckets, her natural optimism renewed. If every minute of her spare time was spent helping the wranglers, Dan would realize that was her main interest. Yes, this would all work out perfectly.

Barney nickered when she entered the barn, leaning against the stall door and stretching his neck. She dropped the buckets and paused to scratch his jaw. He was such an affectionate fellow, always eager to please. Dan was adamant about not shipping extra horses back to his ranch, but while Splash was a super performer, there was something special about Barney.

"No problem," she said. "We'll just have to try harder."

He pressed his head against her chest and sighed, as if accepting he'd be returned to the contractor with the rest of the herd but bore no ill will. His tendon would require special care for at least another month, and she prayed he wouldn't get lost in the shuffle. Under Dan's care, he was kept under confinement, not fun for a horse but at least it gave his leg a chance to heal.

There wasn't much time left to prove Barney was worth keeping. Heck, Dan didn't even want to know his name...or her last one, for that matter. He had experience with so many horses and women, he'd become rather hardened.

She pressed a kiss against Barney's velvety nose and scooped up the buckets. Dan cared. He was just cautious. There was no way someone could act like he did and not have feelings. It was obvious in his kiss, his touch, the way he listened. Like she was the most important person in his world. And for now, that was enough.

Humming, she placed the buckets on the side of the wash stall while Barney watched with curious eyes. Tomorrow this aisle would be much busier. People and equipment would be everywhere. And thanks to Dan, Jenna would see Emily speak on screen.

She already had memorized her script, and clearly Splash wouldn't give any trouble. For Dan's sake, she wanted the scene to go super smooth. Hopefully, the aisle wouldn't flood.

Frowning, she kneeled and checked the drain. It looked clear but Anthony would understandably flip if a flooded aisle caused delays. Lizzie probably knew the procedure to have set construction check the plumbing. Fixing it today would save everyone time and trouble.

Barney snorted, yanking back her attention. Mrs. Hamilton walked down the aisle, her high heels muted on the rubber in the aisle.

"Hello," she called. "Have you seen my husband?"

Emily's glance automatically shot to the apartment door. She scrambled to her feet and brushed at the knees of her jeans. "I haven't seen him. But the lock is still on the apartment so I don't think he's up there."

Mrs. Hamilton frowned and checked her watch. "If he does come by, could you remind him the theater luncheon starts at one?" She glanced at the buckets, her expression softening. "Do you need more shampoo?"

"No, thanks." Emily smiled. "This isn't for me. It's for a horse."

"Well, if you need any more product, I have some in the trunk."

"I'm fine, thanks," Emily said, realizing she'd stopped obsessing about hair or makeup—rather ironic since she'd always associated actresses with glamour. "We're just stocking up for the scene here tomorrow."

"I thought all stall scenes were shot in the main barn?"

"This is the extra one Anthony added, the bath scene when they introduce Billy."

"Ah, yes." Mrs. Hamilton gave a distressed sigh. "You're one of the girls who knew our dear caretaker." Her eyes narrowed on the wash stall. "But Reckless was always bathed outside. And he was moved to the other barn after he acted up."

Emily nodded. Mrs. Hamilton was correct; some of these movie details weren't totally accurate but perhaps Anthony was taking creative license. "I guess it's easier if the apartment door is close to the wash stall," she said, "since my role is to yell for Tracey."

"So they want you by the apartment door." Mrs. Hamilton raised an amused eyebrow. "And I imagine Anthony wants you in a wet T-shirt and that's why he's using a bath scene."

"Probably," Emily admitted. She'd been so excited to read the script, she hadn't asked any questions. And Dan hadn't said much. After Mrs. Hamilton left, she'd turn on her phone and text Judith. She probably knew what everyone in the scene was wearing, right down to the color of halter on the horse.

"Do you want a drive back to the set?" Mrs. Hamilton asked.

"No, thanks," Emily said. "I need to make sure this drains properly before the scene tomorrow."

Mrs. Hamilton gave a polite nod and turned away. Emily pulled out her phone. The battery was almost empty, but it wouldn't take much juice to text Judith.

The indicator light blinked. Five messages. Obviously Judith was excited about her speaking role too. But three texts were from Wally. Her heart lurched as she scanned the terse messages. The first: *Give me a call ASAP*. Then: *Peanut is very sick*. And the last: *Call me. Don't think he's going to make it.*

She pressed Wally's number, barely able to breathe.

"Finally," Wally said, his voice thick with irritation.

"How's Peanut?"

"Not good. High respiration, elevated temperature, stiff neck. He won't stand, eat or drink." Wally sighed. "I don't know what to do. Jenna might fly home if I tell her. And she needs this vacation."

Emily squeezed her eyes shut. No doubt about it, Jenna would jump on a plane, believing her presence would help Peanut. And maybe it would—if she made it on time. Peanut's two favorite people were Jenna and Emily.

"Don't tell her," Emily said, already rushing down the aisle. "I can get home much quicker."

"Aren't you in the middle of a big job?"

"I'm coming, Wally. My phone is almost dead, but I'll be there. If he can just hang on a few more hours—" Her voice broke.

"Okay." Wally exhaled with relief. "He'll be glad to see you. But don't dally."

Emily jammed her phone back into her pocket and bolted from the barn. Poor little Peanut. So many times, she'd cried into his shaggy mane, missing her mother and using him like a giant teddy bear.

She thought he'd live forever. Sure, he had some health issues, but he'd always pulled through. Ponies were tough.

Sometimes they lived well into their thirties. One old Shetland down the road was supposed to be forty-four. They weren't exactly sure how old Peanut was but he certainly wasn't forty. Why couldn't he live as long as the neighbor's pony?

Tears filled her eyes but she waved frantically at the blurred silver car pulling away from the barn.

Mrs. Hamilton immediately stopped and lowered her driver's window. "What's wrong?"

"I have to get to the highway," Emily said, wringing her hands. "Would you mind dropping me off wherever it is you're going?"

"Hop in," Mrs. Hamilton said.

Emily scrambled into the passenger's seat and the car shot down the drive. She buckled her seatbelt, grateful Mrs. Hamilton understood her urgency. This property was so damn big.

"The interstate is only fourteen miles north," Mrs. Hamilton said. "Would it help if I took you there?"

"Oh, yes." Emily sagged with relief. Once she was on the highway, she could hitch a ride much faster.

"Okay. There's an Exxon gas station just off the highway. Your ride can meet you there."

Emily nodded, clutching her damp hands. Wally was great with sick animals. He'd keep Peanut alive. He had to. But her lip quivered and she turned her head, staring blankly out the side window.

"Perhaps you should call your drive and let them know we'll be there in a few minutes," Mrs. Hamilton said gently. She waved at the security guard manning the back gate to the estate, turned onto the secondary road and pressed the accelerator.

Emily nodded, appreciating Mrs. Hamilton's concern but lacking the energy to explain she'd be hitchhiking. "I will. But can you tell Dan Barrett that I won't be able to do the bath scene tomorrow? I'm very sorry but I have to go home."

"Of course," Mrs. Hamilton said. She pulled out to pass a slow-moving van and the car sped along the smooth pavement.

Emily twisted her fingers. Maybe Peanut had eaten something not intended for little ponies. He was always rather gluttonous. Once she'd hidden beer in the hay and he'd bit a hole in every can. She'd skipped the tailgate party that night, afraid he might colic but too scared to tell Jenna why she needed to stay home and sit with him.

A large Exxon sign loomed. She scanned the parking lot, relieved to see several transport trucks.

Mrs. Hamilton veered into the paved rest area and pulled to a stop. "Wait a moment," she said, glancing at Emily. She slid out of the car and opened the spotless trunk.

"Take this." She pressed a pink leather bag in Emily's hands. "There's a hairbrush, deodorant, makeup. And a few bills."

Emily gave a shaky smile. The products were unimportant but the money would be a huge help. She could share gas expenses and possibly find a drive more quickly. "Once again you come to my rescue," Emily said, her voice thick with emotion. "Thank you."

"Will you be returning to the set?"

"Yes, but I'm not sure when." Emily clutched the bag to her chest and inched away. She could hear a truck engine start. Maybe it was heading north. "I'll repay you though, I promise."

"Don't worry." Mrs. Hamilton waved a hand. "Just go. Call if I can help with anything. And good luck…meeting your ride." Their eyes locked and it was clear she knew exactly how Emily intended to travel.

Emily nodded and bolted toward the paved rest area. A man carrying a thermos and a cell phone walked toward a gleaming black truck.

"Excuse me," she said. "I have a family emergency and need a drive to East Virginia. Are you going that direction by chance? I can pay for some gas."

The man barely slowed. "I can't take passengers," he mumbled. "Company rules."

The next two drivers were friendlier but one was heading west and the other intended to grab a nap before leaving. "If you're still here in an hour," the man with the gray hair said, adjusting his Blue Jays cap, "I'd be glad to take you right to Toronto."

Emily's shoulder slumped. One hour felt like an eternity.

The man gave an encouraging smile. "We'd make better time then. The traffic will be good and I'm a safer driver when rested."

"I appreciate it. But really, I can't wait."

"Oh? What's your hurry?" Genuine interest flashed in his kind eyes.

"Our pony's sick." She swallowed. "And my sister will be heartbroken if he dies while she's away."

The man turned, pulled open his cab door and reached for his walkie. He glanced over his shoulder. "What's your name?" he asked.

She told him then listened in grateful disbelief as he spoke on the radio about how his friend named Emily needed to get home to be with her sick pony.

"There." He hung up his mike and rubbed his hands in satisfaction. "We have a lot of animal lovers out there. They know what it's like to be away from home. It might take a few transfers but I expect you'll be home with your little pony in less than five hours."

She blinked. "That's so kind of you."

A truck blared from half a mile down the highway.

The driver gestured with his thumb. "That's your first ride coming now. Hope it works out."

"What's your name?" she asked, scanning the door of his truck. He had a bit of an accent that she couldn't place.

"Big Mike," he said. "I live in Toronto now but come from Newfoundland."

"Thank you very much, Big Mike." She stared at him for another moment. She'd never see this man again, never be able to return the favor. He knew that. Yet his simple act of kindness would make a huge difference. Already her tension eased, knowing she was going to make it back to Three Brooks as quickly as if she had her car.

She raised her hand in heartfelt salute then stepped forward and gave him an impulsive hug.

A blue rig with flames painted on the door rumbled up beside them. Emily pulled open the passenger door and climbed into the seat. The driver was a lady with arms as ripped as any jockey's and a smile that made her feel instantly welcome. There were three pictures on the dash: two of smiling children and one of a black Lab holding a red ball in her mouth.

"My name's Shirley," the driver said. "Headed to Charleston. Help yourself to coffee. I like mine black. Your job is to listen and pour. Can you handle that?"

Emily nodded and reached for the red thermos lying between the seats. "With pleasure," she said.

CHAPTER FORTY

Emily tilted forward on the seat, jagged from caffeine and adrenaline. "You don't need to drive all the way up to the Center," she said, glancing at the driver. Lester had the coolest sleeve tattoos including a colorful Phoenix that extended to his thick wrists.

"No problem," he said. "We made good time. Besides, Allie likes you."

Emily adjusted the purring cat, reluctantly moving Allie off her lap and back onto the blanket. The kindness of utter strangers amazed her. Four trucks, five hours later, and it was impossible to say which ride she'd enjoyed most: coffee-swigging Shirley from Kentucky, Pooper who donated all his gas miles to handicapped children, Eugene who loved to garden, or Lester and Allie who spent their spare time helping out in a tattoo parlor. None were captains of industry like Burke, but they definitely enriched the lives of people around them. Including hers.

The truck rumbled up the cobblestone drive where mercury vapor lamps illuminated pristine flower beds. Lester blew out an admiring whistle. "This Three Brooks is a fancy place. Is your pony a racehorse?"

"No, he's just a pet. But Three Brooks is a rehab center and my sister knows the owner." Jenna was actually married to the owner but Emily was reluctant to admit it, which seemed a little twisted. Before, it had been a major bragging point.

"I grew up in a little trailer just over that hill," she added. "Peanut always had the run of this place. He's a very cool guy and like a member of our family. But I'm not sure how this is going to go…"

Air brakes hissed as Lester eased the rig to a stop in front of the main entrance with the clearly marked doors. He turned toward Emily.

"Sometimes when animals are sick, there's not much you can do. Just be there to hold them. Although I guess it's hard to hold a pony. They're not like a cat." He gave an encouraging smile. "You're here and that's what's important. Good luck."

"Thanks, Lester." Emily swung open the heavy truck door. She didn't know what she could do for Peanut that Wally couldn't. Three Brooks had the most advanced equipment as well as access to the best vets. She only knew that nobody loved Peanut more than her and Jenna. And one of them should be there. "I hope your aunt's operation goes well," she added. "I really appreciate the drive."

She gave Allie a last pat and slid down from the cab. She waved, but once the truck pulled from the curb, she bolted toward the front door. Peanut was probably in one of the stalls close to the hyperbaric chamber. He'd always responded well to oxygen treatment.

She yanked at the door, not surprised to find the entrance locked. It was already close to midnight. Lights glowed from the windows of Wally's apartment above the Center and she turned and jogged toward the end door.

"I'm here, Emily. I heard the engine."

Wally's quiet voice came from behind her. She wheeled, straining to see his face through the gloom. "Where's Peanut?" she asked. "How's he doing?"

"He's in his regular stall in the ship-in barn. Breathing is labored and he's still down. We couldn't persuade him to walk to the oxygen chamber. I thought it best to let him rest. You sure we shouldn't call Jenna?"

"She'd fly back, and she and Burke need this vacation."

"Yeah, I know," Wally said. "I'm just worried. And I hate to keep anything from her. From Burke."

Even though Emily had already turned toward the visitors' barn, the distress in Wally's voice made her pause. She swung around and gave him a reassuring hug. "Don't worry. I'll tell them it was my decision."

Wally patted her awkwardly on the back. "Thanks for coming. I tried to call a couple hours ago—see where you were on the road—but couldn't reach you."

"My phone's dead. No battery charger," she said over her shoulder, already hurrying toward the small barn.

She rushed into the building, straight toward Peanut's special stall, the one with the door Burke had cut low so a pony could see into the aisle. And even though Wally had warned her about Peanut's condition, she couldn't stifle a groan.

He looked defeated, a tiny gray figure prone in the shavings. His eyes were closed and for a moment it seemed that despite the truckers' help, she'd arrived too late.

But then he let out a weary breath and his flank quivered.

"Hey, buddy," she whispered, circling around so she'd be in his line of vision. She crouched down and touched him gently on the shoulder. His eyelids flickered open. But there was no mischievous glint, and it didn't even look like Peanut's eye. More like a lifeless marble.

She squeezed her eyes shut, swept with despair. It was good they hadn't called Jenna. She never would have made it back in time.

Wally appeared in the doorway, the dark circles under his eyes more pronounced beneath the interior lights. "Doc's been in and out. He gave him an antihistamine and Banamine. Pulled some blood. He thinks Peanut might have had a reaction to his needles. Or maybe he's just tired of living. Not much more we can do."

"There must be something." Emily's voice cracked. "What would Jenna do?"

"Just let him know you care."

"But what if he stops breathing?" Her hand shook as she stroked his shaggy neck, so small and vulnerable, bumpy now with hives. "What do I do?"

"Nothing." Wally's voice lowered. "I know it's disconcerting...being the one to see him off. Want me sit up with you?"

She raised her head in surprise. Wally was an old family friend but he'd always been Jenna's buddy, not hers. And clearly he was exhausted. Besides, he seemed to think Peanut wasn't going to make it, and she didn't want that attitude spreading. They had to believe.

"You go to bed," she said. "We'll see you in the morning."

Wally's gaze flickered to Peanut's still form. He gave a dubious nod then turned and disappeared down the aisle.

Peanut's eye closed again. His breathing was shallow but at least he was breathing. She ran her fingers over his head, scratching the base of his left ear where he'd always had a particularly stubborn itch. No reaction. Nothing.

"Just rest, fellow. You'll feel better in the morning." But his ears didn't twitch the way they usually did when she spoke. He acted as if he didn't know she was there.

Fear curled in her chest, and a part of her wished Wally had stayed. Better still, she wished for Dan. Not only did he understand horses but his quiet confidence was infectious. His mere presence made her feel more confident, more capable, affecting her the same way it did the animals.

However, there wasn't much anyone could do. Peanut was unresponsive. He didn't hear her. Didn't see her. Didn't seem to know she sat beside him.

She bit her lip. Dan had talked about horses' keen sense of smell. And Peanut always knew when Emily had carrots in her pocket.

She inched around his prone body, moving her palm closer to his flared nostrils. On impulse, she bent down and blew gently in his nose. He twitched but it seemed more in irritation than recognition.

Her tears pricked. So many times, she'd cried into his neck. Once she'd caught Jenna crying too. He'd been their buddy, playmate and confidante when friends and money had been achingly scarce. Maybe he'd felt a little ignored over the last few years. Jenna was focused on acing vet school while Emily had been chasing smoky dreams. And she knew it hurt to be shuffled aside. He probably didn't realize how much he was cherished.

And so she told him.

She curled up against his back, wrapped her arms around his neck and whispered of bittersweet times. She even spoke of the night her father had slammed her against the sink because she hadn't dressed prettily enough for his poker game.

Jenna had never heard of that incident. Emily had been too ashamed. And scared. Her big sister had always stood up to their father, and he had a very uncertain temper. She'd always feared that one day his hammy fist would crack open Jenna's skull.

But Peanut knew everything. There'd been no secrets from Peanut.

A horse shuffled in the adjoining stall, moving restlessly in the straw and nosing at her water bucket. Emily wiggled deeper into the shavings. Peanut always gobbled up straw if it was used as bedding. Keeping his weight under control had been a constant issue so they only used wood shavings or peat moss.

Overeating wasn't an issue now. She'd never imagined a day when he wouldn't sniff at her pockets, searching for a treat. Never imagined a time when he wouldn't press his forehead to her stomach in that special greeting he reserved for her and Jenna.

She blinked back the well of tears and then gave up, no longer able to hold them back. Besides, Peanut was no stranger to crying. At least maybe he'd recognize her. "If you have to go, it's fine," she sobbed. "But I need you. And I'll always love you.

"And you should stick around and meet Dan. He'd love to see your tricks. He had a pony too until his mother sold him."

She pressed her wet cheeks tighter into his shaggy mane, remembering the Sunday afternoon that Peanut had disappeared. Jenna had marched off, fists clenched, both braids swinging—still in her church dress—and somehow found a way to buy him back. Their father had never tried to sell Peanut again.

"Please stay," she added brokenly. "Stay for Jenna. She'll be back soon. We can wait together."

The horse in the next stall banged her bucket again, but Peanut didn't move. Emily thought his breathing wasn't quite so shallow but maybe that was wishful thinking. Besides, it was hard to see anything through her blurry eyes.

But she kept a loving hand on his neck and recited every happy story she could remember, grateful that he'd been a stalwart presence in so many of them. The night inched past. A lone star twinkled through his stall window but darkness clung to the sky, and morning seemed a fragile lifetime away.

"Tomorrow I'll find a charger and call Dan," she rambled on, her throat painfully dry from non-stop talking. "Explain why I had to leave. But don't you worry about a thing. I can handle it. And I'm not going to fall asleep and let you leave, so don't even try to sneak off." Her voice turned fierce. "Now you listen to me, Peanut."

And whether it was her sudden bossiness or the raised voice, Peanut's ear twitched and for the first time since her arrival, he finally seemed aware of her presence.

CHAPTER FORTY-ONE

Barney was supposed to hold the bucket in his mouth, but every time they filmed the scene, he dropped it on her chest.

I should have practiced the grab trick a little more, Emily thought. She tried to push the bucket away but only felt Barney's tiny nose. *Tiny?*

Her eyes whipped open. She stared up at a muzzle flecked with white and gray. Peanut was alive! And standing.

She scrambled to her feet, almost afraid to touch him. He looked wobbly and his legs were swollen, but he definitely recognized her. In fact, he pressed his head against her stomach, holding it for a few seconds before sniffing at her pocket.

"Good boy," she whispered, her voice trembling with emotion. She scratched him cautiously behind the left ear and studied his flank, checking his respiration. It was a little rapid but much stronger than last night. Best of all, his eyes were wide and lucid, not quite as bright as usual, but he was definitely interested in her presence.

A door slammed. The horse in the adjacent stall nickered and slammed the bucket. Obviously it was breakfast time. A lanky teenager with reddish-blond hair stopped and stared over the door. His freckled face broke into a broad grin.

"Wow. Peanut's up!" he said. "When did you come home?"

"Hi, Charlie," she said, recognizing the local teen. "I came in last night. Are you working here now?"

"Sure am." He thrust out his thin chest. "Wally hired me to feed and muck stalls. It's never busy here though. He doesn't think I'm ready to work with the expensive horses in the big barn." He flushed and the color of his face matched his hair. "I don't mean Molly and Peanut aren't expensive. I think they're the best horses on the property."

"Best loved anyway," Emily said with a smile. Burke had built this ship-in barn so local horses could be treated at free or discount rates. However, the animals in this building certainly didn't match the dollar figures of the elite racehorses stabled in the Center.

"Is that your mare in the next stall?" she asked.

He nodded, his lanky hair flipping over his forehead. "Yeah, that's Molly. She's sore in the hind end again but a massage will fix her up. When is Jenna back anyway?"

"I'm not sure," Emily said, still touching Peanut's head, reluctant to move her hands. The pony was obviously weak but it didn't seem necessary for Jenna to abort her vacation. Now when they spoke, there'd only be positive news.

Emily's gaze drifted over Charlie's worn backpack and the Apple headphones dangling from his neck. "Do you have a charger I could borrow for a bit? My phone's dead."

"Sure." He rummaged in his pack and pulled out a battery charger. "I'll leave it in the feed room. Dr. Colin gave instructions for a mash in case Peanut could be coaxed to eat. I'll get it ready." But he lingered, shuffling his feet. "Jenna told me you had a part in a horse movie. I always thought you were pretty enough to be a movie star."

Emily smiled but felt a slight pang, realizing that filming had started without her. "I actually don't have lines, not anymore. I was going to be in a speaking scene today. I did get to lead a rearing horse though."

Charlie's eyes widened. "Wicked. That's way cooler. Everyone can talk. Not just anybody can lead a horse."

"It is fun," she said, "working with the horses. And my time here really helped. So be sure you listen to Wally. It might not seem that way, but he knows his stuff."

Charlie gave a teenager's typical shrug, backed away and wandered down the aisle. He probably feared she'd break into a lecture. Emily totally understood that feeling. She'd always thought she was pretty damn smart when she worked at the Center.

She turned back to Peanut and began plucking pieces of shavings from his mane. "You're the toughest little guy," she said.

"That he is." Wally's voice sounded behind her. "I'm not sure what you did, but it looks like he'll rebound." He swept into the stall and wrapped her in such an exuberant bear hug it lifted her feet off the floor. "Thanks for showing up."

"But I didn't do anything," she said, flustered by Wally's unusual embrace.

"You came," Wally said, stepping back. "That's what mattered to Peanut. You always come through when it's important." His voice turned gruff. "Let's check his vitals and call Colin. He's going to be amazed. He dropped by four times yesterday."

"By the way," Wally added, "you look great. New hair cut? Anyway, you look nice. I'll be back with a stethoscope."

Emily watched his retreating back, somewhat stunned. Wally had never seen her like this—without makeup. He'd also never once complimented her appearance. Shaking her head, she turned and pulled another shaving from Peanut's mane. "Obviously," she whispered, "he's very happy about your recovery."

She gave the pony a little pat and headed toward the feed room. She'd call Jenna after the vet came, after they were certain Peanut's condition had truly stabilized. However, Dan's call couldn't wait.

The charger was on the table, just as Charlie had promised. Once she connected it to the wall, her phone blinked to life. But she paused, hit with the realization that she didn't have Dan's number. Had never even texted him. After a moment of thought, she called the production company. It shouldn't be too hard to track him down.

"Sorry," the brisk woman at the other end said. "We can't give out personal information."

"But I work for him. He just never gave me his number."

The woman snickered. "Then he must not want you to have it."

Emily fought the edge of panic. "Could you at least ask him to call me?"

"We're not a message service. And the movie is winding down, so there are no new hires." The woman's voice turned mechanical. "If you're interested in future work, please apply through our website." The line went dead.

Emily groaned, paced twice around the feed room, then called Judith.

"You must be crazy." Judith's voice rose in disbelief when she heard Emily had left Hamilton Stud. "I can't believe you left. That you didn't show up for your speaking role."

"This was more important," Emily said.

"But what about looking around Billy's yard? That's important too. Things are starting to happen. And now neither of us is there."

"I'm coming back after it's certain Peanut will be okay. That's why I'm calling. I need Dan's number."

"Well, I don't have it," Judith said, her voice plaintive. "The only contact I have is for the production company. And they're not going to give out phone numbers. That information is protected."

"I know. I already tried." Emily twisted a tendril of hair around her finger. "Dan gave me his business card. But it only has the company info. Do you have Anthony's number?"

"Only select people have the director's number," Judith said, "and I'm not one of them. You shouldn't have been so impulsive. Peanut is only an animal. Isn't your career more important?"

Emily swallowed. She was impulsive, always had been. But Peanut and Jenna *were* more important than any career. And it didn't matter what Judith thought. However, the last thing she wanted was for Dan to think her irresponsible.

"Never mind," Emily said. "I have the casting director's number on my phone. I'll call him."

The casting director was polite and advised the scene had been moved to Friday since they were making changes to the set. He also said, with an obvious edge in his voice, that he would have no problem finding another actress if she didn't want the role.

"I do want the role though, and that's great it's moved," Emily said, elated that she hadn't lost her lines. "But could you give me Dan Barrett's number? We have a sick pony and I just need to tell him—"

"I'll mention it to him when I see him," the casting director said, his voice impatient. "Leave a message tonight and let me know if you'll be back tomorrow." He cut the connection.

Emily wistfully palmed her phone. 'I'll mention it to him' didn't feel very satisfactory. She needed to talk to Dan, the quicker the better. But only the production company had a listed number, and they weren't at all helpful. Everyone else had private or temporary numbers.

Except for Hamilton Stud. They'd been in Kentucky forever and definitely had a public presence. Brightening, she checked the Internet, then called the number on their website.

A real person answered.

"May I speak to Louise Hamilton, please," Emily said. "It's Emily Murphy calling, the groom from the movie."

"She's at a fundraiser now," the pleasant voice said, "but I'll make sure she receives your message."

"Thanks." Sighing, Emily closed her phone. If Mrs. Hamilton couldn't help, she was stuck until she returned to the set and saw Dan in person. But he of all people should understand about the importance of a sick pony... Shouldn't he?

For the next few hours, she hung around the ship-in barn, trying not to chew her lip and worrying alternately about Peanut and Dan. At least Peanut was eating and drinking. His temperature was a little high but out of the danger zone, and the vet was going to check the enzymes.

"This little guy has nine lives," Colin said, inserting the vials of blood in his black vet case. "Yesterday I doubted he'd make it. Guess there's no reason for Jenna to hurry back, not unless she wants to start her practicum early."

He gave Emily a rueful smile. "I'm off to Dubai in six months. Burke made an offer I couldn't refuse. He probably wanted to make sure Jenna could practice close to Three Brooks."

Emily's eyes held his in tacit understanding. She guessed Burke also wanted to make sure Colin was far away and happy. The two men were always cordial but Colin had once dated Jenna, and the vet was an extremely attractive man.

"You're going to break a lot of girls' hearts when you leave," Emily said. "But sometimes you meet the right person when you aren't even looking."

"Sounds like you're speaking from experience, little Miss Emily," he teased. His grin deepened. "Hey, you're actually blushing. Not a condition I usually associate with you. Glad to see it," he added, lowering his voice so Wally couldn't hear. "I hope you're as happy as Jenna."

"Oh, Colin." She reached up and hugged him. Other than Dan, he was the most attractive man in the world, kind but with a steely core that held up even to Burke's powerful personality.

She walked him to his truck and watched him drive away, fervently hoping he'd meet someone worthy in Dubai.

She remained in the barn for another hour, fussing over Peanut and even putting some braids in his unruly mane. However, he was more interested in hanging out with Charlie's mare in the adjacent stall. Peanut's return to his normal gregarious self left her smiling with relief and much more comfortable about leaving.

She wandered into the main building to grab a coffee and visit some old co-workers.

"Are you really working in the movies?" the receptionist, Frances, asked. "I thought you had to be really slim for that."

Emily's eyes narrowed. Frances was full of snide comments and constantly needed to be put in her place. "No, they need all sizes," Emily said, "even big people like—" She paused, choosing not to complete the sentence. Sparring with Frances used to be fun but it wasn't really a healthy sport. One of them always ended up hurt.

"I'm working with the horses. Not on screen," Emily said, "so appearance doesn't matter. It's really cool how they're trained to act wild and can do all kinds of stunts."

"So you're not in the movies." Frances wrinkled her nose and turned back to her crossword puzzle. "You're just cleaning stalls."

Emily nodded. "Yes, and I love it."

Smiling, she turned and walked away. Jenna always reminded her that Frances wasn't mean, just unhappy. Besides, Emily didn't work here any longer so the receptionist's barbs didn't matter. It actually had been nice to see her.

Emily stepped outside. She waved through the office window at Wally then turned and cut across the parking lot and onto the path that led to Emily and Jenna's trailer—actually not their trailer any longer. Burke had built a beautiful home in its place. But it wasn't her home. And now he was building a guesthouse.

Her steps slowed as she trudged along the overgrown path, in no hurry to be reminded that her family home had been demolished. It probably wouldn't sting so much if she still had a bedroom, or even a sofa. After all, the trailer had been sagging. But to be grouped with Burke's business associates in a separate guesthouse hurt.

She scooped up a rock and flung it at an oak tree. She and Jenna had always used the woods as a convenient place to vent their emotions. At least the trees never changed. The rock ricocheted, giving several satisfying bounces, and Emily blew out a sigh.

The house would be locked, of course, and she'd never been given a key. But maybe she could climb in a window and have a quick shower. If it were necessary to stay another night, she'd sleep with Peanut again. Besides, it was mainly the land she wanted to visit. The view from the Murphy porch had always been spectacular.

The trees thinned as the path widened into a clearing. Her steps slowed to a crawl. Burke had razed the shed and kennel, along with the old trailer. It had to be done, but part of her mourned the loss of her home. Of being pushed out.

Pulling in a deep breath, she stepped from the trees. For a second her breathing suspended. The new guesthouse wasn't what she expected. Not one bit. In fact, it looked like an extension of Jenna's house, blended so artfully it was impossible to tell where one ended and the other began. A beautiful deck extended around both homes, so all could share the panoramic view.

It wasn't ostentatious at all. Not bad, Burke, she conceded reluctantly.

She stepped onto the deck and lifted the thick mat. No key. And why would there be? Jenna hadn't known she was coming. In the good old days, they'd never bothered to lock their trailer. Three Brooks had a private road and security was tight. Besides, this place didn't look like it used anything as primitive as keys. In fact, it had an intimidating control panel by the door.

She remembered Burke asking her to speak into a machine. Jenna had insisted they didn't need locks while Burke had been equally insistent they did. Minutes later, they had laughingly slipped into the master bedroom, arms entwined, and Emily had been left rolling her eyes at their abrupt disappearance.

On impulse, she leaned toward the panel. "Hi," she said.

"Hi, Emily." The husky recording was Jenna's and her voice sounded so relaxed and satisfied, Emily suspected Burke had finished this particular recording in bed.

Click.

Emily tilted her head, cautiously eyeing the handle. Something had happened but she didn't want to touch anything that might trigger an alarm. Burke was so protective of Jenna, he probably had rigged a booby trap. Several of them.

The door swung open.

Emily grinned. Burke sure liked gadgets. However, the fact that he had included her voice in the lock deactivation made her feel much better. Almost like she still had a home. Maybe they wouldn't stick her in the guesthouse after all.

She stepped inside and headed for the shower by the pool. Jenna always kept it well stocked, and there'd be no need to deplete Mrs. Hamilton's emergency toiletries. She was hallway across the polished granite hall when she spotted a foyer on the left. It looked like Burke had made another addition.

An archway curved around the side. She veered though the foyer and up the winding steps, walking slowly, staring in confusion. It seemed she was now on the second floor of the guesthouse. But she couldn't imagine they'd want their business associates underfoot.

She pivoted in a slow circle. A welcoming balcony linked the two houses and led into a five-sided turret. She could see the valley, the brook, even old Mrs. Parker's house.

She stepped into the room and for a moment stopped breathing. Could only stare in disbelief. All their familiar treasures were here: their mother's sewing box, the framed picture of their parents, even the carving of Peanut she'd made for Jenna back in the eighth grade. The old porch swing had been hung as well. She'd assumed Burke had thrown it out when he demolished the trailer.

She sank down on the friendly swing, her breath coming in grateful gasps. Nothing had changed, not really. It was all here on this shared balcony—the feeling of home, the belonging, the love.

She rose to her feet and walked into the attached guesthouse.

Her nose twitched. This place smelled familiar, like their old trailer, like someone had been using her favorite perfume. She stepped into the first room. Her hands swept to her face and she gawked in disbelief.

She rushed through each thoughtfully designed room, her cheeks now wet with tears. Her emotions churned with each discovery. Everything was here, her 4-H ribbons, her favorite moisturizer and a creatively designed closet with space for countless pairs of shoes. This was no guesthouse. It was apparent now—Burke had built a sister-in-law house.

Her throat convulsed, and the need to call and thank them was overwhelming. But she jammed her hands in her pockets, aware she had to wait. Otherwise, they'd question why she was home. Colin would be back in the afternoon to re-assess Peanut. If the prognosis was favorable, then she'd call.

She returned to the familiar swing, her emotions whirling. This house, Peanut, Jenna, Dan, the movie... There was much to absorb.

And while the conversation with Jenna might be upbeat, it was hard to feel optimistic about her call to Dan. Or that there'd even be a call. Because unfortunately there was still no response from Louise Hamilton, and try as Emily might, she couldn't help but agonize about what he was thinking.

CHAPTER FORTY-TWO

"So, Emily went to the stud barn yesterday and never came back?" Dan crossed his arms, watching Lizzie for any signs of evasiveness. "You sure she didn't say anything?"

"Positive. We worked with Splash and she delivered the props for the bath scene. I didn't ask her to do that though," Lizzie added quickly. "She offered."

"How did she act? Was she upset about something?"

"No." Lizzie gave an emphatic shake of her head. Her face was flushed but she didn't avoid his eyes. "Like I told you, she was excited about the shoot. And rather helpful. Splash was really good, by the way."

"Yeah, great." Dan ran his hand over his jaw, wishing he could concentrate more on his horses. He'd had a sleepless night even though Louise Hamilton had informed him that Emily was fine and simply needed to go home. But that didn't make sense.

She'd literally worked herself raw trying to earn a shot at a speaking role. To simply walk away was astounding. She'd claimed she didn't want to be an actress, that she only wanted a few lines to prove her success. He'd arranged that. Clearly though, she didn't know what the hell she wanted.

Lizzie cleared her throat. "You sure she left the property?"

Dan wheeled. "What do you mean?"

"All I know is that she left here carrying the wash buckets. She wasn't thinking about leaving. Only wanted to help with the horses. She seemed totally sincere."

"They always do," Dan said, his voice clipped.

"Yes," Lizzie said, her voice troubled. "But now we know what it was like twenty years ago when that other groom disappeared…and maybe nobody looked very hard."

"This is hardly the same thing," Dan snapped. He immediately felt rotten. Lizzie hadn't done anything wrong. He was the love struck idiot who'd let Emily into his life. And it had been a mistake. He knew better. "I'm sorry you wasted your time training her," he added.

"It's fine. She's actually…okay. Did you say it was Mr. Hamilton or Mrs. Hamilton who drove her to the station?"

"Mrs."

"Well, that's a relief," Lizzie said.

Dan stiffened, hit with a jolt of unease. Hamilton was a known lecher and like Lizzie pointed out, there'd already been one missing groom. "Guess I'll ask a few more questions," he said. "Find out why she left so fast. Who she was meeting."

"Good idea," Lizzie said.

But an hour later, Dan still had no idea where Emily had gone. The production company provided her phone number but she wasn't answering. Neither were the Hamiltons.

"Emily didn't call you?" he asked Anthony. "Or your assistant?"

"No." Anthony raised an irritable eyebrow. "And if we hadn't rescheduled that scene, this would have been damn inconvenient. That's the problem with non-union. They jump ship for a better offer."

"Emily isn't like that." Dan folded his arms. "She does everything with heart. There are no half measures."

"Whatever," Anthony said. "But those aren't the kind of people I want around. They always burn you."

"I only want to make sure she's okay," Dan said.

"You're just shocked she left your bed. Don't worry. It happens to the best of us." Anthony jabbed him in the shoulder. "Welcome to the ranks of us mortal men."

Dan scowled.

"Well," Anthony said, grinning now. "If you can track her down, let her know she can still do the scene if she's back tomorrow. We're moving it to the main barn. And I need time to convert a little apartment."

"What's wrong with the stud barn?" Dan asked. "It already has an apartment."

"Hamilton doesn't want the barn used. He's still upset about the fire and wondering what really happened to the groom. Anyway, that's his story."

"Yeah," Dan said, unable to keep the strain from his voice. It was odd that only the Hamiltons knew anything about Emily leaving. He tried her number again but it went directly to voice mail. Her battery had been low so her phone might be turned off. Or dead.

He turned back to Anthony. "How did you know Emily wasn't coming? Hamilton?"

"No. Emily called casting this morning."

"Oh," Dan said, at a loss for words. So she really was fine. She had chosen to leave. She hadn't been kidnapped or forced to quit or developed amnesia.

When he was a kid, he'd half hoped his mother had been abducted by aliens. That she'd been sucked up by a green light in the middle of the night. For years, he'd prayed for super powers so he could fly through the sky and zoom to her rescue.

And naturally he was relieved Emily was safe. But there was no bogeyman to battle. She'd simply made a choice to leave. All perfectly fine. He didn't want or need such a flamboyant woman anyway.

He pressed her number one final time. However, her cheery recording only exacerbated his deep sense of loss. He cut the connection, dropped his phone in his pocket and turned his attention back to his job.

"Peanut's okay now, Jenna," Emily repeated, adjusting the screen of her phone and bringing her sister's face into sharper focus. "He's even trying to reach over the door and grab Molly's hay. All his vitals are better and Colin says his blood work is good. I'll scan the reports and send them. But Colin thinks he's over the hump."

"Thank God." Jenna's relief escaped in a grateful sigh. Seconds later she leaned forward and even though she was four thousand miles away, her confusion was apparent. "Why are you even home, Em? You have a speaking part."

Her voice turned accusing. "You didn't quit, did you? Burke says the movie industry is very tight. They don't forgive performers who aren't dependable."

Emily tried not to wince. Tried not to think of Dan. "It's just a couple lines," she said. "And the casting director said everything is okay as long as I'm on site early tomorrow."

Jenna nodded, her beautiful face softening. "You shouldn't have left your job, but I'm grateful you did. According to Wally, you're the reason Peanut pulled through."

"He would have been fine without me. Colin figures it was a reaction to the spring needles. They all gave him super care."

"Should I fly home?"

Emily shook her head. "No. Stay and enjoy your vacation. Peanut's fine now. Improving every hour."

"Guess we'll have to reconsider his vaccines," Jenna said. "Maybe consider intranasal options. He can't be on the Center grounds if he's not up-to-date, and I'd worry about cutting out the tetanus and West Nile." Her face disappeared as she reached for a pen, and Emily heard a muted discussion about pharmaceutical companies.

Moments later, Jenna reappeared. "No worries. Burke will check into it."

Emily smiled. If her recollections were correct, Burke Industries owned an equine drug company. Peanut's allergies would not be a problem. Jenna winked, and it was obvious they were in complete accord.

"Burke's amazing," Emily said. "I saw the guesthouse. It's not what I expected. I thought... Well, it's just perfect. Thanks to you b-both." Her words tangled with such emotion she could only touch her lips and place her fingers against the screen.

"It's your home." Jenna's voice bubbled with delight. "All yours, whenever you want it. We wanted to surprise you. It was Burke's idea to make the connecting balcony. I didn't even know that was possible. He's buying a local construction company so he can relax in Three Brooks more. This vacation gave us a chance to talk about a lot of things."

Jenna glowed with so much happiness, it was apparent the vacation had been the perfect tonic.

"Are the English races what you expected?" Emily asked.

"We didn't leave the hotel suite for the first couple days," Jenna admitted, her smile rather wicked. "But the races we saw yesterday were super. The fences are huge and how they jump at such speed is amazing. But we saw enough. I'm coming home now."

Emily walked from the feed room, holding the phone in front of her. She'd anticipated Jenna would jump on the first plane, despite assurances that Peanut was out of danger.

"We're all glad you're having a good time," Emily said. "And there's a little guy here who thinks you should stay and enjoy the vacation. You're a vet. Judge for yourself how he's feeling."

Emily tilted the phone while Peanut sniffed at the screen, his eyes bright and curious.

"See." Emily turned the phone back to her face. "He's fine. Even his hives are almost gone. So don't you dare come home. Besides, Burke deserves this vacation as much as you, especially after he built my super cool house."

Jenna's brow furrowed. "Peanut does seem okay. But are you sure, Em? You have your own life. You can't be on call for our old pony."

"I most certainly can," Emily said. "He's like a crusty uncle. And you're not in this alone. There are two of us who love him. If necessary, I can come back, much quicker than you. So relax and have a good time."

"Okay." Jenna's voice faltered. "I just hope you didn't give up too much to come home. But thanks, sis. Just a sec."

Burke's face replaced Jenna's on the screen. "How are you getting back to Kentucky?" His voice was crisp and authoritative. "Wally reported you didn't drive your car. That an eighteen-wheeler dropped you off."

Emily stiffened. It seemed a lifetime since she'd wrecked her car. She hadn't talked to Burke since that happened. No doubt he'd accuse her of reckless driving and grill her about insurance premiums, totally understandable really, considering he'd bought the vehicle.

"I've arranged for a car to take you back," he went on. "Wally has the limo number. You can call anytime." He smiled then, looking surprisingly boyish for a hardnosed executive. "And no matter what you told Jenna, I know it's not possible to walk away from a movie set without repercussions. When we get back, I'll introduce you to a competent producer in California. Just in case you need some new contacts."

"Oh, but I don't want—"

Burke frowned and she quit talking.

"You're unorthodox," he went on. "And often I don't understand you. But you've always had Jenna's back. Whenever she needed it." His voice lowered. "You're blue chip. And I appreciate you, very much."

Emily gripped the phone, barely able to concentrate as he went on about agents and commissions and how his legal team should vet any new agreements. Burke had given her a compliment? And he'd said she always had Jenna's back?

"Let me speak." Jenna's head poked in front of Burke's. "I don't want my only sister living far away in Hollywood," she went on. "You're good with animals. What about being a vet assistant? You haven't tried anything like that yet."

Emily pressed her fingers over her mouth, feeling much lighter than the last time they'd discussed her various careers. It seemed Jenna didn't care what she did. And Burke only wanted whatever made Jenna happy.

"Actually," Emily admitted, "I'm hoping to get a job as a horse wrangler. And then maybe move on to trick training."

"That's great, Em," Jenna said, not missing a beat. "As long as you come home more often, even if it's just for a couple days."

Emily blinked. She could have said she was running off to join the circus; Jenna really didn't care. The only thing her sister wanted was to see her more often. They may have had a piss poor father but Emily definitely could never find a better sister. Or brother-in-law.

"Have a good time in England," Emily managed, her chest fuzzy with so much emotion it spilled into her voice. "I'll visit when you're back. And don't worry about Peanut. I love you both."

The call ended. But Emily palmed the phone long after they'd hung up. It was great talking with them, seeing their faces. However, now that they were gone, her loneliness felt more acute. If only she could see Dan, or at least talk to him.

Mrs. Hamilton hadn't returned her call though. There was one message, but that was from Judith. At least Emily's phone was charged, thanks to Charlie. She pressed Judith's number, needing to talk to someone who knew Dan.

"Did you hear?" Judith asked, her voice thick with relief. "Your shoot isn't until tomorrow. They're not using the little barn either. They have to make a fake door for the scene. Isn't that weird? That Mr. Hamilton won't let them use the bottom of the stud barn?"

"Yes, weird but lucky," Emily said, rather distracted. "Do you think the casting director gave Dan my message? About Peanut being sick?"

"I don't know." Judith blew out an impatient breath. "Does it matter?"

"Of course. He was at Churchill yesterday so I couldn't talk to him before I left."

"He's so busy he probably didn't notice," Judith said. "Just get back here. You can talk to him then."

Emily twisted a strand of Peanut's mane around her finger. She didn't want to wait, didn't want Dan to think she'd disappeared for no good reason. "I'll probably come back tonight," she said, "so I can do the scene tomorrow. Peanut is doing quite well. And I won't have to hitchhike."

"If you're here before dark we can check the area around Billy's cottage." Judith's voice lifted. "Investigators finished checking the rubble, and the area is no longer restricted. But everyone's speculating about the fire. I wish they'd bring in one of those machines that hunts for graves."

Emily turned from Peanut and paced a circle in the stall. She hated to think Billy was a murderer. Sometimes she wished they hadn't found Tracey's duffle bag. "I don't think he would have buried her in the yard. It's too open. And judging by the kennel, there used to be dogs around. They would have dug up a body."

"Yes," Judith said. "There was a bag of moldy dog food in the closet. But where else would he have buried her?"

"I don't know. But not close to the road."

"I'll check if there were any pigs," Judith said, her voice strained.

Emily shuddered at the thought of what a pig could do to a body. "Hamilton Stud doesn't seem the kind of place that would have a pigpen."

"I have to go," Judith said. "The bus just stopped."

"The bus?" Emily asked. "Where are you?"

"At the site. I'm doing background today."

"Then you'll see Dan soon." Emily swung around, so excited that Peanut stopped chewing hay. "Can you tell him that I'll be back tonight? Maybe you could have him call me. Or get his number so I can call him. Please, Judith."

"Slow down," Judith said. "He probably won't give me his number but I can pass on your message. And yes, I'll do it. I won't even go to the background tent first."

"Thank you." Emily sighed with relief. It was quite a favor for someone like Judith to delay her check-in.

"I don't know why you're worrying," Judith said. "Dan isn't the type who gets attached. Bet he didn't even notice that you're gone." Her words turned rushed as voices swelled in the background. "I'll call you later. Bye."

Emily put away her phone and turned back to Peanut. He pushed his head into her chest so she could scratch his shaggy ears. "Judith doesn't know everything," she whispered. "And I think Dan noticed."

Still, it would have been simple for someone in his position to find her number. Yet he hadn't called, not unless it was before her phone was charged. Peanut nudged at her pocket, blithely unconcerned about the lack of calls, and despite her preoccupation with Dan, the pony's interest in treats was an immensely positive sign.

Her phone vibrated. She yanked it from her pocket so quickly, she almost dropped it in the shavings.

"Hello, Emily," the cultured voice said. "This is Louise Hamilton. I received your message. Were you able to meet your drive on time?"

"Oh, yes. Thanks for taking me to the highway." Emily kept her hand on Peanut's neck, drawing support from his stoic presence. "I just wondered if you were able to pass my message on to Dan?"

"Certainly," Mrs. Hamilton said. "I spoke to him yesterday. I do hope everything is okay."

There was a slight question in her voice, but she was clearly too refined to ask details, and Emily's appreciation of the lady grew. "Everything is fine. I'm hoping to return tonight. Luckily my scene was postponed. But I wonder, do you have Dan's number?"

"If I don't, I can get it for you," Mrs. Hamilton said. "Wait one moment while I check with my husband."

Emily squeezed her eyes shut and even Peanut's neck relaxed, as though sharing her relief.

"He's calling Anthony's assistant now," Mrs. Hamilton said, mere seconds later.

A man's voice rumbled in the background. Shortly after, Mrs. Hamilton relayed Dan's number.

"Thank you very much," Emily said. She quickly pressed the number into her phone, wishing there were some way to repay Mrs. Hamilton for her many kindnesses. But she'd worry about that later. Right now it was more important to call Dan.

CHAPTER FORTY-THREE

"Cut!" Anthony said.

Shania nodded at the actor playing Billy, grabbed a bottle of water from her attentive assistant and sauntered off the set, her tight jeans plastered to shapely legs.

"We got the flashback on the second take," she said, stopping by Dan. "I'm glad they added those extra scenes. A famous racehorse is fine, but now we have the human-interest element. And that's what sells movies." She took a dainty sip of water, her black-coated eyelashes fanning her cheeks. "Do you think Billy killed her?"

"Investigators didn't find anything in the rubble," Dan said.

"Perhaps they should dig deeper. Playing the role of Tracey has made me sympathetic toward the girl. It's unfortunate the cottage was badly burned. I heard someone found a duffle bag but then took off."

Someone. Dan's mouth tightened.

"Billy may have been a cross dresser," Shania went on. "Otherwise it's doubtful he'd have Tracey's bag unless it was for nefarious reasons. The only other man who moved around freely was Thomas Hamilton. Let's get together tonight and compare notes." She placed a hand on Dan's forearm and blinked her big eyes. "I gave you information on the ball cap, but my assistants gathered much more research on Tracey. Just think of the headlines if we helped solve this mystery."

Dan gave a dismissive shrug. Shania seemed to think he wanted to be an investigator, probably because of that call he'd made for Emily. "Anthony would want to hear this," he said, "but I'm primarily interested in the horse aspect." He didn't want to shake off Shania's fingers and look rude, but this was a hectic morning and he had a lot to do.

"Oh, but I have plenty of horse research too." Her hand fluttered higher on his arm. "I interviewed three grooms. One of them covered for Tracey the morning she went missing. The poor girl broke her wrist trying to hold Reckless for his bath. That's when they noticed the colt's violent behavior."

"Broke her wrist?" Dan rubbed his forehead. Anthony had requested a quiet horse for the bath scene and that had suited him fine, especially since Splash was safer for Emily to handle. But Emily was no longer here and the movie was taking a darker twist, one that the company seemed keen to pursue. Anthony might want to consider Shania's information, especially since the script supervisor was still making changes.

Dan's phone vibrated and he slipped his hand in his pocket, using the movement as an excuse to free his arm.

"Barrett," he answered.

"Hi, it's Emily."

He hated his rush of relief, the pure happiness he felt at the sound of her voice. "Where are you?" he asked. "Are you okay?"

"I'm fine. It took me awhile to get your number. But Mrs. Hamilton was kind enough to help. Sorry I had to leave without talking to you."

"It doesn't matter," he said, more stiffly now, aware of Shania's avid interest.

"But it does." Emily sounded rather breathless. "Peanut had an allergic reaction and my sister was away and I didn't have time to leave a note."

Dan blinked in surprise. Her pony? Her absence was because of Peanut? "How's he doing?" he asked, remembering the sparkle in her eyes whenever she mentioned her pony.

"Much better. It was touch and go for a bit though. I'm hoping to come back soon, depending on what the vet says."

"Good. How did you get home?"

"Oh, Mrs. Hamilton helped. Then I caught a couple drives," she said, her voice drifting.

"Hitchhiked?" He hated the disapproval in his voice, knew that wasn't what she needed. She'd had enough censure to last a lifetime. "Never mind, Em," he said. "I'm glad you're okay. You and Peanut too." But even to him, his words sounded flat.

"The casting director said my scene with Splash's bath was postponed until tomorrow. So that's good..." Her voice trailed off to an uncomfortable silence.

"It might be postponed even further," Dan said. "And the horse might not be Splash. In fact, from what I'm hearing the bath could be a lot more energetic."

Shania gave a throaty laugh and leaned closer. "I like energetic," she murmured.

Dan pressed the phone closer to his ear, wishing Emily had called at a better time. Five people signaled for his attention, their eyes reflecting various degrees of urgency, and Shania had her hand plastered on his arm again. "I have to go, Emily," he said. "We're in the middle of filming. But I'm glad you and Peanut are okay. See you."

He slipped his phone back in his pocket. Then authorized an extra horse for the upcoming scene, signed for a rush delivery of bedding, soothed the stunt performer who claimed Anthony practiced verbal abuse, and then had Lizzie add some touch-up paint to a horse's legs. Throughout the activity, Shania didn't leave his side…or Emily his thoughts.

"Sorry to bother you," a quiet voice said, so tentative he could barely hear. "I've been waiting for a long time. I just need to pass on a message."

It took him a second to recognize Emily's friend from their trailer stay. "Hello, Judith," he said.

"Emily wanted you to know that she'll probably be back tonight." Judith shuffled her feet, speaking quickly. Her self-conscious gaze bounced from the buttons on his shirt, to Shania, and back to his shirt again. "There was an…animal emergency and she had to leave. But you can call if you want. And if she had your number, she'd call you."

"I just spoke with her. She told me about Peanut." His voice softened. "But thank you."

Judith's shoulders visibly relaxed and she lifted her head, finally meeting his gaze. "That's good. I better report to the background tent now."

Shania made an impatient sound, and Judith scooted away, clearly relieved the message had been delivered. Perhaps Shania's imperious presence had been daunting, especially since Judith lacked Emily's pluck. On her very first day, Emily had sashayed into the cast and crew's dining room, acting like she owned it.

The image of Emily cheered him, along with the knowledge that it must have taken considerable effort to persuade her meek friend to deliver a message in the middle of a bustling set…although Judith wasn't always meek. She was the same woman who'd rifled through his papers, behavior that didn't fit her conformist appearance. He frowned, bothered by the inconsistencies.

"Those extras should know better than to barge up like that," Shania said, clearly misinterpreting his frown. "How about we meet back at the hotel where it's private? You can listen to my interviews and pick out what's important for your horses."

Dan turned back to Shania. "Do you have notes from the groom with the broken wrist? And more information on Reckless's bath?"

"Of course. There are both notes and audio." Shania's voice turned sultry. "And I'd be delighted to show you everything I have."

"I'll send you a daily report," Wally said, holding open the back door of the limo. "But don't worry. The way Peanut is stealing Molly's hay shows he's back to normal."

Emily nodded and slid onto the luxurious leather seat. Burke hadn't skimped with the car. Of course, Burke never skimped on anything.

Wally dropped a new phone charger on her lap. "Thought this might come in handy while you're on that movie location. Charlie picked it up. And the way you were with Peanut—your dedication—well, if you ever need a reference for horse care, I'd be pleased to talk to any future employer. Your mother would be proud of the way you and Jenna support each other." He cleared his throat. "I am too."

He closed the door and tapped the roof of the car.

Emily gripped the charger, staring out the window as the driver eased the car down the manicured driveway. Wally remained on the cobblestones, waving, and his rare sendoff filled her with a sense of belonging.

"Your dad left an envelope from Mr. Burke in the side pocket," the driver said.

"That's not my dad, more like an uncle," Emily said, still waving to Wally. "An uncle I never appreciated enough."

The driver smiled in understanding, his eyes meeting hers in the rearview mirror. "Refreshments are in the fridge. Let me know if you want to stop before Lexington."

Emily nodded and cautiously reached for Burke's envelope. It might be an invoice for the drive—something she could ill afford—but at least travel time back to the set would be minimal.

Dan had sounded so stiff on the phone, as though she'd committed a serious offense. And maybe, in his opinion, she had. However, Peanut was recovering, Wally was happy and Jenna was able to enjoy her vacation. Those things were far more important than any job. Always would be.

Squaring her shoulders, she ripped open the envelope. A golden airline ticket dropped onto her lap. "Oh, wow," she breathed, staring at the pass, good for unlimited air travel anywhere in the USA. No upkeep or gas required. She could go home for vacations. Heck, she'd be able to fly home whenever she wanted.

There was a typed message on a thick white sheet. Obviously Burke's scarily competent office had looked after this.

Flying might work out better for you than car maintenance. Come home often. Do you want a skylight in your bedroom?
Burke

He hadn't written anything about Peanut but his appreciation was clear and by Burke's standards, the note was absolutely gushing.

She folded his letter and reverently tucked it into the side pocket of Mrs. Hamilton's gift bag. She'd been a fool to think Burke resented her visits, that they were in competition for Jenna's attention. Heck, he'd even said 'come home' not 'visit.' And he hadn't mentioned her wrecked car. In fact, his toughest question had been about skylights.

And heck she wanted skylights, sure she did. She wanted to take Dan home, play cards with Burke and Jenna, and then lie in bed and admire the stars. There wasn't a prettier sight than watching the reddening horizon from the porch. But having Dan beside her would definitely move the bedroom view to first place.

She fingered her phone, tempted to call him again. Maybe he'd have more time to talk. But it was only three o'clock, and they'd still be filming. Judith might not be busy though. Emily pressed her number.

"Hi," Judith said. "Is your phone charged?"

"Totally. And I'll be back about seven tonight."

"That's great," Judith said. "I went over to Billy's cottage. Guess who was there?" Her voice rose. "Thomas Hamilton. He was poking around but not in the rubble. He was checking the grass, like he knew there was something hidden."

"Did he see you?" Emily adjusted the heat in the back seat, suddenly chilled.

"No, I hid in the woods. But he knows something. I'm sure of it."

"But the yard is too open. If they dug a grave there, someone would have noticed." Emily lowered her voice, but the driver stared straight ahead, stoically concentrating on the road. "What about Dan?" She blew out a breath. "Did you see him?"

"Yes. I passed on your message. He'd already spoken with you."

"Thanks," Emily said gratefully. "How did Bruno do this morning? Did they finish the rail stunt?"

"He wasn't with any horses. Only Shania."

Emily frowned. "I thought all her scenes were finished until next week."

"Yes, but the producer added some parts with Billy. That's good because more attention could force the police to reopen Tracey's case. The actor playing him is super creepy. I looked him up on the Internet and he did some stalking movies. They're going to show him watching Shania ride."

"But Shania doesn't ride. Would they use Splash? Or maybe Ice?"

"I don't care what horse they use," Judith said impatiently. "I just know Tracey liked to ride around the estate in the evenings. A bunch of grooms did."

Judith sounded increasingly testy and Emily soothed her voice. "That's great. I'm glad everything is going well, and that you have more background work."

"Everything is fine," Judith said. "But you shouldn't have left. You definitely missed your chance with Dan. He and Shania are really tight. She was hanging on him all morning, and he wasn't pushing her away."

"But they're working together. He's just humoring her." Emily paused. "Don't you think that's what he's doing?"

"I don't know," Judith snapped. "And don't you think finding a body is more important than who's hanging on Dan Barrett's arm?"

"Not really," Emily said.

The line turned silent. Then went dead.

Emily sighed but quickly called back. Judith was obsessed about solving the mystery of Tracey's disappearance, and a true friend would be more supportive.

"Sorry," Emily said, as soon as Judith answered. "Of course I'll help you check Billy's yard—wherever Hamilton was standing. And anywhere else you want to look."

"Okay, thanks," Judith said, rather stiffly. "We already checked the apartment. She can't be hidden in the barn. The smell and stuff. Wouldn't horses freak?"

"Like Reckless did," Emily said.

Neither of them spoke for a taut moment.

"But the barn was built a whole year before Tracey disappeared," Judith finally said. "Do stalls have wood floors or concrete?"

"Wood. Concrete wouldn't be good for a Thoroughbred's legs." Emily's knuckles whitened around the phone. "When was the wash stall put in?"

"You think maybe…she's under the wash stall?"

"Well, it slopes funny and doesn't drain," Emily said. "But there's no way they'd go twenty years without having it fixed. There'd be constant flooding."

"Mr. Hamilton moved the three-year-olds after Tracey disappeared," Judith said. "They had some studs in there for awhile but basically there was no access. Until the movie."

Emily pressed against the seat. The phone suddenly felt heavier than a hay bale. "Hamilton must have known," she whispered. "That's why he doesn't want anyone in the apartment."

"So he and Billy could have been in this together," Judith said. "And he's trying to cover up something. We need to check that floor."

"It's not easy to dig up concrete."

"We could pull out the drain and look around. Or you could ask Dan to have the set guys fix the floor."

"But they're not shooting there anymore," Emily said. "There's no reason for the company to fix it."

"Yes, and I bet Hamilton is behind the switch. But maybe we can find something in Billy's yard. Enough of a reason to check the barn."

An authoritative voice hollered in the background.

"I have to go," Judith said. "They're calling the extras. But I'll sneak in my phone. Text me when you get here."

"Would you let me know if you see Dan?" Emily asked. "He was too busy to talk the last time I called."

"Okay. Be sure to ask him about the floor. Gotta go."

Emily put away her phone and peered at the speedometer. The car was highway cruising at just over the limit but it seemed to be crawling. A sense of urgency consumed her. Billy had always been eccentric, his comments rather bizarre.

With dementia, normal filters were removed. He might even have confessed to a dark partnership with Hamilton. *If he'd lived long enough.*

She folded her hands, trying to stop their twitching. But despite turning up the heat, goose bumps snaked down her back. There had been no official announcement about the cause of the explosion. Not yet. But it seemed increasingly possible that Thomas Hamilton might be responsible for more than one murder.

CHAPTER FORTY-FOUR

Emily stared through the car's window at the blur of Kentucky road signs. Not far now. *I'll be there in forty minutes,* she texted to Judith. *Are you still on set? Is Dan there?*

She'd already sent Judith two texts, as yet unanswered, but surely the shoot would finish soon. It might be difficult for Judith to pull out her phone under the watchful eye of the assistant director. Actually it was surprising Judith even dared to sneak it onto the set. That woman was definitely loosening up.

The message light blinked and Judith's text appeared: *Just finished. Dan not here or Hamilton. Going to cottage now.*

The sun was dropping and red tinged the western ridge, but there was still plenty of daylight. And the stud barn had good lighting. Emily clasped her hands, barely noticing her chipped nails and the ridge of calluses. She just wanted the car to move faster.

She leaned forward. "How much further?"

"Twenty-two miles," the driver said. "Is there a back entrance?"

"Yes, we can use the caretaker's driveway. The security guard will let us in with my movie card."

She settled back against the seat, determined not to call Dan yet. He might be finished on set but she didn't want to disturb him during a production meeting. Besides, when she couldn't see his face, it was hard to know what he was thinking. Texting was totally unsatisfactory. What if he didn't answer?

She lasted another interminable six minutes but it wasn't her nature to pussyfoot. She picked up her phone and pressed Dan's number.

He answered on the second ring. "Barrett."

His deep voice seemed to suck the oxygen from the car, and it took a second to gather her senses. "Hi," she finally said. "I'm less than half an hour away. Just wondered if you were busy tonight?"

"Yes, I'm at the hotel. Doing some research."

"Okay." She paused, but he didn't speak and she understood firsthand how he'd become so adept at fending off women. Her chest tightened but she kept her voice light. "Peanut's doing well," she said. "The vet was happy with his blood work."

"Good."

Questions. She needed a question, some way to get him talking. "Did you decide if you're using Splash?" she asked.

"Not sure yet. Shania has some interesting recordings we're checking now."

She squeezed her eyes shut, her chest constricting. Shania and Dan. At a hotel. It was impossible to stop the painful stream of images. And he wasn't making it easy. But his job involved working with actresses, and he didn't need another drama queen. He'd made that clear. Besides, this was Dan. Everyone knew he was famously immune to co-workers.

"Good luck," she said, ignoring a woman's sultry laugh in the background. "I hope you find something that helps."

"We discovered Reckless couldn't be washed inside," Dan said. "And a lot of people knew it. Anthony may cut that scene."

"But was the trouble only in the little barn? Because Judith and I think…" She paused, but her fear tumbled out. "We think Reckless smelled something and that's why he acted up. Maybe we could even find Tracey's body."

"Reckless acted up everywhere." Dan gave a humorless laugh. "But don't worry. Anthony has already guaranteed you a speaking role."

"The role doesn't matter." She fought a wash of despair. She hadn't considered the ramifications of dropping the bath scene. Didn't care if she was ever accepted in the union. But clearly Dan thought that was her main concern.

Of course, at one time it had been.

"Your name is on the actors' sheet for a hotel room," he said. "So at least you don't have to worry about a place to stay."

"Great." She forced some enthusiasm into her voice. "I'm meeting Judith now but maybe I'll see you at the hotel later?"

"Yeah. Give me a call," he said, before hanging up.

She leaned back against the headrest, her tension marginally easing. It wasn't all bad. He wasn't bursting with enthusiasm but at least she'd see him. Surely she could make him understand why it had been so important to go home.

She pressed Judith's number. "I'll be at Billy's cottage in about fifteen minutes," she said.

"Good. There's so much debris lying around here, it's impossible to find a duffle bag. But it looks like there was a small pen about thirty feet from the house. Do pigs use little houses?"

"It's probably just the dog kennel," Emily said. "Is it boarded? Or wired?"

"Nothing like that. Just some rotten planks and a shovel. But it's close to the spot where Hamilton was looking." Judith's voice lowered. "Is Dan coming? This is kind of creepy."

"He's working at the hotel."

"Darn. But at least there are two of us. Maybe we can find something to grab his interest."

"I hope," Emily said. But she blew out a tormented breath, hating to think what Shania might be doing to arouse Dan's interest.

"This is the last interview," Shania said. She reached for the wine bottle and raised a questioning eyebrow at Dan.

"No, thanks." He jotted down another notation. Anthony's decision to include the mystery of Tracey's disappearance required some adjustment with the horses, but fortunately Shania had conducted extensive research. Her reputation of accurately portraying true characters was well deserved. He'd never met an actress who gathered so much material, and his respect for her professionalism mushroomed.

Anthony wanted the horse to mirror Reckless's actual behavior on the day Tracey was reported missing. Splash definitely couldn't be used for that scene, not after reading Shania's notes. And they would have to shoot outside, since by all accounts Reckless had been unmanageable in the little barn. Maybe Emily was onto something about the smell.

"This groom lived in the area," Shania said, "and worked for the neighboring estate. When Louise and Thomas married, the two properties were joined, and Hamilton Stud became one of the largest horse farms in the state. She knew Tracey well and rode with her in the evenings. But she said Tracey stopped riding and turned rather secretive. That would have been a few months after she was given the apartment in the stud barn."

"The two properties were joined?" For some reason that detail bothered Dan, but he couldn't pinpoint his unease. "Sorry," he said. "Please continue."

Shania paused to take a sip of wine then resumed talking. "This groom agrees with the consensus that Tracey and Thomas were having an affair. She claims Tracey was only a mediocre groom who happened to have a special bond with Reckless. And his owner.

"There was plenty of jealousy about Tracey being assigned a Derby hopeful," she went on. "At least five grooms felt they deserved the colt and the bonuses that came with his wins. But they didn't want the...extra duties that came with the apartment." Shania gave a meaningful smile.

Dan scribbled down a notation. Clearly there were plenty of people who resented Tracey, and the missing person case should be re-opened. But he didn't like gossip, and his responsibility related to the colt and how to best simulate the horse's actions. "So this groom confirmed Reckless's behavior changed that morning?" he asked. "The exact day Tracey didn't show for work?"

"Absolutely. A media shoot had been scheduled and the girl I interviewed tried to prep Reckless. But he was too rambunctious. He almost scrambled over the stall door. It took three of them to hold him for his bath. She said it was like he'd lost his mind."

Dan sighed. Based on this information, Bruno would be the best horse. He looked formidable when rearing. Emily would have to evade the horse's front feet as well as deliver her lines, but she would certainly be center stage. It would be a great opportunity, especially since interest in the movie was skyrocketing.

"Media attention will make this a blockbuster," Shania said, as if reading his mind. "Anthony and the producer are masters at grabbing opportunities. It's not just your horses that are affected. He's changed several of my scenes to demonstrate a growing fear of Billy. The timing of the explosion couldn't have been more convenient."

"Not so convenient for Billy," Dan said dryly.

"Yes, and normally I'd give a more concrete thanks. But he doesn't have any children." She gave a dismissive wave of her hand. "Otherwise, I'd start a fund of some sort."

"You still could," Dan said. Billy's death and subsequent rumors about his involvement had boosted movie interest. However, it was still a tragedy, and he wasn't going to let Shania escape with cheap platitudes. "What about Tracey's family?" he asked. "They must have gone through hell and back. This stirs up fresh agony. I'm sure your fans would be quite impressed with your compassion."

"Yes." Shania tapped a thoughtful finger against her lips. "My publicist should have considered that angle. A fund would keep the movie in the news until its release. And Tracey is a more sympathetic figure than Billy—who was no doubt her murderer. That was my pick, by the way." She peered at Dan from beneath long dark eyelashes. "Or did you bet on Hamilton?"

"Bet?"

"There's a betting pool. Hamilton, Billy or the field which includes all the jealous grooms as well as any random creeps. Anthony threw in a thousand bucks trying to stoke interest. The win pool is swelling."

Dan abruptly laid down his pen. There wasn't any winner in this, and he craved fresh air. And maybe someone who wouldn't sell their soul for ratings.

Shania leaned forward, laying her manicured fingers over his wrist. "This conference room isn't very cozy. Perhaps we should order dinner and finish in my suite?"

"No, thanks. I'm meeting someone later." He scraped back his chair and rose. "Thanks for sharing your notes."

She made a moue of disappointment. "At the very least we should join Anthony and Hamilton in the media room. A few pictures would boost our movie. Besides, what's your rush? Your little actress already skipped out."

"What makes you think that?"

"Anthony said so. He was going to give her a speaking role and she blew it. Simply walked away. She's definitely not dedicated."

"Not to the movie," Dan said. "But clearly to other things."

Shania sniffed. "When you're making a movie, nothing can be more important. Not to a *real* actress."

Dan paused. Emily claimed she didn't want to be an actress. He hadn't believed her. Deep down, he'd suspected part of the attraction she had for him was based on his position. Yet she'd dropped everything for a geriatric pony—a family pet cherished by both her and her sister.

"You're right." His voice thickened, and a huge weight lifted off his shoulders. "Obviously she's not a real actress."

Shania glided around the table, encouraged by his sudden smile. "And everyone knows you're all about commitment. We'd make an attractive couple. I could be very committed, at least for the length of the movie."

Dan laughed, still pumped from thinking about Emily and her spontaneous selflessness. But Shania's eyes narrowed with displeasure, and he quickly sobered. "I'm very honored," he said. "But you don't need a horse trainer."

"Of course I don't. But I need you. For now." She grabbed his arm and tugged him in front of a gilded mirror. "What do you see?"

"An astonishingly beautiful woman."

"Not me." Her voice rose. "You! Look at yourself."

Dan's mouth tightened. His mother had passed on some attractive genes but he rather resented it. If she'd been ugly, she might have stayed home.

"I'm thirty-two years old," Shania went on. "I need to be seen with a stud. Besides, you're not married so what does it matter? Or will your little actress be jealous?"

He thought for a moment. Emily constantly saw him with other women. But unlike him, she'd trusted his words, every one of them. "No," he said, letting out a big breath. "Emily's good. Surprisingly...perfect."

"Then, please. A few photos. Just smile adoringly. Besides, you owe me." Shania had already pulled out her phone and pressed a number. Obviously her press secretary, judging from her terse instructions.

"Twenty minutes," he said. "And then I have some pressing business."

Shania cut the connection. "Thirty minutes." She looped her arm through his and gave a triumphant smile. "And be sure to kiss me on the lips when you leave."

CHAPTER FORTY-FIVE

"You can let me out here, please," Emily said, reaching for the door handle.

The driver stopped the car by the wreckage of Billy's cottage. "What a mess," he said, peering through the murky light. "Gas stove?"

"The police haven't released much information yet." Emily grabbed her bag and slid from the seat before the driver could open her door. "Thanks for the drive."

The man nodded. He turned the car and eased along the road until his glowing taillights disappeared into the gloom.

Emily skirted the yellow caution tape that circled the charred ruins. The handle of a pot poked from beneath a blackened beam and a coffee mug, curiously intact, tilted against a skeletal bed frame. She swallowed. Billy's body had been removed but the place felt like a grave—sad, desolate, creepy.

"Judith," she called, scanning the grassy yard. The wide plot of green looked benign, a contrast of color against the scorched cottage, lush even in the fading light. A shovel leaned against a wooden sawhorse, and a clear water hose was neatly coiled.

She checked over her shoulder. The curving drive was visible from every point. Clearly this was a poor place to hide a body, assuming Billy was even involved in Tracey's disappearance. At any rate, they needed more sophisticated help. Judith had probably reached a similar conclusion.

It was surprising Judith hadn't waited though. Emily blew out a frustrated breath. She could have taken the limo directly to the hotel and been there when Dan finished with Shania.

Finished. The word raised all kinds of connotations. But even though he'd been reserved on the phone, his simple statement that he'd see her later filled her with an intuitive confidence. He wouldn't touch another woman until he'd ended things with her. But maybe that was his plan.

She pulled out her phone. It was nearly dark. She and Judith would have to catch transportation to the hotel or they'd be stuck paying for a cab. More importantly, she wanted to see Dan as quickly as possible.

Her phone beeped and a message flashed. But it was from Judith, not Dan.

Come to the stud barn, Judith texted. *Did you tell anyone about the wash stall?*

Not yet but I'll see Dan later, Emily texted back. *Just dropped off at cottage. See you in a sec.*

Emily closed her phone and hurried toward the barn, keen to leave this forsaken place. It would be nice to see Barney and Ted, but there was no need to linger. She and Judith couldn't do much about a concrete floor.

It would be best to relay their suspicions to the police. Dan hadn't shown much interest and Anthony was impossible to approach. Hopefully Judith wouldn't be bullheaded about leaving.

Low-lying clouds blotted the moon, but the concrete drive was smooth and easy to follow. She didn't even need the light on her phone. The welcome glow from the stud barn was already visible through the trees and served as a beacon.

She walked into the barn, swinging the bag Mrs. Hamilton had given her. She'd brush her hair and teeth here, just in case she saw Dan before being assigned a hotel room. But she fervently hoped she wouldn't be sleeping single tonight.

Barney nickered and thrust his head over the door. She paused to pat the friendly gelding. If Dan were half as happy to see her, she'd be delighted. The horse nuzzled at her pockets, his warm breath sweet from the smell of hay. "Do you have any peppermints?" she asked, spotting Judith crouched in the adjacent wash stall.

Judith didn't answer. The cover to the drain had been lifted. A rusty screwdriver lay in a matted tangle of black horse hair. But Judith remained on her knees, her eyes blank.

"Was the drain plugged?" Emily asked. "Was that the problem?"

Judith's gaze shifted. Emily turned. Mrs. Hamilton edged from the empty stall across from Barney. She wore a tasteful pearl necklace, glistening coral lipstick, and pointed a rather stubby-looking gun.

Emily's automatic greeting shriveled.

"You're actually the problem," Mrs. Hamilton said.

Emily gulped, desperately trying to wet her throat. "I d-don't know what you mean."

"You shouldn't have come back here. Shouldn't have made friends with Billy. And it's truly unfortunate you have Dan Barrett's ear."

"But I haven't told him anything." Emily's gaze skittered to the floor of the wash stall then back to Mrs. Hamilton's face. "So there's no need to protect your husband. Or Billy. No one is even very interested."

Mrs. Hamilton gave a humorless smile. "Put down your phone and bag. Sit by your friend."

Emily gaped, too stunned to move. This woman sounded so different. No longer charming, but cold and ruthless. A dawning horror swept her. "It w-wasn't Billy?"

"Move." Mrs. Hamilton gestured with the gun.

Emily lowered her phone and bag with clumsy fingers. She shuffled to a spot beside Judith and dropped awkwardly on the cold concrete. Her gaze met Judith's in a moment of mutual terror before shooting back to Mrs. Hamilton who now inspected Emily's phone.

"I just called Dan," Emily said quickly. "He knows about the wash stall. In fact, he's heading here now."

"Indeed." Mrs. Hamilton lifted a disbelieving eyebrow. "According to my husband, Dan's engrossed with Shania. And I can see your calls. Read your texts."

"But why are you doing this?" Emily shook her head, still struggling to absorb the significance of the gun. "We found Tracey's bag. Everyone thinks it's Billy."

"Yes, poor Billy," Mrs. Hamilton said. "Loyal to the end. But he was supposed to burn that bag. Unfortunate about the dementia. It progressed so quickly. I couldn't trust him not to talk."

A chill settled on Emily's neck. She gaped in dawning horror. "Billy was your man, not your husband's? But his family worked for the estate—"

"My family's estate. Our properties were joined by marriage." Mrs. Hamilton's voice hardened. "And I wasn't about to have it carved up because of that pregnant slut."

Judith jerked forward. "Pregnant?" she whispered, speaking for the first time since Emily arrived.

"That baby should have been mine." Mrs. Hamilton's mouth flattened. "I went to the apartment, offered her money to leave. She grabbed a knife. Ordered me to go. And it was *my* property."

Emily's hands shook. On the other side of the wall, Barney munched hay, the sound of his contented chewing discordant with the terror chilling her limbs.

"So it was self defense." Emily tried to shrug but her cold shoulders were too stiff to move. "No problem," she croaked. "Everyone would understand. Let's go and call a lawyer."

"For six months I watched them through that apartment window," Mrs. Hamilton said. "Giggling and drawing hearts. I thought it would pass, like the others. She claimed I wasn't woman enough to give Thomas a baby." Mrs. Hamilton's voice turned toneless. "I lost my temper... Billy helped me clean up."

Bile climbed Emily's throat. She wanted to plug her ears. Stop listening. Beside her, Judith's breath came in shallow gasps.

"It's okay." Emily forced the words from her dry mouth. "All you need is a good lawyer. Everything will be fine."

"But *he'd* never forgive me. He's already suspicious. Because of this, Reckless didn't make the Derby."

"Tracey was pregnant," Judith whispered, her voice reedy. She sat unmoving, almost trancelike, her words barely distinguishable over her ragged breathing.

"It's no problem. You just need a good lawyer," Emily repeated, nudging her friend in the ribs, wishing Judith didn't belie Emily's words by sounding so horrified.

"What I need is for you to go away," Mrs. Hamilton said.

"Sure." Emily nodded quickly. "We can do that."

Mrs. Hamilton gave a tight smile. "I liked you. I really did. You never flirted with my husband. But you shouldn't have been snooping. Now get up."

The past tense. She spoke in the past tense. A cold sweat prickled Emily's neck. Neither she nor Judith moved.

"They're going to find the body anyway." Emily gripped her sweaty hands so tightly they hurt. "When they run water, the aisle will flood. They'll have to fix the floor."

"I had that scene moved to the other barn. And the apartment closed. Nothing will be shot here." Mrs. Hamilton's coral mouth twisted with dark humor. "Unless it's necessary."

Emily stared into the muzzle of the gun, doubtful her numb legs would even work. "Where are we going?"

"Just for a little drive. Now get up."

Emily reluctantly struggled to her feet and pulled up Judith. There would be no help from her friend. Judith's face was pasty white, her eyes glazed. "It's okay," Emily said. "We're just going to walk to her car."

"There's hay on your jeans," Mrs. Hamilton said. "Brush it off, please."

Relief coursed through Emily and she obligingly swiped at the hay, her arms and legs not quite so boneless. This was comforting. If Mrs. Hamilton worried about a dirty car, probably any fear she'd shoot them was groundless. Besides, there were security guards at both entrances. They'd have a chance to signal for help.

"Good girl," Mrs. Hamilton said. "You just lie where I say and you won't get hurt."

An image of the Lincoln's clean and cavernous trunk flashed. Emily's knees buckled and she grabbed Barney's door for support. Of course Mrs. Hamilton remembered the guards. She didn't want anything soiling her spotless trunk.

Emily shook her head. "We're not going."

"Yes," Mrs. Hamilton said. "You are. Besides, I'm not going to hurt you."

But the woman's gaze flickered, and it was obvious she was lying. Worse, if she was as adept at hiding their bodies as she had been with Tracey's, she might never even be caught. The only witnesses were the two horses.

Emily's fingers clenched around the top of Barney's door. She couldn't think, could barely stand. Barney didn't understand at all and sniffed at her hands, still hopeful for a treat.

Mrs. Hamilton waved her gun at Judith. "You. Step closer. Walk beside Emily."

Emily's gaze darted down the aisle. Burke had enrolled her and Jenna in a self-defense course. The instructor stressed if you intend to fight or flee, do it immediately. There might not be a second chance.

Maybe they could bolt once they were closer to the door. Mrs. Hamilton might miss. And the sound of the shot would bring someone, or at least be remembered tomorrow—or whenever she and Judith were reported missing.

But when would that be? Judith didn't have any family, and Jenna and Burke were in England. Dan expected her at the hotel but probably wouldn't be too surprised if she didn't show. After all, she'd left once before without telling him.

She pressed against the stall, sucking in a ragged gulp of air. Her entire body trembled and she had to get her shaky legs under control. Needed to be ready to run. She could bolt down the driveway and Judith could swerve toward the trees. Hopefully, clouds still covered the sky. Together they could do this.

She glanced sideways, willing Judith to understand. But Judith's eyes were stark against her bloodless face, her arms clamped woodenly against her chest.

"It's okay, Judith," Emily said, trying to hide her own debilitating fear. "We're just going to walk *toward* Mrs. Hamilton's car." She squeezed Judith's arm. "It'll be okay, outside."

However, Judith's horrified gaze remained locked on Mrs. Hamilton's face.

Emily squeezed her eyes shut, fighting a rush of hopelessness. Judith couldn't speak. Couldn't move. She'd never be able to run. And Emily couldn't abandon her.

But she didn't want to die. She had to see Dan again. And Jenna. Needed to thank Burke in person. And Peanut might have another setback. She tightened her grip on Judith's arm, shaking it almost frantically. But Judith was in a zombie state, and Mrs. Hamilton was far too shrewd.

Her eyes narrowed. "If you do anything rash, Emily, I will shoot your friend." She motioned with the gun. "Now keep holding her arm and walk slowly down the aisle."

"Please," Emily said. "You don't need to do this. A good lawyer would get you off."

"Maybe," Mrs. Hamilton said, "but the scandal would kill my marriage. Now walk."

Emily gave Judith's arm another frantic squeeze. But despite her death grip, Judith remained oblivious to any attempts at communication. If only she were as alert as Barney.

Unlike Judith, the horse was totally attentive, not understanding why three people lingered in front of his stall but clearly expecting it might result in a treat. His bright eyes tracked Emily's every movement.

This isn't a movie, Barney, she thought despairingly. There'd be no trick or treat games tonight. But his gaze remained on her hands, as though determined not to miss his stage call.

And he's already shown that he's dependable.

She sucked in a fortifying breath and edged to the side of the stall, tugging Judith with her.

"Keep walking," Mrs. Hamilton snapped, stepping in front of Barney and waving the gun.

"Get it!" Emily said. She pushed Judith aside and charged forward, catching a blur of movement as Barney reached over the stall and grabbed the gun. Mrs. Hamilton's furious eyes held Emily's as she tried to wrench the gun from Barney's mouth.

Crack.

A bullet ricocheted off the steel grill. Barney's head jerked in alarm, his nostrils flaring at the unexpected noise. The gun clattered to the floor.

Emily launched herself at Mrs. Hamilton, rocketed by adrenaline and fear. They tumbled to the floor in a tangle. She grappled with flailing limbs, trying to pin the woman to the floor. But a pointed knee drove into Emily's chest. The impact emptied her lungs in a painful whoosh. For a moment, she couldn't move.

"Bitch." Rage thickened Mrs. Hamilton's voice. She twisted sideways, groping for the fallen gun.

"Looking for this?" a voice asked.

Emily peered up, aching for breath. Despite Judith's odd voice, the gun in her hand looked surprisingly steady.

Emily stumbled to her feet. Mrs. Hamilton rose more gracefully. But she didn't look as beautiful now, even though her clothes and makeup were still elegant despite their rumble in the aisle. Barney edged back to the front of his stall, reassured that the humans were acting normally again. Mrs. Hamilton shot him a venomous look and appeared far from beaten.

"Careful, Judith," Emily warned.

But Judith stepped closer. "You k-killed her. My sister was pregnant and you killed her."

Emily gaped. So did Mrs. Hamilton. But only for a moment.

"Your sister? Really," Mrs. Hamilton said coolly. "Your parents must have been delighted to have raised such a slut."

"My parents died of broken hearts." Judith's voice shook. "They searched and hoped and prayed until they gave up. You shouldn't have done that... She was just a kid. You didn't have to kill her."

"It was humiliating." Mrs. Hamilton spat so vehemently a drop of spittle formed at the corner of her sculpted mouth. "My husband wanted a divorce, all because of a twenty-year-old nobody who'd barely finished high school. He kept sneaking off to the apartment. Even Reckless was infatuated. Well, I fixed it so they both could sleep with her."

Judith flinched. Her gaze shot to the wash stall and the muzzle of the gun quivered.

"Give me the gun," Emily said.

"No. I'm going to shoot her." Judith's voice turned eerily calm. "Otherwise she'll get a lawyer and be out in five years. I did the research."

"Don't. It's not worth it."

"She killed my sister. And her baby. Then buried them like trash. What would you do?"

Emily gulped. If someone killed Jenna... It was too horrible to contemplate. But she shook her head and inched closer. "Don't wreck your life. My dad died in prison. Really, it's no fun."

Judith waved the gun, her voice firming. "Stay back, Emily. She took everything. I have to make her pay."

Barney's ears shot forward. He raised his head and stared down the aisle.

"Of course she needs to pay." Dan's easy voice sounded behind them. Emily twisted, sagging with relief. He looked so calm, as if he handled murderous gun scenes every day.

"What's the most important thing in *her* life?" Dan said, easing between Judith and Emily.

"Her husband," Judith muttered, keeping the gun trained on Mrs. Hamilton.

"Yes, and Hamilton Stud. What will happen when she faces two murder charges?" Dan's voice remained level, but his gaze flickered over Emily and his eyes were arctic shards of blue. "Along with the attempted murder tonight."

Judith's throat convulsed. "I imagine he'll divorce her."

"I imagine he will." Dan edged even closer. "Put down the gun, Judith. Security is on its way. They'll handle this."

"I knew Tracey didn't run away, no matter what the police thought," Judith said brokenly. "She wouldn't do that, especially before the Derby. She loved Reckless. He was all she talked about."

"And clearly the horse knew that," Dan said, easing the gun from Judith's hands.

Mrs. Hamilton immediately swelled with bravado. "I'm calling security," she snapped. "These intruders were in *my* barn. Trespassing, threatening—"

"Don't speak." Dan's voice sliced the air. "Don't move. Don't even look."

His command was low but full of such menace Emily half hoped Mrs. Hamilton would try to say something else. She also hoped Dan would never, ever speak to her in such a scary voice.

As if aware of her thoughts, he reached back and gave her a one-armed hug, his voice instantly gentling. "Are you okay, Em?"

He stuck the gun in the waistband of his jeans and cupped her face. Anger still vibrated from him in waves, but his touch was achingly sweet. "I heard a shot."

Emily shook her head. "It didn't hit anything. It went off when Barney grabbed the gun."

"The horse grabbed it? The Reckless lookalike?" He gave a tight smile. "How fitting."

"His name is Barney," she said. Suddenly it was important that Dan say his name. After all, the horse was a hero. "It's not fair to be nice and then dump him when the movie's over," she went on, her words tripping over each other. "Barney's a good horse and he's dependable. And someone needs to look after his leg."

Dan looked at her oddly then reached for two horse blankets, draping one over her and one over Judith. "We should watch you two for shock. Get checked out by the paramedic. Here are some cars now."

Headlights slashed the dark beyond the entrance. Car doors slammed. Moments later two security guards swept in, their eyes wide, hands close to their holsters.

Dan met them in the aisle. They spoke for a moment in low voices.

One guard walked up to Mrs. Hamilton. She opened her mouth to protest but cast a wary look at Dan and remained silent. The other man accompanied Judith, following Mrs. Hamilton and her escort out the door.

And then Dan's arms wrapped around Emily, and he was holding her so tightly she could barely breathe. "It's over," he said, adjusting the blanket. "But we need to stay here until the police take your statement. Are you cold?"

"Not anymore. But I need to check on Judith." She tried to twist away, her voice choking with compassion. "Now I understand much better. Why she acted that way. Tracey was her sister."

"She's safe," Dan said, keeping her anchored in his arms. "You can see her soon. But they want to keep you all apart until the police come."

His hand caressed her, long strokes from her neck to her lower back, filling her with a sense of safety. It was a good thing he held her though. Her legs wobbled and her head was so light she feared it might float away.

"Barney remembered the grab trick," she said, her throat still painfully dry. "But I was so scared. Still am."

"Me too," Dan said, his voice gruff.

"But why are you even here?"

"Shania's research showed Mrs. Hamilton owned the adjoining estate along with the caretaker's cottage. So Billy was her employee. That raised some flags. And she was always too constrained, even when Hamilton openly ogled the girls."

Emily shivered. She'd never imagined such evil lurked beneath the woman's gracious veneer. Of course Dan was skilled at reading horses, and people. He wasn't blinded by superficial beauty but attracted by other qualities—like dependability and courage.

Qualities she didn't possess. And never would. She'd probably always be a little rash, and she still shook with fear.

She squeezed her eyes shut, swept with hopelessness but needing to explain anyway. "Sorry I left yesterday without leaving a message. My phone was dead. But thanks for coming tonight. Even though you were disappointed that I rushed off for Peanut."

"I would have been disappointed if you hadn't."

"The thing is, I'd probably do it again. I love Peanut and Jenna…" She paused, her eyes widening. "What did you say?"

He held her wrist and studied his watch—it was obvious he was checking her pulse. "We need to get you to the hospital," he said. "They'll treat you for shock."

"Wait." She gripped his arm. "You'd have been disappointed if I hadn't left? Is that what you said? You're not mad?"

"You walked away from an acting job to help Peanut and your family. Admirable in my book." His voice hardened. "But yes, I was annoyed you didn't tell me. Still am. I might have been able to help."

"Oh," she said. So she had some apologizing to do. But clearly he wasn't prone to sulks and maybe, just maybe, he wasn't going to dump her. At least not until the end of the movie. She'd have a few more weeks to work hard and try to make him care.

Heat blossomed in her chest, an odd mixture of fear and hope. "I have a new phone charger," she said. "It'll be easier to call if I have to leave again."

He scowled.

"But that's not going to happen," she added quickly. "I'm a little impulsive, but I'm getting better. And I can be politer with Lizzie and try not to get annoyed, and I won't name your horses or anything—"

"Shush." He pressed a finger against her lips. "Don't change too much. Or you won't be the woman I fell in love with."

Her mouth opened but no matter how hard she tried, she couldn't get enough air. She wanted to pinch herself but all she could do was stare, her breath coming in short gasps.

"That's it. You can't even breathe." He turned her toward the door. "We're not waiting any longer. The police will have to take your statement at the hospital."

"I'm f-fine." She pulled at his arm, trying to see his face.

"You're shivering and your pulse is sky high." He scooped her up and turned toward the door.

It was quite apparent he was the one in shock, not her, but since there was no other place she'd rather be, she wrapped her arms around his neck. "Can you repeat what you just said?"

"We're going to the hospital. I'll call the police from my car. And I love you."

"Oh," she managed, feeling like she was in a movie because surely this moment of such complete and utter happiness couldn't be real. Of course not.

But her eyes watered and they felt like real tears and when she blinked, Dan still looked at her, as if he'd meant every word. And even better, that he'd have no problem saying them again.

"You don't even know my last name," she said. But her words were wrapped in a face-splitting smile, and she twined her arms around his neck, feeling weightless with joy.

"Just because I don't use last names," he said, "doesn't mean I don't know them."

"It's okay." She spoke quickly, in a rush to reassure him. To prove she wasn't a needy actress. "Lizzie said not knowing names was related to a permanence thing. It doesn't bother me at all. And I understand you want to be cautious."

He stopped and cupped her face. "I love you, Emily Ann Murphy. And that Reckless lookalike, Barney, registered name Barkeeper's Choice, I'll be buying him from the stock contractor tomorrow. He'll be waiting for you on the ranch, whenever you want a break from the movies, or from wrangling, or pony sitting, or whatever the hell you want to do."

For a moment she stopped breathing. "But you don't want an actress," she managed.

"I just want you." He trailed a finger over her cheek. "And you'd be happier with a variety of jobs. No reason not to try them all." His smile turned rueful. "The challenge might even keep you out of trouble for a while."

Then his mouth lowered, covering hers in a kiss that started out gentle but turned so passionate she almost forgot about the security guards waiting outside. And when he finally raised his head, her breathing raced and it seemed medical attention might be required after all.

But this was simply difficult to grasp. Horses, acting, wrangling. All with this wonderful man by her side. And a ranch where they could escape. The scope of her happiness seemed too big for a single person.

She tugged in a shaky breath, her gaze swinging from Dan's brilliant blue eyes to the bay horse staring at her over the stall door. Barney's expression was calm and accepting, as if unaware his future had taken a dramatic turn, one full of unconditional love. But she knew.

And when her misty eyes turned back to Dan, he gave her such a heart-stopping smile, it was obvious he knew too.

EPILOGUE

Emily stepped onto the sweeping ranch verandah, smiling as Dan immediately laid down his iPad and poured her a fresh coffee. Hawaii had been nice but Montana was even nicer.

"Let's ride out and check Barney this morning," she said. "He and Splash are probably still grazing by the creek."

Dan tugged her onto his lap. "Sure. And we should round up a few. Find some horses for that saloon fire for the railroad series."

"Okay. But it's my turn to hold the flaming hoop." She snuggled into his hard chest, already feeling an anticipatory thrill, merely from his closeness. He looked like a gunslinger with his dark cowboy hat and stubbled jaw. Of course, some of his family had been gunslingers. The story about his trail-blazing ancestor who had rescued and married a beautiful squatter still made her shiver with delight.

She pressed a kiss against his tanned throat. "Don't shave this morning," she said. "I need to practice love scenes for a cowboy show."

"You're not in a cowboy show."

"I'd still like to practice."

His eyes flashed with a wicked glint. "I'll have the horses saddled in ten seconds flat." But he skimmed a hand over her body, his thumb brushing her breast, and it was obvious he intended to forget the horses and linger on the verandah.

"Our house guests are in the kitchen," Emily reminded him. "Burke is eager for a poker rematch."

"And he'll get one," Dan said. "But not this morning. Will they ride with us today?"

Emily shook her head. "They're sore from yesterday. Jenna did say a ranch vacation was even more fun than the steeplechase. Not sure about Burke's thoughts. He's still trying to persuade Jenna to give him a massage."

"Okay. We'll let Jenna entertain her husband for a bit. Let's go for that ride." His hands lowered over her hips and he effortlessly raised her to her feet.

Emily's gaze flickered to the headlines on his iPad. *Socialite Arraigned in Decades'-old Murder.* She picked it up, scanning the article.

> Louise Hamilton, a bastion of Kentucky society, was arraigned yesterday for the murder of Tracey Walker, the groom of famous racehorse, Reckless. Walker vanished mysteriously decades ago while in the employ of Hamilton Stud. The twenty-year-old murder was unearthed during the shooting of the movie *Reckless*, on location in Kentucky. Police have confirmed the body found beneath a concrete wash stall was that of Tracey Walker.
>
> Animal behaviorists speculate that Reckless's unruly behavior that forced him to scratch from the 1993 Kentucky Derby was related to the presence of his beloved groom's body beneath the floor of his barn. Charges are also expected to be laid in the suspicious death of a caretaker on April 22 although police

remain tightlipped. A spokesperson confirmed Billy Tanner died six months ago on the Hamilton estate in a house fire now considered suspicious. Neither Louise Hamilton's lawyer nor her estranged husband, Thomas Hamilton, were available for comment.

Famed actress, Shania Stevens, who portrays Tracey Walker in the movie is relieved justice will finally be obtained and has established a family support fund that now exceeds three million dollars. "I love all animals but to imagine this remarkable horse screaming for help and being totally misunderstood is mind boggling. The Walker family suffered terribly and my heart goes out to Tracey's surviving sister, Judith, the only relative who has lived to see justice. I am very glad I was able to play a small role in the solving of this crime."

Movie buffs anticipate that *Reckless*, scheduled to open December 26, will be a box office hit. Oscar-winning director Anthony Jenkins says no horses were harmed in the making of the movie.

Emily sighed and closed the iPad. "This is going to be in the news forever. And now that Judith discovered the truth, she's completely rudderless. She's been back to Three Brooks several times since the steeplechase. Actually she's there now, helping Wally brush up the Center's online presence. She sent me a cute picture of Peanut and Wally. Clearly, she's bored."

Dan's mouth twitched. "I don't think Peanut is the only draw," he said.

Emily tilted her head. Wally had sat with them during the steeplechase, not even leaving to visit the sponsors' tent. "Judith and Wally," she said thoughtfully. "Do you suppose…?" She groaned. Dan was much better than her at figuring out people. "How long has that been going on? It's hard to believe I didn't notice."

"You've been busy," Dan said. "Not many wranglers can act, solve a murder, and still keep their man happy."

"Are you happy?" She linked her hands through his.

He stared down, his gaze suddenly intent. "Deliriously."

"So reports that you and Shania were secretly married are off base?"

"Way off."

A familiar glow warmed her chest, the joy rising and edging out the corners of her mouth. She'd never imagined such happiness was possible. She loved every aspect of the movies: the challenges, the travel, even the stress. But most of all, she loved Dan. Sometimes sheer joy made it hard to speak, and all she could manage was a goofy grin. Best of all, he seemed to feel the same way.

"You're not saying much," she whispered.

"Can't help it," he said. And he grinned.

***

ABOUT THE AUTHOR

Bev Pettersen is a three-time nominee in the National Readers Choice Award as well as a two-time finalist in the Romance Writers of America's Golden Heart® Contest. She competed for five years on the Alberta Thoroughbred race circuit and is an Equine Canada certified coach. She lives in Nova Scotia with her family and when not writing novels, she's riding.

Visit her at http://www.bevpettersen.com

Made in the USA
San Bernardino, CA
02 January 2014